3 Days In Rome

3 Days In Rome

Scott D. Southard

Writers Club Press
San Jose New York Lincoln Shanghai

3 Days In Rome

Writers Club Press
an imprint of iUniverse.com, Inc.

For information address:
iUniverse.com, Inc.
5220 S 16th, Ste. 200
Lincoln, NE 68512
www.iuniverse.com

A work of fiction (novel, book, manuscript, words on paper)
that is best when read silently or shouted (yelled, screamed)
in the HOPE that someone higher may hear (sighsighsighsighsigh).

ISBN: 0-595-17967-3

Printed in the United States of America

DEDICATION

Dedicated
to the beautiful real
Toni Lyn Morelli
who graciously allowed
me to steal her name.

With special thanks to my parents; my bro; Head Rooster; The forgiving Management; Emperors (from the lovely matriarch and past patriarch right on down to the youngest cousin); Beatrice130; WMUGirl, she knows ; Second Cousin Dinkel, his Mrs. and their dog, Kitty; Kate or Kay; Gdeadgirl and her Jim Morrison; The minds behind Minds' Ear and the Dante crew; The Super Oatman and his family; Erik and Sarah and his clan; Karaboo; Kristie Girl, Hurricane Bonnie; Anna Fine and the dream of Paris; Sorshakat (A lost soul); The Professors who taught me to mentally breathe at Aquinas College (Professor Chesley, Eberle, Raikes, and Brooks); StevenL750; Ian, Todd, Paul and the others from the A July Party session; Carrington; Steven Allison and his organization; Laura Jordan; Michele H.; Lisa S., the first muse; Susan A.; And Cratchit.

Preface

The top five first responses from people arriving in Heaven-

1. You gotta be kidding me!
2. What's that smell?
3. I have to stay here for how long?
4. Can I get a drink?
5. What? This is it?!

My Introduction

I never expected to die... Well, I knew I was going to die someday (I'm not an idiot), but I just wasn't expecting to die so soon. Twenty-eight years of age is just too soon to take your final bow. However, since I've arrived in Heaven, I've met many people who would argue the opposite. Many of the Roman soldiers I drink with at the local pub claim I'd be a senior citizen in their day... So maybe it's best to get off this point....

TAKE 2

My Introduction

I never expected to die and go to Heaven. My past record on Earth was far from clean-robbery, alleged kidnapping, arson, adultery and I was responsible for an international incident that made me an embarrassment to my country... Just to name a few little problems.

Then there is the whole thing of me being a fugitive on the run.... Those were the greatest days of my life. The adventure. The love. The thrill... Oh, well, I'll get to that later. So how does someone like me end up in Heaven's version of Rome?

Wait!

Get this—

I'm a hero up here! Dead people come by all the time to hear my story. That's the main reason I decided to write this book. Then I can spend more time walking around the streets of Rome without being interrupted to tell another dead person my story.

Let me admit something else here too—I'm not a writer. I know it's pretty obvious but I think it's best I say it before someone beats me to the punch. The author, Henry James (He lives in the apartment across from mine) offered to ghostwrite the story for me (He is just dying to put ink to paper again. He really is an incredible writer. A Hell of a lot better than I'll ever be. He could do wonders with this story. I feel so guilty because when I first met him I really didn't know his work. He was crushed. I guess he expected his name to mean more that it does. So I went to the local library in Heaven and borrowed one of his books. And then another and another and another.... Now it's like I've become a member of some elite literary club. So, who are my friends? Well, how about F. Scott Fitzgerald, Charles Dickens, Sylvia Plath, Virginia Woolf and that's just to name a few…. I sit with all of them at our local coffeehouse, The AfterTaste, and discuss literature and the absence of originality in the post-modern society—we dead people love to complain about the living. I think the fact that I can handle these kinds of discussions is pretty amazing. It's just really good for an ex-con), but no, I need to write this book. It's my story…. Ok, I'm off track again. I'll probably get better at this as I go on. Knock on wood.

So how does someone like me end up in Heaven? Well, God works off a different basis than we mere mortals first thought. Actually, it's really surprising exactly how much different it is. It's almost humorous…. Trust me, you'll get a kick out of this. (James told me to tease my reader in the beginning with hints of what is to come. I think he'll be pleasantly surprised by my use of subtlety in this field.)

However…

I'm still not satisfied with this Introduction. See, I promised myself once I started writing this book I wasn't going to go back. Straightforward! My thoughts as they come out right onto paper. Get the story out quickly (I gave myself a very short time limit on the creation of this work. I'll get to that later too). I'm not a literary great, so why worry about perfection? Granted this first draft-straight-forward style might cause some problems in the future. I may forget things or contradict myself, but I'm only a dead human. I'm not perfect.

Let me try this again-

TAKE 3

My Introduction

I never expected to die and become a romantic hero. While alive, I consistently had the worst experiences with love. It actually got so bad that once I wanted to give up on the entire thing. Just abandon love. Just stop thinking about lust and women's legs (I'm a legman) and just find something else to put my passion to… That reminds me of another reason why I look up to my friend Henry James. He gave up his sex drive for writing. All his energy went right into work…. Probably another reason why he's such a better writer than me. He was a living pen; I was a living heart.

But up here in Heaven, I'm a romantic hero! I can't even begin to guess the number of times people have asked for hugs or even tried kissing me. The Bronte sisters came all the way from Heaven's London just to see me. They seemed a little disappointed that I wasn't a darker, more mysterious man (Personally, I think these girls have some issues they need to deal with… soon. Poor Lord Byron had to go into hiding 3 years after their arrival.) I am not a Heathcliff! Let's make that point clear too. I'm not that kind of a hero. I'm not about to let myself suffer away my days, longing for someone else. I do things. My philosophy is…

Well, that's another thing I'll get to later. I've had two philosophies in my life. I abandoned my first for my second philosophy. You'll see all that as the story goes on. I can, however, give a variation on my philosophy now—just so I can make all of this flow= "Seize the day and all that crap."

God, I can't believe I used an expression like that. That's so unlike me. I hate expressions and cliches. They're almost as weak as pickup lines. I've only used one pickup line in my entire life. I'll get to that later too.

So much to look forward too! As a reader, I know I'd be interested.

Instead of starting this book at my birth and forcing you to follow my entire childhood with all its standard issue traumas and experiences (Like some typical post-modern novel), I'm going to begin this book at the point when I was born for a second time…. It was right before I met the great love of my life.

I was in Rome.

Part 1—ROME

Hello. I love you. Won't
you tell me your name?

—The Doors

CHAPTER 1

So I was 23 and I went to Europe to commit suicide.

Just think about it... Death in Europe! Find a secluded bridge- maybe in Rome or Venice or Paris—make sure it is a starry night. Then I would say a little prayer to God I had prepared. It was very simple. Very neat and to the point. Here it is—"Ok, I give up you win. Amen." Melodramatic maybe, who knows? I, on the other hand, thought it was the best move and decision I have ever made. Isn't that sad? To put so much faith in the idea of one's own death as salvation. But really I never had the experience of living, so what could I judge it against? However something happened. Something I was not prepared to learn about myself.

An Explanation-
I know this contradicts the first part of my introduction. But let me assure you, I am not a psycho-don't worry. There is an explanation to all this. It's not logical, but it explains my mind. See, at this moment I really didn't know what to "live" meant. I was coasting so much of my existence- college girlfriend, job. You, know, everything everyone says you want out of life. But it did squat for me! I was just not made to live that kind of life. So the idea of suicide was more for just ending a mistake. Like using white-out on a grander scale. Very naive and very stupid. I know. I know. That stupidity will unfold all too clear for me by the next few paragraphs-

I was a complete wimp! I wimped out!
How much of a wimp?
I know for a fact I stood on:
    14 bridges in
    9 different countries for about
    <u>+ 42 hours.</u>
And that equals wimp.

Think of it—Forty-two hours of standing on bridges trying to talk oneself into jumping. ("Ok, this time is for the gold. End it. You know you want to. Let yourself go. C'mon, you can do it. Count of 4. 1… 2… 3… No wait. I never liked the number 4. Let's try to count to 5. Here we go. 1… 2… 3… 4… No! Stop! I still don't like 4. How about if I do it this time skipping the number 4? Ok, here we go. 1… 2… 3… 3… 3… 3… 3… 3… 3… 3… 3… 3… 3… 3… 3… 3… 3… 3… 3… 3… 3… You know, I don't think I like the number 3 either.")

And if it wasn't too cold out, I was wearing the wrong clothes or the bridge wasn't the right bridge for me. Etc.…

Originally, I was hoping to have the act completed after two weeks.… By the time this all begins, I had already traveled for a total of four months.… See what I mean about being a wimp?

I was in Rome.

I had just spent the entire evening standing on the God given most perfect bridge in the world. That bridge was truly the finest I had ever seen. And trust me, by this time if anyone had the credentials to judge a bridge that would be me. It was very ancient and looked to have at one time been bright white. Maybe it was marble. (If I was smart, I would have the name of that bridge. Henry James would have done the research. But like I said, I'm not James.)

Before I knew it, it was dawn. The sun was beginning to rise and suddenly…

Suddenly I was touched…. Yes, touched. Right inside. Like an egg was hatching right inside my body, my heart, and my soul. The sunlight did that to me. That beautiful, brilliant dawn.

I was given a gift. A vision. A phrase. A philosophy to end all philosophies. The words to make my life extraordinary. The words to give me the courage and strength to change everything about myself—From how I breathed to how I got up in the morning.

I smiled up at the sun as it shown brightly down into my eyes. And I mouthed repeatedly the phrase that would change my life forever:

"Fuck Them All."

They were the 3 most beautiful words I had ever uttered in my life! More beautiful than the time I said, "I love you" to Jaime Buchman in the backseat of my Ford while a junior in High School. More beautiful than the time I said, "I am sick" to my boss so I could take the day off to go to my first strip club in Canada…. See, instead of giving me a little moment of bliss, like those moments, these words gave me something I could live for.

They gave me a goal.

A goal that was truly my own.

Not a good goal, granted. But at least it gave me a reason to live.

Chapter 2 — Two Hours Later

Oh, Shit! Shit! Shit! Shit! Shitty shit shit!

So, there I was being chased by the Vatican Police. And man were they getting close. *Shit!* Who would have guessed that people in outfits like that could move that quickly? (If you don't know what I mean in regards to the outfits of the Vatican Police I recommend you find yourself a picture of one. They are the ugliest, stupidest and most ridiculous military uniforms in the world) There must've been at least four officers on my tail. *Out of my way! Move it! Coming through!*

By this point, I was finally outside the Vatican. Unfortunately, that didn't make things easier. Believers!

Out of my way! The crowds were Hell to fight through. And it got worse, much worse when those crowds of believers began to realize who I was and what I did. *Let go!* I fought my way through the main square and on to the street. Tourists!

Move It! I was pushing people out of my way left and right. *Excuse me! Pardon me!* Everyone was screaming at me (They were all speaking Italian, I assume they were telling me to stop. Fat chance.). *Shout at me in English! Christ! I don't understand you!*

Suddenly this small Roman police car pulled out in front of me. *Jesus...* I acted quickly and jumped on the hood. *...Christ! Excuse me!* I ran over the top of the car and jumped back on to the pavement. So now, the Roman Police was in on the chase. This was not making my life easier. I turned into one of the side streets…

One of the cops almost got me! He got my shirt from the back. I turned quickly punching him in the face. *Let go of me, you Fucker!* Pow! Square in the nose. He dropped my shirt and quickly covered his bleeding nose. This only seemed to piss off all the other police officers more.

A gunshot went off! *Oh, God! They're firing at me!*

I've got to get out of here! I turned down another street. *These cops are everywhere!*

I quickly turned on to a third street. The cops were still on the other street. It was only a matter of time before… My chance! *Eureka!* In front of me was a giant tour group. I pushed my way in between them and ducked down. The ones closest to me looked down confused. *Shhhh!*

It was then that I heard the cops and the cars speed past.

…………… *Yes.*

I had escaped. I casually (with a forced smile plastered on my face) moved with the group to the next site of their tour.

I have to find someplace to hide out. I had to go someplace that would protect me from going to an Italian jail. I had to go someplace where I could contact my family for help.

Excuse me!… Pardon me…. Yes, hello… Do any of you fine tourists know the way to the American Embassy?

CHAPTER 3

The run through Rome I just described reminds me of something I saw here in Heaven just two weeks ago. "The Famous Run Of The Great Unknown." The Great Unknown? John Lennon penned that name for the man.

Here is what I know about The Great Unknown right now-

He died 3 weeks ago. He was given the apartment next door to Henry James. The angels led him into his rooms as James and I watched from the hallway. It's always interesting to watch this moment. The recent arrivals' faces are always so… so… confused. I mean, they can be excited or happy or annoyed, but it is all just hidden under another level of confusion…. Well, except for this guy.

The face of The Great Unknown was gray. And his eyes were glassed over.

The angels led him into his apartment. They then gave the generic speech (They give it so often it almost comes out in a singsong manner you can almost snap your fingers to it).

"WelCOME to YOUR HOME in HEAVEN. WelCOME to YOUR ETERNITY. WE hope you like your ROOMS, if there are any problems FEEL FREE to fill out one of the COMPLAINT cards down in the LOBBY. On the TV, you can find many EDUCATIONAL Heaven Television stations. On channel 14 is INFO about the AREA INCLUD-

ING interesting TOURIST spots. Channel 18 is the STATION of report-
ing ON the OTHER RESIDENTS. Just LOOK at how HAPPY they all
ARE. WE are all HAPPY here. Enjoy."

Then the angels went out shutting the door behind them.

James and I looked at each other.

This was something new and we both knew it. This dead guy was different. "What do you think happened to him?" I asked James.

"It's hard to say," James said. "I've seen people who were tortured and
murdered who looked more…."

"I know."

We paused. It was all silent behind that door. Nothing at all.

"Should we say something?" I asked James.

"No… He needs to be alone. He needs his Recovery Stage."

A brief interruption to explain "The Recovery Stage."

"The Recovery Stage" is a term used to describe the initial reaction and
amazement of arriving in Heaven. Your mind follows a pretty much standard path during the first few weeks.

1. You look around dazed and excited as if you are expecting to see
   all your relatives lined up to see you. (The angels are really behind
   in notifying the next dead of kin. A good example of this is my
   own personal experience with my grandfather. He didn't know I
   was in Heaven until an entire six months had passed. I didn't
   know this fact until he called me one afternoon and demanded to
   know, "What the Hell were you thinking?")

2. You begin to get excited waiting for all your questions to be
   answered… Actually, you learn nothing from the angels or your
   fellow dead right away (The dead do pass on some knowledge at a
   later time… I'll get to that later in the book).

3. Then you begin to ask questions of yourself. Some good examples
of these questions are:

"I wasn't a good person, how did I end up here?"
"Doesn't God remember that _____ I did? I know that was bad!"
"But I used to always say _____, didn't he hear me? That wasn't good."

A few days later when you realize no one is waiting for you and none of
your answers will be answered by sitting around, you move on. There is
supposedly another stage in development after this one, but I think it's a
load of shit.

"I don't think this is the typical Recovery Stage," I said to James. In my
opinion, he wasn't right about The Great Unknown. He had nothing to
come down from. He was already down. He was more than down… It was
like there was nothing on his face…. But neither of us really wanted to get
into this. Being dead is enough of a pain, who wants more stress?
     Of course, that doesn't mean we weren't a little curious….
     "Maybe we should just look in to see if he is…."
     "No, no." I replied shaking my head. We both took a step closer to his
door.
     "But just a peek, should be ok?"
     "No." I said again to James. He is too much a writer. James used to
(when alive) go to restaurants and just watch people. Their faces. Listen to
their voices. He would create scenes in his mind and all those anonymous
faces became characters in stories and novels. These people would go on to
live other lives without knowing it… It was like he would take a piece of
their soul with his eyes and retrace it on the page….
     We both put our ears against the stranger's door (He wasn't The Great
Unknown yet) and listened to the nothing from the other side.

We must've stayed in that position for at least two hours. Really, nothing else was going on in Heaven. Neither of us knew how much time had gone by until John Lennon appeared on the stairs.

"What the Hell are you two doing?"

We both quickly hushed him.

"What is it?" He asked a little quieter.

I put my finger against my lips and waved him over to the door. We made room for Lennon by the doorknob. He got on his knees, leaned his ear against the door and listened to the nothing with us.

Suddenly a noise.

"Is that water?" Henry James asked me quietly.

"Yes," I replied. "He's filling his bathtub."

"Boy, that's exciting," Lennon replied sarcastically.

We both hushed Lennon again.

And there we were-Henry James, John Lennon, and me listening to The Great Unknown take a bath....

The Great Unknown was in that bath for a whole week! A whole week! We, of course, didn't stay outside the door the entire time. We really only stayed against the door for another hour. We probably would've stayed there longer, but Lennon was demanding answers to the situation. Who was this guy? Why were we both so mesmerized? It was hard for us to explain.

As the bath water continued to move quietly from the apartment day after day, Lennon began to see what was so great about the mystery.

But how does this relate to the Great Run?

Well, here is how that day worked—

The Happy Angels were not happy. See, every sector of Heaven has angels assigned to watch and observe and make sure we are all tranquil. We call these ambassadors of love the Happy Angels. They are one of 3 groups of angels to avoid up here (I'll get to the other groups later). They didn't like that The Great Unknown was not moving from his bath. "It's not healthy," One of the Happy Angels explained to me in the hallway as they knocked on his door.

"Really?" I asked with a slight sarcastic tone. "So he should be happy with the fact he's dead and he doesn't know what his life was about?"

"Exactly," the Happy Angel replied and patted me on the head (Since all the angels are over 8 feet tall you get treated like a child a lot. You get used to it.). "Very good." Idiot.

The Great Unknown didn't come to the door.

They flew through the door (At least, they knocked first this time).

From the hallway, I heard them ask The Great Unknown a series of questions. He didn't answer a single one! Is that cool or what? He stuck it to the angels. He really didn't care about anything!

Then the angels left. Here's where it gets interesting. They began to do some investigating into The Great Unknown.

The Happy Angels had a discovery. Last week Monday, they flew into his apartment again. Henry James and I both stood in the hallway waiting to see what would happen. The angels who went in were clearly happy about something. This is all we heard from the door....

".... So we went to your old home and recovered all the unpublished copies. We then took them to a publisher in Heaven's London. He read the work and was very excited. Well, your work is published finally! Isn't that great? All your books are coming out in print. As we speak they're arriving in all the book stores throughout Heaven..."

And that was when the famous run began!

He sprinted out of that apartment wearing only a pair of shoes and a towel! He knocked both James and me over! Down the hallway! Down the stairs!

He raced down the streets! Knocking down numerous people along the way! He really didn't give a fuck about anyone! It was amazing! Here was a half-nude man running through Heaven as if his life was in danger.... Something like that is just not a common occurrence in Heaven.

The Great Unknown raced into the first bookstore he could!

And there were his five books. Published. Staring right at him. He slowly grabbed one book and opened it. (The book dealer has told this story over a hundred times. James loves the story). He ran his hands along one of the pages....

Suddenly...

Rip!

He ripped his name off the page!   *Rip!*

Then he ripped his name off the cover!

Then he did another book!   *Rip!*

Then another!   *Rip!*

The book dealer (an old man with spectacles that graced his vulture nose) didn't know what to do. We just don't deal with these kinds of situations in Heaven.

Well, The Great Unknown took his name manually off every copy of his books in that bookstore.

He then ran out of that store and into another bookstore! And before the evening was through, he had destroyed every copy of his books in Rome!

Two hours after the run was completed (and he was back in his bath) every damaged copy of his books was sold.

So how did he get the nickname?

Last week, I was sharing coffee with Lennon at The AfterTaste. Lennon was just finishing one of the books (He bought a copy of each). He looked straight up at me (in his moptop haircut), and pointed his finger down at the book until it graced the ripped cover. "This man," Lennon said, "is 'The Great Unknown.'"

And suddenly for all of us, Heaven got a little bit more interesting....

CHAPTER 4

—THE FOLLOWING IS A TAPE-RECORDED MEETING AT THE AFTERTASTE AT NOON ON THE FIRST DAY.

Sound: Tape player clicking on.

Fitzgerald: (puffing on a cigarette).... Has The Great Unknown left his apartment yet?

James: No, not yet, but...

Woolf: (interrupts) What's with the tape recorder?

Me: I want to record our discussion today. Maybe get some useful stuff for my book.

Woolf: Good idea.

Me: (directly into tape player) Okay. It's noon on day one of 3. Everyone is at the AfterTaste for lunch as usual. Sitting next to me is Charles Dickens.

Dickens: Yes?

Me: I'm just saying you're here.

Dickens: To whom?

Woolf: He brought a tape player, Charles.

Dickens: Oh.

Me: (coughing) Next to him is the lovely Virginia Woolf.

Woolf: Charming lad.

Me: And then Henry James, F. Scott Fitzgerald. On the other side is Sylvia Plath. Say, "hi" into the tape player Sylvia.

Plath: (no response)

Me: (sarcastic) Oh, thank you very much, Sylvia.

Sound: Tape player is being put onto the center of the table.

James: So what do you need to discuss?

Me: I began writing the book this morning.

Fitzgerald: (slowly) It's about time.

James: How is it going?

Me: Well, ok, I guess… Of course, I'm taking a different approach to writing it.

Woolf: What do you mean?

Me: Well, I hope to have it done in 3 days.

Pause.

James: What?

Me: I hope to have it done by midnight two days from now.

Pause.

Me: Is everyone ok?

Dickens: You're planning to write an entire book in only a 3-day period?

Me: Well, I figure that way I can get everything out in a quick fashion. I won't have to stress over the work….

James: (interrupting) That's idiotic.

Me: Listen, I know I'm not a writer like you guys are. I'm not expecting to make a great piece of art…. And I also fear that if I spend too much time working on it, it might become a post-modern novel and we all can't stand those and…

Woolf: (interrupting) Writing is an artform.

Me: I know, but this is only a story. My story. It's no big deal.

James: This is ludicrous.

Me: It's how I want to do it.

Fitzgerald: Why only 3 days?

Me: Well, I spent only 3 days in Rome. Also, I fell in love in those 3 days. My life changed forever because of those 3 days. So, I thought it would be a nice way to draw everything together.

Plath: You also died because of those 3 days.

Me: Yeah, I know…. It'll show the effect she had on my life and me.

James: You've lived an incredible life. You have the potential to create a great work about your life and you're throwing that opportunity away.

Me: That's your opinion.

James: It's not an opinion, it's a fact!

Me: Listen, all you guys do is complain about how nothing today is written with any kind of originality. Everything is the same humdrum work. I thought putting myself under the gun would spark something new. You have to like that?

Pause.

Me: Why is everyone so upset about this?

Woolf: This is our artform. We all lived for this. You can't expect us to be impressed by someone who thinks they can do what we did in such a short amount of time.

Me: I'm trying to make something different. I'm not trying to write like you. I'm trying to create a new kind of book. If I wanted to do something like your writing, I would slave over it for 3 years or something like that…

James: Slave?!

Me: Bad choice of words. I apologize.

Woolf: So what kind of advice did you want?

Me: Well…

James: He doesn't want our advice Virginia. He already knows everything.

Me: What?

James: You already said as much. He doesn't want our help. He has
everything already figured it out.

Woolf: Be easy on him, James. He's only a boy.

James: Plus, he doesn't have the time. He has to finish a hundred pages
a day for the next few days. I think he better be going.

Me: But I...

James: (interrupting) But you have so much work to do, don't you?

Pause.

Me: I can't believe you're acting this way!

James: Didn't our friendship affect you regarding the artform?

Me: Of course, it did. I mean I could have done this on film or maybe
tape, but I decided to do a book because of all of you and...

Fitzgerald: (interrupting) I find this all quite ridiculous.

Pause.

Me: Ok, I'll go.

James: Sure.

Me: This tape didn't help at all.

Sound: Tape player being picked up.

James: Well, it's not our...

Sound: Tape player turning off.

CHAPTER 5

—I MADE IT TO THE EMBASSY...

"Do you have a passport?"

"I did," I responded, "I threw it into the river last night."

The man at the American Embassy sighed and looked back at his forms. You could tell he was annoyed with his job. "Why did you do... Nevermind."

"Ok," I replied. I couldn't believe I made it there. I was still catching my breath from the run. It was a little bit of a hike to get there, let me tell you.

"Now," he said looking up. "I need some kind of proof that you're an American."

"Like a driver's license?" I asked quickly.

"Yes," he replied. "That'd be perfect."

"I threw that in the river last night too. Got a good throw on it off the bridge. It skipped right across the water. Better than a smooth stone."

"That's thrilling, but I need something."

"Don't we all?"

"What?" I was just one confusion after another for this man.

"Don't we all need something, you know, deep down, you know, in our hearts. Aren't we all just looking for something?" I asked.

"No." He hung his head and rubbed the temples of his forehead with the palm of his hands. "I need proof that you're an American."

"Well, listen to me," I said. "I sound American, don't I?"

He looked up at me. "Yes, but that can be imitated and…" He stopped in midsentence. He looked at me closer. It was like he was almost beginning to recognize me from somewhere. Suddenly he began to sputter. "Oh, Christ, you're an American! You're an… Oh, my… You came here. You came here! Why did you come here?!"

"I was being chased by the cops. I needed a haven and…" I tried to explain.

His sudden fearful movements interrupted my train of thought. This man was really freaked. He slowly got out of his chair backwards. He almost tripped on the leg of the chair. I really, really stunned him. "Do you have any idea what you just did? Oh, my God do you have any idea what you did by coming here!?"

"I'm starting to realize it's a bigger problem than I first thought it was." I tried to sound reassuring. His movements were quite comic. Like he was physically stuttering. "Wait…. Wait… Wait right here."

He then backed up and ran into an office slamming the door behind him. I was still living under my first philosophy so I really didn't care what was going on in that back office. So I twirled my thumbs as I listened to a group of office workers from the Embassy argue from the other room. Every now and then, an exclamation was loud enough to reach my ears. Some notable things I heard were:

"…International incident…"

"…National embarrassment…"

"…Can we get that asshole out of here?…"

"…When does the ambassador get back?…"

"…If we let him go and it is discovered he is an…"

"…Hide…"

Suddenly the office door opened and a nervous looking bald man came out. He looked down at me in my chair. You could see the sweat as it formed on his forehead and then flow down, down, and off his nose. Drip. Drop. "Hello," he said. You could hear the strain in his voice to stay calm. I think he was worried I was going to snap at any minute.

"Hello," I replied mimicking his tone. I was being a complete jerk. It felt good.

"How are you?" He asked slowly.

"I'm fine," I replied slowly.

"That's good."

"Yes it is."

We paused. "Can you come with me someplace?" He asked.

"Sure," I said getting up. He led me down the hallway and up some stairs. It felt weird and strangely wonderful walking through those hallways. Everyone stopped to look at me. I was like a hero on parade. Well, maybe not a hero. But I was definitely *something* on parade.

The bald man with the sweat opened a door and motioned for me to enter. "Please come in." It was an extremely ugly, old bedroom. Everything looked like it was out of the early sixties. A very, very ugly room.

"It's nice," I lied.

This stunned him. You could tell he thought the opposite (like any sane man would). "Could you wait in here, please?"

"Sure," I replied.

"Someone will be up to help you in a little while." He backed up slowly to the door. Suddenly (like he was jumping) he ran out, closed the door quickly and locked it.

I spent the rest of my first day in Rome in that room. Now and then, someone would come up to give me food, but they didn't know anything. At least they claimed not to know anything. It felt like I was already in prison…. Home, sweet home.

CHAPTER 6 — I'M INTERRUPTED ...

Damn it!

My apartment was raided again by the "Ghost Patrol." God, I hate these angels! They do the same thing every time. First they kick in the door (I have a doorbell for a reason), and then they come in waving their "mighty" badges in my face (Their badges look ridiculous. They're gold and it looks like the main entrance of the pearly gates with two giant wings on either side. If you ask me the shape looks more like a windmill cookie than a badge of authority). To top it all off, their outfits look as silly as the Vatican Police uniforms. It's like they think they're out of a 1940's mystery. Picture this-

An angel in a fedora (halo above hat), in a gray trenchcoat with the wings coming out the back and a wrinkled business suit. It's like they have seen too many Bogart films...

Anyway, so they burst in and....

Wait a second....

Let me do this a different way....

It was a cool, dark afternoon in the afterlife.

I was busy on my typewriter trying to work out another chapter. Trying my best to finish my dime store novel before the end of the third day. I don't carry a gun, but I do take shots of whiskey. I gulped another one and allowed the fine liquid to seep down my throat. The light from the light pole outside my window streamed through the shades painting a picture of black and white stripes on my red carpet (It was actually quite bright outside, but I thought adding this touch might add some proper atmosphere-think film noir… I didn't have any whiskey either. Oh well.)

Suddenly my door was kicked in by two thugs. The Ghost Patrol. Christ, I hate these guys.

"Ghost patrol!" The first one shouted at me waving his badge in my face. "Don't fucking move!"

"I wasn't planning to," I said slowly. I slowly raised my hands above my head. I knew the drill. "See, I'm clean, coppers."

"No, no," the second one said to me. He lowered my hands for me. "We're not here to arrest you." They were playing good cop and bad cop again. I usually love it when they do this. It's so cute… And funny… But not today.

"What do you want then?" I asked. I turned around and went back to typing.

"Look at us when we talk to you!" Bad Cop shouted.

I sighed and turned back around. I really hate these guys. "Ok." I waved my hands in a TaDa fashion. "You have my attention."

"You've got quite the record," Bad Cop said. "We could take you in right now."

"But you won't, will you?" I asked trying to sound scared.

"Shut up," Bad Cop burst out. "I should book you right here and…."

"Wait," Good Cop interrupted. "We came to get his help. We're all friends here."

"Cool, I like friends," I tried to sound excited.

"Sarcastic little…" Bad Cop muttered under his breath. Good Cop hushed him again.

"So what do you want?" I asked, annoyed. "I haven't been a ghost in a while if that's what you want to find out. I've been staying up here in Heaven like any normal happy, dead person."

"Just remember that traveling to earth as a ghost is illegal."

"I know," I sighed. "I know. Can we get to the point?"

Good Cop shrugged his shoulders towards his partner and sat down near me. He had bad breath. All angels for some strange reason have bad breath. It's like breathing in really strong incense from way too close a location. "What do you know about the new kid down the hall?"

"You mean The Great Unknown?" I asked.

They both looked at me,confused.

"That's what we call him," I explained. "What did he do?"

They both looked nervously at each other. Good Cop turned his back to me. "That's none of your business. We're just collecting info on him."

"You're planning to bring him to trial, aren't you? What did he do?" This was getting interesting. I know all about trials and the steps and the procedures. A lot of bureaucratic nonsense, if you ask me. Hell is too full for anyone to be sent there anyway. They basically slap your wrist and send you on your merry way…. But The Great Unknown going down to Earth… Now that's kind of interesting.

"We're not…" Bad Cop began.

"He went back to Earth as a Ghost, didn't he?" I interrupted. "What did he do there?"

"We're not allowed to share that information. We're just collecting info about his personality."

"Character witnesses?"

"Who's asking the questions here?" Bad Cop asked angrily. His wings fluttered angrily knocking over one of my lamps. It broke. Nice.

"That's my lamp," I exclaimed.

Good Cop sighed. "We'll buy you a new one."

"I didn't like it anyway."

"Ok, we were wondering…"

"But a new lamp would be nice," I interrupted.

"We can do that, but we need...."

"One from Paris," I interrupted. "They have nice lamps there, don't they?"

"I think so," Good Cop answered. Bad Cop glared at Good Cop. He walked angrily forward and stared down at me threateningly.

"What do you know about him?" Bad Cop asked slowly.

"Truthfully? Nothing," I replied with a sigh.

"I don't need to repeat your past record to you. You've been caught 3 times taking on the form of a ghost and haunting a said...."

"I know who I was haunting," I interrupted. I was getting bored with this game. I had writing to do. "The man murdered me! I think he deserves a little fear of God, don't you?"

"What he did to you is besides the point," Good Cop sighed. "It's illegal to go back down to Earth. Being a ghost is against the law.... Now are you sure you can't tell us anymore about this Great Unknown? A record is so easy to clean."

"He... likes... baths," I said slowly.

"That's all?" Bad Cop asked annoyed.

"Yes, that's all," I replied. "Now what did he do?"

"We can't share that information."

I threw up my hands in frustration. "Then I guess this conversation is done. Please shut the door on your way out. I'm busy."

Bad Cop moved threateningly forward. Good Cop quickly reached out his hand to stop Bad Cop. They stared each other down. Bad Cop lost. He left the room first. Good Cop walked slowly to the door and turned around to face me. "If you think of anything, you know how to reach us."

"Whatever."

The door shut.

Idiotic angels.

I went back to writing....

CHAPTER 7—HOW I SPENT MOST

OF MY SECOND DAY IN ROME—

"Let me the fuck out of this room!

"You can't keep me in here like this! I'm not in jail! I'm an American! You can't treat me like this! Let me out now, damn it! I know you can hear me out there!

"Let me out of this room! If you don't let me out of this room, I'll break the door down! Don't tempt me! I'll do it! I'll give you until five to open that door!

"Five!

"I'm not kidding! Let me out! I'm dead serious!

"Four!

"Do you want to lose a perfectly nice door!? It'll wreck the hinges on the wall!

"3!

"C'mon let me out! I said, let me out! I'm not kidding here. My ancestors fought for my freedom! I deserve my freedom! Let me out!… What number was I on?….

"Two!

"One more number and you can kiss this door goodbye! Goodbye! No more door! And my tax dollars are not going to pay for a door because you're mistreating a guest!… I'm a fucking guest! Open up!

"One!

"Here I come!"

BANG

"Ok, I need a doctor in here! This really hurts. I think I broke my shoulder blade. It hurts like hell! This is not my fault! I'm suing every one of you for this! This is all your fault! I'm not paying for this medical treatment! Damn this door!

"I really need some medical attention in here! It's my God-given right to have a doctor see me if I need one!

"I'm in pain here because of your door! I can't believe you people did this to me! What did I do to you? Hey! I didn't do anything to you! It's not like I screwed your Grandmother or anything. Not to say your Grandmother isn't attractive or anything, it's just… What I'm trying to say is I'm a good person! I don't need to be treated like this…

"Ok… Ok…. Will it help matters if I admit what I did was wrong?!

"Ok… Ok…. I'm sorry!

"Did you hear me? I said I'm sorry? I admit what I did was wrong! Even though, it was really funny! (Laughing) You've got to admit that, right? Oh, you people know you laughed! It was hilarious! And you think that was funny you should have seen the faces of the Pope and the Bishops around him. Their expressions were hysterical! And…. (Stop laughing).

"Ok…. Ok… It's wrong to laugh. I'm sorry. I won't laugh again.

"I won't…. (Laughing hysterically)… Oh, man, am I a bad person? (Pause)

"I deserve one phone call! I really do. I know I do. I've seen enough prison films to know I deserve one phone call! I want to call my family! I want to call someone! I want out of this room!…

"By the way, who is the idiot who decorated this room? Well, you can tell him from me personally that I think it's shit! Absolute shit! I hope you don't have foreign diplomats in here because this is far from being a good example of American elegance!

"Christ….

"Do you mind if I redecorate in here…. Not too much… Maybe move the bed around. Take down a few pictures or something…. Maybe just a better organization of the room will save the aura of the… The design of the… What is that word I'm looking for?… Hell…

(Bed moving)

(Coughing)

"Don't you ever dust in here!? The floorbeds under this bed are filthy! Disgusting! Oh God, my allergies. I think my throat is closing up. I can't breathe. Oh please let me out. I'm passing out. I can't… I can't….

(Pause)

(Normal sounding) "You guys are really heartless. What if I was really dying in here? What then? You would have a dead person on your hands, wouldn't you? That wouldn't be good. Not good for anyone. Especially for me, let me tell you.

"LET ME OUT, YOU FUCKERS!"

CHAPTER 8

It was the evening of my second day in Rome and I needed to get out. I was going nuts! What made it really intense for me was that the last time I ate was around 10 AM. An entire day without food! Convicts are treated better.... It didn't help that I also knew a party was going on.

A big party. A huge party. From outside my "prison" window I watched as carload after carload after carload of people in suits arrived, pass and wave at the large crowd outside the Embassy; handshakes all around, and inside. Perfect opportunity to escape. Who would notice another person sneaking out of an Embassy on a wild scene like this?

Under my floor, I could feel the bass drum of the band (Smack. Smack. Smack).

I knew 3 things:

1. I had to get out.

2. I had to get some food.

3. I had to get out now!

When I was a kid, I used to sneak into my parents' room (to see my dad's **Playboys**) by bending a clothes hanger and fitting into the keyhole.... And, if by luck or by fate, the keyhole on that door looked exactly the same.... I opened the closet.

The clothing in the closet mimicked the dated style of the room. All the clothes looked like something out of a late Brady Bunch nightmare. Large collars, ugly colors. Bad, bad suits.

I grabbed a hanger holding an awful Hawaiian travel shirt, threw the shirt aside and bent the hanger to my own whims.

Now it's a talent. Careful talent. Of patience... Skill... Damn... Patience again... More patience than before.... God damn hand, stop shaking... Patience...

Eureka!

I left the room.

The hallway was empty. It was an easy escape. Just a walk.... But man, that bass drum was really pumping. It sounded like big band jazz... jazz.... Hmmm.... My mind raced back to my philosophy.... And it did sound like a good party...

Well, I couldn't go to a party like that wearing the same clothes I've worn for two days? I just wasn't in good shape to do that. My clothes were covered with holes and smelled... Fhew... Smelled like sweat. I needed to look good.

I went back to the room and shut the door. I ran over to the closet.

What to wear? What to wear? What to wear?

The only thing that I had even close to a tux in that time capsule of a closet was this light blue monster suit with wide collars... Extremely, extremely uncool. Hideous in every way... I had to wear it. I took it out of the closet and threw it onto the bed.

I decided to take a shower first and then get dressed for the party.

Remember: Fuck them all.

Entering that room was an incredible feeling. I was quite stunning. The diplomats were all (logically) confused by my fashion sense. The members of the American Embassy had a very different expression. It was an expression I happened to know very well. It was the same expression I had when I was dumped for the first time in high school and I felt like my world was falling apart. It was the expression I had when my grandfather (who seemed to be the only person who truly understood me) passed away. They felt like the world had just fucked them.

Fuck them all. I waved at them. "Hello" I mouthed with my lips. I wandered over to the buffet table and began to stuff my mouth. Usually, I'm a very conscious eater. I like to eat with my mouth closed while using all the proper silverware. However, after 10 hours of fasting, I had a different approach… I wiped my mouth, smiled and moved closer to the band. See, I knew if I stood near the center of the party there really was no way they could take me out without a scene.

Strangely enough, no one bothered to take me out. I think they could tell that I wanted a scene. Smart of them, very smart. So, I stood there listening to the band. There were a lot of interesting people at the party. A lot of interesting looks. A lot of interesting languages… And… What… Wait… I… And…

I…

Oh… God…

Bliss.

Revelation…

I saw her…

It was like something reached in and turned on my heart… she reached in and… Beating for the first time…. She… She was…. She is….

The most….

The most wonderful… The most perfect…

I felt instantly…

I…

Pick up… Pick up… Pick up the damn phone… Jesus Christ, James, pick up…

CLICK

Hello, this is Henry Ja…

James! Hi. It's me I'm sorry about earlier today. I didn't mean any disre-
spect. I just had to go my own way….

Yes, how is the book go…

I don't have time. I need your help.

I'll be right over…

No! I don't want you coming over.

Why not?

You'll break my concentration.

You called me.

Listen, James, I need your help. I'm at this difficult point and….

Where is it?

It's when I first see her.

Oh…

I'm having a hard time finding the words.

So, you're at a loss for words?

Yeah.

Why don't you just say that?

What?

*Do this. Describe what she looks like. Make it easy on yourself-make it sim-
ple. Just the fact that you remember the details will impress the reader.*

Ok. Anything else I can do?

What do you mean?

I want the reader to know the feelings. I want them to feel the love.

But you can't think of what to say? You're at a loss for words?

Yeah.

So, say that.

(Pause) That's stupid.

Well, it's your book. You figure it out.

CLICK

She was standing over in a corner of the room talking to two other people (The other two people? I don't remember. I don't care). She was wear-

ing this beautiful sleeveless blue gown. A very dark blue. A very rich blue. It had a low cut and she had on a small necklace with a little red heart on it. It seemed much too simple for the gown she had on. Actually, it seemed like the gown did not fit her. She looked great in it; of course, it's more like she wasn't used to wearing gowns like that. She was fidgeting (She was very careful that no one could tell she was uncomfortable, but, for some reason, I could tell).

She was trying to listen to someone in the group and every time she nodded her head, her black hair got in her face. Her hair was shoulder length and she had a hard time keeping her bangs out of her green eyes. She would use the back of her right hand to brush it off the front of her face.

There was something about her. Something that reached in. Somehow, I felt like something was turned on inside me.... And... And... I was at a loss for words.

Soon my philosophy was going to change for a second time. And this time my philosophy would be permanent.

Pick up, James. C'mon....
CLICK
Hi...
Hi, James. I owe you a drink. Meet me at The AfterTaste.

Chapter 9 — Lame

It was around 2 PM at The AfterTaste—

"So there you are in that blue suit…" Fitzgerald began slowly.

"With the large collars," I interjected.

"And did she see you yet?" James asked.

"No not yet," I replied, "I was still on the other side of the room."

Woolf leaned forward on the table. "Then what did you do?"

"Well, I had to say something."

"Yes?" Woolf asked.

"And I tried my best to think of something."

"Ok…"

"You have to understand my mindset at that moment. I was trying really hard."

James looked up at me from his espresso (which I bought for him) annoyed. "Just get to the point."

"You have to understand that I was in awe. In that little instant, she became my world."

"He's stalling," Woolf moaned.

"She was the reason I was breathing from that moment on."

"Get on with it!" Dickens said annoyed.

"But you have to understand (They all moaned) that I didn't know how long I was going to be at the Embassy. I didn't even know if I was ever going to leave the Embassy. And if I left the Embassy, I didn't know if I could find her in Italy. I couldn't lose her after just seeing her. So the question I asked her seemed very logical at the time…"

"What did you say?" Woolf asked slowly. I could sense the annoyance in her voice.

"I didn't know what I was saying was a bad pickup line. I mean, I knew it was a pickup line. I just didn't think of it as a line. Wait. No, that isn't right. I didn't think of it as a pickup line. Even though, I really was trying to pick her up, but not in the typical sense of pickup. (Everyone moaned louder) I just thought of it as a good question."

"What did you ask?" Fitzgerald asked in a very angry tone.

"So do you come here often?" I asked with a smile. After those words left my lips it felt like everything in the room stopped to center on us. The gravity instantly increased by 20X. And my world fell right on top of my shoulders (which felt extremely weak-made out of paper).

She looked up from her drink at me annoyed. "What?"

It was at that moment that I realized that I just used an incredibly bad pickup line on the woman of my dreams. I quickly tried to cover myself, but I was clearly rambling. I could feel the sweat forming on my palms (my old philosophy was clearly out the window). "I didn't mean that as a pickup line. I meant it as an actual question. Not that I don't want to pick you up, I do. I really do. I mean, wow. Look at you. You're great. Not that I'm just interested in sex or anything. I mean, the sex would be great. Incredible. Life changing, I'm sure. But I want to get to know you. Bond. Talk. Whatever. And I'm stuck here all the time. Well, I, at least, think it'll be all the time. I can't really be certain. I just got here. Granted, most of Italy wants to kill me now, so really I'm not going to be able to leave anytime soon. And what I was thinking…"

"Okay, shut up now," she interrupted with controlled anger.

"Okay," I said slowly, hanging my head. I knew I totally blew this.

"At the moment, you're wanted by the local law and many, many angry and armed people. You aren't supposed to be at this party for the

Ambassadors. If you could please go back to your room immediately before you cause another international scene, I would greatly appreciate it. Now I have to get back to my job." She began to walk away.

"Wait, I…" She didn't turn around. I knew I totally blew it. Lame.

Lame.

Lame.

CHAPTER 10 — LAMER

"But you didn't stop there?" James asked.

"Well, my curiosity was peaked. Here was this beautiful, intelligent woman who had totally taken my breath away. I had to know her name."

"But she made it pretty obvious she wanted nothing to do with you." Dickens stated.

"Yeah, I know," I replied. "But I was so gungho over her I didn't care. See, I figured if I at least got to know her name I could fight to repair my image over the next few days."

"So what did you do?" Dickens asked.

She was over by the punch bowl filling her drink. She was alone. It was a perfect, perfect opportunity. I couldn't let this chance pass me by. I carefully walked up behind her. I could smell her hair. Even her hair smelled great. I lightly coughed.

She turned around. Her face instantly fell into a frown. "What are you still doing here?"

"I'm sorry," I quickly replied. "I was on the way out. Back up to my little ugly room and all. Extremely ugly, ugly room, by the way. Someone should really do something about that room and… "

"What stopped you?" She asked interrupting me.

"You did."

"I was right here," she replied confused.

"No," I shook my head. "I couldn't stop thinking about you. You were haunting me."

I could tell from the look on her face that I was not winning her over. I waited for almost a minute (Well, it at least felt like a minute) for her to ask me a question. She didn't respond at all. She just kept staring at me with the expression I was getting to know all too well.

"What, I mean, is I wonder, if I can get your name."

"You want my name?"

"Yes."

"Why?"

I paused. "Because I'm curious."

"What would knowing my name prove?"

"You know my name."

"The whole world knows your name right now. You caused a major international incident."

For some reason, her stating that made me feel a little cool. Not everyone can pull off something like that. I had to fight to hold back my smile. I think a little of that smile sneaked out because when I looked up at her, her glare had increased.

She continued her explanation. "Everyone. And I mean everyone knows your name. Where you are. And what your ass looks like."

This was new news to me. "What do you mean they know what my ass looks like?"

"A picture was taken," She replied. "It's on the cover of most newspapers."

"My ass is on the covers of newspapers across the globe?" This fact couldn't help but stun me a little bit.

"Yes, it's a lovely picture," she replied sarcastically. She sipped a little from her drink and looked to the side as if to find someone else to talk to. There was no one else there.

I paused and allowed my words to slowly and quietly seep out. "Who would have thought mooning the Pope would cause such a controversy?"

"For Catholics, he is the spokesperson of God here on Earth," She replied annoyed.

"Yes, but he has a butt too," I answered. "I mean, a person does not stop going to the bathroom once they become Pope... Or do they? To tell you the truth I really don't know. The self control would have to be incredible to pull off stopping such a natural function...."

"Listen," she interrupted quickly. "This is a really interesting conversation..."

"It's not as if he doesn't know what a butt looks like," I interjected.

She sighed and kept talking. "I really have to go mingle with some of the representatives here. Please, get back in your room like my earlier..."

"Tell me your name first," I interrupted.

"Why do you want to know my name?" She asked again.

"Why don't you want to tell me?" I asked in return.

She paused and glared at me. I could see her mind was trying to figure me out. She blew some of the hair out from in front of her face, sighed, and told me. "Ok, fine. My name is Toni Lyn Morelli."

Her name couldn't help but surprise me. "Toni?"

"No, Toni Lyn," She corrected.

"So it's one word than?"

"No, it's two."

"So Lyn is the middle name?"

"Yes, but..."

"So people call you by both your first and middle name?"

She was really starting to get upset with me. "What's so hard to under-stand here?"

"It just seems a little..." I began to use the word 'odd' but I noticed the look that was forming in her eyes. It was a look that I did not want to explore. It was actually more intense than the look I had seen earlier. I wisely decided to alter my choice of words. "Different. But in a cool dif-ferent way."

"Now, you know my name," She replied. "So if you could please get upstairs before you cause another scene, I would greatly appreciate it."

"Is Toni short for something?" I asked.

The look in her eyes grew hotter. "That's ok," I replied quickly. "We'll talk about it another time."

I turned and quickly began to leave the room. I may have just ruined my chances with her, but at least I knew her name.

So this is what I knew by this point:

1. Her name is Toni Lyn Morelli.

2. I annoyed her.

3. She's an American.

4. I annoyed her a lot.

5. I was not leaving the Embassy again…. Well, at least not without her…. But would she be here at another time? Is she from the Embassy? Where will she go? These thoughts began to bother me.

CHAPTER 11 — LAMEST

"Just out of curiosity," I asked, "Does anyone know if 'lamer' and 'lamest' are words? Or is it supposed to be 'more lame' and 'most lame'? Because I was thinking of using the…"

Dickens interrupted my question with a moan and a question of his own. "Please tell me you went up to your room and left it at that?" Everyone at the table seemed annoyed with me. Halfway through my last story, James got up to get a drink. He hates hearing about Americans acting like idiots in Europe. Of course, for a while there I represented the king of idiots.

"Actually, I started to go up to my room."

"Oh, no." They all moaned together.

"But I wondered how I could contact her. I mean the Embassy was a big place. She could work anywhere. And what if she worked part-time? Getting the name was not enough."

"But you could have asked someone about it the next day. Why bother her again?" Woolf asked aghast.

"I guess I just had to see her again."

When I entered the room again, I noticed her right away. She was talking to some of the other Anerican diplomats on the side of the hall. She was laughing… Well, she was laughing until she noticed me enter the hall again. You can't help but stand out when you're wearing a bright, ugly blue suit…. Even from that distance, I could read the words on her lips: "Oh, God…"

I walked up. The other diplomats quickly moved away. Like most of the people at the party, they didn't want to be seen with me. I was a walking time bomb of danger and bad press. I could have probably destroyed any one of their careers with only a handshake. For some reason, Toni Lyn didn't worry about her career. She was just annoyed by me and that was enough for her. "Excuse me, Toni," I began.

"Lyn." She ended her name for me. I didn't catch that that was the point.

"Ok," I tried again. "Excuse me, Lyn."

"No, Toni Lyn," She corrected.

"That's what I thought it was," I replied confused.

"Then why did you only call me Toni?" She asked.

"I was trying to be personable," I explained.

She sighed. "What do you want now, Moonboy?"

"Well, I…" I paused and looked confused. "Moonboy?"

"Haven't you read any papers since yesterday?"

"No… They didn't even bring me food. I probably would've eaten the paper if they brought it."

She seemed a little appalled by that. I guess she didn't know how they were treating me. "I'm sorry for that. 'Moonboy' is what they are calling you in all the papers."

I was not only the cause of a major international incident; I also had a new nickname! Like most nicknames, I didn't like it. "Moonboy? Kind of lame."

"Well, what would you've liked?" She asked. Suddenly it felt kind of playful between us. "Assman?"

"No."

"The Crack?"

"Even worse."

"Holy Buttocks?"

"That's the pope's butt, not mine."

She paused. "Well, I'm out of butt jokes." Suddenly the playful nature was gone. "So what can I say now to get you out of the party?"

"Well, I was wondering if you work in the Embassy?"

This question made her laugh.

"See, it's nice to know your name and all, but I need to know how to find you after the party is over. Maybe we can talk sometime or..."

She interrupted me. "Just a second." She put her arm around my shoulder and turned me around to face the party. "You see all these people?"

"Yes..."

"All these people-all these important people, might I add-are here to see me."

I looked sideways at her, confused. I could smell her hair again from this location (Don't be distracted). "You can't be the Ambassador?"

She looked at me annoyed. "Of course not. I'm his assistant."

"How did you get a cool job like that?"

"What do you mean?"

"You can't be more than 22?"

"I'm 21," she replied annoyed.

"But that's such an important job."

"You think I don't know that?"

"But you're so young. I expected you to be a receptionist or something."

This really pissed her off. "I graduated from Yale."

"Wow, I'm sorry. I..."

"I graduated early," she interrupted.

"That's so cool," I replied. I tried to sound apologetic. I had a lot of back-tracking to do in this relationship. "I didn't mean to sound so surprised."

She was talking down to me. "I know you didn't. You just weren't thinking again. I'm just glad you kept your pants on this time. By the way, how did you get past all the guards in the Vatican?"

"It wasn't easy," I sighed. "They were everywhere. It took me hours. Luckily, they stand out in those silly outfits..."

"Listen, that's really interesting and all," she interrupted. "But I've got to get back to the party."

"Where is the Ambassador?" I asked.

"What? You don't think I can handle a party like this?"

"No, it's not that…."

"I've been to hundreds of parties like this." She fidgeted in her dress.

"Hundreds?"

"Well, actually this is my first," she replied. She whispered under her breath to me. "I feel like I'm at a prom or something. A lame prom with no date."

"I'll be your date."

She laughed. "Dream on, Moonboy."

"Shouldn't you be out in the crowds more than over here by the punch bowl?" I asked in the most innocent way possible.

It was not seen as an innocent question. "Are you telling me how to do my job?"

"No," I replied quickly. "I'm just guessing you need to mingle more. I've been at this party for over an hour now and other than me, I've only noticed four other people talking to you. And they were other American diplomats."

This really annoyed her. "It's not as if I wanted to host this party, Moonboy. The Ambassador was supposed to be back this morning, but he had to meet with the President to discuss a major incident that occurred when an American mooned the Pope."

I paused. "So right now the Italian Ambassador is talking with the President about my ass?"

She sighed. "Can you please leave the party now?"

"Can I see you again?"

"I'm a very busy person…"

"Can I ask for you from my room? Or pass you notes or something?"

"I'm an extremely busy person," she said slowly. "So if you could leave now I would greatly appreciate it. I will call security if I have to."

"Why haven't you called security before?"

"You don't know?" She asked me slowly. She seemed really surprised by this. "You haven't looked outside today?"

"I did when the diplomats arrived. There were a lot of people out there to see them."

"The crowds weren't there to see the diplomats," she replied slowly. "They're there to kill you. It's called an angry mob."

I paused. "I..." I paused again. "Me... I..." I paused again. "Oh..." I paused for a third time. "Me?"

"Yes, you, buddy," she replied with a pat on my back. "Some people actually are annoyed when someone moons a religious icon. Now why don't you get back to your hidden location so you can live another day?"

I looked at her. Suddenly my entire focus moved from my existence to her. Maybe it was her eyes. Or maybe it was the fact that she still had her hand on my back. But at that moment, all I cared about was seeing her again. "Will I be able to talk to you again?"

She paused. "For my career's sake, hopefully not."

I turned away from her and slowly left the party. This time I was going up to my room. And this time I was going to stay up there...

6. I was bad for her career.

7. She is much more important than me.

8. Her hair smells really, really great.

CHAPTER 12

—WE'RE NOT DONE YET....

I can always tell when Fitzgerald is getting annoyed with me. He has a distinct way of tapping his fingers on a table and rolling his eyes while at the same time acting perfectly calm. He was acting far too calm at the moment. "So let me get this straight," He sighed. "So you annoyed her 3 times that night. But now you have her name and her job position, however she can't stand you. Am I right?"

"Well, almost." I sighed.

"What part is wrong?" Fitzgerald asked.

"The number of times I talked to her that night."

"Don't tell me you went back to see her again!?"

"Well…"

"Listen, I'm really sorry for bothering you again," I said in the nicest way possible.

"Jesus!" She moaned. "What do I have to do to get rid of you? Do I have to call Security? Or maybe I should let the crowd in from outside?"

"I just have a quick request, that's all."

"What could you want now?" She was extremely annoyed with me. Her face was getting bright red. "You have free room and board. And, technically, we're saving your ass by letting you stay here. So what could you want that could be worth threatening that relationship?"

"A dance," I said softly.

"What?" Her face changed. She looked very confused. I was beginning to think I had seen all of her expressions. Not a chance. This one was flattered and confused combined.

"Just a dance," I repeated.

"I don't understand," she mumbled.

"I'd like to dance with you," I replied.

She paused. "Why?"

I decided to be straight up with her. "Well, I think I may be in love with you."

This floored her even more. She was stunned. Her mouth fell open in surprise. "What... What did you just say?"

"I know its nuts. But I never felt this way about anyone before. I mean, seriously I've never been in love before. I mean, I once dated this girl for a few years. Actually, her name is Stacey and we dated for four years. But I think we were more friends than anything. The sex was ok, but there was really no emotional connection. But this is incredible. Wow. The first moment I saw you I suddenly felt..."

"You love me?"

"... I felt happy. Isn't that odd?" I continued. "I just felt like I've found a missing piece of my puzzle. That's what I was looking for all my life. The thing to make life worthwhile. The reason to get up in the morning. You. I just think you are for me and..."

"But you don't even know me..." She stuttered out.

"I know," I replied quickly. "I'm confused by this just as much as you are. So that's why I want to dance with you..."

"How will dancing solve this?" I could see that I was not only confusing her, I was also freaking her out.

"Have you ever read any Jane Austen books?" I asked quickly.

It was like her mind had to jump onto a different track. "I had to read **Pride And Prejudice** in high school. I liked it a lot. Great characterization."

"Good, good," I tried my best to explain this quickly. "See, in all Jane Austen novels you can tell how well a couple is going to get along by how well they dance together. Dancing equals whether they are a good couple and if they are meant to be together. And I figure if we dance together I can use that to figure out whether I am totally nuts or really in love."

"This is so strange," She mumbled to herself.

"Trust me, I totally agree with you."

She sighed and looked down at her feet. I had no idea what she thought of me or what she was thinking at that moment. I guessed that it probably wasn't good, though. She looked up with a serious expression on her face. "If I danced with you once would you leave me alone?" She asked.

"Yes," I replied.

"Forever?"

"Certainly."

She paused. "Ok, let's do it."

I moved over to stand alongside of her. We watched the band as they finished another song. It was a pretty good big band. Not great. The dance floor was pretty empty. It was almost midnight so many of the older diplomats were gone.

"Next song," she said to me.

"Ok," I replied.

Suddenly the band began to play "Sing, Sing, Sing" by Benny Goodman. A classic fast swing song. Probably the best. However, it is the worse when you want to slow dance with a woman's emotions.

"Ok, let's go," She replied abruptly moving onto the floor.

"Wait," I responded.

"What?" She looked at me annoyed.

"This isn't a slow song," I complained.

"Slow songs are easy. If we can dance to this then I think we'll have a real answer."

I paused.

"Or are you chicken?" she asked.

I grabbed her hand and led her out to the floor. I was going to fast swing dance with her to prove my love.

"Swing dance?" Virginia Woolf asked. "What's that?"

"It's the dance style that goes with jazz music. It takes a lot of practice," I replied.

Woolf looked around the tables at the other. "What does it look like?"

"It's fast," I tried to explain. "It's also coordinated. If you do it right she should be spun and thrown around a lot."

"I think I'll look into this," Woolf mumbled to herself. "Sounds like fun...."

"Did you do that to her?" Fitzgerald asked.

"Oh, like you wouldn't believe..."

I turned her.

I threw her up in the air.

I spun her left and right.

We covered every inch of that dance floor.

We were perfect together. It was like all the barriers between us were removed. We moved in sync. Every thought I had, she was prepared for. Every turn I made, she moved with me. Every step I took, she stepped with me.... It was the most spiritual experience of my life.

And when that long jazz song came to an end, both of us were covered with sweat-we were breathless. People began to applaud us. The band even applauded. She looked up me. Her face was flushed. She smiled excited. "That was better than sex."

"That's because you've never had sex with me," I replied between my heavy breathing. I looked back at the band. "Can we get a slower song?" I called over to them.

The band began to play "If I had you."

"I love this song," I said to her as we began to slow dance to it.

"I thought you loved me," She laughed. I could feel that the tension was gone between us. She was much closer in my arms. I could smell her hair again. Even her sweat smelled good.

And then, at that moment, holding her close, my philosophy changed. This time it was permanent. It would never change again. I would never allow this philosophy to ever be changed. It was:

"All For Her."

CHAPTER 13

"What a sweet scene," Plath said. I could hear a little sarcasm in her voice. I tried not to take it too hard. She sounds that way about most things.

"Then what happened?" Dickens asked.

"Well, we danced for about 3 more songs," I explained. "It was incredible. It was like our bodies were meant to be together. I never stepped on her foot. And if any of you've ever seen my dance skills, you'll know that's quite an accomplishment. We were in sync. It was like finding another part of myself."

"So what you're saying is you were both in love?"

"Yes, Charles," I replied finishing off the last of my coffee. "We were in love."

"Now you stay here in your room," she said to me. After all that dancing she had to walk me back to my little prison. It was like she had to be sure that I was safe.

"Ok," I replied. I felt like a nervous teenager after a first date. Do I kiss her? Do I make a move? Does she want me to make a move? Of course, the sides were a little switched. She walked me to my door. What is the etiquette here? Do I wait for her to make the first move? Or maybe I'm just thinking about this too much? Asking too many questions? Of course, when I looked over at her I could see her mind was racing with the same problems.

"I've got to get back to the party," she said to me softly.

"Ok."

"Ok?"

"Ok," I confirmed.

She smiled softly. Everything was soft with her now after those dances. It was like I found a different person under that hard shell I first saw. A person I always knew was there…. How did I see this inside her? I mean, most guys wouldn't have kept going down there to be mocked and criticized like I did. It's like I wasn't in control of the situation. Another person was controlling my story…. Frankly, I didn't care what that author wanted me to do. I was going to kiss Toni Lyn… I reached out and touched her right cheek. She smiled at me. I leaned softly in and….

Bliss…

Allforherallforherallforherallforherallforherallforherallforherallforher…

A little moment of perfection was there.

We stopped kissing. Slowly, we both opened our eyes.

"Wow," we both said at the same time.

"That was an incredible…" She began.

"Kiss… I never had a…" I continued.

"Kiss like that before…. I can't believe…"

I smiled. "Hi."

She smiled back. "Hi."

"How are you?"

"I'm fine. How about you?"

"Super."

We paused and just enjoyed smiling at each other.

"Get to the next scene," Fitzgerald sighed.

I looked at him annoyed. "I'm trying to create an emotion for the reader."

"They know what you're doing. Readers have seen moments like this thousands of times. The first moment of the discovery of love has been recreated in poetry and plays and stories since the artform of storytelling was born."

"So what's wrong with me doing it?" I replied. "And this is a true story, not a piece of fiction. It's… Forget it, I'm going back to my room."

Woolf and James looked angrily over at Fitzgerald. "Are you going to come back later?" Woolf asked me.

"What's going on here tonight?" I asked.

"It's Bingo Night." James replied.

I sighed. I hate Bingo Night at The AfterTaste. I always lose. But what else is there to do? "Ok, I'll be back later then. I've a lot of writing to do…. Well, a lot of planning to do."

"Good luck," James said quietly. "If you need any help you know where to come." James looked over at Woolf and Dickens-they all made eye contact. "We have nothing else going on…."

As I walked out the door I heard Henry James ask a question of everyone left at the table. "Did anyone else get a visit from the Ghost Patrol this afternoon?"

CHAPTER 14 — THE STORY GOES ON WITHOUT INTERRUPTION...

"You have the most incredible smile," I said softly to her. "I could stand here and look at it all day."

"It's night," she laughed quietly.

"All night then."

"I've got to get back to work, though," she moaned.

"Will I see you tomorrow?"

She paused and placed a finger on her cheek like she was thinking deeply about the subject. "Let's see. I think I may be able to squeeze you in between my important lunch meeting and my two o-clock appointment with the Ambassador... And hmmmm. Then I have..."

"All I am looking for is a 'yes'." I laughed.

"Yes," she said with a laugh. She grabbed my shirt and quickly pulled me closer to her. She kissed me passionately. She ran her other hand through my hair and let out a soft moan... Perfection... Perfect moment. "I really have got to go."

"Ok," I softly replied.

She backed up slowly, bumped into the wall, laughed, turned and ran away.

After she was gone, I turned and entered my room.

I tried my best to fall asleep... I couldn't... I couldn't stop thinking of her eyes.

All for her.

CHAPTER 15

At exactly 5:45PM every evening the sun sets in Heaven. Everything in Heaven outside our control works like clockwork. I opened the shade of my living room and sat on the windowsill. I looked out the window at the street corner below. Suddenly the front door of the apartment complex opened. It was John Lennon. He was carrying his guitar.

John Lennon walked over to the lightpole. He put his guitar strap around his shoulder and leaned back against the pole. He strummed his guitar once and then began to sing "You've Got To Hide Your Love Away."

I went back to my desk and began to write again.

She snuck into my room about an hour later. She quickly shut the door behind her and ran over to my bed. "We've got to get you out of here immediately."

"Why? What's wrong?" I asked. I sat up. I was wearing only an undershirt from the tux and a pair of boxer shorts.

"Someone in the staff is letting in a Mafia hitman. You're going to be killed." As she spoke she ran over to the window and peeked out.

"When?"

"Later tonight."

I got up out of the bed and slowly walked over to her. "How did you find this out?"

She paused. It was almost like she was trying to remember the story. "One of the cooks told me," she said quickly. She walked over near me and lightly touched my arm. "We've got to leave here… immediately."

"You're right… there's no time to lose." I gripped her shoulders in my hands. "We've got to get out of here."

"Right away," she stated again rubbing her hand slowly across my arm… very slowly.

Sex.

"Get dressed. We've got to move now. No time to waste," she said getting out of bed. She quickly began to put her clothes back on.

"I totally agree," I said as I watched her dressing. She has an incredible body.

"If we stay here a minute longer there's a good chance you might die." She looked over at me as she began to button the back of her dress.

I got up off the bed and moved to my clothes. I began to put on my pair of jeans. "Trust me the last thing on my mind right now is dying."

She moved over closer to where I was standing. She looked at me closely in the eyes. "What's the first thing on your mind?"

I laughed.

Sex.

"My God, you're like a locomotive," she said with a smile. She rubbed her hands along my face.

"No, you are," I said holding her naked body close. "I'm just along for the ride. You're the amazing one. It's like working with a professional trapeze artist."

"That's sweet," she smiled.

"You were the artist, I was just that bar that the trapeze artist hangs on to."

"I like your bar." She laughed.

"Thanks," I laughed, "But I meant that bar they do the trick on. The one tied to the top of the big top."

"I think it's called a swing."

"Well, that's what I am. I'm the swing."

"Could you go for another ride?"

"I'm always ready."

"You're an animal…"

> *Sex.*

"Ok, now we really have to go," She stated defiantly. She got up from the bed and put on her clothes in record time

I got up and quickly threw on my own clothes.

She moved over to the door and slowly opened it. She looked left and right down the hallway.

She grabbed my hand and led me out the door. "C'mon, we've got to get you out of here…"

Chapter 16 — Bingo Night

"B34. Does anyone have B34?"

It was Bingo night at The AfterTaste. A lame game, but really there was nothing else to do on a Wednesday night. "I bet you're feeling pretty stupid right now," James said to me.

"B34."

"What do you mean I should be feeling stupid?" I asked.

"Well, that whole, 'I'm going to tell my life story in 3 days nonsense.' This is the first night and you're out and about. It must mean you've given up."

Virginia Woolf leaned over to whisper in my ear. "Don't fret over it. We all say stupid things from time to time."

"G2. The next one is G2."

Virginia Woolf put a token on her card. James looked down at Woolf's card with a glare. He hated losing.

"I don't know what you're talking about," I replied. "Everything's going fine. I'm right on schedule."

"Where are you in the story?" Woolf asked quietly.

"G2."

"We just snuck out of the Embassy. So, I'm right on schedule with the writing. This is a break."

Woolf looked at me as if I was speaking complete nonsense. Henry James coughed a slur under his breath and went back to his card.

"B9. The next one is B9."

"What's wrong?" I tried to get James's attention. "I don't understand why you're having a problem with this."

"My problem is you don't understand what you're dealing with." He replied under his breath. "You're dealing with an artform."

"It's my story. I can tell it the way I want. And I think the best way for me to get through this quickly and with the least amount of pain is by setting a time limit and sticking to it. And I thought using 3 days-the same amount of time it took me to fall in love—was romantic."

"It's romantic," Woolf agreed quickly. "But it's insulting."

"G24. Does anyone have G24?"

"Can we get off this argument please?" I sighed. "I'm getting bored with it."

James looked over at me. "Did you get visited by the Ghost Patrol this afternoon?"

"Yeah," I answered.

James laughed. "When they came by I thought it was for information about you."

"I've been good recently," I replied with a laugh. "I haven't bothered him in weeks."

"O4. Next is O4."

"What do you hope to accomplish with that anyway?" Woolf asked me. She placed another token on her card.

"I want him to be so scared by my visits to his jailcell that he becomes a born-again Christian. And born-again Christians live such boring lives they rarely get up here. Then I don't need to deal with that asshole for all eternity," I replied.

"O4?"

Woolf looked down at her card. She was getting close. She took out her lighter and waved it over the card for luck. "All this negative energy. Why don't you just go see her?"

I paused. "It's too... I can't... I... It's too..."

Henry James leaned over to Woolf. "He hasn't seen her since the day he died."

"Can we please not talk about this?" I replied angrily.

"I think it's important we talk about this," Woolf answered. "It seems to me you have a lot of issues to deal with. It sounds almost like you are still dealing with 'The Pain.'"

I was angry, but I tried my best to hold it back. "'The Pain' is complete bullshit."

"O15. Okay everyone. Who has O15?
Someone's getting close I can feel it.
How are you doing Virginia?"

Virginia shouted back at the Caller. "I'm doing fine. Just keep going."

I looked over Woolf and James. "I'm going to go get a drink. When I get back we're going to talk about something else, ok?"

Woolf and James sighed.

"O15, C'mon people O15?"

I came back with an Iced Drink. These always calm me down.

Woolf was silent for a little bit and looked over at me. "So where did Toni Lyn take you?"

"It was a friend's apartment. She didn't tell me whose it was until later."

"What did it look like?"

"N1. Who wants N1?"

"This looks nice," I said as we entered the apartment. It was quite a large place. Toni Lyn sighed and led me in. I could tell she didn't like being there at all. "So whose place is this?"

"A friend," she replied quickly. I could tell something was on her mind but she didn't want to discuss it.

"Is your friend going to be coming in?"

"Hopefully not," she replied under her breath. She walked over to me and began to unbutton my shirt. "We'll stay here tomorrow. And then tomorrow night, we'll drive to a safer location. We need to get you out of this city."

"Won't that hitman look for me here?" I asked slowly while watching her undress me.

For some reason, what I asked was hilarious. "He won't look here. No one will." She placed her hand on my chest and leaned up to be nearer my lips. "We're safe here. Let's use this time to our advantage…."

She kissed me.

"Did you guys do anything but have sex?" James sighed.

"We loved each other," I replied to him. "And we felt like two kids discovering sex for the first time. Everything was new and perfect between us…. It's hard to explain. We just couldn't get enough of each other."

"N1? N1 anyone?"

"But didn't you guys ever talk?"

"We talked a lot," I sighed. "In that day we learned almost everything about each other. Except our families. That info was to come later."

"Then what did you talk about?"

"The first time I had sex was when I was sixteen," she told me. We were lying on top of her friend's bed. The dawn was peeking through the window. And the rays of the sun swept across the bed and our bodies. We kept out bodies close. "It was awful. Everyone talks about how great sex is. All the movies, all the books. Sex. Sex. Sex. Hell, you would think it was the greatest thing in the world. And there I was at sixteen trying it and I couldn't help thinking of other things. I went over questions for my algebra test. I thought about what movie I wanted to go see later. I just didn't get the thrill out of it everyone said you were supposed to… Well, at least not until now."

"I know what you mean, the emotion is everything," I ran my hands through her hair and looked down at her. She smiled up at me. "Why does it feel so easy to say 'I love you' to you?"

"Because it's true," she replied with a smile. "And for some strange, demented, twisted…"

"This is going to get better I hope," I interjected.

"… wicked, bizarre, odd way," she laughed, "I'm fond of you, too."

"Nice…"

James looked over at me annoyed. "So basically on your third day in Rome all you did was…" He couldn't get himself to say the word.

"I12? How about I12?"

"It was bliss," I smiled wickedly at him. "We were in love. Life was great. Other than the fact the police and the Mafia wanted me for mooning the Pope, life was incredible. I was in love."

"Why did the Mafia want you?" James asked.

"The Mafia is very protective of the pope," Woolf said. "I saw **The Godfather** movies."

"Didn't they kill the Pope in the third one?" I asked her.

"They had the best interests of the church in mind," Woolf replied. "Now be quiet, I'm trying to concentrate."

"I don't know why I bother to play this game," James sighed. He pushed his card away down the table. "So what time did you leave the apartment?"

"After ten", I replied.

"Are you sure your friend won't mind me taking some of his clothes?" I asked her. Her friend (who turned out to be male) happened to be near my size (He was a little taller), and when we discovered that the clothes fit, she handed me a bag and pointed towards the closet.

"I'll take care of it," She replied from the bathroom.

It felt odd to me the fact that she had a key to this guy's apartment and she had no problem giving away his clothes. I wasn't going to get into it, though. I was just happy she was with me and loved me. Why bring up a subject unless I'm sure she wants to speak about it? I didn't want to cause any problems at all. "So where are we going?"

"My dad has an apartment in Venice. We'll stay there until we can contact your family." She replied. She came out of the bathroom. "C'mon let's go." She grabbed the bag of clothes, zipped it up and led the way to the door.

We ran down to her car and got in. Suddenly she paused. "Just a second, I want to do something." She ran back upstairs to the apartment. I waited for about five minutes. Then she ran down. She was panting. "Let's go."

"What I learned later is she destroyed the apartment. She broke the TV, knocked over bookcases, destroyed pictures and left the door wide open."

James sighed and pulled his Bingo card back to himself. "Interesting girlfriend, you have there."

"I would, of course, learn what she did and the reason she did it later," I said. "She was thinking ahead to a possible problem we might encounter... But I was just happy to be leaving with her. We were on our way to Venice."

"Why did she..." James was interrupted by the caller speaking.

"G27?"

"BINGO!" Woolf exclaimed and jumped to her feet. She quickly ran up to the caller.

Henry James looked over at me with a very annoyed expression on his face. "She always wins..."

PART 2—VENICE

Ahhhhhh, Venice.
—Indiana Jones

[The following is a copy of the pamphlet given to the new dead 3 weeks after their arrival in Heaven.]

Greetings!

You're dead.

>>>

Welcome to Heaven, buddy.

Your fellow dead have prepared this pamphlet, so please make sure to keep this out of the hands of the angels. The reasons behind this request will all be explained in detail.

Ok, dig this—Heaven is nothing like you were taught to believe. It is not a place of singing or white gowns or clouds or wings or halos or other nice little frills. Actually, if the real Heaven can be called anything it is this-dusty.

Heaven is made up of five cities. They are all exact replicas of cities on Earth during a specific heyday. For example, the New York City of Heaven is a replica of the town during the madcap 1920's; London is a copy of it in the late 1800's... Etc... Etc.... You can visit any of these towns at any time (Granted, you will first need to get a visa and prepare a statement for the borders explaining in exact detail why you want to visit that part of Heaven).

You will not, I repeat, you will not be allowed to visit the main city of Heaven. God and the Superior Angels no longer like to be bothered by the dead, so don't even attempt to go near the Pearly Gates. We also beg this as your fellow dead, because no matter how bad Heaven is now, it is worse when God is taking notice of it.

Ok, there are some things you should know about in regards to angels. Angels are in a word, annoying. Stay away from them at all cost. There are 3 groups of angels that should be at the top of your list. The first group is "The Ghost Patrol."

As dead, we have the power to visit the living in a form than can only be compared to that of a ghost. You might remember moments like this from your living days. You were home alone and you felt this chill and suddenly you thought you were not alone. Well, you weren't alone. A dead person was visiting. Yes, you too can do this too! Just talk to any of your fellow dead and they'll tell you how. However, doing this is highly illegal. God does not want the living to know the real reason for existence. And having the dead visit with all the answers at their disposal can make matters pretty bad for God. So, the Superior Angels have appointed a group of angels to investigate into any ghost activity and place fines on the people taking part. Hence, the Ghost Patrol.

WHAT TO LOOK FOR:::

These angels wear trenchcoats and fedoras. They look like they are right out of a 1940's mystery film. However, their wings stick out the back of their coat in a very awkward fashion. They usually travel in pairs.

So, if you do want to go back to Earth and see Ma and Pa, please for all of our sake, don't let them see you and for all our sakes do NOT say anything!

The second group of angels to avoid is the Reporters. You will see them from time to time running around holding cameras and microphones. Their job is to make TV shows about how great Heaven is and how much we all love it here. You will notice once you turn on the TV that there are only a few stations and these stations play the same cheesy music over and over again while showing brief interviews with fellow dead. Very, very annoying. And to appear on this station is considered a great embarrassment.

WHAT TO LOOK FOR:::

The Reporters look like a TV film crew. They usually have baseball caps on backwards. The caps will have "HTV" etched on them—That stands for "Heaven Television." The station of God. If you think religious public access stations back home were annoying, you have no idea how much worse it can be.

The last group of angels is the worst. For your own well being, avoid them at all, all, all, all cost. They are called "The Happy Angels." Their job is to make sure we are all happy here in Heaven and they will do whatever it takes to improve a person's mood. Their first step is to answer dreams and wishes. This is not as nice a concept as it sounds. Trust us. If that doesn't work, they give you the drugs. "The Happy Pills" change your personality and give you a forced happy outlook. It has also been known to cause cases of hysteria and hyperactivity.

WHAT TO LOOK FOR:::

There is nothing to look for. They either look like typical angels or worse, they look like us. That's right. They can look like your fellow dead. They can even act like us. Avoid all dead strangers that come up and ask you how you're doing. If this happens, quickly answer that you're happy and walk away.

So, you are in Heaven.

That means you're quite an interesting person. See, everything we knew about Heaven back on Earth iss wrong. Actually, it could be argued everything we knew about the afterlife was wrong. A great example is Hell.

Hell has nothing to do with the living! Kill, maim, steal, it doesn't matter! Hell was set up as a punishment to the dead who had gotten into too much trouble with the angels. It has nothing to do with sins on Earth… Anyway.

Here's the brief story-the Superior Angels were annoyed with the lack of respect from the dead so they assigned the Devils to come up with a place of pain and torture. They then issued a decree—"If you upset an angel they will enter it against your name—a strike, if you will. If you receive 3 strikes you will be sent away for a long time." Creative, isn't it?

Well, as it turns out the Devils are much more interesting than the Angels (Go figure) and the rumors quickly spread of all-night parties, free booze, mud wrestling, trampolines, and discos. Now, Hell is full and if you do happen to decide to wait behind the velvet rope outside their pickup spot (The actual Hell's location is kept hidden), you may be looking at, in the least, 150 years.

That ends the first private report on the afterlife. You will receive a second pamphlet within the next few years (if you have avoided causing a scene) that will go into detail about the Meaning of Life and the truth behind Heaven. The reason any of this is brought up now is to warn you about what you're going to see once you step out onto the streets of Heaven.

It's very likely that you will bump into famous people. Please, don't bother them. Usually, the last thing they want to do is go into great details about the lives they have lived and answer numerous little questions. Chances are, they have already written a book answering all your little questions that can be found in any bookshop in Heaven for free.

Well, that's it for now.

Good luck.

Again, do not allow any angels to find a copy of this pamphlet.

WELCOME TO ETERNITY.

CHAPTER 17

"DO YOU KNOW WHAT THIS IS?" The Great Unknown asked me. They were the first words I ever heard spoken by him. To tell you the truth, I'm pretty sure they were the first words anyone up here heard him speak. So maybe in a way, I should've felt honored that he chose me as the first to bestow his vocabulary on.

I was in The AfterTaste. It was 8AM. I had been up all night writing (See, in Heaven you only have to sleep if you want to. It's not required. So basically, we all do it out of habit. The funny thing is we can still dream. Sylvia Plath has a great quote about dreaming in Heaven. It goes like this, "When I was alive I had nightmares of dying, now I have nightmares about being born." Very cool) and I got bored with my location so I thought I'd come in for a caffeine rush. So there I was drinking my coffee, eating my giant bagel and in walks The Great Unknown.

The second he walked in everyone stopped what he or she was doing and watched him. He just had an air about him that made him noticeable. And then, for some reason, he chose me. He took out of his pocket a folded copy of the "Welcome" pamphlet and slapped it down in front of me. And that is when he spoke the words I earlier quoted.

I paused for a second upon hearing him speak. He looked at me as if I had all the answers. To him, it looked like I was preparing my words carefully to bestow on him-some great words of wisdom. Frankly, I was stunned. So, this is the best I could come up with. Please bear in mind it was 8AM and I was up all night writing. "What?"

He was frustrated. He shook his head 'no'. "WHAT IS THIS?"

Not everyone gets the "Welcome" pamphlet. None of us really knows who hands them out. All we know is that the people who receive them are usually intelligent enough not to discuss them. So, logically, this is the first time I've discussed it with anyone. And the fact I was doing it in a public place did not make it easier. "Sit down," I whispered to him.

He sat down across from me. He was wearing normal clothes. He also looked very well bathed. Strangely enough, he also looked very relaxed. I was going to learn the reason for that later in the day. "HOW MUCH OF THIS IS TRUE?" He whispered to me.

"Well, most of it," I replied. "Of course, it's kind of old. Plus, the writer avoids a lot of key facts that could make a person's death easier up here."

"SUCH AS?"

"Well, when Happy Angels are disguised as us, you can usually tell it's them by their eyes."

"I KNOW," he replied, "THEIR EYES ARE GOLDEN."

"How did you know that?" I asked in a shocked manner. I was about to say that I didn't know he left his room last night, but I stopped myself. I didn't want to look too much like a weirdo.

"I LEFT MY ROOM LAST NIGHT TO HEAR LENNON PLAY, " He said to me. "HE'S STILL GOT IT. AND THEN I TOOK A WALK. I BUMPED INTO A GUY WITH GOLDEN EYES AND…" He started laughing.

"What?"

"NOTHING," He replied. "I'LL TELL YOU LATER."

Interesting. He was actually planning to have future conversations with me. Maybe it was because I was so near his age (He couldn't have been more than twenty-six). Or maybe it's because we lived in the same building. Still, I was very confused by the thought that he wanted to be my friend… I felt strangely unworthy.

"WHAT ARE YOU DOING?" He asked me. He pointed down at my old typewriter.

"I'm writing," I replied.

"OH REALLY." He was very curious. "WHAT ABOUT?"

"I'm telling my life story. The story of my adventure, my life, my death, my great love. You know-all the good bits."

"YOU HAD A GREAT LOVE?"

"Yes."

"LUCKY," He replied. "WHERE ARE YOU RIGHT NOW?"

"Well," I sighed. "It's kind of hard to explain, but me and my girlfriend Toni Lyn…"

"TONI LYN?" He asked.

"That's her name, yes."

"IS THAT ONE WORD OR…"

I was used to this question. I quickly interrupted him. "It's two words. Toni and then Lyn."

"SO LYN IS HER MIDDLE NAME?"

I sighed.

"NEVERMIND. SO WHAT ARE YOU DOING IN THE STORY RIGHT NOW?"

"Well," I replied. "We just escaped out of Rome. We were staying in her father's place in Venice. Just the two of us. No one knew we were there. Not even her father. I guess he was someplace in Las Vegas or something. Anyway, we stayed there about a week."

"SO WHAT DID YOU DO THERE?"

"We basically just hung out and talked a lot."

"I LOVE VENICE," He said to me.

"Me too."

"Do you know what I love about Venice?" I asked Toni Lyn. We were walking down a street in Venice eating ice cream.

"I thought you loved me?"

"Well, that's besides the point."

She looked at me with a comical expression. "Your emotions for me are besides the point?"

"Only in regards to Italian ice cream," I replied quickly. "This stuff is incredible."

"Oh, I agree," she said. "This chocolate ice cream is great."

We paused and savored in the moment of the world's greatest ice cream.

"I wonder why it's so much better than ice cream from everywhere else."

"We Italians do everything better."

I looked over at her and raised one eyebrow. "I can attest to that."

She laughed and wrapped her left arm under my right arm. We were walking over a crowded bridge. After we crossed the bridge, she continued the conversation. "So you love me and Italian ice cream?"

"Not in that order."

"What?"

"Not to say there's an order to my love."

She paused and looked at me with a playful expression.

"Oh God, don't make me choose between the two of you!" I comically cried. "Can't you just accept the fact that I love both of you?"

She paused and watched my performance. "You really aren't an actor, are you?"

"I did a play once," I corrected her.

"Really?"

"It was in elementary school. I played a toothbrush."

"How did it go?"

"I knocked over the kid playing the toothpaste by mistake and he squirted the audience. It was a mess… Everyone left with clean teeth and fresh minty breath, though…. I have this speech from Hamlet memorized. Do you want to hear it?"

No!" She quickly exclaimed. She paused and repeated herself in a more controlled manner. "No, thank you."

"When you want to hear it, just ask," I said.

"Sure," she replied.

We paused and walked for a little longer. There is something perfect about an afternoon in Venice. "Should we take a gondola ride?" I asked her.

"Oh, it's so corny," She moaned.

"But everyone does it," I replied. "It's understood. If I go home and I tell people I didn't take one I'll look like an idiot."

"So you're telling me, when you go home, people aren't going to ask about the international incident or the fact that you were on the run from the police-they'll ask if you rode in a gondola or not?"

"You don't know my relatives," I replied. "It's like them."

"I don't know what the purpose of those rides are."

"They're romantic."

"You've got me here, do you have to try and be more romantic?" She asked me.

"You really aren't fun anymore," I laughed.

"I LOVE MEANINGLESS CONVERSATIONS," The Great Unknown said to me. I thought for a second he was being sarcastic, but he was being serious. I watched him. He was looking around The AfterTaste. There were only a few other people. None of the regulars I hang out with were there yet. Too bad. None of them would believe me when I told them about this conversation. He looked back at me. "CAN I ASK YOU A QUESTION?"

"Sure," I replied.

"HOW DO YOU... HOW DO YOU STAND THIS? ALL THIS?"

"You mean The AfterTaste?" I asked confused.

"NO. THIS. HEAVEN. ALL OF THIS. THIS FASCIST STATE AND ALL."

"I wouldn't call it a fascist state," I said quickly. "I don't know of many fascist states in which the dictator doesn't even notice and control every aspect of his country."

He sighed and looked around again. He looked up at the menu on the wall and looked back at me. "I CAN'T STAND IT."

"And God really has a problem with people thinking of this as a dictatorship."

"WHAT DO YOU MEAN?"

"That's something else they edited from the pamphlet," I explained. "Every two year we have elections."

This stunned him. I didn't hold that against him. This concept usually blows most people away. "ELECTIONS?"

"Yeah," I sighed. "There's actually one coming up in the next few weeks. You 'll probably start to see campaign brochures and signs around any day now."

"BUT...."

"No one runs against him," I quickly added. "Who would dare? So really all you have to do is check him or the other box. But no one checks the other box. Who would dare..."

"WHAT'S THE POINT OF THAT?" He asked.

"As the story goes, when the fighters of the American Revolution started arriving in Heaven they all began arguing for change. See it was pretty rough for them. There were no Heaven versions of American cities yet so they had to stay in Heaven's London. And of course, Heaven's London was filled with British aristocrats. And they were the last people Alexander Hamilton, Thomas Jefferson, Thomas Paine, John Hancock and all the others wanted to be around. So, they began complaining. And supposedly, to make everyone feel more equal God started the elections. The problem is no one had the balls to run against God. Who would? So, thanks to that complaining we have to deal with these ridiculous elections every two years. Which means you spend a few weeks listening to ads and getting angels grabbing you to make campaign promises. Then on the day, you go to a central location in the city where you have to wait in line almost all afternoon to vote," I sighed. "I'm not looking forward to it at all."

"DON'T VOTE THEN," he replied quickly.

I looked at him stunned. "Are you kidding? If you don't vote, the angels worry. They come and ask you if you're all right. If you answer that you're fine, they drill you to find out why you don't like God and... No. No. Who would risk it?"

The Great Unknown sighed. "I'M GOING TO GO GET A CUP OF COFFEE AND THEN I WANT YOU TO TELL ME MORE." He began to get up. He paused and looked at me. "WHY DON'T YOU SAY... WHY DON'T YOU DO SOMETHING?"

I looked up at him. "For her." I paused. "I'm waiting for her."

He smiled, turned and went up to get his coffee. I could read it in his eyes. He was jealous of me.

CHAPTER 18

"He was here?" Henry James asked me. He couldn't believe he missed The Great Unknown by only a few minutes.

I nodded my head without looking up. I was writing again.

"What did you talk about?" Fitzgerald asked. He lit a cigarette and blew the smoke over in my direction. Maybe it was his way of getting my attention. Or maybe it was just his way of annoying me. Either way it worked.

I coughed and looked up at him. "We talked about my book. We talked about Toni Lyn."

"What a surprise," Fitzgerald sighed under his breath.

"And what are you doing smoking in public? That's illegal still if I remember."

Fitzgerald brushed my comment off. "So where are you in the book right now?"

"We're in Venice together staying at her father's place there," I explained and went back to typing. I tried not to feel annoyed by Fitzgerald's attitude. He's a friend. He's just having another rough time. See Zelda (his estranged wife) is in Heaven's New York and every few months or so Fitzgerald will try to reach her by phone to talk. Whenever he calls, Zelda does the same thing. She hangs up…. None of us ask him when this happens. It's easy enough to tell by his mood.

"So let me get this straight," He replied. "Your girlfriend's an Italian American and has a very cushy job with the American Embassy in Italy that we all agree is incredible for someone of her age. And her father has a second home in Venice and you aren't suspicious?"

"Why should I be?" I asked. "Sicily is the Mafia headquarters. And when I asked her about it at that time she had a quick answer."

"He deals in imports," She said with a laugh.

"Importing what?" I asked. We were having dinner at a local restaurant.

"You've got to try this," She said changing the subject. She filled her fork with some of the food on her plate and leaned forward for me to sample. I tasted it. It was wonderful.

"That's great." I swallowed the food. "So what does he import?"

She laughed. "Stuff."

"My favorite," I laughed.

"But what about the fact that she knew about a hitman from the mob coming to get you?" Fitzgerald drilled me. "Didn't that make you think?"

"So who told you again about the hitman that was going to get me that night?" I asked her. We were on a gondola (It took 3 attempts to convince Toni Lyn it'd be fun). These rides can be addictive. The Gondolier seemed surprised by what I asked. He must have been able to understand English. He looked down at me and then quickly looked forward again. Best to pretend he didn't hear, I guess.

"One of the cooks," She replied. She snuggled up against my arm. We leaned back a little more. We were passing another gondola (It can be so crowded on those rivers at night). That Gondolier was singing. We quietly listened to him. After we passed, Toni Lyn sighed. "I love Venice."

"But why would the cook tell you?" I asked her.

"I guess she could tell we were close," she responded. "I really didn't take the time to ask."

"Did you know she was connected to the Mafia?"

She leaned over and kissed me. "I'll be more surprised if she wasn't," she said and leaned back again.

Henry James looked over at Fitzgerald, annoyed. "I'm going to go get a drink. Who wants one?"

I shook my head 'no' and turned my attention back to the typewriter.

"Didn't you learn anything that might've prepared you for what was going to happen later that week?" Fitzgerald asked. He was onto his second cigarette already. Not a good morning for him at all.

"Not really," I replied (patiently). "That entire weekend was a surprise for me…. But I still have a few more chapters before I get to those moments."

"I just can't believe you didn't learn anything of importance before then?" Fitzgerald said and sucked in some more of his smoke.

"Well, I did learn some important things…."

"Like what?" He asked me quickly.

9. Toni Lyn is ticklish.

"Nothing of importance to you," I said to Fitzgerald. I sighed. I was done dealing with him for the morning. I had more work to do. "I'm going to go back to my room. I'll see ya later." I picked up my typewriter and left.

"Stop it! Stop!" Toni Lyn screamed in laughter at me.

"Make me," I replied with a laugh. I was holding her leg tightly under my arm and was tickling the bottom of her right foot with no mercy.

"Oh, stop it!" She screamed again. She grabbed a pillow and whipped it at my head. It missed me.

James came back to the table with his drink. "Where did he go?"

CHAPTER 19

[The Following is the one phone conversation I had with my parents. I didn't know how the call would go so I waited until Toni Lyn was gone from the apartment. This is the first time my parents have heard from me since I went to Europe. They went over four months with no word from me. The call could go any way.]

SCENE—AN APARTMENT IN VENICE. DAY.

I'm pacing the room with the phone in my hand. I'm preparing to call my parents. I stretch and then slowly begin to dial. I walk over to the window and look out. It is a sunny day out. Suddenly the phone clicks.

MOM
(over phone)
Hello?

ME
Hi Mom. It's me.

There is a pause.

MOM
Yes?

                              ME
I need your help, mom.

There is a pause.

                             MOM
Yes?

                              ME
I'm in a little bit of trouble, mom.

                             MOM
You don't think that I know that.

                              ME
I know.

                             MOM
So, what do you want?

                              ME
I need to get home.

                             MOM
Ok.

                              ME
Is there something wrong, mom? You don't
sound…

                             MOM
What? Thrilled? Delighted? Should I be?

ME

What?

MOM

We haven't heard from you in over four months.
We thought you were dead.

ME

I'm sorry about that. I had a lot of thinking to do
and…

MOM

And then we see you on the news. First, I hear
about you mooning the Pope.

ME

I'm sorry, mom.

MOM
(sarcastic)
Oh, you're sorry for mooning the Pope? That's
good to hear.

ME

Mom, I didn't mean to embarrass you.

MOM

You father is a District Attorney. He's a prominent
person. He doesn't need his son mooning important
religious leaders.

ME
I know, mom, I know. I wasn't thinking...

My mom is clearly very upset with me. This is really affecting me.

MOM
Is she still there?! You have to let her go?

ME
She's out shopping.

MOM
Shopping?

ME
What do you mean—'let her go'?

MOM
It's all over the news about the kidnapping.

ME
Kidnapping? What are you talking about?

In the background, my father can be heard walking into the room.

DAD
(in background)
Who are you talking to?

MOM
(to Dad)
No one, Dear.

ME

Is that dad? Dad! Why did you tell him...

DAD

(in background)

I'll be upstairs.

MOM

Ok, dear.

ME

Why did you tell him I wasn't....

MOM

You've ruined him. Do you know that? His career
is over because of you.

ME

What do you mean? I....

MOM

A DA can't have a son who is known for an
extremely rude display. Did you know that he hired
private investigators to try and find you when you
disappeared? We were so worried. And you do this
to him! The kidnapping just about...

ME

Why do you keep saying kidnapping?

MOM

It's all over the news. Why did you take her?

ME
What? You don't mean Toni Lyn, do you?
I didn't…

MOM
Let her go.

ME
I didn't kidnap her!

MOM
Don't yell at me.

ME
I'm sorry. I didn't mean to…

MOM
I don't know you anymore. I thought I
knew you. I…

ME
Mom, I'm sorry for all of it.

MOM
I wish I could believe you.

ME
Why can't you believe me? I'm your son. I wouldn't…

MOM
That wasn't my son who did all that stuff, which I
won't even mention, in front of the Pope.

ME

Mom...

MOM

My son died in Europe.

ME

Mom?

Toni Lyn has come home with groceries. She walks in shutting the door behind her. She walks past me. She pauses. She can tell something is up.

TONI LYN

Is something wrong?

MOM

Is that her?

ME

Yes.

MOM

Did she drive you to this?

ME

I love her!

TONI LYN

What's going on? What are they saying?

ME

Listen I'm sorry for hurting you. It was not my intention. Mom...

                        MOM
          Do you know how many reporters and camera
          men are staked out around our home? Do you know
          that every time we go out we are hounded and
          stared at because of you? Your father is gawked at
          because of you. He was an important person....
          Now he is a washout. A fool.

                        ME
          Mom, I didn't know...

                        MOM
          TV shows debate our parenting skills. Magazines
          discuss us as the worst parents in the world. They
          blame us for you. And no one listens to us!

                        ME
          Mom?

                     TONI LYN
          Honey?

Toni Lyn puts the bags on the floor and slowly walks up behind me.

                        MOM
          And if they did listen, I wouldn't have anything to explain
          you. I don't know why you did what you did. That
          was not my son in those pictures.

                        ME
          Mom, I'm sorry.

Toni Lyn is standing behind me.

TONI LYN

Are you ok?

MOM

Is that her?

ME

Mom.

MOM

And a Morelli! Why did it have to be a Morelli?
You know your father's strong stance against....

ME
(interrupts)
I love her, mom.

MOM

The world thinks you're going to kill her. Her
family is looking for her. Not to mention the
American and Italian officials.... This has killed
your father. He is a walking ghost around the
house. He can't even leave here now. He can't
even leave his own house because of you!

Toni Lyn wraps her arms around me and holds me close. I'm having a
hard time standing up.

ME
I didn't mean to...

> MOM
>
> Well, you did. The only way we have to get through this is to think of you as dead…. You aren't our son anymore. You can't be our son….

> ME
>
> Don't say that…

> MOM
>
> Goodbye.

> ME
>
> No! Wait. Mom. Wait!

> MOM
>
> I'm not your mother.

The phone CLICKS and she is off the line. I slowly put the phone down and turn to face Toni Lyn. She quickly wipes the tears off my face. She then takes me in her arms and holds me tight. Ever so tight.

END OF SCENE.

CHAPTER 20

The Great Unknown knocked on my door at around 3PM. "CAN I COME IN?" He asked me.

"Sure," I replied. "I was planning to take a break anyway." I opened the door and let him in. He wandered over to my desk and began to flip through the pages on it. "No, go ahead. Just read my words." I sarcastically said.

He turned back to look at me. He was excited about something. "I HAVE AN IDEA."

"Ok," I paused. "What is it?"

"I WAS WATCHING HEAVEN TV ALL DAY TODAY…"

"I'm sorry for you," I interjected.

"THANKS," He continued. "AND I GOT THIS REALLY GREAT IDEA. TONIGHT WE'RE GOING TO VISIT THE STUDIO. I NEED SOMEONE TO WORK THE CAMERA."

"What?"

"AND I WAS WONDERING IF YOU WOULD DO IT? THE IDEA OF HAVING THE ACTUAL MOONBOY THERE, IN MY OPINION, IS JUST PRICELESS. JUST PRICELESS."

I didn't understand any of this. What was he thinking? "What would I be filming?"

"ME," He replied. "I ALREADY TALKED TO THIS FILM ENGI-NEER I FOUND AT A BOOK STORE. HE'S GOING TO TAKE

CARE OF THE TRANSMISSION FROM THE STUDIO. SO WE'LL GO ON THE AIR."

"Whoa, whoa." I held up my hands. "You're planning to go on HTV?"

"YEAH," He replied with a smile. "OF COURSE, THE ANGELS WON'T KNOW."

"Illegal broadcast from Heaven?" I was stunned.

"COOL IDEA, ISN'T IT? He asked. His smile got wider...."

"What are you going to say?"

"THAT'LL BE A SURPRISE," He said.

I paused. "I can get in trouble for this. You know I don't want to do anything that will ruin my chances of her..."

"NO NO," he shook his head. "I'LL TAKE FULL CREDIT FOR THIS. PLUS, IT'LL BE AN ADVENTURE. ARE YOU IN?"

It did sound kind of interesting. I mean, this is The Great Unknown. It's got to be legendary. "Sure why not?" I replied. "But I need to be back here by one am. I have a lot of writing to finish before midnight tomorrow."

This confused him. "WHAT? YOU HAVE A DEADLINE?"

"Something like that," I replied. I was not going to discuss this with another writer. I was getting enough grief from the others at The AfterTaste. "But I have a condition."

"WHAT IS IT?" He looked back down at the stack of papers on my desk.

"You have to tell me why the Ghost Patrol is looking for you."

He looked up at me. "OH THAT? I HAD DINNER WITH MY PARENTS ON SUNDAY."

My mouth fell open. "You what?!"

It was Sunday at 6 PM when The Great Unknown knocked on his parents' white, two-story home. His father opened the door. His father was clearly shocked. "Wh... I... Oh... I... Ah... "

"HI, DAD," The Great Unknown said walking past his father into the house. "WHAT'S FOR DINNER?"

"Your mom made pot roast," His father replied. He was too stunned to reply in any other fashion. The Great Unknown stood in the center of his parent's living room and stretched his arms. It felt good to be home.

"WHERE'S MOM?" He asked. His father was, at the time, walking around him trying to figure out whether this was a hallucination or not.

"She's in the kitchen," He replied quietly.

"Who are you talking to?" His mom called from the other room.

"Well, I'm talking to… I'm…" His father didn't dare say his name. "Honey?"

His mom walked out of the kitchen wiping her hands on the end of her apron. "What's wrong with you, dear? I can't understand…" She froze in midsentence.

"HI MOM," The Great Unknown said with a smile. "DINNER SMELLS GREAT."

"It's your favorite," His mom replied in a stunned fashion. "Pot roast."

"GREAT." The Great Unknown walked over to his mom and kissed her on the cheek. "I KNEW I COULD ALWAYS COUNT ON A GOOD MEAL ON SUNDAY. THE FOOD IN HEAVEN IS LOUSY."

It was at that moment that his mother decided to faint.

"HEAVEN IS REALLY LAME," The Great Unknown said over dinner. "IT ISN'T FUN AT ALL."

"You don't say?" His mom said. She was still too stunned to believe what was going on. She was having dinner with her dead son.

"I LIVE IN THIS REALLY DUSTY APARTMENT COMPLEX IN HEAVEN'S VERSION OF ROME."

"Is it a nice apartment?" His father asked.

"NICE TO A POINT, I GUESS," He answered with his mouth full. "I LIKE MY BATHTUB." He swallowed his food. "THIS IS REALLY GOOD, MOM."

"Thanks," His mom said quietly. She was so confused she didn't know whether to finish her meal or ask another question (And what question would she ask?). So, she instead played with her food.

"AT LEAST I LIVE NEAR SOME INTERESTING PEOPLE," The Great Unknown continued. "MY NEXT DOOR NEIGHBOR IS HENRY JAMES."

"You mean from my office?" His father asked.

"NO," The Great Unknown replied, shaking his head. "I MEAN THE WRITER."

"What's he like?"

"I REALLY HAVEN'T TALKED TO HIM YET. I ALSO LIVE NEAR THE ONE AND ONLY MOONBOY."

Both of his parents looked at each other. "You live near Moonboy?"

The Great Unknown nodded his head and ate some more food. "I JUST LOVE YOUR COOKING MOM."

His mom looked over at her husband. Through their eye contact, they made an agreement. "Honey, we would like to ask you a question?

"SURE MOM."

She was very careful in how she worded her question. "Honey… Dear… When you got in that car accident was… was it truly an accident?"

The Great Unknown put down his fork. "WHERE DID THAT THOUGHT COME FROM?"

"Well," his mom began.

His father finished the thought for his wife. "We all know, son about how she got engaged to someone else. We all know how much that affected you."

The Great Unknown rubbed his face with the palms of his hands. He spoke quietly to himself. "YOU THINK I COMMITTED SUICIDE, DON'T YOU?"

His parents looked quickly at each other.

"WELL, I DIDN'T. I WAS LOOKING AT THE ROAD. I ADMIT MY THOUGHTS WERE ON HER. BUT I WAS MORE CARELESS THAN ANYTHING ELSE. I HAD NO INTENTION OF DYING."

"Really?" His mom asked. This thought seemed to cheer her up.

"YEAH MOM," The Great Unknown replied. He tried to give them a reassuring grin. However, he couldn't hide that there was still a great level of pain on his face.

The Great Unknown was standing at the front door. "WELL, I'VE GOT TO GO." He turned back to his parents. They were both holding back tears. "OH, DON'T CRY. DON'T CRY." He gave his mom a hug. His father placed his arm on his shoulder as he hugged her. They stood that way for a minute.

"NOW I'VE REALLY GOT TO GO," He sighed. He wiped away a tear. "I MIGHT GET IN TROUBLE FOR THIS VISIT, SO I DON'T KNOW WHEN I'LL BE ABLE TO SEE YOU AGAIN."

His mom reached over and touched his face. "You take care of yourself, ok?"

"SURE MOM," The Great Unknown said. "GOODBYE DAD."

His dad tried to smile. "GOODBYE."

The Great Unknown smiled and turned. He began to walk away. Suddenly he stopped and looked back at his parents. "COULD YOU GIVE HER A MESSAGE FOR ME?" He paused as he tried to put all his thoughts and emotions together. "TELL HER… TELL HER SHE WAS ALWAYS ON MY MIND. RIGHT UP UNTIL THE END."

"Ok," his father said. "We'll tell her."

"AND THEN ADD," The Great Unknown said with a wicked smile. "I HAVE MORE IMPORTANT THINGS TO THINK OF NOW."

"So you died for love too?" I asked The Great Unknown. Asking this question seemed to wake him up from his story. Suddenly all the pain of her was wiped off his face. He had his game face on again.

"THE BEST OF US DO," He replied with a smile. He got up and headed into my kitchen. "YOU MIND IF I HAVE A GLASS OF WATER?"

I listened as he poured himself a glass. I couldn't help but feel a little jealous of the closeness he had with his family. I know I could never see my family again. They wouldn't greet me with welcome arms. When The

Great Unknown came out of the kitchen, he could tell something was on my mind. "WHAT IS IT?"

"Nothing," I replied.

He finished his glass quietly. "SO ARE YOU GOING TO BE THERE?"

I sighed. What the Hell. "Sure, I'll do it."

He quickly walked over to my apartment door. He was excited about this. "GREAT." He began to open the door.

"You know you're lucky."

"FOR WHAT?" He asked me looking back in my room.

"Your parents," I replied. "You're lucky you have parents that love you."

"I'LL SEE YOU TONIGHT," He said and shut the door.

When Toni Lyn came home from shopping, she found me lying on the ground. I was in the fetal position. Lying next to me on the floor was the phone. It was off the hook. "Oh, my God," She ran over to me. "What happened?"

"My... My parents..." I couldn't get the words out. She could tell I'd been crying. She sat down on the floor by me and moved my head over to her lap. She ran her hands through my hair. "They... They..." I tried to begin. It was too painful to even say.

"It's ok," she sighed to me. "I'm here. It's ok."

We sat in this position for a few minutes. We were both very quiet. Then she began to hum a song to herself in time to her stroking my hair.... Ever so lightly stroking... back and forth... softly...

"They changed their phone number," I said quietly.

She didn't respond. She just kept humming and lovingly rubbing my head. She didn't have to say anything more.

CHAPTER 21

At 11:30PM, I was interrupted in my writing by a knock on the door. I sighed and looked over at my clock. "Fuck," I moaned to myself. I didn't know it was that late. It's amazing how distracted you can become by writing. I stood up and stretched. Another knock. "Just a minute," I called. I sighed and walked over to the door. It was F. Scott Fitzgerald and Henry James. "What are you two doing here?"

"The Great Unknown told us to meet him here," James said with a whisper. He looked left and right like he thought he was being watched. "Can we come in?"

"Sure, why not," I sighed and let them in. Earlier, I felt kind of exciting to be taking part in this stunt with The Great Unknown, but, now, I was beginning to have second thoughts. Not because of the job itself (Whatever that was), I was sure it would be interesting, It's just I only had an evening and a full day to finish the work. I still had to talk about Lake Lucerne and Amsterdam. And then there is the ending...

Both James and Fitzgerald aimed right for the stack of paper on my desk. They both took a hand full of the stack and started reading through the copy. "What is with you writers?"

They both looked up at me with an expression I can only compare to that of a child that had been yelled at by their parents. "So we can't see where you are?" James asked in a very meek fashion.

"Well...."

"We just want to help…" Fitzgerald interrupted with a smile. His attitude was much improved from the morning.

"Sure, why not," I sighed. They both went quickly back to reading my words. I, on the other hand, went into my kitchen to get a drink. "Do you know if anyone else is coming?" I called from the other room.

"All I know about is the 3 of us and someone he's bringing who knows how to work the studio. Someone he called "The Engineer." James called to me.

"Everyone seems to have a nickname these days," I moaned and entered the living room again.

"Have you seen Sylvia Plath recently?" Fitzgerald asked me.

"Not since yesterday morning," I replied. "The last time I saw her was when I brought the tape player to The AfterTaste." I could tell by the expression on my partners' faces that this was not a memory they wanted to revisit. "I was planning to contact her tomorrow. I have this idea I wanted her help on for one of the ending chapters…"

"Well, what's going on with Plath is she's holding a revolt," James said quietly.

"A revolt?"

"A small one," Fitzgerald sighed.

"Against who?"

"Who knows? Who cares?" Fitzgerald sighed. "It won't really matter anyway. Once the Happy Angels figure out what she's doing they will put her on the pill and that'll be it… She claims The Great Unknown inspired her to the idea."

"But what is she doing?" I asked again. I didn't get an answer. The door. I went and opened it. And there was the Great Unknown (wearing a very interesting white suit with a cane) and a very hairy thin man. "Hello," I said.

"HEY," The Great Unknown said with a smile. He patted me on the head as he walked in. He was in very good spirits. "THIS, MY FRIENDS, IS THE ENGINEER."

The Engineer did not look like a man who knew anything about a TV studio. He looked like a man who had not even seen a TV before. He was wearing a red flannel shirt, an old pair of jeans, and big boots. His beard was black and thick just like his hair, which made it hard to tell where the one started, and the other began.

"So how are you doing, Engineer?" I asked in my best attempt to sound casual.

"The Engineer if you don't mind," he replied with a gruff.

"That's what I said," I replied.

"No it isn't," He replied again.

"What do you mean?" This was incredibly annoying.

"You forgot the 'The'," He sighed.

"Oh, I'm so sorry," I sarcastically moaned. This was all childish.

"It's ok," he said, "I won't hold it against you, *The* Moonboy."

It was at this moment that Fitzgerald wisely placed his right hand on my shoulder. He could tell I was ready to deck 'The Engineer.' I relaxed and sighed. He removed his hand.

Henry James walked around The Great Unknown checking out his garb, "So why are you dressed like Mark Twain?"

The Great Unknown smiled. "Because I figure what I'm about to do tonight is the same thing he would have done, if he wasn't hiding in the Outback…"

A Note-

Dense forests and mountains surround every one of the five cities of Heaven. They were placed there by the angels in the hope of persuading the people in Heaven, it is a bad idea to try and leave that city. These miles and miles of acres of forestry are called the "Outback." The Outback did just what the Angels were hoping they would. They have convinced many people it is a bad idea to leave Heaven. It, however, has done the opposite for a small number of others. It has given the others a perfect refuge to hide out it in. Miles of mountains and dense forests is ample territory for hiding. And to all the angels' horror, they did such a good job making the forest difficult that angels rarely find the people hiding there. Mark Twain was one of the first people that went into the Outback. He has not been seen since. Rumor has it, he is living in one of the tallest peaks near Heaven's London and he has completed over 50 new novels.

"TIME TO GO," The Great Unknown said. He stuck his cane out in front and pointed it at the door. "LET'S MAKE HISTORY...."

Henry James leaned over at me. "Do you have any idea what we're doing?"

"No idea, at all..."

CHAPTER 22

It was midnight and we were inside the HTV Headquarters. "Just like angels to trust people and not lock their doors," I sighed.

The Great Unknown laughed. "IT'S LIKE THEY'RE SETTING THEMSELVES UP FOR THIS."

The Engineer patted The Great Unknown on the back. "This way to the studio." We followed The Engineer to the site. It was very eerie being in those hallways. There were no guards, no security. It was just empty. So, unlike everything back on Earth. The Engineer led the way in. When we reached the outside of a studio, The Engineer looked back at us. "I'll come and get you when I'm ready to go. It should only be a few minutes." He went in to the studio.

We stood around silent for a few seconds. The Great Unknown looked over at Henry James, Fitzgerald, and me and smiled, "SO I HAD SEX WITH AN ANGEL LAST NIGHT."

"You what?!" James blurted out.

Fitzgerald and I began laughing. "How did that happen?" I asked.

"WELL, I WAS WALKING DOWN THE STREET LAST NIGHT—IT WAS ABOUT 2AM—AND SUDDENLY THIS DEAD GUY CAME UP TO ME. I HAD NO IDEA WHERE THIS GUY CAME FROM. IT WAS LIKE OUT OF THIN AIR. VERY FISHY, RIGHT? HE LOOKED ME UP AND DOWN AND ASKED ME HOW I WAS DOING."

"He was a Happy Angel," Fitzgerald explained.

"YEAH, I KNOW THAT NOW," The Great Unknown sighed. "ANY-WAY, I KNEW SOMETHING WAS UP. THE MAN HAD GOLDEN EYES. THAT'S NOT NORMAL. SO, I DECIDED TO TEST THIS GUY. JUST HAVE SOME FUN, YOU KNOW. SO I SAID TO HIM I WAS REALLY SAD."

"How did he respond?" I asked with a laugh.

The man with the golden eyes' face fell into a frown. He looked over at The Great Unknown with a worried expression. "What's wrong? Is there anything that you want?"

"WELL, THERE IS SOMETHING," The Great Unknown replied with a very heavy sigh. "BUT I NEVER CAN EXPECT THAT DREAM TO COME TRUE."

"All dreams are possible," The man replied. His voice had a strange tone to it. It was almost like he was speaking through a harp or some guitar strings. There was music behind his voice. "What is your dream?" He also had the most incredibly bad breath.

The Great Unknown sighed and looked at his feet. "WELL, WHEN I WAS ALIVE I WAS NEVER TRULY EVER... WELL... I WAS NEVER... SATISFIED."

The man with the golden eyes looked confused. "What do you mean? You didn't have a good meal?"

"NO, I'M NOT TALKING ABOUT EATING..."

"Drinking?"

"NO, NOT DRINKING."

"You weren't satisfied with your job?"

"NO, NO," The Great Unknown replied with a laugh. "I'M TALK-ING ABOUT SEX."

The man with the golden eyes looked worried. "What sexually troubled you?" When he asked this question there followed a rustling noise under his coat. It sounded almost like wings readjusting themselves under fabric.

"WELL, I'VE ALWAYS HAD THIS FANTASY AND…"

"What is it?"

"IT'S KIND OF EMBARRASSING," The Great Unknown said. He looked away like a nervous child. He was playing a game, but the man with the golden eyes could not see that that was happening. He thought this was all legitimate. "I'VE ALWAYS FANTIZED ABOUT… WELL…"

"What, my child?"

"ANGELS." The Great Unknown quickly stated. "I WANT TO FUCK AN ANGEL."

The man's mouth instantly fell open. You could see this was an odd request and one he did not often hear. "That's…"

"I KNOW IT'LL NEVER COME TRUE, "The Great Unknown replied quickly. "BUT IT'S ALWAYS BEEN MY DREAM."

"I have to go," the man said quickly. He scurried away down the street. The Great Unknown laughed under his breath and continued his late night stroll.

Later that evening, The Great Unknown received a surprise at his apartment. Waiting for him was an angel standing in his living room. "HELLO," The Great Unknown said in a confused style, "CAN I HELP YOU?"

The angel was beautiful. She had long flowing light blonde hair (that seemed to move under it's own wind. Flowing left and right. What was moving that hair?); Her skin was a brilliant bright white (It seemed to shine with it's own light); Her eyes were a bright silver; and she was wearing a sexy red nightie. She held out her hands to him welcoming him forward. As she reached out her hands, her wings opened to their full length. She was quite the sight to behold. "Tonight your wish comes true."

The Great Unknown laughed under his breath and moved forward. "Ok." The angel made the first move. She wrapped her arms around him. Ok." He mumbled again. Then she began wrapping her wings around him. The Great Unknown looked down at the wings as they surrounded around him. "Ok."

The angel leaned in and kissed him….

"You made love to her?" I asked confused. This was the first I had ever heard of this happening. This might have been the first time this has *ever* happened.

"OH, YEAH," he replied. He took out a pack of cigarettes and lit one. "TWICE." He took a puff of his cigarette. "AFTER IT WAS DONE SHE ASKED ME IF MY WISH WAS GRANTED? I REPLIED THAT THE OTHER ANGEL GOT IT WRONG. MY SECRET WISH WAS TO MAKE LOVE TO TWO ANGELS." He laughed at his own joke. "I CAN'T WAIT TO SEE WHAT IS WAITING FOR ME IN MY APARTMENT WHEN I GET HOME TONIGHT." I laughed with him.

Henry James looked angrily at the both of us. "What is wrong with your generation?"

The Great Unknown and I looked at each other and then back at James. "What do you mean?" I asked him.

"Nevermind," he sighed. "Just nevermind."

Fitzgerald lit his own cigarette and laughed under his breath. "I might have to try that sometime."

I looked back at the Great Unknown. "That could account for that weird harp noise I heard last night while I was writing."

"YEAH," The Great Unknown laughed. "I WAS TUNNING HER HARP."

"I really don't understand your generation," Henry James sighed and stuffed his hands in his pockets.

It was at that moment, that The Engineer poked his head out the door. "We're ready."

It looked exactly like what you would expect a studio to look like. There was a little set in front of the one camera. There was a giant sound mike near the camera. We were really not given time to observe everything in there because The Engineer instantly began to give orders. "Fitzgerald," He called.

"What?"

"You see that sound mike?"

"What's a sound mike?"

The Engineer sighed and walked Fitzgerald over to the mike whispering instructions to him the entire time. I leaned over to The Great Unknown. "Are you nervous?"

"LIKE YOU WOULDN'T BELIEVE," he said, "I WOULD WET MYSELF IF I WASN'T WEARING ALL WHITE."

When The Engineer walked back over to us, he grabbed me. "C'mon The Moonboy."

"Just Moonboy would be fine," I replied. He dragged me over to the camera and gave me some simple instructions on how to work it. Basically, I just had to hold it steady. "I think I can handle that." The Engineer walked back to The Great Unknown and Henry James. I looked over at F. Scott Fitzgerald. He had headphones on his head and he was trying his best to hold the mike up.

I gave him a thumbs up!

He stuck his middle finger up at me.

The Engineer grabbed James by the collar and said, "Ok, writer you're coming with me. Just do what I tell you."

"I think I can handle that."

"You'd better," The Engineer moaned, "Or I'll get you reborn just so I can go back and kill you. You got that."

They disappeared up into the studio control room.

The Great Unknown moved over to the chair sitting in front of the camera. He sat down in the seat, got comfortable and laid the cane across his lap. I had no idea what he was going to say. But I knew it was going to be big. Really big. And there was no way to go back now.

Suddenly from the studio, I heard The Engineer speak through the speakers of the studios. "We'll be ready in 3 minutes…"

CHAPTER 23

"Dinner will be ready in 3 minutes," I said to Toni Lyn. I was making my famous casserole dish. It was my own secret recipe.

"How can this be a secret recipe?" She asked me in a joking manner from the other side of the room. "I saw everything you put in there. And let me tell you there were no extravagant mixtures being used in that pot."

"Ah, my pretty young thing, don't doubt the master chef," I said in my best French accent, "Simplicity is the spice of life."

"What does that mean?"

I paused. "I really don't know. But it sounded good, didn't it?"

She got up from the couch and walked over to me in the kitchen. "How much time did you say we had again?"

"About 3 minutes," I replied. "Why?'

"Well, I'm going to go buy some simplistic red wine for your simplistic meal," She said.

"I don't know if red wine will go with this meal," I said as I checked on the oven timer.

"I wasn't thinking of how it would go with the meal," she said as she moved towards the door. "I was thinking about how it would go with me."

She smiled back at me, waved and walked out of the apartment.

I turned back to the oven. For some strange reason, I always get an incredibly warm feeling whenever I create tuna casserole. It almost feels like I am creating a work of art in every dish. Each bite to be cherished, loved, and considered as its own masterpiece in of itself. Every person has a purpose in life, my grandmother would say (I don't know what she says now that her grandson has caused an international incident and is being searched for throughout Europe for kidnapping) and maybe my purpose was to cook this meal. In my little imagination, I pictured myself somehow releasing a cookbook for casseroles. It's a best seller. Everyone buys a copy. I'm on TV discussing my dish and no one cares about my past. My food brings peace and understanding to the world. I'm a hero for cooking! Then come the movies, the TV specials, the sitcom, and the rock album. Then I'm an old man in my large mansion with Toni Lyn by my side (For some reason, in my dreams, she still looks incredible even as an old woman) and I feel at one with all the world.

Food=Peace

It was these silly thoughts that were going through my head, when the apartment door opened and two men entered. They were both Italian. The one standing in front was a little smaller than the one behind (Of course, since they were both taller than me I don't know what right I have to judge something like that). The one in the front was wearing a very smart suit. He had a short haircut and slicked black hair. He was smoking a cigarette and seemed to know his way around the apartment. The other one stood like a statue behind his partner. He kept his hand in his pocket in a very awkward position…. I, of course, would learn later that he was holding a gun.

I am the King of Naive. No one is more naive than I am. In walks what anyone (who has watched at least one Mafia film) would say were Mafia thugs and it doesn't even register with me that there is a problem. How naive, am I? Get ready for this————

"Hi, you must be friends of Toni Lyn. She's out buying some wine for the meal. I'm making my famous casserole dish. Well, it's not famous yet, but one can always dream, can't he? Sit down. Sit down," I said with a very, very stupid smile…. Whenever I think back on this moment, those words mock any sense of intelligence I think I have.

As you would expect, my words surprised the two gentlemen in front of me as well. I guess they were expecting me to make a run for it, or try attacking, or maybe they expected me to jump under the counter and pull a gun. They did not expect me to invite them to dinner. They looked at each other to see what the other wanted to do. The one in the front (who was clearly the leader) turned back to me and smiled. "Sure, we'll stay for dinner."

They sat down on the stools outside the kitchen counter. They looked at each other and smiled. They seemed to be enjoying the thought of their prey cooking them dinner…. And what a glorious meal it would be…

I walked over to them and stuck out my hand for them to shake. "Hi, I'm…" I began.

The smaller one interrupted me. "We know who you are."

I laughed. "I guess most of the world does."

"I'm Jon," the smaller one said, "I'm sure Toni Lyn has mentioned me."

I shook my head 'no.' "No, never heard of you. And you are?" I was asking the other one this when I turned to shake his hand.

"He's my friend," Jon answered for him.

This remark confused me a little bit. "Ok…." I didn't get too much time to think about it though because my timer began to go off.

BBBBBBBEEEEEEEEEEEEEEEPPPPPPPPPPPPPP!

"My casserole!" I exclaimed and ran to the oven. I opened the oven and reached in without oven mitts (stupid). "Hot!" I reached quickly up and grabbed the oven mitts wrapping them over the corners of the dish. I lifted the dish up carefully (Such a work of art) and placed it on top of the oven. I opened the lid. It smelled Heavenly….

"That smells good," Jon said from the counter.

"Thanks," I replied. "But we have to wait."

"For what?" Jon asked.

"For Toni Lyn to get back," I said. "She should be back in a few minutes."

I moved over to the counter to face my newfound friends. "So Jon can I ask you a question?"

"Sure," he replied (It's amazing, looking back, how at ease he was during this next conversation).

"Your name. Do you like your name?"

"What?" His grin was very awkward.

"Maybe it's just me," I began, "But I've always had a hard time taking people with the name 'Jon' seriously. It's such a boring name! How are we supposed to believe that such a person, with such a boring name is a worthwhile part of society? It's like his mother doesn't even give a damn about her own kid enough to think of a real name."

"What?" His grin was very, very awkward.

"Nothing against you or your mother, but it's such a common name. Such a boring name. I had this same problem with the Jons in my high school. They were everywhere. People always refer to the expression 'Every Tom, Dick and Harry,' but how many people do you really know named Harry and Dick these days? Not that many, right? And they aren't easygoing names either. They have a little danger to them. Harry. Dick. Manly aspects to the male body. But Jon. All that comes to my mind is a toilet. I guess I just have a hard time taking someone serious when their parents only care enough to name them after a toilet."

"What?" His grin was very, very, very awkward. His friend made a move inside his coat. Jon reached over and touched his friend's arm in a reassuring fashion.

"No offense," I quickly stated.

"None taken."

"Good."

"Like I can complain. The entire world is calling me 'Moonboy'? What a lame name is that," I sighed. "Could make an interesting comic book though, couldn't it? *Now it's time for the adventures of Moonboy!* " I laughed.

He laughed too.

His friend did not.

Jon paused in his laughter. It was like he recognized something about me. "Nice shirt," he said slowly... very slowly.

I looked down at the shirt, "Thanks, I'm borrowing it from one of Toni Lyn's friends."

His right hand was a tight fist. "Really?"

It was at this moment that the apartment door slowly opened and Toni Lyn walked in. Her expression and mannerism could only be compared to that of an animal knowing that it is walking into it's own deathtrap.

I, on the other hand, was still playing good host (Naive. Naive. Naive). "Hey, Honey. Some of your friends stopped by. Hurry over here. Dinner is ready."

She did not respond to me. "Hi, Jon."

Jon walked over. "Doll." He reached over and tried to touch her face. She squirmed back (almost as if a snake was touching her).

"Honey?" Jon said in a very loving (and very controlling fashion). "Aren't you glad to see me. I've come to save you?"

"Save me?" She asked annoyed. "You don't think I can take care of myself?"

"Dollface," He whispered. He touched her face this time. "I wasn't thinking that at all."

It was at this moment that I finally woke up to the idea that something was up. Something that was not good. Something that not even my casserole could fix. "What is going on here?" I started walking around the counter to where the two of them were but Jon's friend stopped me. He held me back with one arm and an expression of pure disgust.

"I love you, honey," Jon said.

"You don't think I know what I'm doing?"

"I didn't say that." Jon said. He tried to sound very reassuring. "We all trust you. Your dad and I just wanted to check up on you. You've been getting a lot of attention that is, well, very unlike you.""I know what I'm doing."

"And how do you think it feels for me," Jon tried to sound hurt. "Having my fiancée running around Italy with such a character."

And when that magic word was spoken my entire view of the situation changed. I was angry. I was so, so angry. I was angry at the world and life and him and her and everyone under the sun. At that moment, my philosophy almost went back to my first choice with dire consequences. I saw myself diving at Jon and strangling him.... If you can't guess, the magic word was "Fiancée."

And yet, I tried to stay calm. Maybe I was just hearing things. It happens to the best of us, right? Every now and then, we all hear things spoken that really weren't said at all. "Did he say fiancée?" I asked. I added a light laugh at the end of my question. Maybe it was all a joke? That's it, a big awful joke. Ha.

"Unfortunately," Toni Lyn said with a sigh. She looked over at me. She looked really sad that she had to tell me. I had no idea how I looked to her. I'm sure I must have looked at least a little dumbfounded.

"What do you mean 'Unfortunately'?" Jon asked annoyed.

"This is an arranged marriage Jon," Toni Lyn shouted angrily at him. "You couldn't have expected me to just follow orders on this one."

"Fiancée?" I mumbled under my breath. The word was so foreign to me. The concept was beyond me. She was going to marry someone else. Be with someone else. Love someone else.

"It was your father's decision," Jon replied angrily. "It's good business!"

"I don't even know you Jon!"

At this moment, he grabbed her hair. He pulled her hair until her ear was aligned with his mouth. "You are mine," he said slowly.... It was also at that moment that I snapped!

I jumped at Jon. My sudden movement seemed to surprise Jon's friend because he did not move quick enough to stop me. I was able to get to Jon. I punched my elbow into his stomach. On impact, he let go of Toni Lyn's hair.

Toni Lyn quickly looked over at Jon's friend. She could see that he was pulling a gun. "Wait. Stop!" She shouted at me.

I was far from listening to anyone's reasoning by this point. With my other arm, I was able to get a punch in at Jon's nose.... Jon's friend was standing behind me but I had no idea he was there. I didn't care. All I cared about was the person that took Toni Lyn away and actually hurt her.

"Don't kill him," Toni Lyn shouted at Jon's friend.

Jon's friend nodded to her in understanding and.... Pain.

Darkness.

I had no idea how much time went by when I came to again. I was sitting in a chair. At least, I could tell that. I tried to get up but I couldn't. I was tied to the chair by something. I tried to ask what was going on but I couldn't. My mouth was covered. I tried to move my hand to remove the tape off my mouth, but couldn't.... I was firmly taped with duct tape to one of the kitchen chairs. I was facing the wall. I tried looking left and right. I was against a corner. I couldn't see anything.

It was at that moment that I began to listen to the noises going on around me. The first noise I heard was silverware. And I heard chewing. They were all having dinner without me....

Jon: So why didn't you just let the hitman into the Embassy like you were told to do and we would have been done with him?

Toni Lyn: What all of you failed to see was the perfect PR opportunity in front of us. So many people associate our name with crime. Just think of it Jon. A well-known nut kidnaps the daughter of a famous American and is saved by her fiancé. Brilliant. You cannot ask for a better way to clean your name than that.

Jon: Then why didn't you let me kill him a few minutes ago?

Toni Lyn: Because we can't kill him in private because people will then be suspicious. They'll see it as just another Mafia hit. But if we could stage the final scene and rescue so that it could be caught on film and in pictures. Now there you would have something. We would be on the covers of every magazine in the world. We would be interviewed on every talk show. You would be a hero, Jon.

Jon: Why didn't you tell your dad this idea?

Toni Lyn: I haven't had the chance to call him. This idiot won't leave me alone. He follows me around like a lost puppy. This guy is so head over heels over me that it's not even funny… And if you guys killed him, there you would have ruined this.

Jon: So what did you expect your dad to do? The second he heard someone was using the phone in his Venice apartment you knew he'd figure out you were here.

Toni Lyn: I know. I know. But I needed the idiot to call his parents. I had to get him more alienated from the world. His parents acted just like I expected them to. All he has in the world now is me. He would do anything for me.

Jon: You need to call your dad now. You need to tell him this idea.

Toni Lyn: I'll do it tomorrow.

Jon: What are you going to tell him to do?

Toni Lyn: Another PR opportunity. He's going to go out on the news. And he's going to cry. That's what I'm going to tell him to do.

Jon: (coughing) Cry?

Toni Lyn: Yeah, cry. He's going to show that he loves his little girl. And all he wants in the world is for her to come home safe and in one piece. Just like any good father. Just like any good American.

Jon: I don't know if he'll go for that.

Toni Lyn: I'll explain it to him. Don't worry about it.

Jon: And why did you do all that to my apartment?

Toni Lyn: Did you report it?

Jon: What?

Toni Lyn: Did you report it?

Jon: Why would I report it?

Toni Lyn: I did it so we would have evidence he was psycho. God!...
Nevermind, we'll just bring it up in a television interview later.
Pause.
Jon: I've got to say one thing for the Moonboy.
Toni Lyn: What's that, my love?
Jon: He does make a good casserole.

10. Toni Lyn is connected to the Mafia.

11. Toni Lyn is planning to kill me.

12. Toni Lyn was using me.

13. Toni Lyn is engaged.

All these facts combined with the pain helped to give me the only
escape I could hope for.
I lost consciousness.
I went off into the beautiful nothing.
There was no pain there. No worries. And if I were really lucky there
would be no dreams either.
Falling away....
Nothing....

14. Toni Lyn is engaged... but not to me.

CHAPTER 24

I recovered consciousness a few hours later. It was already evening. Everything in the apartment was dark. I was alone in the living room and I was still tied to the chair by the duct tape. I had no idea what kind of physical condition I was in. Most of my body hurt and I felt weak. Actually, every aspect of me felt weak. My entire world (in all the corny glory this sentence can represent) was falling apart.

Toni Lyn was engaged.

She was going to marry this man. Screw the fact her family is connected to the Mafia and she was supposed to let in the hitman that was supposed to kill me that night. Those facts meant nothing to me... All that affected me that evening (not the pain, not the fear of my approaching death) was the fact that she was promised to another. She was engaged to that man.... As the hours of that evening slipped by, I allowed my thoughts to sink deeper and deeper into that realization. Maybe all I thought we had was just a delusion I created for myself. I was pretty desperate for a goal to live for. That is pretty obvious, isn't it? Maybe I played right into her hands just like I heard her describe to Jon over dinner.... Maybe I didn't really hear that conversation? Let's face it; I was in pretty bad shape. There is a chance that it didn't happen.

It was when I had those thoughts running in my head that she snuck out of the bedroom. She snuck over to me in the chair. I looked up at her.

I had no idea what to expect from her at that moment. As she looked down at me, I could read that she felt the same way in regards to me.

She leaned down and whispered all of this in my ear:

*Don't be mad at me. Please don't. I'm sorry. I do love you. I love you so… I… See you must understand I didn't get engaged to Jon because I wanted to. That was a decision by my father. It was good for the business. See Jon's family is not connected to our family and the engagement was looked at more as a business merger than a marriage… God, it sounds like something out of **The Godfather**, doesn't it? I claim it is true. I don't love Jon… Everything throughout my life has always been mapped out for me. From schools to colleges. My grades to the right teacher. Everything was laid out for me. And when you grow up in that environment you don't look for change. Change is not an option. I was following a path. I was given this life by being born in the right family. I wouldn't even have that job at the Embassy if it weren't for my family… Everyone I have ever met has been connected to us and they all are sure to act a certain way around me. Predictable. Straightforward… And then you came in. The most unpredictable, annoying, bothersome soul I have ever met. All I could do was hate you for going against everything I knew. All I could do was fall in love with you. I love you. Don't doubt that for a second. We'll get out of here. I promise. It won't end this way. It won't end here. I have never felt this way about anyone or anything before. It's like… It's like I feel alive. Truly alive, with all the energy and unpredictability that comes with living free. I can't stop this feeling. I can't go back now to the way I used to be. I won't let myself go back. I'm a new person because of you. You've changed the world for me… My god, that sounds lame, doesn't it? But it's true; I swear it's true. I can't remember how I felt before this. How did I live before this? Everyday's an adventure with you. Everyday means something. Before, the days would just slip by and I wouldn't think about them. The days, the months, the years falling away like layers of skin on a snake. I treasure these days. These are the days of my life. We'll get out of here. We'll find someplace to live where they can't find us. We'll get a house and a job. Change our names. Start our own* *life. Maybe in Switzerland. We could go there. Or Amsterdam… It'd be easy to hide there. The possibilities are endless where we could go. Just picture it, honey, the two of us living happily someplace. Growing old together. Just the two of us. That's my dream. That's what is going to get you out of here. How does your face feel? Does this hurt?… I'm sorry. It doesn't look too bad, honest. Your eye isn't black, which is a good thing. Did you lose a tooth? No? Good. I don't know what the chances are of us getting dental insurance someplace. (Laughing lightly). We'll get out of here, start a home, get dental insurance and live, I swear.*

She kissed my cheek.

Trust me on this. We'll get out.

She kissed it again.

She turned and headed back to the bedroom. She looked back at me, smiled and then went in. She shut the door behind her….

I was able to fall asleep then.

For the next few days, I watched her live (They moved me around from the wall on the next morning). It was a strange feeling. Almost like watching a TV show that is going on all around you. You can't say anything to the people around you, you can't interact. Life was going on all around and I was watching. I watched as she spent the next day and the next playing happy fiancée to Jon. I watched as they discussed when they were going to kill me. I watched as they all casually discussed how they were never going to feed me. I watched as she kissed him…

Two days of being tied to a chair with no food, no water. When my clothes began to stink after the second day, Jon's bodyguard carried me into the shower and turned it on over my head. It felt so good having the water flow down onto me. I would have sold my soul at that moment to have been able to open my mouth and taste the stream coming down….

He then worried that maybe the water would affect the tape so he put more on me. Two layers of tape holding my mouth and my body in one place.

Then I was placed back in the living room.

I watched as Toni Lyn called her father. She apologized to him for all she did. She did her best to explain it. She claimed by taking me away from the Embassy like that would make me look more psycho to the public. Plus, she claimed it was good PR for her and the family. Careers and images could be built out of this moment, she claimed. Her father—the worried All-American Dad trying his hardest to get his little girl back. Her—the educated politician who fights for her freedom and captures her kidnapper. Her fiancé, Jon—The dedicated lover who stopped at nothing to save his love. She made it all sound like a TV movie… Of course, she didn't know how to pull off the ending that would make it all believable. So that's why she argued with Jon that I should be kept alive. And once they think of how to pull off the murder as a heroic moment, they then can end the charade…. And she argued that waiting a few more days to do it would build suspense… It was very surreal to hear the woman of your dreams discuss you as a PR tool…. It may have been because of her family that she got that job in the Embassy, but she definitely had a talent for politics.

Two days of this… I would lose consciousness from time to time. And sometimes I pretended to lose consciousness just so I didn't have to live in the pain of the moment.

One thing I did to get by during those two days was to relive movies and songs in my head. If you concentrate hard enough you can remember quite a lot. Maybe not every scene is up there but you do get a good chunk of the actual thing. My two favorite things for this (Or what turned out to be the easiest for me) were **The Wizard of Oz** and The White Album of The Beatles. It was very surreal to watch Toni Lyn walk around her fiancé like a lovebird while I heard in my head the scene for "Somewhere Over the Rainbow." Another memorable moment was when the bodyguard was getting ready to go out one afternoon. He was wearing all black and all I could think of was "Blackbird." Happy songs and happy memories to hide the danger that surrounded me.

From the lack of food on that second night, I began to think maybe… Just maybe, Toni Lyn was playing me for the moron. I heard all the stuff that she told her dad. It was getting hard not to believe it. Think about it- right from the start she knew the effect that she had on me. It would've been so easy to use me…. I forced myself to stop thinking these kinds of thoughts. Even if they were true, this was not what I wanted to be thinking while I was dying. I forced myself to think of happy thoughts as I watched Toni Lyn cook her fiancé and his bodyguard a beautiful spaghetti dinner…. I love spaghetti.

CHAPTER 25 — HIS SPEECH

I SPEAK TONIGHT ON BEHALF OF MY FELLOW DEAD. MY NAME IS NOT IMPORTANT.

WE ARE A WHIPPED RACE.

WE ARE WHIPPED BY LIFE.

AND WE ARE GIVEN THIS COMPLACENT IMMORTALITY BECAUSE OF THE SKILL WE USED IN SUFFERING THROUGH OUR MORTALITY.

BUT I AM NOT HERE TO COMPLAIN ABOUT HOW LIFE IS RUN. THAT CAN'T BE CHANGED FOR ANY OF US HERE. OUR END IS ALREADY REACHED. WHAT I WANT TO COMPLAIN ABOUT IS THE WAY WE ARE THROWN TO ETERNITY.

HEAVEN IS A FASCIST STATE.

HOW CAN MAN HOPE FOR HAPPINESS WHEN ANY SENSE OF FREEDOM OR FREE WILL IS CAST ASIDE FOR AN ENFORCED HAPPY STATE OF MIND? THE CONCEPT OF JOY HERE IS ALMOST AS LUDICROUS AS THE FREE ELECTIONS THAT ARE HELD EVERY TWO YEARS.

WE ARE FORCED TO LIVE THROUGH THIS WITHOUT COMPLAINING, WITHOUT OBJECTING. IF WE DO OFFER THE SLIGHTEST OBJECTION OUR MINDS ARE MANIPU-LATED BY PILLS OR OTHER METHODS PUT UPON US BY THE HAPPY ANGELS.

IS THERE A BETTER WAY FOR HEAVEN TO BE RUN?

SADLY, I DON'T THINK SO.

WE ARE NOT A RACE THAT CAN BE HAPPY DOING ANYTHING FOR AN ENTIRE ETERNITY. WE BREED OFF OF CHANGE. TO REMOVE THE CHANGE IS TO REMOVE WHAT IT MEANS TO BE HUMAN. BUT YET OVER A MATTER OF TIME WE CAN BECOME USED TO CHANGE AS WELL.

SO IS THERE ANOTHER OPTION AVAILABLE? NOT THAT I CAN THINK OF EXCEPT THAT OF NOTHINGNESS.

YES, NOTHING.

SO WITH THAT THOUGHT IN MIND, I BEG GOD TO ALLOW US THE CHOICE.

IMMORTALITY OR NOTHING. ALL I ASK IS FOR THE CHOICE.

I'M SO TIRED....

[At this moment, he bowed his head and a thousand years seem to fall over his face.]

I'M SO TIRED....

[At this moment, the angels pulled the plug and everything went to static.]

CHAPTER 26

I was awakened up by a kiss. I opened my eyes to find Toni Lyn smiling down at me. "We're getting out of here," she whispered.

"How...." I was about to ask her how we were going to pull this off when I suddenly realized I had the duct tape off my mouth. This distracted my train of thought. "I..." I adjusted my mouth around. It felt so incredibly good to have my mouth free.

Toni Lyn had a knife and she was cutting away all the tape around me.

First, my left arm was free. I stretched it up almost bumping her in the head. "Sorry," I whispered.

"It's ok," she sighed and began working on the other arm. As soon as my right arm was free, I bent down and helped her to work on releasing my legs.

"What about Jon?" I whispered.

"I put sedatives in the pasta sauce," She whispered back. "I can have secret recipes too. They'll be out for hours. And if that doesn't work I have his gun." She placed it on my lap as she worked more on my legs. "There. You're free."

I slowly stood up. It was almost too much for me. I grabbed on to the back of the chair so I didn't collapse. "I feel so..."

"You haven't moved or eaten in two days. You'll feel fine in a few hours..." She moved herself so she was under my arm for support. She slowly lifted me up. "C'mon honey, we're going away."

"Just a second," someone yawned. We turned to face the speaker. It was, of course, Jon. Why can't things happen easily for us? "You're not going anywhere," he yawned again.

Toni Lyn quickly raised her gun and pointed it at him. "We're getting out of here Jon."

"I can't let you do that." He was really tired. He was having a hard time standing up. His determination to stay awake was really quite impressive.

"We're getting out of here. Just move slowly," Toni Lyn whispered in my ear. We began to walk to the door. She kept her eyes directly on Jon. She never once let that gun drop. Jon slowly (very slowly) tried his hardest to move around to get to where we were. His movements were more defined by his moving from one large object to another for support. Each movement would be followed almost simultaneously by a large yawn.

"Your father's never going to let this happen Toni Lyn." He said slowly. "He'll find you." Jon sat down on a chair. He was too tired to get up from it. You could see the frustration in his face as his mind tried to fight with his body.

Toni Lyn sighed. "I'm sure you're right Jon. But this is what I want. I love him Jon. And if you have even the slightest feeling for me you'll let us go." We were at the door. "Get the door," she whispered to me.

I reached back with my right arm and opened it. We moved around to the front of the door and began walking out.

"Stop, Toni Lyn!" Jon called. "You come back here. You're mine, Toni Lyn. Toni Lyn, your father…. Toni Lyn, you can't do this."

Toni Lyn only sighed in return and shut the door. We walked to Jon's car and she unlocked the doors by remote. "I always liked his car better." She helped me into the passenger side and she got into the driver's side. As soon as she sat in the driver's side, she turned to me and smiled. She reached over and gave me a quick kiss.

She started the car and we were gone.

I leaned over onto her shoulder and fell asleep. At that moment, I felt safer than I had ever felt in my life…. I had beautiful dreams.

A few hours later as we crossed the border into Switzerland in her fiancé's stolen car, I realized something. And I think Toni Lyn realized it too because she reached over and took my hand. Neither of us said it but we both knew it... All we had in the world was each other now.

I looked around the new land in front of me. I smiled. "I think we're going to love it here."

"I think so too," She said. She gripped my hand harder. "It's so beautiful here. We're going to love Switzerland..."

PART 3
—LAKE LUCERNE

We hated Switzerland.

–Moonboy

*[The following is a copy of the
campaign brochure for the
reelection of God.]*

HEY

YOU!!!

YEAH YOU!

THE ONE

READING

THIS!

Have you thought about whom you would vote for in this election?

Yeah, it can be a pretty tough decision.

There are so many questions that you need to answer before casting that all important vote. Some such questions for example could be "What does the candidate's past record look like?" or "What does the candidate promise to do during the next term?" or maybe even "What has this candidate done for *me* lately?" Let's take these questions one by one with the only candidate—GOD.

"What does the candidate's past record look like?"

In the beginning, GOD created the Heavens and the Earth.

Wow! Talk about a hard worker!

GOD is not only a hard worker but also a hard worker with a vision. How many other candidates can claim to have had such elaborate goals and succeeded at them? Not very many, we're sure.

GOD is also the author of the most popular book in history—The Bible. Who can claim that this book hasn't touched them in some way or another? His words have been used for support, comfort, love, and, more importantly, hope. Clearly the work of a leader that cares about everyone.

GOD's past record has touched every one of us in someway—From creation to death. It's hard to argue against that kind of success.

"What does the candidate promise to do during the next term?"

GOD has agreed during the next term to allow all of us to survive for another two years.

How many other candidates have the power to promise something like that?

**"What has this candidate
done for me lately?"**

Well, let's think about this one carefully—If it wasn't for GOD there wouldn't be any life, love, Earth, sun, moon, rocks, air, TV, trees, grass, plants, homes, people, puppy dogs, kitty cats, CD's, water, cola, cars, computers, digital watches, music, dancing, bikes, exercise, painting, books, plays, movies, VCR's, refrigerators, microwaves, ovens, dish washers, dishes to wash, forks, food, macaroni & cheese, sex, chocolate, light bulbs, airplanes, space shuttles, stars, pillows, couches, beds, baths, toilets, faucets, garbage bags, bananas, ice cream, whipped cream, strawberries, gasoline, mountains, statues, chairs, curtains, carpets, spatchules, lizards, roller coasters, blankets, wool sweaters, underwear, bow ties, keys, angels, toasters, bagels, towels, paper, postcards, stamps, letters, pens (erasable and non), hammers, screwdrivers, alcohol, nails, telephones, mortgages, homes, apartments, hugs, kisses, happiness, hot, cold, laughter, the wheel, rakes, sports, afterlife, and, basically, everything else you can thing of.

Wow! GOD has done quite a lot for you lately. Can any other candidate compete with facts like that?

Of course not!

GOD.

HE CREATED YOU.
NOW IT'S TIME TO
SAY THANK YOU.

VOTE GOD.

CHAPTER 27

"That was incredible!" Fitzgerald laughed.

James in reply mumbled something under his breath. The 3 of us had escaped through a back entrance of the HTV studio and were currently sprinting away. We had no idea what happened to The Great Unknown and The Engineer. But they were the last things on our mind at the moment. We were all living in the moment of what we had just accomplished. And each of us had a different view of the situation. Fitzgerald was excited. He was probably the most excited I have ever seen him since we first met 3 years ago. He was laughing and screaming as we ran through the alleys. James, on the other hand, wanted nothing more than to escape the possibility of capture. He was nervous, and as he ran he would continue to look left and right as if an angel was waiting for us around every corner with happy pills in their shinning hands.

I, on the other hand, had a more relaxed feeling about what had just happened. I knew the gravity of what we had just done. And I knew it was something that had to be done.… But I felt tired about it. Maybe it was the knowledge that tired me or maybe I felt the words of The Great Unknown a little too close. Maybe I felt tired like him. Maybe I was ready to just abandon this for what he asked for. The nothing.

All for her.

All for her.

I couldn't do that. I shook the thought off and continued running. Fitzgerald was talking the entire time I was thinking. I had to take a few seconds to catch up to his words. "…. stuck it to them. He really did. He told them. The first person to actually have the balls to tell it to God and I was there to witness it. Do you have any idea how historical that moment was? And we were there. We lucky few!" Fitzgerald then screamed at the top of his lungs in triumph.

"Please, be quiet," James whispered angrily at him. "The angels are probably looking for us right now. And who knows what they'll do to us?"

"What're you scared of James?" Fitzgerald shouted at him. "Hell is full."

"I'm sure they could make room if they wanted to," he mumbled back. Ever since I've met him, James has always debunked the rumor of Hell being a party spot.

This made Fitzgerald laugh harder. "What's so awful about Hell anyway? Pain and torture only mean something with the threat of death behind it. You've just got to accept what's being done to you and get used to it. It's just a matter of perspective. There's nothing that can hold us back now. All I needed were his words to open that realization in my head. We're immortal! There are no limits to what we can do. I think I may go back to Earth and…"

"No!" I shouted at him. I stopped running.

Fitzgerald and James both stopped and looked back at me surprised. "What is wrong?" Fitzgerald asked.

"You're not going to Earth," I said angrily. "You are *not* going to speak to anyone down there."

"Why not? I have every right to."

"If you do…" I tried to think of a threat that would work against a dead person. "I will burn down The AfterTaste." It was the best I could come up with on short notice.

Luckily, that made him take notice. "Ok. I'm listening to you now."

"No one is ruining her chances of coming up here to Heaven. No one is ruining her chances of finding me here waiting for her. And if you go down there now and break the glass between our two worlds, you'll ruin it for us. I won't let you do it."

"The Great Unknown went down there and had dinner with his parents," Fitzgerald said. My reaction confused him.

"That's different," I explained. "I had nothing to do with that."

Henry James walked slowly over to me. "That's why you won't go see her as a ghost, isn't it? (I turned away from him.) You're worried that if you see her you won't be able to let her go again. 'The Pain' is eating at you that badly…"

" That's not it," I interrupted. "I've no problem with fighting or working to change the living environment in Heaven, but the second we try to break that glass, God'll get worried. It's one thing to ask to disappear, it's another to ask to change all of reality."

Henry James looked over at Fitzgerald. "He's right."

Suddenly, we heard the sound of flapping above our heads (Christ! Here it comes). "Please wait," the angel said as it landed in front of us.

Henry James looked like he was going to get on his knees and beg for mercy. I quickly placed my hand on his shoulder for support. Whatever this angel was going to do we'd experience it together. He could feel that message through the grip of my hand. He straightened up…. Fitzgerald on the other hand did not need any of my friendly support. "Well, look here. An actual angel. What can we help you with this fine night?"

"I'm looking for someone…"

"Aren't we all?" Fitzgerald replied. He flung his arms out wide as if he was speaking to a crowd. A crowd that wasn't there.

His gestures seemed to confuse the angel. It was obvious that this angel was not used to dealing with us dead. It's an artform dealing with us. You need to be both strict and patronizing or just patronizing. This angel wasn't educated in that fact. "I'm sure any of the Happy Angels can help you, my poor soul in your quest for happiness. I'm looking for a young gentleman. He is about 5'10", black hair, clean shaven, looks to be about twenty-five and…"

Fitzgerald grabbed me and pulled me forward. "You mean like this?"

The angel was confused by this bold gesture. Almost as confused as I was. Of course, I was more annoyed than confused at that moment. "No, my poor soul. The dead I am looking for is wearing a white suit."

"What's wrong with this young gentleman?" Fitzgerald asked ('Let me go Fitzgerald….").

The angel tried to control the situation. "Well, your young gentleman is very nice. However he is not the young gentleman I am looking for."

"But look at how clean he is." Fitzgerald grabbed my head and turned it left and right for the angel to study. I let him do it. He was a loose cannon. I had no idea what he would do if I made a move.

"He is very clean."

"And handsome?"

The angel sighed. "Yes, he is handsome."

"And he is…."

The angel interrupted him. "He is however not the young gentleman that I am looking for. I'm sorry, poor soul." The angel began to flap his wings.

"Wait a minute!" Fitzgerald let go of me. He was upset. I guess that maybe he was expecting them to be after him as well. They didn't see him there. They didn't know he had anything to do with it. Fitzgerald wanted to be on the chase too. "Hey, wait a minute there!"

What I wanted to say at that moment: *Just go, please, go. Disregard my friend. He had a hard life and he is a little upset. But he's happy here in Heaven. He is happy to be here. We are all happy to be here. Don't change anything… Please, don't change anything….*

The angel held it's position in midair and looked annoyed down at Fitzgerald. "Yes, poor soul?"

"Why do you keep calling me that?" Fitzgerald demanded.

"Isn't that what you all are?" The angel asked. Those had to be the most humane words I have ever heard from an angel. It was a strange feeling. It is obvious when speaking to an angel its understanding of what is good or bad, but compassion from an angel? This was something new... Can angels feel? It never seemed like they could before... Maybe... I brushed that thought off. I had to keep the separation in my head.

Strangely enough, after it was all over and the angel was gone, Fitzgerald was still satisfied with that confrontation (Even though it had nothing to do with him except him acting like a jerk). "This all deserves a celebration."

"You think so?" Henry James asked meekly. I forgot about him standing back there. He looked extremely pale. His right hand seemed to be shaking.

Fitzgerald walked over to James and placed his arm around his shoulder. "Yes it does my friend. Follow me to The AfterTaste." He led James past me. He looked casually at me as he passed (Never an apology). "Are you coming, Moonboy?"

I sighed and walked behind him. Around me in the night sky, I could hear the sound of angels flying. They were scouring the city for the Great Unknown (Where was he?). I pictured him running through muddy alleys (like I did in the real Rome so long ago) as teams of angels flew behind him. Now and then, I could see him grabbing a garbage can to whip back at them. Maybe he would trip and they would all fly down and... Don't worry about him. Brush it off. He did this to himself. He set himself up for this. I can't get involved. All for her.

Fitzgerald smiled and pointed down the street. "I have a surprise all lined up for you, (he emphasized his last words in his own particular way) *you poor poor poor poor poor poor poor poor poor poor poor poor poor poor poor poor poor poor poor souls...*"

CHAPTER 28

—[VIRGINIA WOOLF AND CHARLES DICKENS ARE ALONE AT THE AFTERTASTE AND THEY ARE TRYING TO LEARN HOW TO SWING DANCE.]

Music: Glen Miller's "In The Mood" is playing in the background.

Woolf: You have to feel the beat.

Dickens: I feel it.

Woolf: You're not feeling it.

Dickens: Well, I'm trying to feel it.

Pause.

Woolf: Ok, I'm not supposed to lead.

Dickens: When I tried to lead, you were almost injured.

Woolf: Just concentrate on the rhythmn.

Pause.

Dickens: Should I....

Woolf: What?

Dickens: Should I try to spin you?
Woolf: Go right ahead.
Pause.
Dickens: That wasn't too bad.
Woolf: It's the easiest of moves.
Dickens: It's my first time trying this, love.
Woolf: Just keep up with me.
Pause.
Music: Song ends.
Woolf: You're getting better.
Dickens: Get out the book. Let's learn another move.
Woolf: Oh, I don't know….
Dickens: What can it hurt?
Woolf: Me.
Music: Glen Miler's "American Patrol" comes on next on the record.
Pause.
Woolf: It's a simple move to move into a…
Dickens: Where should my hand be?
Woolf: Here… No, not there!
Dickens: Sorry.
Woolf: Pervert.
Dickens: I didn't mean anything by…
Woolf: (interrupting) Ok, our arms go up. We move alongside each other. Good…. Turn in a circle.
Dickens: This is fun.
Woolf: Stick out your hand like this.
Dickens: Like this?
Woolf: Shake the hand.
Dickens: This is really fun!
Woolf: Now I move out and we're back to where we started.
Dickens: I've got rythmn. Look at me… Do you hear laughing?

"Very nice," Fitzgerald laughed as he entered The AfterTaste. He began clapping his hands in appreciation for their hard work. "Very nicely done."

"It's our first night of trying," Woolf explained. She went over to turn off the record player. Dickens went to a chair and sat down. He looked out of breath. "I really like it," Woolf said to me in excitement. "I will thank you for this as soon as I get the dancing down."

"Yes, thanks a lot," Dickens added. I could sense a little sarcasm in his tone.

"Now, now, now, it's time for my surprise!" Fitzgerald said as he moved behind the counter. "I hid this under a plank in the floor." He disappeared behind the counter. It sounded like he was struggling with a piece of wood (Heard a few interesting swear words too). Suddenly he popped up from behind the counter with a big smile on his face and a bottle of actual bourbon in his right hand. "Behold!" He waved his hands in front of the object like a hand model on a gameshow.

Everyone was clearly awed by the beautiful object. This was rare. Very rare. Alcohol has been banned for years in Heavens (Ever since the incident when a group of drunk dead went down to earth and hung out in the Haunted Mansion at Disneyland and scared people). "Is it real?" Henry James asked quietly. He moved forward towards Fitzgerald.

"You bet your soul it is," Fitzgerald replied. He grabbed some glasses from behind the counter and began to pour us all some shots. "C'mon, one for each. Come and get it, people. Come and get it."

We all slowly moved over to the counter. We all held up our glasses staring at the beautiful gold liquid inside. The liquid almost seemed to glow in the light of that coffeehouse. Beautiful, just plain beautiful.

"To The Great Unknown!" Fitzgerald said and took his shot of bourbon. We all followed.

Gulp!

Instantly, we all reacted in disgust. When you've gone years without a drink (Some of the others have gone actual decades) that first swig of pure bourbon can put hair on not only your chest, but your nails, eyes and tongue.

"I… I need… I need to sit down," Woolf gasped out. We all moved over to our usual round table. Fitzgerald was the only one that really didn't seem phased by the drink. He smiled and brought the bottle with him. His smile unnerved me.

"You two didn't look too bad," I said to Woolf and Dickens.

"Well, we hope to maybe start up a dance club and…" Woolf began to say.

"Wait!" Fitzgerald interrupted. "We're going to talk about the speech and nothing else tonight."

No one spoke. We all looked around at each. That was not a moment we all wanted to debate and philosophize over. The discussion of what was said was going on within ourselves.

Fitzgerald was clearly annoyed by the lack of participation. "Come on. Someone must have something to say?'"

Woolf looked over at me. "So where are you in your book?"

Fitzgerald threw up his hands in frustration. I didn't pay attention to him, I answered her question. "We had just arrived in Lake Lucerne, Switzerland. To us it looked like the perfect place to hang out. It's almost completely surrounded by the mountains. And it is really quite a lovely little town. But… How do I put this? There's something wrong with Switzerland. That country just isn't right…"

CHAPTER 29

"There is something wrong with this country," I sighed. We were in Lake Lucerne, Switzerland outside a small hotel. The hotel was near the bottom of the Alps. We were getting out of our beautiful stolen car.

"What do you mean?" Toni Lyn asked. She put on her sunglasses. Since we escaped Venice a few days ago, she wouldn't appear in public without her shades.

"I've been through most of the borders in Europe but only crossing through Switzerland did I see actual machine guns. I thought this was the great neutral country? And what about all those bomb shelters in the mountains? It's like they expect us to blow up the world (She sighed). Why do you sigh? You know this is odd. I think there's a conspiracy or a plan going on that we don't know about. It's all very unnerving."

"What do you mean?"

"Well, we all know about the Nazi accounts that are here in Swiss banks. Maybe it's all connected."

"They let us in," She replied matter of factly.

I paused. I had no witty response to that. "You're right."

"Let's go get a room."

I grabbed our bags and followed her up into the quaint hotel in front of us.

"How much!?"

"Is there a problem?" The person behind the desk asked in broken English.

"That price is outrageous!" Toni Lyn exclaimed.

"Is that for the week or the night?" I asked him. I couldn't believe it either.

"It's for the night," he sighed. "It's a very reasonable price."

"It'll be a cold day in Hell before I pay that amount," Toni Lyn shouted angrily at him. "Get the bags, we're getting out of here." She stormed out of the office.

I picked up the bags, smiled at the person, and followed her out the door.

Two hours later-

"So how's the weather in Hell?" The person behind the desk asked with a smile. He enjoyed the fact that we came back to his hotel. He was going to gloat.

"It's fucking cold," Toni Lyn quickly stated. "Now can we get a room?"

"Let me see if I have anything available... Hmmm... Looking... Looking... Let me... see... Something.... Wait, here's something... No, that's a broom closet...This room might be available..."

"Just give us the room," Toni Lyn sighed.

The person behind the desk, smiled in a very evil fashion as he held out the key. "Have a pleasant stay."

Toni Lyn grabbed the keys and we stormed out of the registration office. "Fuck you," she mumbled under her breath.

"I hate this," she stated loudly. We were in our room and she was looking around that cheap hotel room with a glare of annoyance. "I can't believe I am paying this much for this shit hole. Why is it people fill a hotel with old shit and suddenly that makes it worth more to stay there? These aren't quaint antiques. This is shit. This is all bullshit." She paused. "Ok, I'm not making sense anymore. God damn it."

"It's the cheapest room in the city." I walked up behind her and wrapped my arms around her. "It's going to be ok," I replied. "We'll stay here a day and leave. There's always Amsterdam."

She sighed and leaned back into my arms. "You're right. I just need to relax."

That night we decided to go on a walk along the mountain and enjoy the starry night. Toni Lyn was already outside waiting for me (I had to use the bathroom first). When I passed the registration desk, I got a strange look from the person behind the counter. It was... It was as if he knew me (No way. Shit!). "Hello," he said quietly to me. "How do you like your room, Moonboy?" (Fucking shit!)

I stopped in my tracks. "I don't know what you're talking about..."

"Yes, you do," he replied (he waved for me to come closer to him). "And I think if you don't want to get caught, you'll stay here a little bit longer than you were expecting."

"You're blackmailing me?"

"And your board maybe a little higher than the other guests. I hope you don't mind."

"I can't believe this," I sighed.

"Believe it, Moonboy." The man replied. "I'll be up later to discuss the fees. So don't be out too long." I sighed and walked towards the door. I had to talk to Toni Lyn about this. She wasn't going to be happy. We needed to get out of here, but how could we do that without getting caught? "And by the way," the person behind the desk called. "Tell your girlfriend it's a cold season. A very cold season."

I exited the hotel. "I hate Switzerland," I mumbled to myself as I walked over to tell Toni Lyn the news. She smiled over at me.... That smile wasn't going to last.

CHAPTER 30

"We hated Switzerland." I sighed and leaned back in my chair. "A lot."

"I can understand you being unnerved by the blackmail," Woolf said. "But that's not a good reason to hate an entire country."

"Oh, by the end of our week there, we had many good reasons."

"For example?" Dickens asked.

"Lame national landmarks," I said sticking up one finger, "is number one."

"That's it?" I sighed. "That's the big national landmark of Lake Lucerne, Switzerland? It's just a dumb lion carved in the side of a mountain."

"It's pretty lame," Toni Lyn agreed.

"It's not even that large a sculpture. Why am I supposed to be impressed by this?"

"I don't think we're supposed to be impressed," Toni Lyn tried to explain. "I think we're supposed to be moved."

"Moved? Are you moved by this?" I waved towards the carving.

"I'm not," Toni Lyn sighed. "I think it's ridiculous. Lions don't cry."

"Look at him. Have you ever seen an animal so emotional? That's one sensitive lion."

"Maybe that's why we're supposed to be moved by this? His emotions are supposed to touch us. Are you touched by it at all?"

"I'm more confused by it than anything else." I leaned forward to read the words under the carving of the lion. "It lists a bunch of names. It looks like it's in memory of a battle."

"They must have lost," Toni Lyn replied. "If they won the lion would be dancing with a party hat on its head and a bottle of champagne in its right paw."

"Now that would be an interesting carving!"

"Ok," Woolf said. "Then?"

"Number two," I said while sticking up two fingers, "everything is expensive."

"The price of a CD is over 30 American dollars," Toni Lyn shouted. She just went into a record store to buy the new They Might Be Giants CD and sadly came out without it. She had been looking forward to buying that CD for a few weeks now. But recent events have delayed that purchase.

"What do you mean?" I asked her.

She spoke slowly. "It costs over 30 American dollars!"

"How can they charge that much?" I asked stupidly.

"How am I supposed to know?" She replied. This was really upsetting her. "Because they're bastards, maybe."

"It's like those damn watch stores. Who wants a watch that costs more than a car? Buying something like that for yourself is nothing more than financial masturbation."

This description cheered her up a little. She smiled, grabbed my arm and led me away from the store. "This is why I keep you around. You keep me sane."

"God knows that's a full-time job," I sighed... "Ouch!"

"How this little country viewed money was ridiculous," I continued to explain. "It's like they believed it grew on trees and everyone had it...."

Stupid metaphor, I'm sorry. But it's ridiculous. I mean just look at how their money looks."

"What kind of a country has bright pink money?" Toni Lyn held her dollar up for me to examine. We were sitting around our hotel room trying to figure out how to get out of the blackmail situation that we were in. Our discussions into the problem continuously had a way of being distracted by other subjects. We just loved talking to each other.

I pulled out my wallet. "I have yellow. Here's a blue one. And this one looks like a rainbow." Saying 'rainbow' had a strange effect on me. I was instantly reminded of how I listened in my head to "Somewhere Over the Rainbow" while she was with her fiancé, Jon.

She could tell something was affecting me. "Is something wrong?" She leaned over and took my hand.

"Nothing," I shook it off. "I'm fine." (I wonder where he is right now?)

"I thought he was counting the points?" James whispered to Dickens. Dickens hushed him in return. He was listening to me.

"…This country doesn't deserve it's cool mountains," I explained (I was clearly on a tangent now). "It's a strange little backward country. And we hated it. While we tried to think of a plan to get out, we tried every tourist trap in the book. We went to the top of mountains and screamed to our heart content."

"AHHHHHHHHHHHHHHHHHHHHHHHHHHHHH!!!!!" I looked over at her and smiled.

She smiled back. "Good one." She took a deep breath. "AHHHHHH-HHHHHHHHHHHHHHHHHHHHHHHHHHHHHHHHH!!!" She looked over at me.

"I have shivers," I held up my hand. I began to shake it. "Look, it's actually shaking. That's the effect you had on me."

James was going through his wallet. He was distracted by the financial problem. He took out a handful of Heaven Money. He sighed. "I'm sure Switzerland's currency looks better than this."

"Well, at least, their money actually means something," Dickens sighed.

A Note about Meaning Something-

Up until the 1930's, Heaven had a blossoming economy. Everyone was happy and everyone was filthy rich. For those that came from harsh financial backgrounds all worry about funds were swept away. Financial bliss for all.

However, that all changed in the 1930's when the beaten stockbrokers (who suffered from heart attacks or suicides) from the great crash arrived. They saw in the booming economy a mirror of the days they experienced in the 1920's. Suddenly, throughout Heaven, hundreds of financial schemes erupted.

And soon, through their own methods (illegal and legal), a class structure was born in Heaven. The poor once again found themselves suffering and the rich once again found themselves flaunting their money around town. Soon all the problems that follow a class structure of Haves and Havenots began to appear. Prostitutes were walking the street corners and people were making runs back to Earth as ghosts to steal anything the rich might want to purchase on the blackmarket (from drugs, to real alcohol to famous works of art).

Almost 20 years went by before the angels began to take notice of the situation. And what the angels did was really quite clever. They flooded the market with currency. They dropped it from the sky (The "Money Flybys" they were called), they handed it out on street corners and they would stand in stores handing it out to customers.

Soon the entire population was again rich. This did not make the moguls happy at all. They tried their best to correct the problem. They tried to create taxes, enforce inflation and other such notions. But the angels caught them before they could pull off any of those neat tricks. The angels passed an ordinance that nothing in Heaven could ever cost more than one dollar.

At this point, many of the moguls began to fall into depression. Some even attempted to double commit suicide (a real waste of time). It was at that moment that the Happy Angels stepped in with their pills and suddenly everyone was happy again.

By the 1970's, this enforced happy economical state changed the perception of the storeowners around Heaven. Stores and restaurant doors were left wide open every night. It's possible now to walk into any store you want at any time of the day, hang around and take whatever you want without anyone being there. A good example of this is The AfterTaste. I rarely see the owner of The AfterTaste after 6PM. And yet we hang out there at all hours of the night.

I have yet to tell if this lackadaisical attitude of the owner's is one of a perception of security or one of trying to keep the customer happy. Unconsciously, it might actually be because no one cares anymore.

CHAPTER 31

Fitzgerald sighed. He was really enjoying the bourbon. "So what did you and Toni Lyn do? You couldn't stay there."

"We knew that," I sighed. "And we went through all our options. We discussed maybe getting a job, saving enough money for a bribe and then get a place of our own. Even though we hated Switzerland any place together was ok."

"Maybe you can get a job?" Toni Lyn asked. She leaned over on the bed and patted me on the chest.

"That's pretty risky. I'm wanted by everyone it seems and I don't speak the language which might make the interviewing process difficult."

"You could pretend to be mute?" she replied hopefully.

"But I still wouldn't understand what they were asking me," I sighed.

"You could pretend to be deaf too."

This was getting worse and worse. "Well, what if the interviewer knows sign language and tries to talk to me that way. I don't know sign language."

She moaned. "I guess then you would need to be blind too." She began to rub the temples of her forehead. She was clearly frustrated.

"So I would need to pretend to be mute, deaf and blind to get a job." I paused. "Well, what kind of job would I even attempt to apply for?"

"I don't know," she replied, "But I'm sure you'd stumble around a bit."

Henry James got up from his seat and went over to the Jukebox. He chose a piece by Mozart (James loves his classical). "How many options did you come up with?" He asked as he came back.

"Actually not many," I sighed.

"Here's an idea," I said. "We could be one of those couples that have sex for money."

"You want to have sex with other people?" She asked me stunned.

"No, no, no," I said shaking my head. "Some people pay to watch others have sex."

"You think people would pay to watch us have sex?" She asked.

"I think we're pretty good."

"I'm not complaining, mind you," she replied quickly. "But we aren't exactly in the ranks of porno stars."

"What do you mean?" I asked. "It's just sex."

"Well, people usually like to see people with…." She worked hard to find the right words. "Ah… natural… bonuses…"

"Not all the time. That'll be our hook."

"What?"

"Come see a couple make love who are actually in love!" I moved my hands like a banner across the door. "You'll be able to feel the love in the air!"

She paused to let the words seep in. "You know, in today's world I think some people may actually pay to see that…."

"See." I stated proudly.

"But where would they sit?" she asked.

"Well, we would have to build a little stage around the bed." I walked around our hotel room. "And we would need more chairs. Of course the hotel staff may be curious to know what we're doing…."

"I'm sure they'll be."

"Plus we'll need to buy a few boxes of tissue."

"You think we'll actually make the people cry?" her eyes went wide with the thought of our love moving people to tears. Unfortunately, I had to break that bubble of illusion for her.

"The tissues wouldn't be for the tears, Miss Morelli."

She paused to let that new image sink in. "Next idea."

"None of these ideas are realistic," Henry James sighed.

I shrugged my shoulders. "What can I say? I was horny."

"So whose idea was it to rob the hotel?" Dickens asked.

"I've got an idea," Toni Lyn said slowly. "It's not a good idea, but it's the easiest one for us."

"What is it?" I asked. I laid back on the bed behind her kicking my legs up in the air.

"'We rob the hotel," she replied slowly.

I ran my hand along her back. "You're nuts. "

"No," she said quickly. "It could work. One of us distracts the clerk while the other raids the safe."

"How will you distract him?" I asked raising an eyebrow.

"Who said I'll distract the clerk?"

"I don't know who else could do it," I replied. "Guys aren't exactly distracted by other guys."

"Yeah," she replied, "But can you bust the safe?"

I paused. We were in new territory here. "You know how to bust a safe? But you seem so clean cut and innocent, " I said sarcastically. We had never discussed her involvement in her father's underground activities so far. Just one of those topics both of us thought was not worth the pain.

She frowned at me. "I haven't killed anyone yet."

"Yet?"

"My uncle used to crack safes. He taught me how. The safe they have here shouldn't be too complicated."

I paused. "Of course, neither of us planned to burn down the hotel…"

"How did it happen?" Dickens asked quickly.

"And how did you get the safe?" Woolf asked.

"It's kind of hard to explain." I looked around the group. "Actually, I stole a copy of the hotel's blueprints for help in the writing. Maybe I should get it, so you'll know what I'm talking about."

They all looked around at each other. None of them wanted the story to end, but they all knew having the blueprints there might help (I am not the king of careful descriptions).

"Well, go then," Fitzgerald said. He waved his hand towards the door behind me. "Hurry back."

I got up from my chair and headed for the door. "I'll be back in a little bit."

"And don't do anything interesting," James shouted after me. "Just go to your room and come back. No adventures!"

I looked back at him and crossed my heart. "No adventures." I left The AfterTaste.

James sighed and looked around at the group. "I just know he's going to have an adventure and I won't be there."

"I'm sure you could catch up to him," Woolf said with a smile.

James frowned. "My song isn't done on the jukebox. I can't leave until it's over. It wouldn't be right."

CHAPTER 32

I was troubled. I walked down the streets of Heaven's Rome quietly. I had my hands stuffed in my pockets. I didn't bother to look up at the buildings, the moon or the people passing by (Sigh. Deep thoughts. Deep thoughts. Can't you just feel them coming?).

See, something big was going on here. And as I sat there with the group in The AfterTaste and they all began to hint at the potential of The Great Unknown's speech, I began to question my goals in all this.

All for her. Is this more than our love? Is this more than my desire to wait for her? Then there is the problem that if God decides to give us nothing without the choice. I might... She might... Nothing. Everything would be worthless then. All my days and dreams. Even her.

Yet, I didn't know Heaven's truth. There was a mystery out there that I still had to uncover. I once heard James hint at it, but Woolf quickly hushed him. Why were we in Heaven? Many of us were atheists in life and, well, some of us had lives that were far from Christian. Look at me! I mooned the pope and caused a major religious incident! Why am I in Heaven?

What is the meaning of life?

There was a moment when I first arrived at Heaven that still haunts me. I remember it clearly. I was standing in line at the registration office (It looked a lot like a typical Department of Motor Vehicles office. Same long lines. Same "happy" workers. The difference being that behind the main desk was a large gold door). And I kept thinking of how I was going to go to Hell. And that with all the fire and all the pain, I would keep thinking of her. And the absence of her would hurt more than all the flames of Hell combined. There was no way to escape the true torture of that.

In front of me was a very happy older woman. She was holding a cross in her hand and she kept whispering, "Thank God. Thank you, Jesus," under her breath. I remember clearly the discussion she had with the angel (who looked to hate his job) at the desk. The angel was chewing gum. "So what is your name?"

"My name is _____," she said in a very happy way.

"Let's see." He turned to his clipboard. He began to flip through the pages on it while making comments like this: "Typical childhood... Raised in a private school. That'll hurt your points... Dated same guy throughout high school.... Didn't give it up, did you?... Oh wait, you gave it up on your honeymoon... Then... Let's see... Kind of boring... Yadayadaya... Kids... *yawn*... Church work... Singing in choir... Boring... One pet...." He sighed and looked back up at her. "I'm sorry. You only got a one. Not very good, I'm afraid."

She was understandably confused. "What?"

"I'm sorry," the angel repeated. "Good luck next time." He then looked back at me. "Next."

"What?" she cried. She looked around as if this was all a joke. An angel in a security outfit came over and took her arm (This was all beautifully coordinated by the staff. It was obvious that they were used to these circumstances). He led her quietly and quickly out of the building. I watched her go. I had no idea what was going on and my mind didn't have the capability to try and figure it out.

"Name?" The angel asked me. He blew a bubble with his gum.

I gave my name.

He popped his gum in surprise. "Moonboy," he mumbled to himself. "Excellent!" he shouted. He reached over and shook my hand. "Wow! I'm impressed." Everyone in the building turned to look at me. I didn't know how to respond to all the attention. After the death I just went through the last thing I wanted to be was a freak show.

He stopped shaking my hand and quickly began to write on the form paper. "We've got room in Rome. That'll be perfect for you. A lot of the artists and writers live there. They'll love to have someone around like you."

"What's going on here?" I asked him.

He looked at me and waved to the gold door opening up behind him. "Welcome to Heaven, Moonboy."

I walked through the door. And suddenly… I was standing in Rome. It was Just like the Rome I remembered on Earth. Everything was the same. The McDonalds. The statues. It was all very surreal. Suddenly from above flew down two angels. They grabbed me and lead me through the town and to my apartment. They then gave me the speech (like the one to The Great Unknown)… The rest is history….

What did all that mean? It must mean something. All of this must mean something. It was easy to be cynical about a situation when you are stuck in it. But when you realize that situation possibly doesn't have a point, the cynicism changes to fear.

I opened the door to my apartment building and began to walk up the stairs. To distract these disturbing thoughts I counted the stairs as I walked up.

There were twenty-four stairs.

I walked over to the door of my apartment. The door was unlocked. I slowly opened it (here it comes). No angels were there, but waiting for me on my couch was The Great Unknown. He didn't look in the best condition. His white suit was stained with dirt and mud. He jumped up from the couch with the excitement I was used to seeing in him over the last day.

And suddenly all my dark thoughts were replaced with an image of her. I needed to see her again. Even if the point of all this existence was nothing I needed to see her again. Feel her again. Hold her close again. I'll worry about finding a point after I have her again by my side. "You can't hide here," I said to him.

"WHY NOT?" His smile fell to a frown. That wasn't what he expected me to say.

I tried to avoid his eye contact. (All for her). "I can't let you."

"C'MON, IT DOESN'T MATTER WHERE I STAY. THEY'LL FIND ME ANYPLACE. AND I CAN'T PICTURE A BETTER PERSON TO HAVE STAND NEXT TO ME WHEN THEY COME WITH THE PILLS." He walked over to me and placed his right hand on my shoulder. "THE GREAT UNKNOWN AND MOONBOY STANDING TOGETHER FORCING THEM TO PUSH THE PILLS DOWN OUR THROATS."

I looked up at him. He was disturbed. He wanted to get caught and I had to say as much to him. I had to be honest. There was nothing to lose. "Why do you want to get caught?"

His smile fell into a frown. "I DON'T KNOW HOW ELSE THIS CAN GO. I HAVE TO BE A MARTYR. IT FITS THE PLOT."

I was sickened by this comment. "This isn't a story. This isn't a book. You're a real person."

"BUT I'M THE GREAT UNKNOWN, THIS IS MY DESTINY."

I paused. Suddenly it all made sense. "So this is how you avoid all your emotions? You've abandoned the person who died for a character. You hide yourself in this made-up person. This hero for the masses. This isn't the real you, is it?"

He looked angrily at me. "YOU HAVE NO RIGHT TO ANALYZE ME."

"Why?" I asked calmly. "I know what you're going through."

"WHAT DO YOU MEAN?"

I walked over to the couch and sat down. "I lost my love too."

He paused looking down at me. "THIS IS NOT ABOUT LOVE."

I looked up at him. "Everything is about love. Anything else is worthless…"

He walked over to me. I could read in his eyes that he thought he had me on something. "IF YOU HAVE A BETTER IDEA, I'LL LISTEN."

"I do," I replied with a smile. I got up from the couch. I grabbed my backpack and began to stuff it with a few odds and ends for my writing— a notepad, some pens, and the blueprints I promised the group. "We're about the same size I think. Go into my bedroom and change your clothes. Preferably something you can move quickly in."

He ran into my bedroom. I heard my closet door being opened. "WHAT IS YOUR IDEA?" He called to me from the bedroom. I could see he was excited to hear my option. Maybe he really didn't want to become a martyr after all.

I zipped up my backpack. "We're getting out of here. I'm taking you to the Outback."

"WHAT?" He walked out of my bedroom. This actually surprised him. That strangely felt like an achievement considering how many times he had surprised me in just the last day. He stammered. "WE'LL NEVER MAKE IT. THEY'LL CATCH US. WE DON'T HAVE A CHANCE." He actually was worried. But I could tell he liked the idea of getting away. He liked this idea a lot.

"Let's go," I said and walked to the door. "I know Rome. I'll get us there."

"JUST A SECOND," He said after stopping outside my apartment, "WHY ARE YOU DOING THIS?"

I looked back at him. "I'm sick of martyrs."

I closed the door behind him.

When we reached the outside of the apartment building, we both began jogging. "Follow me," I whispered to him. "I know this town like the back of my hand."

"REALLY?" He asked.

"I especially know how to run through this town when you want to avoid attention," I said

We jogged quietly for a few more minutes. When we reached the third alley the Great Unknown asked me a question between his heavy breathing. "CAN I ASK YOU A QUESTION?"

"Shoot."

"IF EACH OF THE HUMAN CITIES IN HEAVEN ARE SUPPOSED TO REPRESENT A HEYDAY OF THAT CITY WHY IS THIS A MODERN ROME INSTEAD OF THE ROME OF THE ROMAN EMPIRE?"

"That's an interesting story," I said.

An Interesting story
"The Modernists and the Ancients Debate"

Heaven's Rome used to be the Rome of the Roman Empire. It was rich and majestic with it's many white columns and marble streets. It was an incredible sight to be seen and quite the tourist attraction. Dead people would travel to it daily to stare at the classic beauty of it and get their picture taken with a man in a toga. And everyone was happy.

That is, everyone was happy until the late 1980's. See, it was at that time that the dead started arriving into that city that were used to the spoilings of the modern technologies and stores. They complained of the lack of normal grocery stores, they protested the enforced toga dress codes, and they cried over the lack of electrical outlets. For the modern man, Rome was beautiful but a Hell to live in.

So, it was with those thoughts in mind that a group of the strongest protesters voiced their dispute to the angels. The angels decided that this was best left up for the dead to decide for themselves. So each side of the argument chose representatives to take part in the great debate.

This was quite a major scene in Heaven's history. Every day, people throughout the five cities of Heaven tuned into the TV station to watch the recent debates, openings and arguments. They booed or cheered over every point that was brought up by each side. Witnesses were brought in to discuss the artistry of both modern and ancient Rome. Artwork was shown over slides to illustrate the growth of the classic styles of each time period.... Etc, etc.

This went on for about two weeks until the Modernists came up with a brilliant and subtle strategy. They began to supply lunches as a friendly gesture for the debates. On the first day they brought in McDonald's, on the second they brought in Kentucky Fried Chicken, on the third they brought in Subway, on the fifth they brought in Pizza Hut... Etc. This went on for about a week and a half. And then suddenly they stopped bringing in these free meals.

The Ancients, of course, complained.

The Modernists smiled and said quite matter of factly that in the Modern Rome these foods are readily available in any fastfood restaurant on every corner. They are, they pointed out, however not available in Ancient Rome.

The debate was quickly over.

The Ancients signed the paper and as everyone slept that night, the angels turned Rome over to the Modern times.

Conclusion-

Since the construction of the Modern Heaven's Rome, the average weight of the Roman has increased by 45 pounds.

"THAT IS AN INTERESTING STORY," The Great Unknown said.
"I know," I replied. "Take a left at the corner...."

Chapter 33

"I DON'T THINK I'VE RUN SO MUCH IN MY LIFE," The Great Unknown said. I could tell he was already getting out of breath. I slowed my pace so he could keep up with me.

"I'm used to running," I replied. "When I first arrived in Heaven I used running to release my anxiety. Plus it feels good to run in Rome. It reminds me of the run that got me to her."

SHE REALLY MEANS THE WORLD TO YOU, DOESN'T SHE?" He asked between his quick breathing.

"Everything," I answered.

All for her.

Time to jogmovemovemovemoverun....

20 Minutes later and...

I stopped running and bent over, resting my arms on my knees. "Oh, God." We didn't make it.

"FUCK." The Great Unknown fell to his knees. It almost looked like he was praying. His hands moved from in front of himself to behind his head. He was exhausted. "FUCK." In his mind he could already feel the pills going down his throat and all the thoughts that made him unique disappearing. He saw himself from outside of himself. He saw himself recreated in almost a comic character. He saw himself without his self-esteem and pride.

"I've been sent to find you," The angel said quietly. "The Happy Angels want to talk to you."

The Great Unknown looked up. He looked like he knew the angel. She was a very beautiful female angel with the most incredible hair (How did it move like that?). His mouth fell open. "OH MY…."

The angel suddenly acted surprised as well. "I… I… Hi…"

"HI," The Great Unknown whispered.

I looked between the both of them. Something was going on here between them. Can The Great Unknown not surprise me? "What's going on here?"

"Why didn't you come home tonight?" The angel asked quietly. "I waited for you."

"I'M SORRY," The Great Unknown replied. "THERE WAS SOME-THING I NEEDED TO DO."

"I know all about it," The angel replied in a huff. "You stood me up. You made me feel like a complete idiot." (Were these actual emotions? Where did this angel get emotions?)

"I'M REALLY SORRY." The Great Unknown got up from his knees. He held his hands out in front of himself as he slowly moved forward to the angel. "I DIDN'T MEAN TO HURT YOU."

"You made all of us angels look like idiots on TV, " She sounded like she was going to cry (Is that really a tear?). "Why did you do that?"

"WHAT I DID, I HAD TO DO," He said. He was very close to her.

"Do you really…" She couldn't get herself to say it. "Do you really want to go into noth… noth…"

He moved closer to her. They began to whisper among themselves. I couldn't hear what they were saying. This angel really was emotional. In just this night alone, I'd seen two angels act more real than I have in the entire 3 years I have been in Heaven. My mind raced with new questions regarding these lifeforms that I only thought of before as stooges for a strict moral code. Are they like us? Do they like this? How do they see reality? How do they see us? How do they feel? What do they do when they are not bothering us? How do they live like this? What do they love? I kept wondering these questions until my mind was put on a pause by the incredible sight in front me... He.. The angel...

They were kissing.

He had his arms around her waist and her wings were beginning to flap. They flew up a few feet then came back down. It was... To see this sight was... Wow.

They stopped kissing. It was one of the strangest and most incredible sights I had ever seen. They whispered a little bit among themselves some more and then... Then she flew away.

The Great Unknown stuffed his hands in his pocket and walked back to me. "SHE GAVE US TWENTY MINUTES. LET'S GO." He turned and began jogging.

I jogged up to him. "That must have been some kiss."

"I USED TO PLAY SAXOPHONE." He looked over at me. "ALL SAXOPHONE PLAYERS ARE INCREDIBLE KISSERS."

"And I thought it was just good for jazz," I said to myself.

The Great Unknown laughed and we continued to run into the night....

CHAPTER 34

An hour later I was standing on the border of the Outback with The Great Unknown. "WHAT A BEAUTIFUL FOREST," The Great Unknown sighed. It did look great tonight. The full moon (which was always full) was shinning down over the mountain and the woods. Somewhere over in the distance a wolf howled. "WAS THAT A WOLF?" He looked at me surprised.

"No," I replied. "It's a loudspeaker they've got about a mile into the woods."

The Great Unknown laughed at this. I joined him. It was funny to think of the angels going to all that trouble of planting a loudspeaker by a mountain and then finding a power source. All that work just to create the sound of a wolf's howl to scare us dead away. What could a wolf do to us dead anyway?

The Great Unknown turned back to the woods. "SO IS THERE ANY-ONE FAMOUS HIDING IN THESE WOODS?"

"Other than you?" I laughed.

"CUT THAT OUT," He laughed back.

I slowed my laughing (Time to get a little serious. Time to get a little misty.) "Fitzgerald told me that Hemingway went in there a few years ago, but of course knowing Hemingway he could be anywhere," I said slowly. "He's not the kind of soul that can be held."

"It would be cool to bump into Hemingway," The Great Unknown said to himself. "I wonder what he's like?"

"Well, if he didn't bring his razor with him, pretty hairy I'm guessing."

The Great Unknown didn't respond to my little (very little) joke. He continued to stare out at the woods.

"Rumor has it, " I said continuing the conversation, "That the entrance to Hell is in this Outback. That, of course, can't be proven. Who knows? Maybe the angels spread that rumor? Sounds like something they would do, doesn't it? Since Hell was filled up a few hundred years ago, we've all lost track of where it is. Maybe the angels are forgetful like the rest of us dead. Or maybe they don't care either." I shrugged my shoulders. After this evening, I had a hard time telling anything anymore. "I do know where the line is for the pickup spot for Hell... It's a *very* long line at the pickup spot."

The Great Unknown seemed intrigued by this conversation. "HAVE YOU EVER SEEN A DEVIL?"

"Once," I replied. "I was jogging on the East Side of Rome where the pickup spot is located. You saw the line, right? It goes around the block 3 times. Anyway, a limo fell out of the sky. Literally fell. It was the impact of the vehicle that caught my attention. Out of the limo appeared two devils. They look exactly like the old drawings—Dark red skin, black hair, and goatees. They are about 5 foot, 2 inches tall. One was dressed in a gold suit; the other was dressed in a one of those jogging suits. They reviewed the first ten people in line, turned away 3 of the older dead, piled in the seven and flew straight up in the air."

The Great Unknown paused and slowly smiled. "HELL? THAT MIGHT MAKE AN INTERESTING VACATION."

You can't be serious," I laughed. "There is always the chance Hell could really be Hell and not like the disco everyone claims."

"EVEN IF IT WAS ALL FIRE AND BRIMSTONE, SO WHAT?" He looked over at me. "SERIOUSLY, WHAT COULD THEY DO TO ME? I'M ALREADY DEAD."

"Fitzgerald said the same thing earlier," I replied. "If so many people think that way it makes you wonder how successful a real Hell actually can be."

"AND WHO KNOWS? MAYBE I CAN SAVE A FEW OF THOSE POOR DEAD SOULS."

"Set some free?"

"I WOULDN'T BE THE FIRST TO SAVE SOME POOR SOULS FROM HELL. HEAVEN MIGHT BE A LITTLE MORE INTEREST-ING WITH A CRIME SPREE ON ITS HANDS." He reached out to shake my hand.

"You should have read the pamphlet better," I smiled. "You might have a hard time convincing some of them to leave." I took his hand and slowly shook it (His palm was sweaty). It was odd to think I've only known him for two days.

"I'LL BE BACK TO READ YOUR BOOK."

"Thanks," I replied. "I hope it'll be worth the trip."

I'M SURE IT WILL BE." He turned and headed into the woods. "JUST REMEMBER ONE THING AS YOU ARE WRITING. THIS, BY THE WAY, IS THE BEST ADVICE ANYONE CAN EVER GIVE YOU REGARDING YOUR WRITING. BE TRUE TO YOURSELF." He began to run into the woods. "I LOVE A GOOD CLICHE!"

For some reason, I just had to say something more to him. "Hey!"

He stopped to look back at me.

"Tell Hemingway I said hi!"

He smiled, waved and disappeared into the brush.

CHAPTER 35

"And then he was gone," I finished. I looked around at the others. They were all sitting on the edge of their seats during my story of getting The Great Unknown to the Outback.

"So he's gone," James sighed.

"I don't think so," I answered him. "I think he's just taking a break. He'll be back and maybe then he'll be himself for a change."

Fitzgerald took another shot of his bourbon. He refilled all of our glasses. "The bastard," he mumbled under his breath and drank the shot.

"What do you mean?" Woolf asked.

"He's a bastard!" Fitzgerald said angrily.

"It's the alcohol," Dickens explained.

"No, it's not," Fitzgerald replied. "The Great Unknown is a bastard."

"Just a few hours ago you were toasting him as a hero," I responded.

"That's when I thought he was actually standing for something."

"He's standing for something still," I said quietly. "In a different way."

"He ran away." Fitzgerald poured himself another glass. "And he left all of us to deal with the results of his speech."

"You wanted him to be a martyr!" I was angry with Fitzgerald.

"What?" He returned with just as much anger.

"You wanted him to suffer. You wanted him to get caught and hurt so you could stand on the sidelines and cheer. Now that he's gone, you don't want to be forced onto the field. You're a cheerleader who doesn't have the balls to play in the game."

Dickens looked over at James confused. "I don't understand the metaphor that he's using?"

"It's football," James explained quietly.

"It doesn't sound like football to me," Dickens mumbled to himself.

James was about to explain the difference between the term "Football" in America and Europe but was interrupted by the intensity that the argument had grown to. "I stood by him. The angels were chasing me too!" Fitzgerald shouted.

"Oh, please," I sighed. "You were like a kid after going to a really good movie. You were living in his moment. You were living in the thrill of him. It had nothing to do with you. The angels don't even know you were there."

"Damn you." He stood up and pointed at me. "Damn you!"

"You know what this is really about?" I asked him. "Huh? You really want to know? You wish you thought of what he did. You wish that was you on that screen tonight preaching that sermon to God. You're angry that he thought of it and you didn't. And if it was you, you would have made a big show of getting caught and then everyone would proclaim you a hero. He has instead done the opposite and that pisses you off. He isn't playing the role like you would."

"You immature hack," Fitzgerald said slowly. "You dare to say that to…"

"Ok, ok," Woolf interrupted. She got up from her seat. "That's enough, you two. That's enough. Let's all sit down."

Fitzgerald and I stared at each other for a little bit longer (jerk) and then we slowly sat down. I leaned back in my chair and he poured himself another drink. He liked his bourbon.

"Now," Woolf said calmly, "Why don't you tell us about the fire. How did that start?"

I opened up my backpack and took out my blueprint of the hotel we were staying in at Lake Lucerne, Switzerland. "I brought the plan like I promised and…" I was interrupted

Ring.

The phone rang. It took all of us by complete surprise. Who would call any of us at 3:30 AM here? We all looked around waiting for someone to do something. Should we pick up the phone or let it ring? Who would it be?

Ring.

"You're the closest," James said to me.

I sighed and got up. This is so typical. I was the youngest so I do the work.

Ring.

I picked it up. "Hello?"

A beautiful female voice spoke very nervously. "Did he make it?" It took me a second to place that timid voice. Could it be? It must be. It was the angel. It was HIS angel.

"Yes," I replied. "He made it to the Outback."

"Good." She sighed in relief. "Thank you."

She hung up.

I put the phone back down and slowly walked back over to the table. Odd… Odd night…

CHAPTER 36

— THE GREAT PLAN AT WORK

"Ok, here is how the plan worked," I said quietly. I unfolded the blue print I had of the hotel. Fitzgerald took another slow drag off his cigarette and leaned in over the blueprint. James readjusted himself in his seat and leaned in as well. Woolf and Dickens just looked at each other and shrugged their shoulders. "First off let me say that everything about this plan was perfect for us. 1. We were able to not only get our money back from our blackmailer but also make a profit at his expense. He deserved it. And, 2., the proper authorities will learn once we're safely away from that hotel that it housed a fugitive without notifying them. Very cool all around. Are you ready?"

They all nodded their heads.

I pointed down at the bar of the hotel. "This is where Toni Lyn was stationed."

The bartender leaned over the counter to Toni Lyn. "Do you want a drink?"

"No," she replied and turned away.

"Then why are you here?" The bartender asked suspiciously.

She looked back at him annoyed. "I came here to sit down, ok?"

He leaned farther over the counter. "Isn't there a chair in your hotel room?"

She glared at him and spoke slowly. "That chair is not as comfortable as these bar stools."

"Couldn't you sit on the bed?" He asked.

"Ok, ok," Henry said. "Now where were you?"

"I was up in our room." I pointed at the blueprint where our room was located. "Right here on the second floor."

"How did the fire start?" Fitzgerald asked.

"Well, that was one of our problems," I said. "See, I don't smoke, but it had to look like I smoke... A lot. We had the trashcan filled with newspapers. And all I had to do was smoke a cigarette down to almost the end and then throw it into the trash."

"Easy," Fitzgerald said. "I've done it a few times by mistake myself. Very easy to do."

"You would think," I sighed. "But after the third cigarette I still couldn't get it to start."

COUGH. COUGH. HACK.

"Why do people smoke these things?" I was pacing the room puffing on my fourth cigarette. *Ew, my stomach.* I was starting to feel sick. "Oh God, I think I'm going to throw up..."

Oh God. I ran into the bathroom....

"Did you throw up?" Dickens asked.

"No, not yet."

"So you were in the room trying to start a fire and Toni Lyn was waiting in the bar?" James asked.

"And she was starting to get nervous," I said. "See we had this all keyed to go at about 9:30PM and it was almost 10:00 PM. So, she was starting to get annoyed at me. Like maybe I wimped out or something. Plus, the bartender was annoying the Hell out of her."

"You know some people might want to use that chair?" The Bartender hinted to Toni Lyn.

"You can't always get what you want," Toni Lyn said and looked away. She was not going to let this guy annoy her. She had more important things to deal with then an overweight, balding man named Sven.

"Yes, but at a bar you're supposed to get what you want. Who would go to a bar that wouldn't serve them? See it's all based on customer service. They ask for a drink and I give it to them. They get what they want."

Toni Lyn glared at him. "Leave me alone, all right? I'm not thirsty."

"So why are you here then?" he asked again. He paused and looked her over. "Are you a prostitute?"

"WHAT?" Toni Lyn exclaimed.

"Well, are you?" He asked again casually.

"Of course, not," she said quickly.

"Well, if you were you're doing a lousy job of it…"

"So when did you get the fire started?" Woolf asked quickly.

"The fifth cigarette," I sighed. "So picture this. There I am—sick to my stomach. I almost threw up once so I looked like Hell. I could barely stand up. I was swaggering left and right trying my best to finish another cigarette. I think I was even chanting to myself just to keep going…"

"Must smoke. Must smoke. Must smoke. Must smoke. Puff baby, puff baby, baby, puff, puff."

"Catchy," Woolf laughed.

"Then it happened," I drank a little of my glass of bourbon (Fitzgerald was sharing again). "It started on fire. I jumped up and down in excitement…. Unfortunately, that only upset my stomach more. So I had to find someplace to throw up…"

Henry began to rub his head. "Oh, no. I can see where this is going."

"…So I threw up in the trashcan. It extinguished the fire."

"Fuck! Fuck! Fuck!" I screamed and fell back on the bed. "God damn," I moaned. *I'm such a moron! Damn it! Ok, ok, think of the big picture. You have to do this, big boy. You have to do this. I have to do this for Toni Lyn. She is expecting this.* I looked at my watch. *Ok, I'm a little behind schedule. All for her. All for her. All for her…*

I reached over for the pack.

"So I was upstairs smoking my sixth cigarette. Toni Lyn on the other hand was downstairs getting into a very strange argument."

"So are you telling me I could not pick up someone wearing this out-fit?" She angrily asked the bartender and…

"Whoa, whoa, whoa," Fitzgerald said waving his arms.

"What?" I asked him. I hated interruptions and that is all I was getting here.

"What was she wearing?"

"I don't understand."

"He was criticizing her clothes and we have no idea what she is wearing. A few details would be nice."

"Well… I told her it was a bad idea to wear the outfit. But she thought it was cool and…"

"What are you talking about?" Woolf asked.

Toni Lyn walked out of the bathroom as proud as can be. She was wear-ing all black. She had on black pants, a black turtleneck, black shoes and even a black snowcap. She turned herself around happily in front me.

"You can't be serious," I laughed.

"What?" She asked. She was not happy with my response. "Don't you like my outfit?"

"You look like a burglar," I said waving towards her (I was sitting on the edge of the bed). "It's obvious."

"Yes, yes," She quickly agreed. "But when I remove the hat." She took off the snowcap. "I look like a normal person."

"Just a happy go lucky Satanist," I sighed.

"And then," she laughed. "When I put on the hat I become a burglar." She put it back on. "See, now I 'm a burglar. Watch out!" She took it off. "Now I'm just a normal Joe."

"Who's Joe?"

And when I put it back on, I'm a burglar again. Run away!" She put the hat back on and stuffed her brown hair into the cap.

"Wow, just like Clark Kent and Superman," I laughed.

"The outfit, in my opinion, is perfect," She turned to the mirror on our door. She looked at herself happily.

"You can't be serious," Woolf sighed.

"Yes, I am," I replied. "So she was wearing an all black outfit down there with her cap stuffed in her bag by her side."

"She had a bag with her?" James asked.

"Her backpack, it had her tools in it," I explained quickly.

"Tools for what?"

"For the safe," I sighed.

"Ok, ok," Fitzgerald groaned. "So she is wearing all black and her clothes are being mocked by the bartender."

"Well, you might be able to pick someone up," he sighed. "But to get them to pay is another story."

"I don't think the outfit would be a problem. I'm a natural beauty."

He began to clean the counter with an old rag. It was obvious he was not enjoying this conversation. "I won't argue that. But look at you. You're wearing all black. You look more like you're going to rob someone than seduce someone."

Toni Lyn awkwardly laughed and looked at her watch.

"Flames," I looked at Fitzgerald. "I had flames. Now this is when it gets really interesting."

"It gets more interesting than this?" James asked with wide eyes. I knew what he was thinking. He has written many works about stupid Americans acting like idiots in Europe. Toni Lyn and I were about to take the cake, the gold medal and the grand prize. Time to make everyone back home proud to be an American.

"I had the fire going, but I was in bad shape. I struggled to get out of the room. It was filling up with smoke and the last thing I needed with my stomach was smoke."

"Oh, god," I moaned and began struggling to the door. I fell down against it. *Must reach the doorknob. Must open the door.* My hand lazily reached up for the knob. I struggled to turn it.

Come on you can do this. This is no big deal. It's just a stupid doorknob. You've turned hundreds of these in your lifetime.

I opened the door. I leaned against the wall and caught my breath. I struggled over to the smoke alarm. It was about two doors down from me and it was right near the stairs, so in a perfect world and a perfect situation, I could run down the stairs and be gone.

Pull alarm! Pull the damn alarm!

I grabbed the little alarm in the tips of my finger and leaned all my weight into it. And… And… And… It went off!

I weakly smiled to myself.

I did it! I really did it!

And then I collapsed on the floor.

"At the same time I was struggling to get out of my room to the alarm, Toni Lyn was beginning to take part in a strange contest."

The bartender leaned across the counter at you. "See, I'm guessing you can't pick up that man over there."

"Which man?" Toni Lyn asked.

"Him." The bartender pointed at a man at a table on the side. He was drinking by himself.

"That would be easy."

"If you can get him to offer you money," The bartender said. He took out his wallet out of his pocket and laid some money on the table. "I'll give you this."

"Are you serious?" Toni Lyn asked.

"Sure go give it a try."

"I don't have to do anything, right?

"Of course, not," He replied. "Just get him to offer you money."

Toni Lyn got off her seat, straightened her clothes and began to walk over to the man when...

"I have an open seat right here at the bar!" The bartender called. Someone ran over and took Toni Lyn's seat. She stopped and looked angrily back at the bartender. He smiled, shrugged his shoulders happily. "So what would you like?" The bartender asked his new customer.

Toni Lyn began walking back to the bartender and her old seat. She was upset and she was ready to...

And that's when the alarm went off!

"So you're here on the ground passed out," James pointed at the blue-print near the stairs of the second floor. And he moved his hand over to the bar. "And she's over here in the bar." And then he moved his hand to the registration office. "And the small safe is over here?"

"Yes," I sighed. "All she had to do was get over to the safe in the confusion and we would've been golden."

"But something stopped this, I'm guessing?" Woolf asked.

"It turned out the bartender was noble," I sighed. "Can you believe it?"

"Come on, Miss," the Bartender said. He jumped over the counter and took her hand. "We've got to get out of here."

"No!" She shouted quickly. She needed to find an excuse to stay in a fire. 'I need to get my bag."

He grabbed it off the floor and handed it to her. All the tools banged around inside it. The noise confused him, but he didn't ask her about it. "Now let's go." He held her right arm in his hand and led her out the building with all the other guests.

"Now what neither of us knew," I said. "Was that the fire in our room was spreading. This was no longer a simple trashcan blaze. The fire jumped to the drapes and then to the bed sheets and soon the room was all in flames. And then it spread over to the next room and the next. This hotel was going down. Neither Toni Lyn nor I expected the entire hotel to be such a fire hazard. Considering the hotel owner is also a blackmailer, I guess we should've expected him to cut a few corners in public safety. But we didn't mean to burn down the entire building. We just wanted a distraction and, boy, were we getting one."

Virginia Woolf looked up at me from the blueprint. "Oh, my."

"You can say that again."

Toni Lyn was the first of us to realize how bad the fire had gotten. When she reached the outside, she turned and looked back at the building in a hope of finding a way to get back in and that was when she saw the fire and the smoke coming out of our room. "I need to get back in there," she whispered to herself.

She snuck around the crowd of guests and ran to one of the side door entrances. Everyone was outside the main entrance so no one saw her when she got back in…

"Didn't she worry about you?" Dickens asked.

"She had no reason to worry," I replied. "My escape from the fire was perfectly planned. Our car was parked, with all our bags in the back, outside the entrance by the stairs. All I had to do was run down. So, in her mind I was already outside the hotel in the car waiting for her. That, however, was far from the truth."

When I came to, I was still feeling weak. However, I still was able to quickly realize how bad a condition I was in. There were flames all the way down the hallway. *Oh shit! I'm going to die!* I began to crawl on my hands and knees to the stairs. *If I can get to the stairs, I can get out of here.*

However, because of my condition I could not move very fast. *I'm so going to die! And I'm going to be cremated too. I don't want to be cremated! Crawl, man, crawl!*

"Now, (I took a breath) she made it to the registration office. It was as we expected—Empty (We kind of assumed that our blackmailer was more interested in saving his neck than hanging around the office). She found the safe sitting on his desk in the office in the back. She opened her backpack and began to work on the safe…."

"So you're crawling to safety?" Fitzgerald asked.

"Yes."

"And she's working on the safe?"

"Yes."

"And then what?"

"And then," I sighed. "The fire department showed up."

I reached the stairs. *Oh, no!* The fire had already spread there. There were flames all the way down the stairs. I lay back down on the floor. *So this is how it is going to end? I feel so at peace. This is how it was meant to be. I can go like this. I loved a great love and I died for her. I wonder what my last memories will be of. Probably her over and over again. I wonder what will happen when I die. Is there a Heaven? Is there a Hell? Where would someone like me go? All I want is to be near her. But I'm stuck. I'm doomed. I don't have the strength. I do feel so at peace right now. So very rested and I can just…*

Suddenly from down the hallway, with an axe in hand, ran a fire fighter.

"Get your ass over here and help me!" He ran over and lifted me up. "Where the Hell have you been?… Oh, thanks, by the way."

"Nice," Fitzgerald moaned. "And how were things going with her."
"Not very well, " I said.

"Fuck you safe!!!" She threw the last of her tools at the safe. "God damn you to safe Hell!!!" She screamed. For the life of her, she could not get it open! Maybe it was all the distractions going on around her. Or maybe it was because she hadn't attempted to do something like that in years. The fact is she could not do it.

She was so upset that tears were starting to form around her eyes. She went over to the safe and wrapped her arms lovingly around it. "Why won't you open?" She asked it. She rubbed her hands along the back of the safe like she was trying to soothe it. "Don't you like me safe?" She leaned over and kissed it. "See, I'm nice. You want to open for me right?" She leaned in and kissed it again and…

A fire fighter burst into the room. The hallway outside was filled with flames. He paused in his thought. I guess the sight of seeing someone making out with a safe during the middle of an inferno confused him. His confusion could be heard in his voice as he casually said. "Ah, excuse me, ma'am. But we really have to get out of here. There's this fire and all."

She picked up the small safe, put her backup over her shoulder, and walked over to him. "Lead me out please." She looked down at her safe (Best to play nuts). "C'mon safey, we've been saved by this nice man."

"Ok," The firefighter sighed to himself and led her out through the front.

"Now by the time she made it outside the hotel, everyone was scattered all around. So no one really noticed the fact that she casually walked away to the side with a safe under her arm. She walked past the bartender, our blackmailer, the cleaning crew, everyone. Not one of them gave her a second thought. She walked over to me where I was waiting for her by the car. I had puked once I got outside so I still looked bad. The firefighter gave me a blanket, which I had wrapped around my shoulders. We looked at each other."

"Hello," I said.
"Hello," she said.
"Ready to go?" I asked.
"Yes," she said. "I'm ready to go."

"We got into the car and drove away. Picture that: There we are in a stolen red sports car; I looked like hell with black stains all over my face and clothes; she was wearing all black with a safe on her lap; And behind us was a huge fire. Just picture that." I sat back in my seat.

All the writers looked around at each other and then back at me and then back at each other and then back at me. Dickens was the first to speak. "That was… very interesting."

"To say the least," Woolf agreed.

We all paused to let the moment that just happened sink in. Fitzgerald leaned forward. It was like him to figure out the one point I forgot to include. "But how did the police discover that the hotel owner was allowing you to stay in his hotel?"

"That was Toni Lyn's brilliant idea," I said smartly. "It was the perfect conclusion."

A week later————————————————

"Excuse me, sir," the police officer said to the Police Chief in the Lake Lucerne Police Station.

The Chief was leaning back in his chair reading the newspaper. "What is it?"

"We received this in the mail and…"

"What is it?" The Chief asked again. He put down his newspaper. He hated being interrupted.

"You should take a look," The police officer handed the Chief a photograph.

The Chief sat up in his chair. He looked up at the Police officer, stunned. "Get my car!"

I stood up from the table, spread my arms wide and bowed. "Taaaadaaaa!"

CHAPTER 37

"Then what happened?" James asked in excitement. He leaned further across the table as if being closer to me would help the words reach him that much faster. Everyone at the table was very much into the story. I could see it in their eyes.

"Well, we took off for Amsterdam," I replied. I needed to leave. It was 3:30AM and I had a lot of writing to do tonight.

"What about the safe?" James asked.

"The entire time I drove to the border, she played with the safe and she was having a bad time with it."

The following speech was censored by the Angel Publishing Board for Decency in Writing.

"This EDIT safe is the EDIT safe in the entire EDIT world. If it was a human I would EDIT and EDIT and EDIT it for all this EDIT EDIT. This is the biggest load of EDIT I've ever EDIT experienced. EDIT this safe! EDIT! EDIT! EDIT!" Toni Lyn looked like she wanted to throw it out the car window.

"What if we bought some explosives?" I asked her.

"So we bought some explosives and blew the door off," I said.

"Just pull the trigger down," she said walking back to me. We had the safe sitting by itself in this field (It was a field filled with cows eating. The cows didn't pay attention to us and there was no one around except the highway in the distance, so it seemed perfect) and we were standing a safe distance away. We were both tired with the entire safe problem. We just wanted this over with so we could get on with our lives. We felt that blowing off the safe's door for us was like helping a butterfly get out of its cocoon. That's what we were doing and we were ready to be done with it. Get this over with.

"Are you sure the dynamite is placed on it right?" I casually asked.

The fact I asked that question really annoyed her.

"Nevermind," I said quickly to cover the question.

"Just do it," She said to me and covered her ears. I pulled the trigger and....

Wait a minute....

IT'S TIME FOR A POP QUIZ!

1. Let's say you're about to set off an explosion in a field filled with cows. What do you think will happen?

A) The cows don't pay attention and continue to go about their merry cow business.

B) The cows tell us how bad such explosions are for the environment.

C) The cows run away in a panic.

D) None of the above.

E) All of the above.

Let's see if you're right....

BOOOOOOM!!!!!

The door flew right off!

We did it!

However, neither of us expected what was going to happen next (We would have failed in the pop quiz). We were both shocked.

"Where are all those cows running to?" I asked her.

"I didn't even know cows could run," was the only response she could get out. For there were two dozen cows sprinting as fast as they could away down the field! The cows knocked over the fence surrounding the field! Right through that electric fence! Then the cows sprinted right out onto the busy highway!

"Oh my God," I exclaimed as we watched all the cars and the frightened cows collide in the distance (All we could hear were skids, bangs, and mooooooos).

"Get the money," she said quickly. "I'll start the car. We've got to get out of here!"

I ran out into the field and grabbed the money out of the safe and sprinted back. She was already in the car and revving the engine. "Let's go!" She shouted at me as I jumped into my seat. "Go! Go! Go!"

I shut the door and we were gone!

The correct answer in the pop quiz was C.

I got up from my chair and began to fold the blueprints. I really had to go.

"What then?" Dickens asked.

"We went to Amsterdam."

"But what happened there?"

"That's what I need to work on," I replied. "I really have got to go."

"But tell us first," Woolf begged.

"I can't," I sighed. "I need to tell that part of the story alone." They all looked so disappointed. They looked like children who were denied a present at Christmas. "I'm sorry. I need to be alone."

"What time do you think you'll be done?" Henry James asked me.

"Maybe 11AM." I began walking to the door. "But I really have to go."

"Good luck with the writing," Woolf called after me.

I turned back to her. "For me, it won't be writing. It will be living through the moments in dreams." I walked out the door.

Woolf looked over at Henry James and Charles Dickens. "He is quite the romantic little fellow, isn't he?"

They both nodded their heads 'yes.'

PART 4
—AMSTERDAM

When you dream, what do
you dream about?
—Barenaked Ladies

THE AMSTERDAM POEM

When I dream
I dream of Amsterdam
And the forty days
Spent there with her.
I think of her hair,
Her smile,
Her laugh,
Her tears,
Her inner beauty,
The way she would say
Everyday
Was only for us-

My heaven is nothing more
Than my fight
To recapture the dreams
And the days
Of holding her hand.
I wait here
Counting the days
Until I can feel that grasp
Once more
And feel that feeling
Of needing nothing
But her-

I relive those moments
Now on these pages
Giving you the moments
We shared so dear (like dreams).
From the opening grin
To the touch
When I left her my soul
To care for-

I wish only for you to feel.
I hope only for you to try
Believe
In everything we felt.
Watch the forty sunsets
On our days with me-

So welcome my friends
To the only things
That make my eternity bearable-

Welcome to my dreams—

CHAPTER 38

1:23 PM
She smiled at me when we first drove into Amsterdam. We first went to a local bank and exchanged our money for the proper currency. We pretended to be newlyweds on our honeymoon. It was all very sweet and the bankteller totally bought it. (kiss, kiss, honey).

2:14PM
We found this quaint bed and breakfast in the outskirts of the town (It is run by an older woman with a British accent. We didn't ask her how she ended up in Amsterdam, but she told us her life story anyway. It had to do with WWII and her parents moving there for military reasons. Exciting stuff). We again pretended to be newlyweds. I even carried Toni Lyn across the threshold into our bedroom to make the performance official. The old lady thought it was very romantic. We decided that this was the best place to stay until we could find a secluded apartment and a job (knock on wood) in town. We hope to stay here only a week.

3:00PM
We made love. We agreed that it was an 8.

5:12PM

Went downstairs to have dinner. It turned out the lady was an incredible cook. She smiled sweetly at us as we entered the room. She knew what we were doing upstairs. 8's can be pretty loud. She asked why we didn't have our rings on. Toni Lyn quickly stated that we were afraid to have them stolen while in town (It's amazing how fast her mind can work). She also added a sweet comment about how we really didn't need the rings because we were married in our hearts. The old lady bought the line (I dug it too) and after she left the room Toni Lyn stuck her tongue out at me-nice. After dinner we went on a walk through town and took pictures of each other in front of every little windmill we could find. And every now and then, we would sneak kisses behind anything that could hide us. Very official honeymoon material.

7:45PM
Back up in room. We made love again (only a 5 this time. Nothing to complain about. A 1 for us was still better than any sex either of us had experienced before we fell in love. We were magic together) and then took a bath. The bathtub was large. Great bubbles. Toni Lyn wanted to buy some candles ("I want some red candles. The really big kind") for next time.

9:32PM
We watched **Casablanca** on TV. It was dubbed. The person reading the part of Rick over Humphrey Bogart's voice was awful. There is only one Bogart. However, the person reading Ingrid's part was pretty good. The accents matched perfectly (no surprise there).

11:05PM
Fell asleep in each other's arms. It was a good day.

CHAPTER 39

On our second day, we decided to take a walk in the redlight district of Amsterdam. It's almost become a tradition for young adults on vacation to visit here. Here all inhibitions were left behind. And that is literal.

So as we walked around we both ended up saying things like:

Look at that.
Wow!
Is that really what I think it is?
I can't believe... I don't want to believe it.
She was really a man?
Is it possible to fit that MUCH in?
I'm offended by that and a little turned on.
I'm guessing that would hurt.
I'm close with my pets but let's be reasonable.

Then we found one of the legendary marijuana bars. This was a new topic of conversation for us to dive into. Neither of us wanted to be the first to admit that we had actually done it before.

She said: "I wonder how strong the stuff is here. Not that I would have anything to compare it to."

I said:"I totally agree with your line of questioning, but since I've never done it I would have nothing to compare it too…. as well…"

She said: "I bet you it's strong."

I said: "Oh, yeah and good. Not that I would know."

She said: "It's got to be cheaper."

I said: "And it's legal which is nice compared… Not that I worried about that when I was back in the United States… I mean, because I wasn't doing it…"

She said: "I wasn't thinking that at all."

After playing back and forth like this for a few minutes we finally looked each other straight in the face and said:

You want to get high?

"Oh, my god! That is good stuff," I laughed. I smiled wide. I smiled really, really wide!

She spread her hands out to their full length and swung herself around in a circle. "I feel great!" She bumped into another person walking down the street with one of her swinging arms. "Oh, I'm so sorry sir. I'm so sorry." She turned back to me and laughed. "I totally punched that guy!"

She came over and took my arm. She looked right up at me with her beautiful eyes. "I love you."

"I know," I replied. I ran my hands through her hair. "I won't hold it against you."

"Actually I might like you to hold it against me," she said in a very deep (overly accented) voice.

We laughed and began walking down the street together.

"Did you buy some to go?" She asked.

"Oh, did you want some too?" I asked suspiciously.

She pinched my arm and reached into my pocket to take out the stash. "I like Amsterdam," she said as she placed it in her coat pocket.

CHAPTER 40

—[OUR THIRD DAY IN AMSTERDAM IS SPENT "RELAXING"]

She lit up another joint. She took a slow drag off of it, held it in for a few seconds and slowly let it out. We were very open on this topic now. "I've smoked marijuana at college, but none of the weed I tried there was ever as strong as this stuff. This is really good stuff…."

"Pass it here," I said holding out my hand. We were sitting on the back porch of our small bed and breakfast watching the day slip away.

Toni Lyn looked over at me and smiled. "I've got an idea."

"What?" I asked.

"Let's have a serious conversation."

I laughed. "Maybe next time we should make that decision before getting high."

"No, no, it's perfect. We're uninhibited with this stuff. We can truly say what's on our mind."

"Are you telling me you've not always been open with me?" I asked raising one of my eyebrows.

It seems that the realization that we never discussed our experiences with drugs opened up the door for many fields of conversation she never considered before between us…. Even so, she was slowly going to ease us in. "Well," she joked, "I really didn't want to steal from that hotel in Switzerland."

"It was your idea!" I laughed.

"Yes, I know," she paused. "But that doesn't mean I liked the idea."

I took another drag and laid back farther on my lawnchair. "So what do you want to talk about?"

"Hmmm," she thought for a second then continued. "I really can't think of anything."

"Well, we've got to think of an important topic soon or we're going to waste all our important time with meaningless, boring chit-chat."

"I know, I know…"

"Not to say talking to you is boring or meaningless."

"I didn't think you meant that," she paused. "Did you think this conversation was meaningless and boring?"

"Not at all," I said. I looked up at the clouds above our heads. One of them looked like a duck. I like ducks.

"Ok! I got an idea," she stated proudly.

"What is it?" I asked.

"Abortions."

"I can't discuss that…."

This confused her. "Why can't you discuss abortions?"

"It's a personal belief that I can't discuss it."

"You're no fun anymore," she said a little annoyed by me.

"Would you like to know the reason I can't discuss it."

She looked over at me. "So you can discuss the reason why you can't discuss abortions?"

"Yes," I answered while nodding my head. "It's all very logical."

She waved her hand motioning for me to give her the all-important information, "C'mon give it to me."

"I have a penis."

She paused. "I know that."

I laughed. "I know you know that."

"It's very nice."

"Well, thank you. I'll be sure to tell Mr. Winkie."

She laughed. "Mr. Winkie!?" She almost rolled over; she was laughing so hard. "I think I may have to rename him for you."

"What? You don't like the name Mr. Winkie?" I asked.

"It's not very masculine."

"Well, there's a Mr. in the name. It's not as if I was calling him Mrs. Winkie. Mrs. Winkie is not masculine. Mr. naturally changes that to masculine." I tried to explain.

"I can think of a better name than that. Will you let me rename Mr. Winkie?"

I sighed reluctantly. "Ok, go ahead."

"Cool…."

"But on one condition," I interrupted.

"What is it?"

"I get to name your breasts."

"Ok," She sighed.

"Both of them," I stated.

"Both of them!?" She shook her head no. "That's too much."

"If you accept I'll throw in my right elbow."

She paused. "So let me get this straight. I let you name both of my breasts and I get to name your penis and your elbow?"

"My right elbow," I corrected.

"Throw in your tongue and I might consider it," she said.

"Why do you want to name my tongue?"

"Why do you want to name my breasts?" She responded.

"Because they are so spectacular that they deserve a name. Hell, they should be blessed in a cathedral."

She laughed at this. "So you would create a special service at a church to bless my breasts?"

"The Catholic church has a special service for everything else in the book, why not?"

She laughed harder. "Well, make sure to bring that up to the pope the next time you decide to sneak into his quarters in the Vatican and moon him."

I paused. "Well, maybe I will."

"That I'd pay money to see," she said pointing at me.

"How much would you pay?"

She lay back in her chair. "At least fifty. I don't know if I would go as high as a hundred though."

"Why do I feel a little insulted by that?" I said slowly to myself.

"What did you say?"

"Nothing…." I looked up at the clouds again. There was one that looked like a large castle. I like castles.

"So why won't you discuss abortions," she asked after a few seconds.

"I feel that men don't have a right to take part in the debate."

She looked over at me. "I want to kiss you."

I looked over at her. "Really?"

"Yes."

I laughed. "Are you sure?"

"Yes, I think that comment deserves a kiss."

I leaned over my chair and kissed her lightly on the lips. "Wait," she said. "I want a longer kiss than that."

"Ok," I said and leaned in again. We kissed for a few minutes. "That was nice," I said.

"I just christened your tongue with his new name," she said proudly.

"Which is?"

She sat up straight in her chair and spread her arms wide. "It is now called 'Tigger.'"

I paused and frowned. "How is Tigger more masculine than Mr. Winkie?"

"Haven't you ever read the Pooh books?" she asked.

"Yes," I responded, "I have read the Pooh books and saw the bad Disney films too. I just don't see how that makes it masculine."

"Well," she said slowly. " Maybe it's not that masculine, but it's a good name."

"So are you saying I use my tongue like Tigger bounces?"

"On a good day, yes," she agreed.

I looked up at the clouds again and sighed. "I guess I can live with that name for my tongue." One of the clouds looked like a gun. I looked away from that cloud. I don't like guns.

"Now here's a question for you," she said across to me. "Let's say your girlfriend was pregnant."

"You're pregnant!?!" I looked quickly over at her.

"No, no, no," she replied quickly shaking her head. "I'm trying to create a situation for further debate."

"Oh, I see what you're doing…" I leaned back in my chair again.

"So you had this girlfriend and she was pregnant."

"You mean you."

"No, let's say you had another girlfriend."

"I wouldn't have another girlfriend. I love you."

She paused. "Ok, that's sweet, but you're really annoying me."

"I just want you to know that I wouldn't cheat on you."

"I guessed that."

"I care that much."

"Can I continue?"

"Sure."

She coughed and continued. "Ok, and she got pregnant. And she decided that she didn't want to have your baby. She wanted to abort your baby. You would then have to discuss that, right?"

"Is that something you would do?" I asked her.

"Of course not," she replied quickly.

"Then I don't have to answer that question."

"What?" she screamed frustrated.

"I claim no comment."

"You are no fun anymore," she said.

"You said that before," I replied.

"Because it's true."

"And you stole that line from me!" I said a little annoyed.

"Frustrating man," She sighed.

"So then why are you here?"

"I have nothing better to do…."

"Neither do I…." I looked up at the clouds again. One of the clouds was shaped like a tree. I like trees.

We basked in the glow of the weed and the moment for a second. She was the first to speak. "What would you name my breasts?"

"I really don't know. I haven't really given it that much consideration."

"Why do I feel a little insulted by that?" she slowly asked herself.

"Well, what would you name my elbow?"

"'Elbow.'"

"What a lousy name!"

"It's an elbow! It doesn't deserve a name."

"How rude," I stated loudly.

"Keep talking like that and I would ask you to hold Tigger." She paused and then laughed at her joke.

"See, you can't take that name seriously either!"

"It is pretty lame," she laughed. "But the name stays! Because he is bouncy and fun! Yes, the name stays…."

"Ok, ok…."

We were silent again for a few seconds. I was the first to speak this time. "Guinevere and Juliet."

She looked over at me confused. "Who?"

"That's what I would name your breasts."

"Juliet and…."

"And Guinevere." I took another drag. "The two most classic female romantic characters in all of history. That's how perfect I think they are.

It's as if the spirit of those two great, beautiful souls exist in them." I looked over at her.

She reached over and took a hit from my joint. "That's pretty good."

"I try my best."

We paused again. Another cloud passed overhead. This one looked like a truck. I am mildly amused by trucks.

"Pinnacle," she said quickly.

"Won't work," I stated, "It's the name of a company that makes golfballs."

"Oh, yeah." she replied slowly.

"And we are not dealing with my testicles right now."

"Ok, Ok…" She paused again. "What if your sister was pregnant?"

"I don't have a sister," I replied quickly.

"Just for this debate, let's say you do have a sister."

"I wouldn't have sex with my sister."

"I didn't say you did."

"If I had a sister, I would really be appalled by that thought."

"That's not why I was asking… Oh, nevermind."

"You know if that is something you're interested in I'm sure we could find some of that action somewhere here in Amsterdam."

"I said nevermind," she stated again.

The sun was beginning to set. The rays of red and gold spread over the fields and the streets in front of us almost like a wind. Naturally, we both reached over and held each other's hand. This was a good day.

"How about Tigger?" She asked.

"You already used that name," I replied.

"Oh, yeah," she laughed. "I forgot…. Man, this is good stuff."

CHAPTER 41

We stayed in bed for the entire day. At one point I played with her hands with my fingers and I moved my fingers…

    in

          out

   around her

      hands

            touching

         out

weaving my fingers

   around her

           delicate

      precious

           hands….

"I love your fingers," I said quietly. "I love your hands."
She sighed and laid herself more on top of me.

CHAPTER 42

HIM	LIST	HER
So what are you doing?		*I'm making a list.*
A list of what?		*A list of things to do.*
Really?		*Really?*
No joke?		*You didn't expect us to wander around and around like a vacation forever, did you?*
(Sigh) No I guess not.		*Ok, then...*
So what's first on the list?		
	1. Sell the car	
No way.		*Yes way!*
But it's such a cool car.		*I know.*
It's a great car.		*Yes, but it's a hot car.*
I guess so.		*We can't drive around in a stolen car forever and expect to get away with it.*
So how do you expect to get rid of it?		*I expect we'll be able to find something in the redlight district. There seems to be everything there.*

And if not we
should at least be
able to find some-
one to have sex
with it.
What's next?

*No joking, this is serious
time.*

2. Find a place
to stay

What are you
planning for this?
Ok.

*Has to be someplace we
can blend in.*
*And someplace they
won't pay attention to
us.*

So what are you
thinking?
You want to live
in the redlight!?
I guess you're
right.

Someplace downtown.

Who'd notice us there?

*And it'll be only for a
few years. Once we get
all the Mafia and law off
our tails we should be
able to move out. Then
we can get fake IDs,
perfect our knowledge of
the language.*

Wow.
I just realized...
That we really are
never going home
again.

What?
What?
(Quickly) Next point.

3. Find a job

Ok, this will be
hard.

*Yeah, I know. But we
can't live off this money
forever. We need to find
a legal way to supply our
income.*

Hard labor, I'm
guessing.

*I don't think you'll be
wearing a suit anytime
soon.*

What about you?

*I'll probably be a recep-
tionist. Or maybe I can
work on one of those
phonelines.*

(Pause) You mean
those...
Yeah.

*Don't you think I have a
sexy voice?*
*And they make good
money.*
*Sex. You can say the
word. It is sex.*

It just feels odd to
think of you as
talking about....
I'm sorry I...

I...

*I'm just throwing out an
idea.*
Next point.

4. Fake ID's

Oh, good one.

*Exactly. We need to cre-
ate new identities.*

How will we get
these?

*I say we start with the
redlight district, I'm
guessing there are a lot
who are running from
their past.*

I'm guessing
that'll be the easy
one to do. What's
next?

5. Learn Lan-
guage

Oh, man. That's
going to be tough.

*We've no choice. And
the worst of it is we need
to be fluent. There can
be no question of our
identity. We can't sound
American anymore.*
Something like that.

Reinventing our-
selves?
(Pause) It's sad.
I just wish we
didn't have to. I
feel bad about...

It's exciting.
Don't feel bad honey.
*The mooning thing
brought you to me. I
don't regret you doing
that at all...*

Really?

No thanks.

(Pause) Do you want the truth?

The mooning thing's not the main problem anymore anyway. We need to hide from my family.

A little like Romeo And Juliet.

A little...

Any more points?

One More.

6. No more drugs

Really?

Yes, really.

Why?

Drugs make us dimwitted and slow.

I know...

And once we move into the downtown we need to have active brains. Nothing can distract us....

You're right, you're always right.

You're not bitter about that are you?

No, I'm just glad one of us is.

We'll get through this...

I know.

Just like Romeo and Juliet...

What?

If they survived and escaped the town.

Sweet...

I have my moments too.

CHAPTER 43

There are days when one thing, one small thing, of your lover or wife or husband or significant other can capture your imagination and hold you for the entire twenty four hours as strong as a grasp on your arm and make you wonder and marvel at how such a piece of perfection had been created there and that miracle could be anything from a laugh to a nod to a way they hold their hands to, like me, a smile that reaches in and brushes your soul and on the fifth day she had that power over me as we walked through all the touristy spots in Amsterdam and I kept trying my best to bring that smile back and back again with jokes and comments ("Do you really think Windmills are that productive? "Can you eat a tulip?" "Don't you think they could have found something better to have made shoes out of than wood if they really tried?" "Do you think dikes had the same second meaning then as they do now?") and now and then these comments would make that beautiful result which would produce that brilliant smile and I would feel alive, refilled, tranquil in that little glow-and this confused her, for she knew she was doing something to affect me but she didn't know what it was and I was not going to tell her because I was a little embarrassed by it, so I kept going and going, throwing out as many one liners as I could to bring about another little blessing and this went on and on for the entire day until she finally, after smiling quite large (and noticing the severe ecstasy that it brought up in my soul which seemed to radiate out through my eyes), turned her head to the side scratched the side of her right ear, and asked, "What?"

CHAPTER 44

—ONE MORNING IN

THE REDLIGHT DISTRICT....

I had to walk out of the store. She followed me out. It was obvious she was confused by my departure. "I'm sorry," I said to her. "Dildos almost make me feel inadequate."

"That's silly," she laughed. We were walking down the redlight district of Amsterdam. We were just in one of their famous sex shops where she took the opportunity to look at a wide assortment of dildos.

"It's not silly. Think about it from my perspective. No man is that long... And it's always hard. How can any man compete against that?... And the ones that shake at the same time, that's physically impossible!"

She laughed again. She wrapped her arms around my right arm and leaned against me as we walked further down the street. "Wait a second." She said. She pointed at one of the store windows across the street. We quickly crossed over the street to it. It was a window for a brothel. Behind the glass, a woman was laying down on a bed nude. "Will you look at that?" This seemed to fascinate Toni Lyn.

"You're sick," I said to her.

"What has to happen to a person to make them take such a turn in their life. I mean, you don't exactly major in this in college."

"Some of my friends did," I said.

"You know what I mean," she responded.

"Actually, I'm serious," I commented. "It's called a liberal arts degree."

The girl behind the glass noticed we were looking at her. She came up to the window and began to dance in front of us. "Will you look at that." Toni Lyn said again. She looked over at me. "Do you find this sexy?"

"Loaded question," I stated quickly. "I respond, 'no comment.'"

She paused for a second. "I want to talk to her."

"What?" My mouth literally fell open in astonishment. "You want to talk to her?"

"Yeah," she said quickly. She began to lead me into the brothel. "I want to hear how she became this."

"I don't think there is an application to fill out." I tried to stop her from pushing me in. This is the last place I wanted to go into with Toni Lyn.

"C'mon," she said still trying to pull me in. "I just want to see what drove her to such a life."

"Listen, if this so interests you we can go back to our room and I'll pay you for sex and then you'll know."

"Very funny," She said and pulled me through the door.

"Clean" is not the first word I would use to describe the brothel. Actually, it would be the last word in my choices. Everything had the look of being covered in some kind of a past lotion. Like there was a shine from it off the furniture and the walls. Whatever the lotion was it was long gone, but the shine remained. There was a condom dispenser on the wall. Strangely enough, there was one right alongside it for fake tattoos. I was about to ask Toni Lyn her opinion on where people liked to put those tattoos, when I noticed she was no longer next to me…. She was over talking to the prostitute that was in the window. The woman was putting on some clothes.

So, while Toni Lyn talks to the prostitute I'll take this opportunity to describe the room a little bit more for you. It was definitely a slow morning. The girls were all wandering around the building with a look that can only be best described as boredom. There was a round table over by the stairs where five of them were playing cards. It looked to be poker. Now what is really interesting is the different outfits these girls were wearing. They wearing every different outfit that seemed to emphasize every different form of fetish out there—From domination to a schoolgirl nighty, for example. And the different looks. Some were really quite stunning. Some really could have been models. It really was a little mindblowing to think that women like that would have sex for money. It's just so odd that in a world like our's that... Oh, sorry, Toni Lyn is coming back....

Toni Lyn skipped back over to me. "She agreed to talk to us, but the second a real customer comes in, she'll have to go. I guess Tuesday mornings are always slow around here."

"She speaks English?"

Tony Lyn looked at me annoyed. "No, I learned fluent Dutch in five minutes.... Of course, she speaks English. She's American."

"She's American?"

Toni Lyn sighed and led me over to her. "C'mon genius."

"He's kind of cute," the prostitute said when I walked over.

I looked over at Toni Lyn, "Well, she does have good taste."

Toni Lyn wrapped her arms around my right arm. "He's taken, Cassandra."

I looked over at Toni Lyn, "Her name is Cassandra?" I laughed at that. What a fake name. It sounded to me like one of those ridiculous names porno stars have.

"You don't like the name Cassandra?" Cassandra asked interrupting.

"Oh, no, it's nice."

Toni Lyn leaned into my ear and whispered. "It's her real name, love."

"Thanks love of my life," I said to Toni Lyn.

Cassandra sighed sadly to herself.

"What is it?" I asked her.

"I can't remember the last time I saw such a happy couple in a brothel. It makes one wonder what has happened to all the morals around the world."

I looked over at Toni Lyn a little confused. "She's got a good sense of humor."

"Well, duh," Toni Lyn said. She turned to Cassandra, "I apologize for my boyfriend here."

"It's ok," Cassandra sighed. "So what brings a couple like you to Amsterdam?"

Toni Lyn and I could only look at each other and laugh…

"I was born in the south part of Minnesota into a very conservative family. I was quite the tomboy in school. All my friends were boys and I hated dolls. I even once cut my hair and almost gave my mother a heart attack in the process…. I was that bad a kid. School bored me. I was a good student. Don't laugh, I received great grades ("I wasn't laughing." "Shhh, she's talking."). Now around the end of high school I began to sprout. And suddenly all the boys that were my friends were suddenly chasing me around. It was like in a matter of moments that I lost all my closest friends and exchanged them for love interests—Of course it wasn't all at once. We would flirt and touch. I would want to play games and they would want to sit and talk and watch TV. I lost friends because I didn't sleep with them. I lost friends because I would. It was a mess. My senior year of high school was the worst in my life…. Seriously, I didn't lose my virginity until I was 18. Now when I went off to college I became a little experimental sexually. I tried everything. I even once made a video tape with a boyfriend who after we broke up sold it to a film company. Now here is where my story turns to the dark side. I had a roommate who became an escort as a way to earn extra cash. See the great thing about being an escort is you don't have to have sex with the man. They basically are just paying for your company. These men are just paying to feel loved.

Sad, huh? Well, after seeing how much she was making I decided to give it a try and suddenly I was making twice as much doing that than I would have earned with my liberal arts degree ("See," I whispered to Toni Lyn). Then I began to hear about the laid back attitude of Amsterdam and how much a person like me could earn. So, I came here. I figure that I can do this for five years and then retire for the rest of my life. I want to get married and have kids, I just don't want to do it on his terms. See my mom used to always take orders from my dad. It seemed more like an army than marriage. When I leave here with a full pocket, I'll be able to live my life the way I want. In just five years…"

Toni Lyn leaned her head against my shoulder. There was a warm message to me through this simple gesture.

"But how do you get through the day?" I asked.

"Let me show you," she said. "Come on upstairs…"

"Now see this is what I do. Right over here. See on the side of the bed. I've a tape player hidden there. Right there between the mattress and the box springs. See. Now when the man is starting to get ready to stick it in, I reach over and casually take one of the headphones… See it's the kind that sticks right in your ear. I just lazily stick one in my ear like this. There. And I then press play on the tape. Now, I hide the noise from the tape with my moans. I'm pretty loud… Hmmmm. Mmmmm. Oh, yeah, baby…. That's it…. It really doesn't matter what I say as long as it's a little dirty. So while he's fucking me, I'm listening to Mozart. See, Mozart is the only thing that excites me anymore. To keep myself wet I need to hear the music and concentrate on it. The point is not whether I have an orgasm or not (at least in the mind of the customer), it's that I stay wet so I don't get a rash or something. Now the interesting thing I've learned is that different pieces of Mozart affect me in different ways—'The Magic Flute' makes me playful; 'Jupiter Symphony' makes me passionate; 'Don Giovanni' makes me aggressive; And so on and so on…. Now I have this so down that I can read exactly what a customer is looking for and while they think I'm getting ready for them while they wait outside, I'm really getting my tape ready so I'll perform to their standards…. However, from time to time… When I want to have a really good time. When I want to have an orgasm. And I really want to scream. At those moments I put in 'The Marriage of Figaro.' By the end of the overture, the customer has gotten his money worth. And between you and me, (sigh) I would pay them."

The day seemed to flow on and on in a very smooth pace as we continued to talk to Cassandra. The girls were still getting very little business. So Vicki (a redhead in a white teddy who had a Southern American accent) was making her specialty for lunch (I couldn't tell what it was, but it involved a lot of hamburger) and we were invited to stay. Now as we were eating a strange business proposal was put before us.

See Cassandra is a smart woman (rumor has it in the brothel that she already has over a million American dollars in Swiss banks) and she could see a business opportunity between Toni Lyn and me. "I'm guessing something is going on between you two love birds that you haven't told us."

Toni Lyn stopped eating and looked up skeptically. It has been such a nice morning that the idea of someone doubting our generic honeymoon story seemed to annoy her. "What do you mean, Cassandra?"

"All of us are in a lifestyle we don't want to be known for," Cassandra sighed. "That's pretty obvious. And you both seem like smart kids…."

Toni Lyn and I looked at each other (whenever something strange comes up we naturally turn to each other for the answer). "What do you mean?" I asked slowly.

"Well, I don't have time to handle the books anymore and Toni Lyn here seems to be quite the intelligent beauty," Cassandra said. She pointed her fork at Toni Lyn as she said this.

"Thanks," Tony Lyn responded.

"You know accounting, right?"

"I took a course in it while at Yale," Toni Lyn replied.

"I would have been happy with a yes," Cassandra moaned.

The other girls at the table laughed.

Cassandra raised her hand and the laughing stopped. This was her place and you could feel that. She continued her proposal. "And we need an extra bodyguard for the evenings," Cassandra sighed, "And trust me in this business you need at least one man around at all times. A man intimidates the aggressive freaks."

"You want me to be a bodyguard?" I asked.

"Where would we stay?" Toni Lyn asked before I could get an answer.

"Right here," Cassandra said. She waved her arms around. All the girls smiled at us. They seemed to like the idea of us being there.

"Are you serious?"

"We have the room," Cassandra explained quickly, "And it certainly seems that you have a need for a place to hide out."

"I don't…." I began.

"I don't know either," Toni Lyn interrupted. "Trust me, I think your offer is great Cassandra and we…"

Cassandra held up her hand motioning Toni Lyn to stop talking. She grabbed a piece of paper and wrote a numerical figure on the paper. She pushed the paper over to Toni Lyn. "This is how much you would make a week. And your room and board will be free."

Toni Lyn held the paper up for me to read.

I was shocked.

Toni Lyn looked back at Cassandra. "We'll take it."

And that is how Toni Lyn and I became part of the "Cassandra's House of Pleasure" in the redlight district of Amsterdam.

We went back to our little bed and breakfast and took a bath. A nice long bath (I promised to buy her the candles as soon as we sold the car). We were both preparing for what we would experience in our new home. This might be the last time we would feel clean for a long time.

That night we fell asleep close.

At midnight I woke up and thought about what all this might mean for us. It was going to be strange.

Tomorrow we were going to be moving into a brothel....

CHAPTER 45

"I just realized something…" I looked over at her. She was softly starting to fall asleep against me (The bed given to us in the brothel was strangely very comfortable—I don't know why that fact surprised me). It was a 7 tonight for us. Very good. It was a very good day all around. We were able to sell our stolen car…

"Don't worry, I trust this guy," Cassandra said to us as she led us down the street. It was a beautiful warm day outside. Both Cassandra and Toni Lyn wore shades. Neither wanted to be recognized (I tried not to feel bad about that).

"What's his name?" I asked.

"Slim Jimmy," Cassandra explained. "He used to work in New York City until certain circumstances required him to move. Of course, that's the story of most people here, darling." She sighed and walked a little ahead of us.

Toni Lyn grabbed my arm so we could walk a little more behind her. "I need to talk to Cassandra about my family."

"Why?" I asked.

"I have to make sure this guy is not connected," She explained quickly. "Wait here, ok?"

I stood in my tracks and watched her walk up to Cassandra. They walked a little ahead of me and talked among themselves. I couldn't catch what they were saying but I could read some of the body language. Cassandra—Reassuring everything is ok. Toni Lyn—A little worried… They stopped talking and waved me forward.

"So why does he go by the name 'Slim'?" I asked. I was going to start a new line of conversation away from the family and the fear of capture.

"No clue," Cassandra answered quickly (What kind of an answer is that?). "Ok, here's the spot." She was standing outside a very dirty garage door down a dark alley. It all looked very illegal. In other words, it looked perfect. She knocked on the door in a certain fashion: **Knock, knick, knockknock.**

Nothing happened. It was quiet. We looked at each other. Suddenly this door on the side of the garage creaked open. Cassandra smiled and led us from the dark alley into a darker office.

As I passed Cassandra (I could tell something else was up), I whispered to her, "What else did Toni Lyn say to you?"

"She told me if I call you darling again she'd kill me," Cassandra said with a smile. She followed us into the shady, dark car dealership.

…. this afternoon for a tidy sum and…

"This is a beautiful vehicle," Slim Jimmy said (He spoke in an interesting fashion. It almost sounded like his lips had a hard time keeping up with the words). It was obvious he was happy with the purchase ahead of him. What happened is he drove us back to the Bed and Breakfast where the car was parked out on the street. Slim Jimmy was walking around the car with a very ecstatic look. Oh wait a minute… I didn't paint a picture yet of Slim Jimmy. Well, his name is a joke name because he was anything but slim. He was grotesquely overweight. And for the poor (I don't mean financially) man his clothes didn't hide the fact. They seemed to emphasize that point, because his body couldn't stay in the clothes. It kept sneaking out from under the fabric (*"Hello"*) or around the belt area (*"Here I am"*). Watching the man move was like watching jello dressed in clothes and forced on a treadmill…. Ok, that's enough.

"But we need the full work to be done on this," Toni Lyn said quickly. "It needs to be painted. All the numbers need to be scratched. It can't be traced at…"

Slim Jimmy looked up at her annoyed. "What? You don't think I know how to do my job?"

"Sorry," Toni Lyn said.

"Trust me," Slim Jimmy said (he was happy again), "No one will know where this came from."

He ran his hands along the hood. He looked up at us with excited eyes. "I might want to keep this car. Can I drive it?"

After we finished driving him around (I still don't know how a man of his physical extremes fit in the front seat of that sport car), it was obvious that we had a good sale on our hands. A very good sale.

…we used some of the money to buy some necessary supplies…

Shopping List.

1. New bed sheets.
2. New pillows.
3. Ear plugs.
4. Weights (I have to make sure I look threatening).
5. Calculator.
6. Big red candles.

…to make our bedroom more of a home for us (Who knows how long we will be staying there).

"What's that honey?" She sighed happily.

"We just had sex in a brothel," I said matter of factly.

This statement quickly brought Toni Lyn back to full consciousness. "Oh, my God." She said quietly to herself. She sat up in the bed and wrapped the blankets over her body. It was almost like unconsciously she thought hiding her naked body might hide what we just did and where.

"Yeah, it's pretty deep."

"It's not as if our sex was dirty like that," She turned to me and said quietly. I could see that she was begging for me to agree.

"Well, technically there is probably not that much difference between what they do and what we do." (Shit! Could I sound more stupid?)

"Oh, God." She said. It turns out I said exactly the wrong thing to her (Genius). She covered her face in her hands.

"Honey, oh, honey," I wrapped my arms around and tried to comfort her. It was strange at that moment how delicate she felt in my arms. Her heart was breaking. All the realizations of what we had to go through down the line seem to break down on her and come out in those tears.

"What would my mom think?… My mom." She looked up at me with tears in her eyes. "I can never see my mom again."

I held her closer to me. "It's ok…It's ok… It's ok…" I softly said to her as she began to let out all her grief.

"This is not me. I don't belong in a place like this. I'm smart. I'm a good person. I had so many dreams that I wanted to achieve. I wanted to run for office. I wanted to be a senator. And now look at me, I'm hiding out in a brothel in Amsterdam. Oh, God. What did I do with my life? What did I do?"

I slowly began to rock her back and forth in my arms. She grew quiet. She was still crying and I could feel her lightly shaking in my arms. I slowly moved us back down on to the bed and slowly….

Slowly….

She fell asleep in my arms.

All for her.

CHAPTER 46

—THE NEXT DAY WE

HAD A TALK ABOUT NAMES...

Her: Have you ever thought about what would be good names for kids?
Me: You're pregnant!?
Her: No!
Me: Then why bring it up?
Her: I'm curious.
Me: Are you thinking about having kids?
Her: No!
Me: Yes, you're thinking about it or you wouldn't have brought it up.
Her: Nevermind.
Me: I don't think a brothel is the best place to raise a kid.
Her: I'm not planning to have a child.
Pause.
Me: Seriously?
Her: Yeah.
Me: What do I think are good names?
Her: Yeah.
Me: Male or female?

Her: Let's start with female and go from there.

Me: I like Juliet.

Her: (laughing)

Me: What's so funny?

Her: That's what you named one of my breasts!

Me: So?

Her: You would name your daughter after my breast?

Me: It's not as if the breast didn't take part in her conception. Let's give the boob its due…. No, I'm not high today!

Her: I wasn't thinking that.

Me: Sure you weren't…. I like the name Juliet and it works for us to have a daughter named that.

Her: Go on.

Me: Well, you have the whole forbidden great love theme that comes with the name Juliet and in many ways we are living a life like that. Seizing our love and seeing where it takes us.

Her: I don't want to commit suicide.

Me: I don't either.

Her: Are you saying you wouldn't commit suicide for me?

Me: No I would…. You won't ask will you?

Her: No!

Me: (phew).

Her: Juliet?

Me: And every time you would see her or hear her name, you would think of our love and the time we spent together. It's perfect to me. She would be a creation of our love and her name would be synonymous with great love past and present. Perfect.

Her: There is some perfection and beauty in that.

Me: I have my moments.

Her: What would you name our son? Not Romeo, I hope.

Me: Of course, not. I don't want my son being beaten up in school. Romeo is just asking to be punched.

Her: And it's such a pretty name. It's too bad.

Me: Boys shouldn't get pretty names. They should get butch names.

Her: Like what?

Me: Well, how about Sid?

Her: (laughing) Sidney!

Me: (correcting) No, Sid.

Her: That's a butch name?

Me: Nevermind.

Pause.

Her: Max?

Me: Golden Retriever name.

Pause.

Her: Well, maybe we should just have a girl.

Me: I only hope that she has your eyes.

Her: Smooth…

Me: I always have my moments….

CHAPTER 47

This is how I look at work—

I wear tight shirts (mostly undershirts) and loose jeans so I can move quickly. I have on sunglasses (This, Cassandra explained, is so the customer never knows if I am looking at them or not. This way they are afraid to make a move). My hair is slicked back. I am wearing comfortable shoes. My arms are usually crossed in front of me. I use the palms of my hands against my arms to help accentuate my muscles in my forearms. I breathe strength and intimidation.

This is the way I speak at work—

"Excuse me…"

"Let her go…"

"Sir, we are all in here to have a good time…"

"Wait right here…"

"I'm sorry sir you must go…"

This is whom I work with—

There are twelve girls (including Cassandra) at the House of Pleasure. I work with two other bodyguards (We alternate our schedules around each other except on busy weekend nights when we all work) and Toni Lyn handles the books.

This is what I think to get the right cocky attitude—

"All these men are scum. Look at them begging for sex as if it is the greatest thing in the world. What a bunch of losers. Fuck them. I can take anyone of them if I wanted to. They are so beneath me. They say Moonboy is a bad mother… Watch your mouth! But I was talking about Moonboy. Then I can dig it. So bad, I'm so bad… Groovy. Hip. Powerful. Tough as nails (What does that mean anyway?). I am the man. The man! Man-o! And Man-o was his name-o. Ok, Ok, Keep your head on the job. Be strong. Ok here comes a character. A problem here, maybe? They better not hurt any of the girls. These girls are like my sisters. How dare this man think that he is worthy enough to sleep with any of them. Yeah, you buddy! I'm watching you! Yeah, you freak!…"

This is what I think to get through the day—
"All for her."

CHAPTER 48

Nothing can ever compare with the junk mail one receives in Amsterdam. And once you see some of this mail you pray to God nothing ever does. These little bundles of information make the magazines you hid from your parents under bedsheets and inside dresser drawers look as bad as hiding a copy of the New Yorker or The Atlantic (Except of course that your magazines in the long run had more interesting works of fiction). Once your senses allow you to get past the extreme graphic nature of these pictures, you can't help but be even more impressed with what this mail promises. From phone numbers to special addresses each of these free smut surprises claim that their pictures are only a starting point and that there is something more wonderful waiting for you just by following their simple directions. What? More personal than a close-up of a woman's privates? More daring than a dozen women dressed like army privates making out? More lurid than a woman performing acts in a grocery store that can't help but make you wish you never go shopping again? (And who by the ways looks at food this way and finds it a turn on anyway? Remind me not to go to that person's house for dinner.)

   All this mail is disturbing and Cassandra would get dozens of these ads a day delivered right to her door. No wonder she paid Toni Lyn and me the big money! Toni Lyn may be fixing all her books and working on her stock purchases, but secretly Cassandra was glad she never had to see another one of those ads again. It was Toni Lyn's job to go through her mail now, not her's. It was one thing to be a prostitute; it was another to have to deal with the smut that comes with it.

So every afternoon at a quarter past one, Toni Lyn would make the long walk to the door and pick up her daily "surprises" waiting for her under the mail slot. Every day the little sigh that would escape her lips would be just a bit louder and louder with more disgust hiding behind it. And then, she would turn, look up at all of us and realize once again that she was living in a brothel. Basically to her it was like someone was handing her shit and then asking her to rub her own nose in it…. And she did it. She did it everyday.

Except for the sigh, the real pain she would hold in. She would hold the mail closely to herself and walk past the prostitutes, past the other body-guards, past me, and right up the stairs to our rooms.

Now on our tenth day in Amsterdam, I couldn't take it anymore. I knew Toni Lyn too well. I knew what this was doing to her. And I knew she would never admit it to me that it was bad. She was taking all this for me without one complaint. She was taking this for us. So on that fateful day I followed a few minutes after her to our room…. And inside I found Toni Lyn crying….

I walked over and sat on the bed next to her. She had all the mail spread across our bed. All these creations of a perverse mind were spread across the place where we made love.

She was holding one ad in her hand. And she had it gripped so tightly that it was almost crunched into a ball. I slowly reached over and took it from her fingers…. It was of a little girl and, in one word, it was sick.

"I don't know what is more disturbing," Toni Lyn said between her sobs, "that someone was perverted enough to take such a picture or that there is a market out there for such shit that this asshole would make a profit of it."

I hugged her.

We both knew.

Someday we were going to have to get out of here. Neither of us could ever start a family so near such a perverse atmosphere (And I don't just mean the brothel, I mean the whole of Amsterdam). Neither of us would feel safe. For Toni Lyn and our own fears, we would have to go someplace far away from the man (or men) that would take such pictures. Then and only then would either of us feel worry free again (As if you can truly get away from perverts).

At that moment I made a promise to her that brought back the smile I loved so much. "From now on I'll get the mail for you Toni Lyn," I said, "I promise you won't see this kind of smut again."

She looked up, smiled and hugged me tightly. She didn't have to say a word. I could read from her tight grasp that she was very thankful.

CHAPTER 49

—(ON SOME OF THE SLOWER DAYS TONI LYN AND I WOULD MAKE LISTS. ON THE 11TH DAY WE MADE THIS LIST.)

100 THINGS WE BOTH LIKE

1. **Casablanca** (Not the dubbed version).
2. Kraft Macaroni & Cheese.
3. **The X Files.** (Especially the episodes with the Smoking Man).
4. Shakespeare.
5. **Star Wars.**
6. Bananas (But not Banana bread).
7. **Sesame Street.**
8. Van Gogh paintings (The more colorful the better).

9. Exercise.

10. Jazz.

11. The Beatles. (The best, period)

12. Oreo cookies.

13. Chicago Cubs. (My home team!!—Toni Lyn)

14. Soccer.

15. Mozart. (But not to the extent of Cassandra)

16. The smell of a new car.

17. A good bath (With red candles around, the big kind).

18. Being inside during a thunderstorm.

19. A fireplace.

20. Christmas trees and white lights.

21. **It's A Wonderful Life** (What's Christmas without that?.. Oh yeah, the baby Jesus.).

22. Mint Chocolate Chip Ice Cream.

23. Jane Austen.

24. Swing dancing.

25. Charlie Brown and Snoopy (Lucy Van Pelt is a jerk, though).

26. Simon And Garfunkel.

27. Dr. Seuss.

28. ~~Windmills.~~

28. Trenchcoats.

29. Red lingerie (As long as it is comfortable—Toni Lyn).

30. No smoking signs.

31. A full moon.

32. **Seinfeld** (Newman rules!)

33.Kurt Vonnegut

34.Sunsets.

35.Japanese animation.

36.Caffeine (The world's favorite drug-time to give it it's due).

37.Refrigerator poetry.

38.Dishwashers.

39.**Alice In Wonderland** (That so warped my mind when I was a kid—Toni Lyn).

40.Woody Allen films.

41.Monty Python.

42.Glen Miller (need something to swing too).

43.Benny Goodman (need to add the other man then too).

44.Friends (Do you mean the show or the real thing?).

45.Trust (You're getting a little deep now—Toni Lyn).

46.Watches not made in Switzerland (AMEN!).

47.Autumn leaves.

48.Memories.

49.Making love.

50.You (I pointed at her).

51.You (Then you too—Toni Lyn. We are too cute).

52.~~Tulips.~~

52.Cookies.

53.New clothes.

54.Volkswagen Beetles (The old ones, not the stupid new ones).

55.A good pair of shoes (Not heels!—Toni Lyn).

56.Forest trails.

57. Frisbees.

58. **The Tao of Pooh** (I love that book—Toni Lyn).

59. Corn Flakes.

60. Late night television.

61. Making lists.

62. Radio drama (I love that stuff).

63. Love notes (Who is writing you love notes?).

64. Holding hands.

65. Utensils (You're scraping the bottom on that one.)

66. Dreams.

67. **The Graduate.**

68. George Eliot.

69. Privacy from the real world.

70. Nat "King" Cole (Sexiest voice in the world—Toni Lyn).

71. Luscious Jackson (fun to jam too)

72. Sherlock Holmes.

73. Edgar Allen Poe.

74. Sunbathing.

75. Swimming.

76. doorknobs (doorknobs? That is really stretching—Toni Lyn).

77. Marching band shows (So I was a band dork in high school. Sue me.)

78. Pineapple-Orange Faygo.

79. London. (Dirtiest and greatest city in the world).

80. Yale (Wooohooo!!! Yeah, baby!!! My school!—Toni Lyn).

81. Masterpiece Theater.

82.Jackie Chan films.

83.Crab cheese wontons (It's an appetizer at Chinese restaurants).

84.Strong German beer.

85.Bridges (Some bridges are really nice; trust me, I know).

86.Photographs.

87.Children (The magic word again).

88.**The Te of Piglet** (sequel to **The Tao of Pooh**).

89.**The Empire Strikes Back** (If you can have the sequel to Tao I can have the sequel to **Star Wars**).

90.All Indiana Jones movies and TV shows.

91.Marx Brothers.

92.Big, soft pillows.

93.Philosophies.

94.**Rent.**

95.Apple trees.

96.Poetry (Classic poetry not that post-modern crap—Toni Lyn).

97.Oasis (When they are trying to be The Beatles).

98.The Dave Matthews Band.

99.The Barenaked Ladies (The band—Toni Lyn).

100. Love (Oh, yeah I almost forgot about that… Ouch!)

CHAPTER 50

Even though Toni Lyn and I knew we would never go home again, neither of us could hide the fact of how sad this made us. Actually, we almost seemed to relish in this pain together. Over the days, we would buy each other little presents that would remind of us of our days back home. And each of these presents would bring out another little story for us to share part of our past.

A good example of this is when I bought Toni Lyn a Chicago Cubs baseball cap (I found it in a sport store in a cleaner area of Amsterdam while running errands for Cassandra). Toni Lyn came from Chicago and the cap brought tears to her eyes. She ran her fingers across the rim of the cap and slowly adjusted it to the right size. Then she placed it on her head, backwards.

"When I was about five my uncle took me to a Cubs game. It was a great day. He bought me a hot dog and taught me how to keep score. I didn't know anything about baseball before that day. It was the first game I had even seen (See, in fear of having me kidnapped my parents rarely let me out of the house unless I was well protected). But with my uncle, it was different. No one, and I mean no one, would attempt to touch my uncle. My uncle was the greatest living hitman. Actually, the person I was supposed to let in to kill you at the embassy was one of his students. But on that afternoon, I didn't know that about him. He was my uncle and he took me out for a day at Wrigley Field. As we walked in he grabbed a cap from one of the vendors and stuck it on my head like this—backwards. He held me out in front of him and proudly looked me up and down in that hat. He said, 'Now you look like a catcher. That's how a catcher wears his hat.' I had no idea what he was talking about but I felt cool. I felt cool that I looked like a catcher. So there I was with a big smile on my face holding the hand of the most dangerous man in Chicago…. It was a good game. The Cubs actually won. I sang 'Take me out to the ball game.' Well, I tried to sing it; I didn't know the words. It was such a great day in my childhood. One of the best…. Thanks for the hat."

CHAPTER 51

—[IF IT'S A SLOW NIGHT, I SOMETIMES STAND ON THE STREET CORNER AND HAND OUT THESE FLYERS.]

Hey, there good looking!

Are you looking for a good time tonight??????????????

Cum to **Cassandra's House of Pleasure** where we have **over a dozen beautiful girls** who are looking for a good time tonight. That's right, over a dozen! We have here a girl for every desire or fetish you might have.

Let's meet the girls!!!!

Have you been a bad boy? Do you need **discipline**? Do you need a **spanking**? Then you should see our own dominatrix—Mistress Wang.

Mistress Wang learned the art of control and pain from ancient Chinese masters.

Do you like **innocent girls**? Well, if you have the time, you should meet our new girl little Sue. She's barely eighteen and she's really **shy**. She's only been with us a week and she's looking for a cute older man to teach her the ropes.

Do you like a good time? Would you like to be with the **wildest** girl in Amsterdam? Then when you **cum** in ask specifically for our own Cassandra! She can never get enough.

Vicki is straight from the Good old **South** of America. She likes country, line dancing and cowboy boots. She loves to dress up like a **Southern belle** and act out any Gone With The Wind fantasy you might have. When you get done with her, you *will* give a damn.

Cat is an **animal**. Oh, she may look like a woman and talk like a woman but she is all **primal**. Get her in bed and she scratches and bites and leaves her mark. **Grrrrr…** You will feel her claws for weeks after your visit with her.

Are you a little curious? Well, Maria is the perfect girl for you. She is a sexy girl with a little bit **extra** down below. If you would like a surprise like that make sure to ask for Maria and she will help you investigate into your **curiosity**.

Alisha likes to use her mouth. She just can't stop putting things in it. She just loves to **suck** and **kiss** and **lick**. Her problem is that she has a hard time finding something to stick in her **mouth**…. Can you help her solve this little problem she has?

Stacey is athletic. She can bench press almost 200 lbs! She can jog over 15 miles! If you see her she will be sure to give you a **workout** you will not forget. **Cum work your muscle** with Stacey.

Liz is a natural redhead and has all the fiery **passion** of one. When she seduces she takes control and gets just what she wants. And tonight **she wants you**!

Missy used to be a swimsuit **model**. She can strike a pose and bend to your every wish. Be her camera tonight. Smile for the man, Missy! Good girl.

Do you want to learn a thing or two tonight? Ask for Alice. Alice will be your **tutor** and teach you all the **ins** and **outs** of the bed. This will be a lesson you will be sure to enjoy. It's time for the final exam.

Ingrid likes to talk **dirty**. She always says what she wants to do and when. It's so **hard** to keep her mouth sealed. If you like to hear a dirty talk ask for Ingrid. You won't believe your ears!

Our last girl is Emma and she is looking for love. She will make you feel all **warm** inside and out. When you want sex to be more than sex see Emma.

See **Cassandra's House of Pleasure** has a girl for everyone! How could you refuse?

Cum on in!!

Show this flyer at the door and save 10% on the Entrance fee!

Cassandra's House of Pleasure
It doesn't get better than this.

CHAPTER 52

I blame myself.

There is no one else to blame. Toni Lyn's security should always be my first concern and there is no excuse for what happened that night. I screwed up. And for all eternity I will feel like shit because of it. Just remembering what happened that night makes my stomach hurt....

It was a busy Thursday at the House of Pleasure. I was on duty watching the door. Toni Lyn was done working for the evening but instead of watching TV upstairs in our room, she had decided to sit down stairs on a couch and read a book. She wanted to be near me. And as the evening went on, we would steal glances at each other. She would look up from her book and smile or stick out her tongue. I would slowly lower my sunglasses and give her my sexy gaze...

At around 10:30 PM a group of college age men wandered into our little brothel (Frat boys). 3 of them didn't have ID. It was a mess, especially since it was obvious that they were of age and they were drunk out of their minds ("I'm not saying you are not eighteen, I just need some ID."). The girls did not seem excited by the evening to come. They all looked pretty much annoyed by it, but of course they hid it under their smiles and their sexy gestures and walks (When you spend all your days with the same thirteen girls you can pretty much learn to read things like that).

The boys were fascinated by the place. Four of the boys got by my station but I had a problem with two of them ("Any ID? A college ID would be fine. I just need to see something. Rules are rules."). It was the four that I should have been worried about.

Well…

See, for some reason a woman dressed in a sweatshirt and a pair of jeans wearing a Cubs cap and reading a copy of a book by Vonnegut was very sexy to one of them. So this drunk frat boy walked past all the women in the lingerie and headed to the girl relaxing on the couch with a book…

I didn't see all this. The first I knew of what was going on was when I heard Toni Lyn's scream:

"Get the Fuck off of me!"

I bolted from the door!

Cassandra knew something was up and ran away from the boy she was talking with. Cassandra's goal was to stop me from hurting this man….

I grabbed the man off of Toni Lyn and threw him up against the wall. I gave him two punches in the stomach. He was pretty drunk and the punches made him vomit (On both me and himself). He fell to the ground and vomited again. Some blood trickled out of his mouth as well.

I don't know what I was going to do to him at that point. I was obsessed. Maybe I was going to start kicking him. Or maybe I was going to dive on him on the floor and… But I was stopped. All it took to bring me back was a touch on my shoulder from Cassandra and the following words: "Toni Lyn. Help her. He's done. He's done now. Go help Toni Lyn."

I turned away from the asshole on the floor and looked over at Toni Lyn. She was… (Oh, my god, it's painful to remember that look.) She was so pale… Her clothes were… (No, I don't want to remember this anymore. Oh, please let me forget this. Why must I remember this? Oh please God)… She struggled to stand up….

I ran over to her and caught her in my arms. We held each other close. She began to cry against my shoulder. I slowly took her up in my arms and carried her up to our room.

As I was walking up the stairs, I heard Cassandra trying to get control over the room. "It's ok, it's ok. She's fine. Sorry for all that. 10% discount...."

CHAPTER 53

"Cassandra! Cassandra! Wait!" I shouted. I was breaking the first rule of working as a bodyguard at a brothel.

RULE #1: Don't interrupt a sale.

Cassandra was walking up the stairs with her customer and I was running up behind her. She looked back at me. She was upset. "What is it?" She tried to hide her annoyance from the customer. But I could still catch hints of it in her voice.

"Cassandra, I'm sorry," I said. "I need to talk to you about something." She looked at me even more annoyed. I was breaking the second rule.

RULE #2: Don't take the prostitute away from the customer.

"Again, I'm sorry, Cassandra, but it is important." I would not be breaking these rules unless it was important and she knew that.

She sighed. "Ok, ok…" She turned to the customer. "You wait right here." She playfully touched his nose. "I'll be right back."

She walked down the stairs to me. "Make it quick or I'll have to play The Marriage of Figaro for this clown."

"Toni Lyn and I need the weekend off."

This stunned her even more. I was breaking rules right and left. I just threw away rule number 3!

RULE #3: Ask for vacation time in advance, especially weekends.

"What?" She asked.

"Toni Lyn is still a little shook up about what happened yesterday. I need to get her away from here for a few days. She doesn't even want to leave her room. She feels like shit. Her self-esteem is gone. It's like she is falling away right in front of my eyes. She is losing her playful and aggressive side. It's like she is losing her will to go on. I just need to get her to relax. Get us together, you know. I'm really sorry but she needs this and…."

Cassandra interrupted me with a sigh. She looked back at the customer and back at me. "Ok, whatever. But be back on Sunday before five."

I quickly agreed. "Thank you Cassandra. Thank you."

She ran her hands through my hair. "And have some fun you two, ok? Now get out of here before I fire you." She turned back to the customer, slid her right arm through his left and led him up the stairs.

I looked happily around the room. No one else was paying attention to what just happened. I sighed, and went back to looking tough.

CHAPTER 54

—[TONI LYN AND I ARE IN A BATH IN A HOTEL IN A NICE AREA OF AMSTERDAM. THE LIGHTS ARE OFF IN THE BATHROOM. WE HAVE RED CANDLES LIT AROUND THE TUB.]

My bathtub speech

"Toni Lyn, I've been thinking about this a lot and about our problems. See, we are whipped by this environment. We are out of our element. We are the type of people that live off the cuff and we like to be in control. Really, we're not in control right now. And we've also created this mind game for ourselves and it isn't helping... Well...

"Let me take this one at a time. See, it started when we pretended to be married at the bed and breakfast. No, I do want to marry you someday, just hear me out. See marriage is a pretty serious subject. A subject we both don't take for granted. We both grew up with the idea that when we get married it is for life and that is important to us. And what are the logical steps after marriage? Well, then you settle down in a good job and get a house and then a dog and then some kids. Well, maybe first the kids then the dog unless you are allergic to dogs, then you might get a cat, but to tell you the truth I don't like cats. Cats really don't give a damn about you. All they care about is… You're laughing. That's good and I'm getting off topic. What I'm trying to say is that once that magical possibility was mentioned our perception of our situation changed. We stopped living in the moment. We started worrying about our future and what we were going to do. Let's be honest to each other, we don't know what is going to happen here. We might get found someday. I don't know and neither do you. So we've got to go back to enjoying the days again. We've got to put the other thoughts on hold for a little while. I will marry you, I swear. I want to spend every waking moment with you. God, I've never felt like this about anyone before. Don't doubt that love, please. But it's safer for both of us to not think about it. It's the only way we can go back to being what we were.

"The second thing I have to bring up is the girls at the brothel. You might not notice this, but the girls there love us being around. They do. Didn't you notice how they always watch us together? They watch us hug and hold hands and they look so envious. Toni Lyn, they will never have a love like ours. Hell, most people won't have a love like this. And what we are doing for those girls is giving them hope again. I know it's odd to think that we fugitives are giving hope to a bunch of prostitutes, but's it true. Look at Cassandra. She's as hard as a rock with those girls. They can't get away with anything. And here we are with a weekend off to relax. I broke 3 rules for this weekend! And she gave it to us. And you know what else? Not one of the girls complained. They all wished us a good time and told us to come back soon. They love us being there. It's strange to say this but we are becoming almost a family. Don't laugh, I'm serious. Forget about the dirtiness of what is going on and all that and just think of the people.

Vicki's bad cooking, Wang's sick sense of humor, Cat's not-so-tender side… Look you're smiling! See, what I mean. Forget they're prostitutes. We could really have fun staying there with these people. They want to be our friends. So let's have fun. Let's find things that we can all… Don't get that look! I don't mean that. I mean we could play games, maybe get a pool table in there or air hockey or fussball… Or maybe some boardgames. It would all help the time go by faster and that is what is important… Let's have fun again. We need to find a way to have fun again…

"Ok, about what happened two days ago. I know what you're going to say Toni Lyn, but it's my fault. I'm taking the blame for it. I can't hide what happened. Toni Lyn… Toni Lyn… Ok, ok… It could have been worse and… I know he didn't rape you, but he did assault you and… Toni Lyn… Whatever you want to say… Whatever you want to believe about that. But I will say this…. I promise no one will ever hurt you again. I swear that on my soul.

"You are all I have Toni Lyn and you are all I want. These weeks with you have been the greatest of my life. I was reborn when I met you. You will always be safe with me around. I love you….

….

….

….

"Pass the soap…"

Chapter 55

—(We made another list for therapy.)

100 THINGS WE BOTH DISLIKE

1. Spinach.
2. Country Music.
3. Banjos.
4. Stephen King.
5. Most sitcoms.
6. Beavis And Butthead. (Worst show in the world. An embarrassment to our generation—Toni Lyn.)
7. Broccoli.
8. Cleaning.
9. Waxing.
10. Sponges (What do you have against sponges?—Toni Lyn).
11. Frat boys.

12.Blackmailers.

13.Hotel Owners in Lake Lucerne.

14.Lake Lucerne.

15.Anything dealing with Lake Lucerne.

16.Murderers (Unless they are family—Toni Lyn).

17.Spinach (We already said that).

Toni Lyn put the list aside. "Did we really already say it?"

"It's number one," I replied.

"Wow," She sighed. "I guess we might not be able to reach a hundred on this."

I sighed and leaned over the floor by her (We were sitting on the floor of the hotel room together). "You know what this might mean?"

"What?"

"We might actually be nice people."

"Oh my God!" She laughed.

"I know," I replied. "Makes you wonder what the world is coming to." She leaned over on the floor and kissed me. She smiled. "Do you feel better?" I asked her.

"I feel better," She replied. "I don't feel great. But you're right. We just need to have fun being together again. Once we can move away we can then start to get more adult."

"See, I can be pretty smart from time to time."

"Who would have guessed that?" She asked with a hint of sarcasm.

I grabbed one of the pillows off the bed and threw it at her. I am happy to state that I did make my target.

CHAPTER 56

When Toni Lyn and I returned to the brothel on Sunday, all the girls were sitting around watching the TV in the back office. We kind of guessed it would be slow. One of the reasons why the surprise Toni Lyn and I brought with us was so perfect.

An explanation-

See tourist season actually is pretty slow in the Autumn. So even though they still do great business on the weekends, the weekdays and the Sundays can just drag on and on. When Toni Lyn and I first learnt that this is the slow season, she said something that made everyone at the dinner table laugh, "What? Perverts come in season? You mean, like strawberries or peaches?"

"Hey girls," I said as I poked my head in the door. They all looked back at me and then back at the TV. "Cassandra?"

Cassandra looked back at me. "What is it?"

"Well, Toni Lyn and I wanted to thank you and the girls for taking us in so we bought something for the House of Pleasure." My statement seemed to capture the attention of the girls.

"What is it?" Cassandra asked. I could tell she was a little skeptical about the situation.

"Come on and see," I said beckoning them away from the TV.

"This better be good," Wang said under her breath, "The X-Files are about to be on and I like to take notes." Anyone else saying that would have made me laugh, but Wang saying that made me shiver a little bit. She has one of those senses of humor that is hard to distinguish between the humor and the truth.

When they all reached the main lobby of the brothel, Toni Lyn removed the sheet we had covering our surprise. "Taaadaaaaa!" She screamed.

It was a Fussball table!

"Cool!" Vicki said. She ran over and ran her hands along the edge and the handles of the sticks. "I haven't played one of these since I was in high school."

"This is very cool," Stacey said. All the girls nodded among themselves and joined Vicki at the table.

Cassandra was the last to move. She looked over at me. I could see she wanted to discuss this a little bit. "Now what are we…"

"Cassandra," I interrupted. I was ready for this. "It's a slow season and once we do get customers in we can move it into the back office. None of your customers will be distracted by it, I swear. Plus it makes the girls happy. And happy girls make happy customers."

Cassandra was almost sold on the idea. She looked over at Vicki, Cat, Toni Lyn and Alice who were all playing with it. "It does look fun."

"And we can have a competition," I said (One thing that is easy to read in the personality of Cassandra is that she is a competitive person. You learn that after the first night of being a bodyguard. Cassandra does not like to lose a customer to another girl. She will get in there with her hands and her looks and her charms and just win that guy back. And if she could do that with men, I couldn't help wondering what she would be like with Fussball).

"Competition?" She looked over at me and smiled. "That might be acceptable…"

Toni Lyn and I were back up in our room. She was going through her backpack (where we keep our money). "You know that Fussball table used a lot of our safe money."

"I know," I sighed, "But we had to do it. We already discussed this. And we still have the car money." (The car money is part of our investment to buy a house someday. We both swore we would never touch it).

"I know," she sighed back at me.

I sat down on the edge of the bed and began to untie my right shoe. "And you chose the Fussball table." I said and pointed up at her.

"I know, I know," She moaned comically. She turned her back to me.

I slowly began to untie my left shoe. Something was up with her. She was about to do something. I could feel all of this in the air....

"You know I never did pay you back for that pillow fight back at the hotel room," she said (Is that a little evil I hear in her voice?).

"Yes?" I asked slowly.

She turned back to me and... "AHHHHHHH!!!!" She screamed and tackled me off of the bed and onto the floor!

As I struggled to get her off me (And she worked to pin me down), I kept shouting, "Ok, you win. You win. Oh God! You win... Don't bite!"

Chapter 57—The First Annual Cassandra's House of Pleasure Fussball Competition!

1.
2.
3.
4.
5.
6.
7.
8.
9.
10.
11.
12.
13.
14.
15.
16.

Sign up!!!
Starts Tomorrow!!!

CHAPTER 58

—(RESULTS OF ROUND ONE OF THE FIRST ANNUAL FUSSBALL COMPETITION)

The Official Scorecard

Game 1
Wang

       Wang

Sue

Game 2
Cat

       Cat

Emma

Game 3
Toni Lyn

       Toni Lyn

Stacey

Game 4
Liz
                    Maria
Maria

Game 5
Me
                    Vicki
Vicki

Game 6
Ingrid
                    Cassandra
Cassandra

Game 7
Missy
                    Missy
Alisha

Game 8
Alice
                    Alice
Slim Jimmy

Highlights

The evening was all strangely… very… sexy. There is nothing like watching women in lingerie performing a sport. You want to cheer them on in the event and you also really want to cheer them on. But Lingerie-Fussball… Well, in a sport where they quickly move left and right and… Well… Lingerie-Fussball puts mud wrestling to shame.

The first round involved eight different games over the course of the evening. Picture little Sue (Funny thing is she is actually in her early thirties) in her white teddy with her blonde pigtails taking on Mistress Wang in her dominatrix outfit. Then there was Cat in her sleek tights taking on Emma in her sheer nightie. It was a hard evening for any man to act as a bodyguard and keep score at the same time. Toni Lyn thought the entire evening was hilarious. However, I think she got more of a thrill watching me pretending not to watch the amusements. She would almost roll over in laughter every time I made comments like "I'm just watching the ball" or "I need to watch the game to make sure there aren't any fouls."

"Sure you are," She would laugh, "Sure you are."

Everyone had a great time that night. It was like all the weight and depression that comes with working in such a field disappeared and was replaced by the feeling of just a normal group of friends having a good time. Even Slim Jimmy came by (It turns out the reason Cassandra knew him is because he is quite the regular at the House of Pleasure). So it was a great evening all around…. Well, at least until I played my game. I didn't make it to round two… Not that I'm bitter about that. I mean if Vicki can live with the realization that she is a cheater God speed to her… I'm not bitter about this, I didn't lose fair and square, mind you…

Ok, ok. You want to know what happened? I'll tell you. I think it is really unfair when a man is playing Fussball against a girl in lingerie for the girl to keep having her breasts fall out. Plop! That is not a fair distraction. I'm sorry if that is harsh (or maybe sexist) but when that occurs the playing field should stop until the boobs are put back. The ball should not stay in motion! It's just unfair. There I am standing with this big stunned look on my face and she's playing like there's no problem. Like it's normal for her breasts to be out in the open while playing Fussball.

The first time it happened (I will give her that) was a mistake. So granted, maybe in a grand scheme of things she can have that first goal. But eight goals and eight peep shows later, I think it's time for someone to throw down the rulebook!

And what about those comments she kept making? Like, "Boy this game is making me hot." or "You know, you are really great at handling a stick." And I'm not going to even begin to describe how she would play with her handles when she knew I was watching her hands... Just evil... Just unfair.

And get this, every time I complained about it everyone in the brothel would laugh as if I told the funniest joke in the world!... Ok, maybe it is odd for a guy to ask a girl to cover her body in a brothel, but we had a game going on.

Sigh...

Round Two is going to be held the next evening....

CHAPTER 59

— (RESULTS OF ROUND TWO

OF THE FIRST ANNUAL

FUSSBALL COMPETITION)

The Official Scorecard

Game 1
Wang

       Cat

Cat

Game 2
Toni Lyn

       Toni Lyn

Maria

Game 3
Vicki

       Vicki

Cassandra

Game 4

Missy

　　　　　Missy

Alice

Highlights

Tonight's round was a little more intense than the previous night. You could feel the tension in every game. These women were playing for blood. There were no longer any little teasing and flirtatious threats, now everything was backed by grunts, anger and tension.

I had no idea what brought this aggressive attitude forward. It was almost like this was no longer just a simple Fussball game. This was a definition of one's importance. And when customers actually did come in and show interest in a girl in the competition, the girls were less than ecstatic. But to save their job they would still disappear upstairs with the man. I will say this though, the girls that did go upstairs, came down very quickly and the men looked like they were thrown through the ringer. What the girls did to speed up the process and still have the customer so satisfied confused and (definitely) caught my attention. I was going to have Toni Lyn casually ask one of the girls about it, but she didn't want to be bothered either.

Round Two was just as important for Toni Lyn. She stood on the side closely watching each of the games. During the first game, I went over and stood next to her. This is what she said to me: "Watch Cat. See she favors that one handle, that's her major line of defense. Once a person gets past that line for her, you are pretty much golden. But the trick is getting past her. See Wang doesn't see that. She is trying to just fling it across the playing field. You have to sneak past that line of defense; you can't just throw past it. Cat is too ready for that. See. Every time. Every time. See, what I mean..." I sighed and went to the other side of the room.

There were some interesting highlights in the evening. The first thing that comes to my mind is Toni Lyn's victory dance. It was quite incredible. She jumped on the couches and the chairs and belted out "I am the Champion," by Queen at the top of her lungs.... When the girls began to offer Toni Lyn dollar bills, I interrupted the number ("Elvis has left the building. Elvis has left the building so go back to your Fussball!").

The second thing that jumps to my mind was the way that Cassandra threatened Vicki's job during their game. "You know it's hard to find work in nice brothels like this one…. And if, say, people were to hear rumors about you… Dealing with drugs or punching customers it could really hurt one's career, don't you think?.. No, no, I know you don't do those kind of things, but it would be sad if such rumors started and you lost your job… I'm just thinking out loud…"

Vicki still won.

"I think it's amazing how great all the girls are at Fussball," I said to Toni Lyn. It was evening and we were back in the room. "Of course, if I was smarter I would have assumed that considering what they do for a living."

"What do you mean?" Toni Lyn asked.

"Well, think about the Fussball playing field. It's a bunch of men, no faces, no arms, and you manipulate these men with sticks—coming out of their body, mind you—to your own bidding. These men are under your control. See what I mean? It's almost poetic how perfect it is that prostitutes would be great at this game." I chuckled quietly. I took off my shirt.

Toni Lyn didn't see the humor in the situation. "I'm good at Fussball too."

I paused. Was she serious? I looked back at her face. Yes, she was serious. "Yes," I said slowly, "You are good at the game too. I was just making a point."

"A point that says they are better than me."

"I didn't say that," I said calmly. She still had her game face on (Oh, no). I knew I had to be careful in what I said (I was still a little bruised from a few days ago when she tackled me). She was into this too much. "I think you're going to win the competition."

Toni Lyn smiled. She was no longer upset. "Do you think so?"

"Yes," I said, "I want you to win."

"Great," she began to undress too.

"Yeah, great," I sighed under my breath and got under the covers… Maybe I should have argued for the Air Hockey table… Oh, well…

CHAPTER 60

—(RESULTS OF ROUND 3 OF THE FIRST ANNUAL FUSSBALL COMPETITION)

The Official Scorecard

Game 1

Cat   **Final Game**
             Toni Lyn

Toni Lyn
                          WINNER!!!
Game 2   _____
Vicki
             Vicki

Missy

Highlights

Cat versus Toni Lyn was an incredible game! And I'm not just saying that because I'm madly in love with one of the participants. Here were two contestants who played with two different forms of attack. First off you have Cat who does live up to her name. She is totally primal. Every turn of the handle and ever move of the ball seemed to be followed by a growl or a grunt. It was a lot like watching a cougar attacking a smaller animal. She was pouncing on that table and the ball was her prey. Every hit she gave of the ball was powerful and aimed.

However, Toni Lyn thought her way through the game. Just watching the intensity of the game and her gaze, you could see that every bit of her concentration was centered on the game in front of her. She planned her moves, corrected maneuvers and performed with a skill that would have made every Professor she had at Yale impressed.

Toni Lyn was right about Cat's game. The trick was to sneak past her line of defense. And as the game went on, she used this knowledge to her advantage. In the end, this was a game that Toni Lyn could be proud of and her victory was well deserved. She was going on to the finals…

The problem though was that Toni Lyn was going up against Vicki. Vicki is an evil player at the game. That is one of the things I have discovered not only first hand but by watching every game she played since then. She finds a weakness and attacks it. She also had a very evil talent for finding the right annoying thing to say to distract her competitor. She has gotten more goals from default (in my opinion) than for any other reason. The final match is truly going to be one hell of a battle.

In good boyfriend standing, I decided to pep my woman up for the final round.

My Pre-Game Pep Talk

Me: Don't doubt for one second that you can't do this.

Her: I didn't say I was doubting myself.

Me: (pause) Good, good, that's the spirit.

Her: Are you saying I should doubt myself?

Me: No, not at all.

Her: Was that a snicker?

Me: What? Anyway, you just got to be brave and think positive.

Her: Will that help me win?

Me: No, but it'll help your self-esteem.

Her: Ok, you're being really funny, but this is not helping.

> Vicki: You're going down Toni Lyn.

Her: Says who?

> Vicki: Says me.

Her: Ok, I just wanted to make sure.

Me: Tough words.

Her: She doesn't have a chance. She's just playing mind games on me.

Me: Is it working?

Her: Of course not!

Me: Good super. That's great.

Her: You really aren't helping me here.

Me: Just make sure to have fun.

Her: Fun? (pause) How about win?

Me: Well, you can always dream.

Her: And I like to dream you know and… Hey, wait a minute.

> Vicki: Are you going to wimp out on me, Toni Lyn?

Her: Of course not, I'll be right there.

Me: That's great. Walk right over there like a man.

Her: I'm not a man, genius.

Me: Well, then just walk.

Her: Say at least something reassuring, funnyman.

Me: I like your haircut.

Her: Thanks.

Me: On to Victory!

Her: Yeah!

Highlights

Vicki dropped the ball for the beginning of the first half. The second that ball hit the table it sounded like an explosion erupted from it! Every man was moved against itself. Everything was being swung around with a furious abandonment. See, Toni Lyn knew the only way she would have a chance against Vicki was to play aggressive to such a point that Vicki could not find ways to distract her (She said this to me earlier today when I was trying to start a discussion over recent political activities in the USA). So she played with all the anger she could. Watching Vicki keep the ball back was like someone trying to hold back a wave on a beach…. However, she did it. So when that timer went off we were still at a game of 0-0.

My Halftime Pep Talk

Me: That was great.

Her: I did it. We're still at a tie. I can actually win this. I can't believe it.

Me: Have some water.

Her: I'm not thirsty.

Me: But I got this great sports bottle.

Her: But I'm not… (forced drinking).

Me: See, isn't that cool?

Her: You got water all down my shirt.

Me: This is such a great bottle. It only cost me…

Her: You got me all wet.

Me: See, the bottle has many different functions.

Her: (pause) Are you high?

Me: No, no. I'm just silly.

Her: Great, just great. When did this start?

Me: I don't know. I guess I'm just having fun.

Her: This isn't fun. It's Fussball.

Me: What?

Her: Fussball is a way of life.

Me: I guess so.

Her: It's my destiny.

Me: Groovy. Here have a towel.

Her: I don't want a towel.

Me: But you said you're wet?

Her: I kind of like it.

Me: Ok. Then wrap the towel around your shoulders like this.

Her: Why?

Me: Athletes do that.

Her: Like this.

Me: Perfect.

Her: This should be in the Olympics.

Me: Do ya think?

Her: Yeah, it should be. If they can have Table Tennis, they can have Fussball.

Me: But if they allow Fussball just think of all the games that would request entry. You would have Air Hockey, and Pool. And then board games like Monopoly and Clue…

Her: (interrupting) All those are shit compared to Fussball.

Me: So you like this game?

Her: Hell, yeah.

Me: Well, get out there and win one, Tiger!

Her: What did you call me?

Me: Tiger.

Her: (pause) Why?

Me: I thought it sounded right.

Her: Why?

Me: It's an aggressive animal?

Her: Uh huh?

Me: Like you are, out there.

Her: Ok.

Me: And it's…

Her: Nevermind… I need to get my game face on again.

Me: Ok.

Her: Be quiet now.

Me: Ok.

Her: I said be quiet.

Me: I said Ok.

Her: So be quiet now.

Me: I am.

Her: You're not listening.

Me: What are you talking about?

Her: Be quiet.

Me: Ok.

Her Augh! If I lose this game, I'm blaming you.

Me: That doesn't seem fair.

Her: Here's your towel back.

                            Vicki: Are you ready to lose yet, Toni Lyn?

Her: In your dreams, Vicki.

Me: Are you sure you don't want the towel.

Her: What? No.

Me: Ok.

Her: Say something to get me ready.

Me: Ok…

Her: C'mon, quickly.

Me: You have pretty eyes.

Her: Do you really think so?

Me: Yes.

Her: That's very nice, but it doesn't help.

                                   Vicki: Tick, tock, tick tock.

Her: Countdown to your destruction, Vicki.

Me: That's witty.

Her: Thanks. (She grabbed my face and gave me a big kiss). This one is for you, honey.

Highlights

Wow.

That's all I got to say—Wow.

It was just… Wow.

Ok, I need to say some other things…

Well, the second half was just as intense. But Vicki prepared herself with distractions before the second half began. It was like she used the halftime to prepare lines. And these lines were great distractions like "Did you know that you are the only girl that lives here that has sex for free?" or how about this "There's been a secret camera in your room for the last few days and I've some advice for you if you like?" and then there is "I think your boyfriend would look good in a dress, don't you?" See what I mean? These are great distracting lines! It was the last line that did in Toni Lyn. Vicki said that line while she had the ball in the offensive and so when Toni Lyn looked up to respond with something like "That is so ridiculous…." Vicki scored!

A few minute later the game ended. 0-1.

Vicki was the victor!

That's when the victory celebration for Vicki began. Cassandra bought some champagne and poured some glasses for us all. Toni Lyn didn't drink her glass… She was understandably upset.

Back in our room later

Her: I can't believe that!

Me: I told you she's a cheat.

Her: But it was a great game, why ruin it with cheating?

Me: She doesn't see it that way. She sees it as a weapon.

Her: I can't believe it I… What are you doing?

Me: I'm looking for a camera…

Her: She was joking.

Me: You never can be certain. A person could make some serious money with a sex tape in this area.

Her: That's silly. These people wouldn't do that. It's just… Well… I'll look over here.

CHAPTER 61

—[AND ON THE 24TH DAY...]

In The Morning—

"Just a second… *cough*… I'm almost ready…"

"C'mon," Toni Lyn sighed. She was sitting on the edge of the bed watching me prep myself up for my performance (No, I don't mean that!). "You've been bragging about this since I first met you and…"

"I said I was almost ready…" I sighed and paced once back and forth again. "Ok… *cough*…" I looked at her seriously. I slowly raised my hand in front of my face… I then lowered the hand. "To be…" I paused and then emphasized my next words. "… or NOT to be…" I raised my hand and pointed at her. "That is the question." I raised my other hand and shrugged both my shoulders. "Whether 'tis nobler in the mind to suffer the…" I acted out shooting an arrow with a bow. "…sling and arrows…" I pretended like I got hit by the arrow and collapsed holding my chest. I began gasping for air like I was dying. … of… *cough*… of outrageous fortune…" I got back up and raised my hands like I was boxing. "or to take arms against a sea of troubles, and by opposing…" I punched out in front of me. "… and end them." I pretended to look scared. "To die,.." I pretended to sleep, "to sleep-…" I then spread my palms up in front of me as if I was trying to get something in front of me to stop. "No more…"

"Stop! Oh, please God, stop!" Toni Lyn laughed. She fell off the bed. "My side hurts!"

At Breakfast—

Hi, girl and boy." It was Liz. She was dressed in normal clothes today. It's strange how a person can get used to seeing someone in lingerie. It actually took me a few blinks to figure out who I was looking at. It didn't help that she had a dark wig on that was hiding her bright red hair.

"What's up Liz?" I asked casually as I ate my Frosted Flakes.

"You two are coming with me today," Liz said.

Toni Lyn and I looked up from our cereal bowls at each other. This was something new. "Where are we going?" Toni Lyn asked.

"You're getting your fake ID's," Liz said, "It's a present from Cassandra. We're leaving in about an hour…."

About An Hour Later—

"We're going now!" Liz called to Cassandra. Cassandra was playing Fussball against Vicki ("Now Vicki I know how much you like working here, but if you say one word during this game I'll fire you on the spot.") It looked pretty intense (You know how competitive Cassandra can be).

We exited the House of Pleasure and shut the door behind us. "How long will it take us to get there?" I asked Liz.

"About thirty minutes," Liz said casually and began walking ahead of us.

About Thirty Minutes Later—

"This is the place," Liz said. We were standing outside a door in a dark alley of Amsterdam (How many dark alleys does this city have anyway?).

"Who is this guy, Liz?" I asked.

"Can we trust him?" Toni Lyn asked.

Liz laughed. "Fatty?" She began opening the door. "You have nothing to worry about when it comes to Fatty." She motioned for us to follow her. "C'mon in…"

Behind the door was a photography studio. A really nice photography studio! It also looked extremely well cared for. The walls were all a stainless white and there were cameras covering the desks. Around the back wall were a mess of broken sets. They looked to be mostly remains of beds and couches.

Fatty McKenzie ran over to see us the second we entered the door. 'Marvelous, just marvelous. Look at them! They're marvelous. Marvelous! Marvelous. Liz, they're marvelous."

Liz sighed, "That's super, Fatty, but…"

"Marvelous, just marvelous."

"But, Fatty, Cassandra wants them to keep their clothes on during the shoots."

Fatty laughed and shrugged his shoulder. "Well, a man can dream. So marvelous." Here's some info on Fatty McKenzie. Well, first off he wasn't fat. He was quite thin. He was also American (Is anyone in Amsterdam Dutch?) and talked in a very fast manner. It was strange hearing him speak. It was almost like the words went faster than his lips could go. Fatty was quite the popular photographer in the area. Other than having the skills to make the best fake IDs in town, he was also the premier photographer of pornography around the world. How popular are his pictures? Well, if he was to take a picture of you nude, it will not only be seen in Amsterdam, but by the end of the week it would be on 3 websites, two magazines in the USA and in cheap magazines in every third world country and …. Fatty is waving us to another side of the room.

"This guy is a trip," Toni Lyn whispered to me.

"Stand here," Fatty said. He stood us in front of this white wall. He walked around us. "Ok, now speak."

"What do you want us to say?" I asked.

"Marvelous," Fatty exclaimed. He turned to Toni Lyn. "Now you speak."

"What?" She asked confused.

"Marvelous," Fatty said with a smile. He turned to Liz. "They sound too American. I'm going to have to make up passports, visas, American driver Licenses and…"

Liz sighed. It was obvious she was not a big fan of Fatty's. "Whatever, Fatty. Just as long as it's done by the afternoon."

Fatty frowned. "Ok, whatever. For you I'll do it, Liz. But the next time I come in, you'll owe me." (That's why Liz couldn't stand him. He was a regular customer of her's. No wonder Cassandra sent her instead of coming herself).

Fatty turned back to us and quickly clapped his hands. "Ok, we're going to take 3 pictures of each of you. I have different shirts in the back I'll need you to wear. Also, I would need you to do something with your hair in each picture so it doesn't look like it was taken the same day and… Who wants to go first?"

"I guess I will," I said raising my hand slowly.

"Marvelous," Fatty said excited, "Marvelous!"

An Hour Later-

The pictures were done. Posing for Fatty was like watching a hyper rabbit in motion with a camera jumping around you. He moved so quickly that I could only compare it to physical stuttering at an accelerated rate. If how he acts while photographing is anything like how he is in bed, I can understand Liz's dislike of him as a customer. Right now Toni Lyn and I are sitting on a couch near the back wall. Fatty is over on the other side of the room sitting at a desk. It looks like he is working with some documents in front of him. Liz walked up to us. She sighed. "Do you know what people have done on that couch?"

Toni Lyn and I both quickly got up.

"Over here! Over here!" Fatty shouted. He waved to us. We slowly walked over to him. "Marvelous! Marvelous! So what do we call you?"

"What?" I asked.

"What will be your new names?"

I looked over at Toni Lyn. We never discussed this before. You think we would have planned something ahead of time. "What do you think?" She asked me.

"I don't know, what do you think?" I asked her back.

Liz sighed. "You two didn't plan this?"

Fatty clapped his hands together. "I got an idea." He grabbed a pen and pointed it at me. "Quickly name all the fiction characters that come to your mind."

"Hamlet," I said.

"Heavens, no," Fatty said quickly.

"Luke Skywalker."

"No."

"Bilbo Baggins."

"No."

"Sherlock Holmes."

"Not a chance."

"Gatsby."

"No."

"Pip."

"Please."

"Winnie-The-Pooh."

"Is 'The' the middle name? No."

"King Lear."

"No."

"Bertie Wooster."

"Of course not."

"Frankenstein."

"No."

"Han Solo."

"No."

"Captain Ahab."

"No."

"Raskolnikov."

"No."

"Candide."

"Love the book, but no."

"Opus the Penguin."

"You want to be a penguin? No."

"Indiana Jones."

"No. Indiana? No."

"Actually his real first name is Henry. Indiana is the name of his dog and he had people call him…"

"Henry Jones?"

"Yes, that's his name."

He paused and took a breath. "Perfect." Fatty wrote that down on a pad. "You're now Henry Jones."

I looked over at Toni Lyn. "Cool." I paused. "You can call me Indy for short."

"Ok, Indy for short," Toni Lyn sighed.

Fatty turned to her now. "What'll be your first name, Mrs. Jones?"

"Mrs. Jones?" Toni Lyn was surprised; she looked over at me and back at Fatty. "We're not married."

"Ok why do you travel together?"

"Well, we are in love and we are best friends and…"

"Where did you meet?"

"Well, we met in…."

"And are you planning to get married?"

"Well, someday and…."

"And why aren't you married yet?"

"We aren't…"

"Do your parents like you traveling like this?"

"They don't really…"

"You see," Fatty said turning to me. "There are too many questions. If you're married all those questions that you can get stuck on during an interrogation disappear. No one questions a marriage."

He made sense. Toni Lyn was still stunned. I looked over at Fatty. "Can we talk in private for a second?"

"Go right ahead," He sighed. "Marvelous!"

Her: Oh, my god.

Me: I know it's a lot.

Her: But we'll be married.

Me: I know.

Her: You and me, husband and wife.

Me: I totally know.

Her: But we discussed this just a few days ago. We were planning to wait to discuss this, I mean this was just confusing us earlier and we were having so much fun and…

Me: Breathe in and out, Toni Lyn. It's going to be ok.

Her: Why are you so calm about this?

Me: Strangely, enough I kind of like the idea.

Her: Why?

Me: One it keeps us together. And we'll always have an alibi for each other and I guess I really love you a lot.

Her: But we'll be married on all our documents.

Me: If it makes you feel better think of it this way—We are actors…

Her: You can't act.

Me: I know, I know. But hear me out. These are parts we'll be playing for the public. Inside we'll still be us.

Her: Keep going…

Me: And once we get out of the House, we can then really get married. Then the characters will be real.

Her: I get it… Yeah, that makes sense.

Me: And there is some beauty in the thought that in another reality, in another land we are married. And in that parallel universe—if you will—we will always be together.

Her: You're so smooth.

Me: I try.

"Ok, we do it," Toni Lyn said.

Fatty clapped his hands together. "So what's your first name, Mrs. Jones?"

"It could be anything, right?"

"Well, it can't be Henry," Fatty sighed.

"How about Kimberly?"

"Ok, Kimberly…"

"No, wait!"

"How about Maggie?" She turned to me. "Northern Exposure was always my favorite TV show and when I was in high school I wanted to be Maggie O'Connell."

"Maggie Jones?" Fatty asked.

"Henry and Maggie Jones does sound like a couple," I said to Toni Lyn.

"Ok," Toni Lyn said.

"Why didn't you put Northern Exposure on the list?" I asked her.

She shrugged her shoulders. "I guess I forgot."

"Marvelous!" Fatty exclaimed. "Now I'll need at least 3 hours to pre-pare all the documents. So if you 3 could go out and visit some stores or whatever."

The 3 of us began heading for the door.

"Just a second," Fatty called. We all stopped and looked back at him. "Can you stay Liz? I might have need of your *cough* services later."

Liz sighed and looked over at us. "He's an incredible tipper. I'll see you later." She began to sexily walk over to him as Toni Lyn and I left the building.

Later That Afternoon—

Toni Lyn and I were holding hands as we ran over to see Cassandra. She was sitting on the couch in the back office getting a back rub from Vicki. This image stunned me for a second so Toni Lyn was the first to speak. "We would like to say thanks, Cassandra. That was so nice what you did for us with the fake IDs."

"Well, I really like you kids," Cassandra sighed. She was really enjoying the massage. "All the girls like you being here. So, I thought it was the right thing to do… A little lower please… By the way, if either of you want anything talk to Vicki today."

"Why is that?" I asked.

"She lost at Fussball to me," Cassandra said, "She's my slave girl for the day…. And she gives great massages…"

"Really?" I asked.

Toni Lyn quickly clinched my hand in a tighter grip (Ow!). "No, thanks, Cassandra. We'll be fine." We started leaving out the door.

"Now you two," Cassandra called after us. "Make sure to come down to dinner. We've some surprises lined up for you tonight… A little lower… There's the spot."

At Dinner—

Cassandra stood up at the dinner table. "Attention. Attention everyone. I would like to be the first to introduce you all to Mr. and Mrs. Henry Jones."

All the girls began to clap. I looked over at Toni Lyn. She was sitting across the table from me. I smiled at her. She stuck her tongue out at me.

Suddenly, all the girls began to hit their glasses with their silverware. They wanted us to kiss. I got up from my seat and Toni Lyn got up from her's. We leaned across the table and kissed each other. They all applauded.

Cassandra looked over at Vicki. "Can you get the presents for our newlyweds, slavegirl?"

"Presents?" I asked stunned. The problem with me saying this is I was still kissing Toni Lyn at the time. We stopped kissing and looked over at Cassandra confused (It's odd how much our minds are in sync. Most of our actions are done in a coordinated fashion).

"You didn't need to get us presents," Toni Lyn quickly stated.

"We wanted too," Maria said in her deep voice. "We thought it would be fun to celebrate the marriage of your alteregos."

"But we didn't even have a ceremony," Toni Lyn said quietly.

"Thanks but…" I began to say when I was interrupted by the vision of Vicki walking in carrying a bunch of presents under her arms.

From Cassandra we received a red nightie.

I held the woman's nightie in front of myself. "I don't think this will fit me."

From Mistress Wang we received a… Well, I don't…. know…

I held up the strange object for Toni Lyn to inspect. "Isn't this what they put on horses so they won't be distracted by things around them?"

From Sue we received some lotions.

"Thanks, my hands were feeling a little rough." I rubbed some on my hands and… Hot! Hot! Hot! "What kind of freaky lotion is this?!"

From Alice we received some boxer shorts.

"One of my past customers left those behind," Alice explained. "They glow in the dark."

From Maria we received some red candles.

"I love candles and red is my favorite color," Maria said.

"Mine too," Toni Lyn responded excited.

From Alisha we received some colored condoms.

"When you get married you are supposed to get something blue," Alisha explained. "There is a blue condom in the pack."

From Stacey and Missy we received... Cool!
"You once told me about the game," Stacey explained. "You made it sound like fun.
"You're right," I said excitedly. "This game is the best!" They gave me a copy of How To Host A Murder. It is a game where you become a character in a mystery for the evening as you try to solve a murder. Great stuff.

From Vicki we received a book.
"A book of helpful hints on playing Fussball," I sighed. "Thanks Vicki."

From Cat we received some handcuffs.
"Those are the real thing," Cat stated. "I used to date a cop."

From Ingrid we received a bottle of champagne.
"I thought you two could drink it tonight," Ingrid said.

From Liz and Emma we received some white lingerie.
"Is there a reason people keep buying me lingerie?" I comically asked. "Are you all trying to tell me something?"

"I think we have some champagne also left over from last night," Cassandra said quickly. She turned to Vicki. "Check the kitchen, slave-girl."
Vicki sighed and went into the kitchen to get the bottles. She came back with 3 bottles. She poured us all some glasses.
"You have to love a job where you drink champagne every night," Missy laughed. "I love the bubblely."
Suddenly all the girls began chanting: "Speech. Speech. Speech."

I sighed and stood up.

"When I was a kid I loved to pretend. I loved to make up characters for myself and act them out. I remember once I played house with this girl down the street. What was her name? It doesn't matter, but anyway I was really good at it. And then there was the time I played doctor and… Ok, that's another story… And then there are my years as a teenager and a young adult. I pretended hundreds of things then-many times alone. I pretended to be a happy worker and a happy lover and… Well, I guess what I'm saying is that I love you Toni Lyn (All the girls sighed). And there is nothing I would like more than to pretend to be your husband for all my days to come…"

In The Evening—

"When you got up this morning did you think you would have a fake reception and honeymoon?" I asked Toni Lyn. We were back in the room. "We had all the goods bit without the ceremony. I guess we'll catch up to that later… I just didn't see this… Did you see this coming at all?"

She shook her head no. "I had no idea. I thought I was going to have to spend the entire day hearing you attempt to act. And then I would have to lie through my teeth—'Oh, that's great. I see an Oscar in your future, dear.'" She sighed. "This is much nicer." She held up the two pieces of lingerie she received. "Which do you think? Red or white?"

"I think white," I replied. "I think you should wear some white today."

She smiled. "I agree." She began walking to our bathroom. "I'm going to change. You light those candles and open that champagne, ok?"

"Are you sure you want some more champagne?" I asked. We had quite a few bottles of this stuff down stairs.

Toni Lyn let out a silly giggle and disappeared into the bathroom.

I began to open the wrappers around the candles and scatter them around the floor when suddenly…. singing? Is that singing?

*"You must remember this
A kiss is just a kiss.
A sigh is just a sigh…
The same fundamentals apply
As time goes by…"*

Toni Lyn quickly came out of the bathroom. "What is that?"

I hushed her quickly. "The girls are singing to us…"

Toni Lyn moved over closer to me. "They sound good." She was right. They did sound great together. It must have been at least four of the girls… No wait I hear five of their voices. Alice, Ingrid, Maria (on bass), Sue and Alisha… They were singing acapella. Very nice.

I love this song. "How did they know to sing this song?" I asked Toni Lyn.

"Vicki saw our list of our favorite 100," Toni Lyn figured out. "She must have seen Casablanca on the list…"

I reached out my hand to her and slowly moved her forward. She was an angel. She truly looked like a perfect angel in that white lingerie and in the light of the candles. Perfection. "You look incredible, Mrs. Jones," I said. I took her in my arms and we slowly danced together with the music. Our bodies softly swayed against each other. So natural, so right.

"Thank you, Mr. Jones, She replied with a sigh.

"As time goes by…"

"I love you Mrs. Jones," I said.

"I love you, Mr. Jones," She said.

CHAPTER 62

(Picture the sound of really long nails
scratching along a chalkboard.)

Wang removed her fingers from the chalkboard and smiled evilly. "Ok, I seem to have your attention. Listen to me! Honeymoon is over! Now you must learn Dutch and I will teach you. And you will learn or else." She unbuckled her whip from the side of her dominatrix outfit.

("She won't use that, I'm sure," I whispered
to Toni Lyn.)

Suddenly I felt something zip past my ear! Oh, my God she tried to whip me!

"Next time, I take your ear," Mistress Wang threatened. "There will be no talking in my class unless I talk to you. Let's test that."

(Silence.)

"Good," Mistress Wang said with her evil smile. "Now this is the class schedule. We will meet 3 days out of the week. And on those days, you will be given an assignment to perform before the next class. If you get one question wrong, you get one whip. If you get two, you get two whips. It's mathematics, you should be able to figure the rest out by yourself."

I stood up. "You can't do that."

"Are you planning to get some wrong?" Mistress Wang asked. She was playing with her whip in a manner that unnerved me.

"No, of course not," I replied sheepishly.

"Then you have nothing to worry about… Sit down!"

I sat down.

"Any other statements?"

(Silence.)

"Excellent," Wang moved over to the teachers desk (See, we were in her bedroom. For some reason, some of her customers like her to act as a mean teacher. So she already had the desk and the chalkboard. She even had these little student desks that we were sitting in. I tried my best not to think of what might have happened against these desks. There was a small blood stain on the edge of my seat…) "Now I have some questions for you. Maggie?"

(Silence.)

"Maggie?"

"Oh you mean me!" Toni Lyn replied startled. She stood up. "Sorry."

"Yes, you should be sorry," Mistress Wang replied. "That is your name now. You must respond quickly to that name. No more Toni Lyn."

"Yes, ma'am," ~~Ton~~ Maggie replied quickly.

"It's not enough to have the IDs and the language you must also become these new people. For now on I will only call you by your new names and you must do the same. Understand Henry?… Henry?"

"Oh, yes, sorry. Sure, no problem. My mind was elsewhere. Fpppp! Gone. But now I'm back. Yes, Henry am I," I replied quickly. I stood up and looked over at Maggie. She looked back at me. We were not looking forward to this at all.

"I have prepared both of your homework. You will not work together! You will not ask others for help! If you do it will cost you one whipping! Understand?"

"Yes," we both replied in sync.

"Yes, what?" She asked quickly.

"Yes, Mistress Wang," We both replied.

"Very good… Not get your homework and go! I don't want to see you again today! Go!"

We both grabbed our homework off her desk and bolted for the door.

——*Later That Night…*

"Toni Lyn?" We were in our bedroom. I was working on my homework on the bed and she was brushing her teeth in the bathroom.

"I'm not responding to you," She said with her toothbrush in her mouth. She spat out. "You must call me 'Maggie.'"

"Well, *Maggie*." I emphasized her name. "What did you get for number forty?"

She walked out of the bathroom. She looked very surprised. "You've got to be kidding me."

"I can't figure it out," I sighed. "It's like it's all in a foreign language or something. Ha! Pretty funny, eh? That's humor and… You're not laughing."

"I can't help you," She stated simply.

"What? C'mon," I sighed.

"No, Henry, I can't," She replied. "I'm not going to get whipped. I love you a great deal but that thing could really do some damage."

"You're taking her threats seriously? She knows we live in the same room together. She has to assume we'd work together. It was a hollow threat."

"Hollow threat? She almost took your ear off!"

"Toni Lyn, that's no…"

"I'm not Toni Lyn anymore!"

"Ok, Maggie," I sighed.

"Now put the book away, I'm going to put on the red lingerie and I want your full attention when I get out."

"I'm not done with my homework and…"

"Now!' Maggie stated abruptly and went back into the bathroom. She shut the door behind her. "And light those candles! I want it damn romantic when I step out!" She shouted from behind the door.

I sighed and began to light the remaining candles from last night. I'm starting to believe that Mistress Wang may be becoming a bad influence on Mrs. Jones.

CHAPTER 63

— [FOR SOMETHING FUN TO DO TO KILL TIME TONI LYN AND I MADE A LIST OF ALL THE STRANGE/COOL NAMES AND NICKNAMES THAT COULD COME TO OUR MIND...]

OUR 100 FAVORITE NAMES.
1. Spunky.
2. Red.
3. Toni Lyn (Please—Toni Lyn).
4. Moonboy (Will I ever be able to live that down?)
5. Ringo.
6. Sherlock.
7. George Eliot.

8. Beautiful (It basks in kissup corniness. I like it—Toni Lyn).

9. Fat boy (I used to call one of my old friends this. He hated it. I wonder what he's doing now?).

10. Ophelia (Why don't people name their girls this anymore?)

11. Harmony.

12. The Verve (Can we name rock bands?)

13. Indy.

14. Vincent.

15. Keats.

16. Robin.

17. Luke (Would you really name a boy Luke?—Toni Lyn).

18. Ilsa.

19. Rick.

20. Juliet (You really like that name, don't you?—Toni Lyn).

21. Sexy

22. Honey.

23. Dearest (Sounds like a nickname my grandmother would use).

24. August.

25. Autumn.

26. Dollface (I feel like a gangster when I say it to a girl. Cool).

27. The Sun King.

28. Elizabeth.

29. Queen (Stop laughing—Toni Lyn).

30. Snoopy (That will be a great man's name!).

31. Austen.

32. Dexy.

33. Genius (Oh, I like that nickname. Thanks for mentioning that).

34. Duke (Can't you just feel the power?).

35. Romeo (Good nickname, bad real name).

36. Alice (Only when used in connection with Alice In Wonderland— Toni Lyn).

37. The Rain King (Would you rather be The Rain King or The Sun King?—Toni Lyn).

38. Tigger (Ha!).

39. Ally.

40. Killer (Why is this always a good nickname?).

41. Aragon, son of Arathorn, Isildur's heir (Oh, my God! My fake husband is a nerd!—Toni Lyn).

42. Darcy (I love Pride And Prejudice—Toni Lyn).

42. Cat.

43. Wolf.

44. Big Boy (Why are you laughing, Toni Lyn?).

45. Viola.

46. Frankenstein.

47. Dracula.

48. Benedick.

49. Han.

50. Picard.

51. Mulder (Have you got all the sci-fi out of your system yet?—Toni Lyn).

53. Leia (Now?—Toni Lyn).

54. Scully (Now?—Toni Lyn).

55.Chewbaca (You're pushing it—Toni Lyn).

56.Darth (C'mon!—Toni Lyn).

57.Lando (That's it! Give me the pen—Toni Lyn).

58.Yoda (I said give me the pen-Toni Lyn).

59.Spock (The pen?—Toni Lyn).

60.Jabba the Hutt (You've had your fun, now give me the pen—Toni Lyn).

61.Obi Wan (Give it here—Toni Lyn).

62.Q (Hand it over, Moonboy!—Toni Lyn).

63.Sisko (That's it! Prepare to wrestle!—Toni Lyn).

64.Emma (I do believe you've learned your lesson—Toni Lyn).

65.Steely Dan (Do you mean the band or the… ah… other thing? You know… From Burroughs?).

66.Marvel.

67.Fly.

68.Dreamer.

69.Lover.

70.Maggie (Cool—Toni Lyn).

71.Henry (Cool).

72.Mr. Jones.

73.Mrs. Jones (Too sweet—Toni Lyn).

74.Elmo (Oh, good call!—Toni Lyn).

75.Big Bird.

76.Ernie.

77.Bert (Hand me the pen).

78.Grover (Hand me the pen, Toni Lyn).

79.Cookie Monster (C'mon).

80.Kermit (Toni Lyn).

81.Snuffleupagus (Ok, you're pushing it).

82.Oscar (We get the picture, Toni Lyn).

83.Fozzie (That isn't even Sesame Street).

84.Miss Piggy (Hand me the pen!).

85.Gonzo (That's it!).

We weren't able to finish the list. See, after that final muppet I dove at her and we began wrestling for the pen and… Well, we got a little distracted.

It was a 9.

Chapter 64

On the 27th night, Toni Lyn was softly falling asleep against my shoulder. She sighed, "The days seem to fly by like dreams changing in the night.. All I seem to remember are a few images and moments and you... Like today at the barbecue..."

"I can't believe you're wearing an apron?" Toni Lyn laughed. "In that apron I can't help but get a glimpse of you at the age of forty with a bald spot standing in front of our grill in our backyard with utensils displayed proudly as a group of our little kids run around with mud in their hands..."

The apron said, "Kiss The Cook." I sighed. "If you want good food, don't mock the apron of the cook. It's so wonderfully tacky and generic... Come and get it!"

"I'm so happy you found the old grill," Alisha stated at the table. "I haven't had a good barbecue since I left my father's farm in Kentucky. This is really good."

"That reminds me," I stated. I stood up. "Can I have everyone's attention please? Excuse me... Ah... Thank you. I'll be passing around this hat. Feel free to donate any funds you feel suitable to the meal that..."

Everyone threw their old sticky napkins at me. "'Hey, Hey, watch it! You're going to ruin the apron…" Toni Lyn threw the most napkins. 3 of her napkins stuck to the apron—That seemed to make her happy.

"Cassandra, we've got this great idea," Toni Lyn said during dinner.
"What is it?" Cassandra asked casually.
"Murder," Toni Lyn said with a smile.
Cassandra in surprise dropped the food that she was holding. Her mouth fell open. I think it was the first time either of us have seen Cassandra truly surprised by something (Always something new). And considering what she does for a living, that's kind of an achievement. "What are you talking about?"
"Actually, it's a game," I quickly jumped in. "We were given it at our fake reception two days ago and…"

What I remember most from the evening is the way Toni Lyn would eat her barbecued chicken. It's not that the way she ate was sexy or different, but that it was such a deliberate attempt to be dainty. She tried. She tried her hardest not to get her hands dirty on the sticky barbecue sauce that covered the chicken. She would use only two fingers, one from each hand. She would have these fingers positioned on either side of the leg and then ever so slowly, so slowly, she would raise it to her lips. And after taking that bite she would quickly move the chicken back to the plate. Then her fingers moved quickly to her napkin, wiping them before starting all over again. Something about all this planning and maneuvering intrigued me.

"Your lips are sticky," Toni Lyn said after kissing me.

"I'm not cleaning this grill," I stated to everyone (they were quickly leaving the table to go elsewhere). "Wait! C'mon back here! Someone's got to clean up! Ok, someone has got to at least help me clean up… Someone…" Toni Lyn ran out of the dinning room the fastest. I heard her laughing as she scampered up the stairs to our bedroom.... I sighed and began to pick up the table...

Toni Lyn sighed again and fell asleep against my shoulder.

Chasing more dreams…

CHAPTER 65

MURDER!!!!!!!

SIGN UP TODAY FOR CASSANDRA'S
HOUSE OF PLEASURE
HOW TO HOST A MURDER PARTY!

Name   Would you prefer a male
                        or female character?

1.
2.
3.
4.
5.
6.
7.
8.

SIGN UP NOW BEFORE ALL THE
PARTS ARE FILLED!

CHAPTER 66

There's been a murder!

At one of Paris's luxurious galas of the 1930's, an unexplained murder took place. Tonight you are one of the suspects in the crime. Did you murder the unknown American businessman? And if not you, who did? Can you find the killer before he kills again?

Starring

Cat as Officer Jack Bentley. Jack is a decorated war hero on a secret mission in Paris. Why is he at the gala? And how does he know the victim?

Ingrid as Sylvia Dennis. Sylvia is a rich American student traveling by herself through Europe on Daddy's money. That night she was seen arguing with the victim. What did they argue about?

Liz as Vincent Beaulieu, the painter. Vincent is famous for not only his painting but also his temper and his heavy drinking. Was the American considering buying one of his paintings? Did he make a comment that pushed Vincent one step too far?

Maggie Jones as Mary Fairchilde, the Duchess of Pettygold. The Duchess is responsible for the gathering so everyone this evening is connected to her. So how does the mysterious victim relate to her?

Wang as Franz Strauss the German diplomat in Paris. What secret is he hiding regarding France and Germany? Does the victim relate to this secret? And what would happen if France learned of Germany's intentions?

Sue as Rochelle Fliss the French parlor maid. What did she see that night? What is she not telling the cops? And why is she working when her shift ended 3 hours ago?

Henry Jones as Buck Sanders, the famous American actor. Buck is known worldwide for his portrayal as villains in cowboy movies. What brings such an actor away from Hollywood and uninvited to a gala in Paris?

Emma as Stephanie Bird, the ballerina. What is a famous Ballerina doing at a party when she is supposed to be performing the same evening at a theater over five miles away?

CHAPTER 67

SCENE—1933. A RICH BANQUET HALL IN THE HEART OF PARIS.

Elegant. Charming. The Hall sparkles with all that makes Paris truly Paris.

A jazz band is performing popular slow songs of the period, but none of the partygoers notice. They are busy discussing the new fashions of the day, the politics and threats that are emerging from Germany and the depression that still haunts the Colonies across the sea.

One of the main attractions of the party is the rich and luxurious Mary Fairchilde, Duchess of Pettygold. She is clearly the star of the party and everyone takes their time to greet her... Even the slanderous (and uninvited) Buck Sanders, Hollywood's favorite villain and cowboy.

BUCK
Greetings, ma'am.

FAIRCHILDE
Hello, Mr. Sanders... I'm glad you decided
to come to...

                                BUCK
                            (interrupting)
            Buck.

                              FAIRCHILDE
                            (aghast)
            I beg your pardon!

                                BUCK
            Buck. You can call me "Buck." My name is
            "Buck." My father is Mr. Sanders.

                              FAIRCHILDE
            Oh, yes! I thought that is what you meant.

                                BUCK
            What's your name, Duchy?

                              FAIRCHILDE
            I'm Mary Fairchilde, the Duchess of Pettygold…

                                BUCK
            Nice to meet you, Mary.

    The Duchess is, of course, a little upset by an American commoner
calling her by her first name. But she was properly raised and she can hide
her annoyance well.

                              FAIRCHILDE
            So what brings you to Paris….
                            (slowly saying name)
            Buck?

BUCK

French tail, Mary.

FAIRCHILDE

What?

BUCK

I heard French girls are easy, so I thought
I would come here and bag a few…

FAIRCHILDE

I beg your pardon!

BUCK

I'm sorry, ma'am. I don't speak all shiny and nice
like I'm sure most people you know do. See I was
raised on the street.

FAIRCHILDE

That is awful.

BUCK

It's ok, once you get used to dodging traffic.

FAIRCHILDE

You're teasing me, Buck.

BUCK

I'm sorry, ma'am. I don't mean to. Thanks for
not throwing me out.

FAIRCHILDE

You're very welcome. Have you tried any of the
delicacies that are offered on the tables over….

BUCK

I'd rather talk to you right now…

FAIRCHILDE

Oh, if you wish…

The Duchess quickly looks right and left to see if anyone notices her
dilemma. None do. They are all too busy with their own conversations
and really none of them want to deal with the notorious Buck Sanders.

The band begins to play "I Could Write a Book."

BUCK

What a pretty song…

FAIRCHILDE

Yes, it is quite fetching…

BUCK

I could write a book about you Mary.

FAIRCHILDE

Buck…

BUCK

It would be so easy to do. I could do it in a matter
of days, not even weeks. It would just flow out of
me like a breath.

FAIRCHILDE

I fear to think what it would be about…

BUCK

It will be about your eyes, Mary and the way
you play with your hair when you're nervous…

FAIRCHILDE

Now, Buck…

BUCK

You're doing it right now…

FAIRCHILDE

Sir…

BUCK

And how right from the first moment I saw you
I knew I was only for you…

FAIRCHILDE

Oh, my, you are most kind, Buck.

BUCK

I'm just a man in love, speaking his mind, Mary.
Do you read?

FAIRCHILDE

I have been well educated, Buck.

BUCK

A yes will do. I reckon you have read a book by a
Miss Jane Austen called **Pride And Prejudice**?

FAIRCHILDE
Yes, I have read all of her work.

BUCK
There is an interesting thing about the book….

FAIRCHILDE
There are many things interesting in it, Buck.
It is a classic. She is one of the great writers
of my country.

BUCK
Right… Well, anyway, do you remember the scene
when Elizabeth and Darcy dance?

FAIRCHILDE
A famous scene.

BUCK
And we all know they are meant to be hitched by
how well they dance together?

FAIRCHILDE
Enchanting…

Buck removes his cowboy hat and bows down in front of the Duchess.
Many of the other people at the party take notice. Was he actually
attempting to ask the Duchess to dance?

BUCK
Will you dance with me, Mary?

FAIRCHILDE

Why Buck, that is very flattering but I must sadly
decline. I am the hostess and my duties are for…

BUCK

Just one dance, Mary. No one will notice…

FAIRCHILDE

Mr. Sanders…

BUCK

(correcting)

Buck…

FAIRCHILDE

…Buck, yes, I can not…

BUCK

But if we dance well together it means we
are meant to be together. And I would love for
you to ride away with me into the sunset…

FAIRCHILDE

But Buck, my duties…

BUCK

You are Hostess to me too, right?

FAIRCHILDE

Yes, even though you were not invited, I…

                            BUCK
Make me happy then. Dance with me Mary…

                         FAIRCHILDE
Buck, I…

                            BUCK
And even if doesn't work out I can still go
home and brag that I danced with an actual
Duchess. You'll make me so happy…

The Duchess leans over to Buck's ear. Everyone near strains to hear what is spoken, but it is lost to all save the two involved.

("What are you doing?" Maggie asked in whisper. "We have to stay in character." "All I want is one dance," I replied with a smile, "And then I promise I'll go back to hating you and all rich British chicks." "Ok, deal," Maggie said.)

Then suddenly to the horror of all around the unimaginable occurred. Buck Sanders slowly took the Duchess of Pettygold's hand and dared to wrap around her noble waist with his other arm. Everyone was appalled! How could they not be? This was not done in British society! Especially not in such a public place and away from one's own court and rooms. She was sure to see herself on every scandal and people section of every newspapers across the world. What was she thinking, they all questioned each other. Families and royalty have fallen for less than this. And the Duchess is no fool to such knowledge. She has been well bred. But at that moment all there could do little more than bask in the confusing beauty of the moment… A cowboy was dancing with a Duchess and strangely, they danced perfectly together.

Absolutely perfectly.

CHAPTER 68

The next day Toni Lyn and I went to a sport store… Well, see a few days ago part of the Fussball table was wrecked. It seems Vicki and one of her customers got a little too excited on top of the table. It really was all Vicki's fault. The customer was shy so he asked what would turn her on and she mentioned the table… The rest is history. So, Toni Lyn and I were sent out by Cassandra to fix the beloved table.

Now while we were in the store, Toni Lyn found a bunch of old soccer jerseys. She excitedly went through the rack of clothing until she stopped at one that caught her attention. She took it off the rack and lovingly eyed the fabric in front of her. She turned to me and told me the following story.

"I grew up around soccer.

"My family lived in both Italy and America so we always kept up with international soccer. I was the only girl in school that knew anything about it but I didn't care. I loved the sport. I idolized the players. The walls in my bedrooms both in Italy and America were covered with soccer posters.

"My hero was Roberto Biago. He was incredible. He was just the finest soccer player ever. He could do anything with the ball. It was all magic with him. Watching him was like watching a great ballet, it was a dance.

He was that graceful. I had everything that had his face on it. I had posters, magazines, books, shirts, jerseys, you name it, and I had it.

"While other girls around my school would gossip over the latest teen heartthrob I would proudly wear my soccer jerseys and feel like the queen of the world.

"For my tenth birthday my family decided to surprise me. We were in Italy at the time and it was a nice day. I remember it so clearly. They had cheesy decorations all over the garden of my grandmother's estate. There was a large table set up and all the family was drinking and eating and having a great time when he arrived. Roberto Biago walked into my party! There he was standing there! Right there. He was wearing his Italian uniform and was holding a soccer ball.

"I was floored. I was totally blown away. It was my hero, my crush, and my idol right there…

"Now here is the catch. He was terrified. Oh, he tried to hide it and I admit I didn't figure out his fear for awhile (I was on such a high), but it was there. His laughing was awkward and he kept looking around nervously.

"We played around with the ball together. He was nervous. His voice shook when he talked.

"Soon my dream moment of meeting my hero was becoming an embarrassment. He was just so uncomfortable being there.

"And it was at that moment that I began to realize something was different with my family. I grew up really fast that day…

"That night I took down all the posters. I was blaming him for making me feel bad because of how scared he was, but it was really not his fault. I was lashing out… It was then that I began watching more what was going on around me… My parents created such a shield around me that it took me awhile before I figured out anything….

"It was quite the loss of innocence moment. Meeting your hero and having him be scared of your family and then learning exactly why he was terrified of your family…. Do you know how I found out most of the stuff about my family?

"This is the kicker.

"My mom saved news clippings. She had a notebook filled with these clippings that she kept locked in her desk. She was saving them like people save photos in a photo album! It was like they were proud of the crimes they got away with! So on that fateful evening I sat there and read about all the evil my family did… Yes, quite a loss of innocence…

"I had this exact jersey back at home. See, it's his….

"Holding this makes me feel like a kid again…

"No, I don't want to buy it …. You can't go back again."

CHAPTER 69

There is a common Hell in the life of all children-the dreaded shopping excursion with mom. Any child raised in America in the last fifty years knows the Hell I discuss. For there you are in a public location with a too loving mother who is choosing clothes that are far from what you would consider cool. As she hands you outfit after outfit you steal glances left and right dreading the approach of the school bully or best friend that would haunt your recesses with jokes aimed at your less than cool wardrobe. Then you escape into the dressing room where you put on the clothes you would not give to your worst enemy. The pain you feel as you look in the dressing room mirror can never equal (It only hints at) the embarrassment that waits for you outside the dressing room with your mother as she prepares to fall in love with you all over again....

Now take that feeling of lost control and embarrassment and multiply it by twelve and you will know what I felt like when I went shopping with Toni Lyn, Liz, Alisha and Missy.

Store after store after store they took me to. Having me try on one outfit after another and when I was fully clothed, I would have to walk out of the dressing room to all of their amusement. Where a mother was happy to just see you standing there wearing her little outfit, these girls wanted more. They would beg me to "Work it;" Or "Turn around;" Or "Show us your butt;" Or "Do a little dance." I was their living Ken doll and they knew it.

I would complain.

Oh, yes I would, but my complaints were never heard. They were only used as jokes or punchlines later. So how did they keep me going for the entire day? That might have been the most ingenious aspect of the situation. They used my emotions for Toni Lyn against me. See, every time I would complain (as I put on another pink polo shirt and khaki pants), Toni Lyn would step forward and say something like, "I know this is bad honey. But do it for me, ok? You know how much I love you right? You love me, right?"

Cruel.

Most cruel

By the afternoon, the day began to get worse. Things were brought up that mentioning here still make me squirm in pain. Moments like: "I wonder what he looks like dressed like a sailor." or "I found this kilt! Have him try it on! Oh, bagpipes! There are bagpipes with it!"

Over the course of the day, my outfits began to change from 80's yuppie to 40's swing dancer to 90's alternative to Halloween. I experienced it all. Every outfit, every time period that could be thought of adorned me at one point or another.

By the time we reached back to the House of Pleasure, I knew what Hell was. My childhood memories of my excursions with my Mom had become fond memories to be remembered over hot cocoa and a fire in the fireplace.

However the pain did not stop there. At dinner all the girls re-hashed the different outfits. And the description of each outfit would bring howls of laughter as I sat there with my face turning red.

In the evening, Toni Lyn hugged me and thanked me for a wonderfully exciting day. In the back of my mind, I could see myself telling her how the day really felt to me. I could see myself comparing it to my experiences as a child in a store with my mother. I could see myself doing all that and more (maybe even engaging in our first argument). But I didn't.

Instead, I said plainly, "'Yep, you owe me one." And then went to bed.

Even then, I knew we had little time together left and I was not going to ruin these days for either of us with a meaningless argument. I was more mature than that… Or so I thought, for I stayed up all night (as she slept lovingly near me) thinking of the embarrassments of those moments, biting my own tongue and listening to the sex going on in all the rooms around ours….

CHAPTER 70

—(And then I had a

vision of applause...)

"Are you nuts?" Toni Lyn asked when I first brought the idea to her.

"I think it's a great idea," I quickly stated. She walked away from me into the bathroom. She began to brush her teeth. It was morning.

"It's absolutely ridiculous," She stated between brushing. "A product of a disturbed mind."

"It's a great idea," I walked over to the bathroom doorway. "Some of the girls here really have a talent. You saw the acting ability of some of the girls during the Murder game."

"A talent show in the redlight district of Amsterdam?" Toni Lyn asked. She hoped restating my idea aloud would turn me against it. She filled her mouth with mouthwash and began to swish.

It didn't. "I know it's a little out there…"

She gargled and spat out in the sink. "Oh, it's out there all right."

"But it'll be great for the girls," I explained. "They all have different skills and talents that aren't really put to use here in this lowly dive… Well, except for Mistress Wang, but you know what I mean. This could really help their self-esteem."

"Think about what you're saying for a second," Toni Lyn leaned against the sink and made eye contact with me. "You want to hold a talent show in the redlight district of Amsterdam. Just think for a second how such a show will be taken. Just think for a second of what kind of an audience you would have. I know, your intentions are the best, I totally believe you there. But it's just not possible…"

"I still think it's possible," I replied. I had a strong opinion on this. "Maybe the audience we'd get would be questionable, at best, but they would adapt to the surrounding. The girls can win over the audience."

Oh, my," Toni Lyn exclaimed and turned back to the sink. "Bend over the sink so I can throw some water in your face."

"Well, I bet Cassandra will like the idea." I stated and walked back over to the bed.

"I have a pretty good idea how Cassandra will reply," Toni Lyn said quietly to herself. "She'll probably say…."

"You're mad. You've totally lost it. You're under a delusion of Euphoria. Let me give you an idea how bad this idea is. Your mind is here (She held her right hand out to the side) and sanity is over here (She held her left hand out to the other side). Darling, and please don't tell Maggie I called you that, you've lost it. Take my advice. And take it as the advice of someone who experiences lunacy and psychos first hand on almost a daily basis-go upstairs, take a bath, and bang you head against the wall until you come back to our reality!"

I paused. "Ok, you don't like the idea and…"

"You're darn tooting I don't like the idea." We were in the main hall of the brothel. The other girls were starting to take notice of our discussion. Cassandra leaned over by me and began whispering. "Listen, I love both you and Toni Lyn. You two are great kids. But this just can not happen in this area. This is not the kind of area that holds talent shows. Talent shows are held in small towns with a normal culture. What I mean is this is not middle America. We are in the dirtiest, most perverted area of the world. Every fetish in the world roams this street with no fear of law or imprisonment. This is not the place that would take warmly to a talent show where people sing songs by Bette Midler."

I sighed. Why was everyone having such a hard time grasping my vision? "The right people will come to the show."

"The right people don't go to brothels, Henry," Cassandra sighed. "The right people don't live in Amsterdam. So the chances of you having the right people show up to see a talent show in a brothel in Amsterdam is pretty slim."

"I think it would be great for the girls."

"What did you think they were going to do?" This part seemed to intrigue her.

"Well, they can sing," I quickly stated. "I know some of them can sing."

"Ok, what else?"

"Well, I know some can act. Maybe a few can do a scene from a play."

"Acting, singing, what else?"

"I don't know," I said, "I guess it depends on the different kinds of talents the girls have."

"You mean like fucking?" Cassandra asked. "You'd like them to fuck on stage."

"Of course not," I replied appalled. "This would be a more…" I tried to find the right word to finish my thought….

"If you say 'wholesome' or 'family orientated,' I will slap you back to reality myself." Cassandra was starting to get really annoyed with me.

"Well, can I at least bring the idea up with the girls," I sighed. "Maybe they will like it?"

Cassandra flung up her hands in annoyance and began walking away. "Sure, whatever, go ahead. Share your lunacy with everyone!.. I can just see their reaction to it already. They are going to be…

Stunned.

The girls were all stunned. Some of them actually had their mouths fall open in surprise. Wang scratched her head. They all looked among themselves to see if they just imagined what was just discussed. When they all saw how shocked the others were they all turned their attention back to me.

"Well?" I asked. I smiled wider. (Maybe I am going nuts?).

Nothing.

Nothing.

Nothing.

"I kind of like it." It was someone in the back that said it. All the girls looked back at the voice. It was Sue in her blonde pigtails. "It might be fun," She said quickly (As if to support her own sanity). She began playing with her pigtails. When that did not turn the attention away from her, she went on the defensive. "What?!"

Nothing.

Nothing.

"It would be something interesting to do," Ingrid stated slowly.

Nothing.

"It definitely hasn't been done before," Alice said simply.

"It'd be nice to be known for something other than the horizontal tango," Emma sighed.

"I think it's extremely out there and because of that I like it," Liz stated proudly.

"I've a question, Henry," Wang said quickly.

"What is it?" I asked.

"Can I use my whip?"

I paused. Would you say no? "Of course you can Mistress Wang."

"Then I'm in," Wang stated.

Soon all the girls were discussing excitedly what they were going to do and what they wanted to do.

Somewhere in the back of the room, under the sound of the excited prostitutes I heard the clap of Cassandra's palm slapping her forehead in frustration. The girls liked my idea! My vision was going to become a reality. I couldn't wait to get back up to my room and rub my success in Toni Lyn's face by sarcastically saying…

"And you called me mad," I laughed proudly at Toni Lyn. We were back in our room. It was evening. She was again brushing her teeth (We don't have a dental plan at the House of Pleasure-which is odd if you consider some of the actions the girls use their mouths for—so we have to be extra careful in regards to our teeth.).

"Oh, you're mad," She said with her toothbrush hanging out of the side of her mouth. "You're definitely off your rocker."

"Mad like a Van Gogh," I said proudly.

I opened the window over our bed and allowed the sounds and the night air of Amsterdam to come in. I had this strange feeling of immortality because of this vision.

Toni Lyn walked into our bedroom and looked at me standing there in front of the window. "You really are happy about this, aren't you?" She asked.

I turned to her with a smile and reached out my hand. She took it. I swung her around until she was in my arms in front of the window. I pointed out at the streets below us. "I hate to say this, but I think this is our home."

"My home is with you," Toni Lyn said quietly.

Pause.

We both started laughing. "My God that was corny!" I laughed.

"I know, I know," Toni Lyn Laughed. "I just had to see what that sounded like."

"Funny… Funny…Whew…"

CHAPTER 71

The Try Out List for "The Talent Show."

NAME   TALENT

_____   _____

_____   _____

_____   _____

_____   _____

_____   _____

_____   _____

_____   _____

_____   _____

_____   _____

SIGN UP BABY!

CHAPTER 72

— (HALFWAY THROUGH THE FIRST

REHEARSAL FOR THE TALENT SHOW

I GAVE THE FOLLOWING SPEECH.)

My Show Speech

"Ok, that's it cut! Cut! Cut!" I stood up and jumped up on our makeshift stage. I picked up Cat's clothes and handed them back to her. "Take this." I turned back to the other performers. "I don't want to say this one more time. The… Clothes… Stay… On! They do not come off. In the middle of a Romeo And Juliet scene where are your clothes? They're on! In the middle of a song where are you clothes? They're on! And where are your clothes when you're performing a dance from Swan Lake? Yes! They're on! Not off! It's not Nude Swan Lake… Or would that be feather-less Swan Lake? Nevermind. The point is your clothes are forever on. Well, not forever on, but while they're on stage they are on. I mean, you have to take off your clothes sooner or later or… Just a second…."

"What?

"What?

"Ok, if your talent is stripping you can take your clothes off, but only if it's decent and mature and artistic…

"Just out of curiosity, how many people here are stripping?

"Oh dear God! You people must have other talents than that…. I'm sure you do, just think…. For example, when you were in high school did you do anything… OK, that was not a joke. What did you do instead of taking off your clothes?…

"You lost it at that age? You must be kidding.

"Ok, ok, back to the subject.

"The point of this show is to allow the people of Amsterdam to see another side of you than the skin. What you are below and underneath, in your soul, in your mind…. I know most people don't care about what's going on under there, but we've got to make them care. You're all more than that…

"How about this? This might explain what I mean? When Toni Lyn… Sorry, Mistress Wang… When Maggie and I came here, I admit I had a hard time seeing you as people beyond the flesh. There was something unreal about all of you. Like you were not human…. Wait, this get's better. Then over time Maggie and I got to know all of you. We've gotten to know the real people. The real yous… Ok, I know that's bad English but it's true. You're all our friends. You're more than friends; we take care of each other and help each other…

"Ok, I'm getting a little teary…

"I'll be fine…

"I'm fine…

"I want the people of Amsterdam to know how damn luck they are to be with you girls. I want them to know how special you are. I want them to see you as I do. They are not having sex with only a piece of meat and breasts; they are having sex with real people. Beautiful, funny, warm real people….

"So let them see another side of you during the show. Don't be afraid to show your other talents. I want to hear you sing. I want to see you dance.

I want to see you perform whatever else you do to the best of your ability. Impress and surprise them just like you do for me everyday….

"There.

"That's all I had to say…

"Now, I'm going to go get a much needed beer…"

Chapter 73

—Second To Last

Night of Rehearsal....

"Maggie!… Maggie!…" I was waving at Toni Lyn as she was working on the stage. "Try to lower the curtain a little on the left…. A little more… A little more…" The curtain collapsed in a pile on the ground. "Ok, that's a little too much."

"Wang! Wang!" I shouted interrupting her practice.

"Yes, yes!" She glared at me. "What is it, you little man?"

"I think you're great, really I do…. Little man?"

"Get to the point, Henry!"

"When you throw the knives could you possibly change what you shout when you throw them?"

She angrily sighed. "What is wrong with my shout?"

"I think it's wrong to shout, 'Die' during a knife throwing act… Maybe that's just me, I don't know… Look at poor Sue, you made her wet herself…"

"See Emma you must become the swan when you dance. The elegance of the swan must sing from your soul through your feet. Dance the dance. See watch how I move and sway like the bird. Watch my arms see how they move like…. No, I'm not gay! Stop laughing."

"That's looking great, Maggie," I was shouting at the stage. She was placing a set up on stage for the Romeo and Juliet scene that Cat and Vicki were doing.

"Thanks," Toni Lyn said back to me. She had her Cubs cap on and one of my old T-shirt (one of the few that remained from my old backpack).

"Can you just maybe try to move it a little more to the right?"

She looked back at me annoyed (She tried to hide the annoyance. Like she can hide anything from me). "Right?" She then mumbled something under her breath to herself. I didn't bother to ask what was said.

"Yeah," I said, "Just a little…"

The set collapsed to the ground.

"Ok, that's a little too much…."

"Can I shout, Ahhhhh!" Wang asked me. I was sitting there watching Cat and Vicki act on stage and Maggie sat down next to me.

"What do you mean? Just "ahhhhhh?""

"No, I will try to put more danger and anger behind it than that. Like this: **Ahhhhhhh!!**"

The action on the stage stopped. Everyone turned to look at Wang.

"That's may be a little too loud," I sighed.

Toni Lyn and I were sitting in the audience quietly watching Cat and Missy performing a scene on the stage. Toni Lyn leaned over to me and whispered, "It's odd…"

"I think they're doing great," I whispered.

"No, not that," Toni Lyn whispered. "It's that when you think about it. This is all odd."

"How do you mean?"

"Here we are in a brothel in Amsterdam watching two prostitutes perform a scene from Beckett's **Waiting For Godot**."

"I guess that is a little odd," I laughed back.

Pause.

"They're doing a great job, aren't they?" I asked her.

"Wonderful," She replied.

The girls were in the middle of singing "Seasons of Love" from the musical **Rent**. It was Toni Lyn's idea. She loves the musical. Also, it seemed like a classic way to end the show. Picture it—All the girls walking out in their costumes from the night, holding hands and singing together such a positive song about love…. Granted, it's sad to think of the life the have to go back to after the song is completed…

Toni Lyn leaned over by me and whispered. "I wish I could be on stage."

"You knew you would feel this way after you recommended this song to them…"

"I know," she sighed back. "I set myself up for this. I love this song."

Cassandra came up to me after rehearsals. "I will have the programs tomorrow."

"Who is making them?" I asked. I had my clipboard in front of me and was reviewing the sets backstage (I looked really important). I turned to her. "No wait! Let me guess. Skinny Billy? Potty Toddy?"

She frowned. "His name is Sigmund and he works at Kinko's copy center."

This was just as surprising. "They have a Kinkos in the redlight district of Amsterdam?"

Cassandra sighed. "They had the best rates. I'll have them tomorrow, director." She walked away.

I looked down at my clipboard and shook my head. "Kinkos….."

Back in our room—-

Toni Lyn was walking around our room a little frustrated. "I wish I could take part in the show...."

"It's safer..." I began to explain (We've discussed this before).

"I know it's safer, I just wish I could be taking part in the show, that's all." She sighed. She stood still with her legs separated and began to stretch. She was stiff after the day's work.

And as I watched her moan and stretch her tired muscles... There was something... She was sweaty.... She was still wearing that old white t-shirt of mine. She had her cap on backwards and her hair was sticking out around the base of the hat.... It was odd how it all seemed to move in slow motion for me—How she removed her hat, wiped her brow and stuck it back on.... All I could say was "Wow."

She looked at me confused. "What?" (I can't hide anything from her.) Suddenly she started hysterically laughing. "You can't be serious? This turns you on?"

"Hi, there, baby." I tried to sound sexy. I laid down on the bed and began to strike sexy poses on the sheets and under them... This only made her laugh louder. After my sixth pose, I looked up at her annoyed. "Hey, this is good stuff. Fatty would pay big bucks for a talent like this."

"So this is your talent?" She laughed. "Maybe it's a good thing we aren't in the show..." She walked over to the bed. I smiled (I still got it). "Move over," She said and sat on the edge of the bed. She then proceeded to face away from me and take off her shoes.

I watched her from the back as she leaned over the shoes. I could read from her body language that something was really bothering her. "What is it?"

She looked back at me (She knew she couldn't hide anything from me for long). "I was just wondering if we were going to perform in the show, what our talent would be. I just can't think of many options for us. You can't act."

"Hey!" I protested. She looked at me annoyed. "Ok, I agree with you there."

She sighed and laid down on the bed alongside me.

"Well, there is something we're really good at."

She looked over at me. "I know," she sighed even louder, "but we already told the girls that can't be done on stage."

CHAPTER 74

Cassandra's House Of Pleasure
First Annual Talent Show

A Private Show for close friends and associates

Hosted by Cassandra

With directions by Henry Jones.
Sets by Maggie Jones.

-A selection from **Swan Lake**.
    a dance solo by Emma.

-"Minnie The Moocher."
    sung by Missy.

-The Balcony scene from **Romeo And Juliet**.
    Cat= Romeo.
    Vicki= Juliet.

-"Sonata OP. 13 in C Minor" by Beethoven.
    a solo piano piece performed by Cassandra.

-"Wind Beneath My Wings."
    sung by Alisha.

—15 Minute Intermission—

-"Rockin' Robin."
    Highlights from **Grease**.
    "As Time Goes By."
    sung by Alice, Ingrid, Maria, Sue and Alisha.

-Knives and Whips on Parade.
    performed my Mistress Wang with her lovely assistant Sue.

-A scene from **Waiting For Godot**.
    Cat= Estragon.
    Missy= Vladimir.

-The Fight for Beauty—An experimental dance number.
    dancers= Stacey and Liz.

-"Seasons of Love."
    The entire cast.

————

Toni Lyn was in the bathroom getting out of the shower. It was at that moment I started the CD Player.

She walked out of the bathroom confused. "What are…" She didn't finish her sentence. She was too confused by the fact I was standing there in a tux. She started laughing. "What are you doing?"

"I'm going to dance with you," I replied.

"What?" She asked confused.

"This is what we would have done in the show. We would have danced."

"Ok," she replied slowly. "But I'm naked."

"I know, come here." I held out my hand.

"I'm wet," She stated quickly.

"It's Maria's tux. Quick before Nat begins singing." I held out my hand.

She slowly reached out and took my hand. Her towel dropped. I smiled at her and we began slowly dancing....

"A Thousand Thoughts
of You"
-Sung by Nat "King" Cole.

A thousand thoughts of you
Will haunt me ever after
The music of your laughter
Will serenade my heart-

A thousand thoughts of you
Will roam the night and find me-
The chains of love will bind me
To dreams that won't depart-
Your face-
Your smile-
The moonlight in your hair-
Your lips.-
I'll see them everywhere-

A thousand kisses too
Will keep me reminiscing-
For there will be no dismissing
A thousand thoughts of you-

A thousand kisses too
Will keep me reminiscing-
For there will be no dismissing
A thousand thoughts of you-

"I love dancing with you," I said. "It's like we are making love on the floor."

"I feel so elegant with you..."
"I'm going to dip you," I interrupted.
"That's certainly different when you're nude."
"Funny man..."

"Fred Astaire eat your heart out..."
"I do admit we are elegant together..."

"This is what Jane Austen meant," she said softly to me, leaning her head on my shoulder....

"Great writer," I sighed...
"The best."

I smiled at her.

She smiled back.

"We would be the best thing performing," I said happily.

"Oh, yeah," she agreed. "We're incredible…"

"And we really don't want to make the girls feel bad…"

"So it's probably better we don't dance for them…"

"I agree…"

We paused and just happily looked at each other. So much perfection. Everything I have ever loved about being alive came from these moments with her. These little moments of blessing. "I love you, Mrs. Jones," I said softly.

"I love you, Mr. Jones," she replied.

We kissed….

CHAPTER 75

The show began exactly as I expected it would. Although Cassandra limited the audience to friends of the performers, it was still filled with many people from the adult industry. So when the curtain went up, the air was quickly filled with the applause and catcalls that you would expect at the beginning of a burlesque show. And the matter wasn't helped when Cassandra (playing Host) proceeded to greet the audience with dirty and low brow humor.

As a director, I was ready for all this. That was one of the reasons I opened with Emma dancing to Swan Lake. She is a great dancer and her grace and elegance couldn't help but set the serious mood for the evening. Her dance changed the audience. I watched the faces from the crowd and you could see the expressions changing from one of sexual interest to one of respect. When her number ended the audience was silent. And then slowly the applause began. She had won over the audience. She did it. From there, we just had to keep it fun.

The next number livened the party up a little. Missy came out and sang the song "Minnie The Moocher." It's hard not to have fun with this song. The audience sang right along with her. By the end of the song, the audience was clapping in tempo.

And from there, the first part sped on. The scene from **Romeo And Juliet**, made members of the audience weep. Cassandra wowed them all with her amazing performance of a piano piece by Beethoven. And the first part ended with the almost high school talent show standard of "Wind Beneath My Wings" which Alisha dedicated to her dead mother (How can a person not be moved by such a thought?).

So, by the end of the first part of the evening, the entire atmosphere of the audience had changed. These were no longer adult entertainers and suppliers; they were just another audience, enjoying another regular show. When I went backstage during the intermission to compliment the girls, the air was buzzing with the excitement. They were loving this. Everyone was smiling and running around in controlled excitement. Toni Lyn ran over to me and gave me a kiss. "This is working out wonderfully," She said to me.

"What can I say?" I replied. "I'm a genius."

I then gave the girls a quick pep talk ("You're doing great! The audience loves you! Keep it up! I'm really proud of all of you!") and then went back to my seat.

The second half seemed to fly by (Time flies when you're… You know the rest). It began with five of the girls singing together. It was the five that sang outside Toni Lyn and my door on our fake wedding day—Alice, Ingrid, Maria Alisha and Sue. What was really cool was when they went into their last number they dedicated it "to the Joneses." Toni Lyn held my hand tightly as they sang "As Time Goes By."

Then came the heart stopping knife throwing and whip showcase of Mistress Wang. When she stepped out on stage the audience applauded until she shouted, "Stop applauding!… Good. Now shut up and watch!" And they did just that. Who would do otherwise? And as the act went on the audience grew more and more in fear of Wang. It got to such a point that when she was over with her act she had to tell them to "Applaud now!" And of course, they did. She smiled wickedly, shouted "No encores!" and went off stage.

Then began the part of the evening Cat demanded. As she said at our first discussion of the play, "If I have to play that damn, smoochy Romeo I get to do Godot. Period." And she did. It was only a little bit of it but

Cat pulled it off. And she went through the emotions and serious comedy of it with all the gusto she had available. All Missy could do was keep up with her lines (And she really tried). Cat was actually trying to make it as an actor in New York when a need for money moved her down another path. When she took her bow, you could see she got something from that moment. A part of her that she had cut off so many years ago smiled. I've never seen someone so happy with herself before... Beauty.

The next dance number I was initially a little worried about. Here we were giving the audience just what they originally wanted—Nudity. Would we lose the mindset we just put in them or would they return to their earlier desires? As the clothes were torn more and more off (It was supposed to be a very symbolic dance. Through the number we see Liz changed from a smartly dressed professional woman to a naked, cowering woman by the force of society which was represented by Stacey). Happily, there were fewer hoots and hollers than I expected (You had to assume there would be a few).

Then came the ending. It was the ending Toni Lyn thought up. The ending she would've wanted to take part in. The cast casually walked out on stage and sang "Seasons of Love" from **Rent**.

Then the applause came.... Wait, it didn't just come, it erupted! You could not hold back the smiles from the girls as they bowed again and again to that thankful audience. It was a beautiful moment and you could see that beauty in everyone in those smiles.

Perfect.

A Scene from the Cast Party—

Cassandra got up on the table. She had her wineglass in her hand. "Excuse me! Excuse me! Can I have your attention? Please... Yes, you too... Thank you... I just wanted to say thank you to two very special people. All you girls know who I mean. Since they came here, they've changed this little brothel into more than a brothel. Well, we are still a brothel. I mean we still do the nasty and all but, what I mean… Oh, God! Look, I'm even talking like Henry!"

All the girls laughed.

I looked around confused. "What's that supposed to mean?"

"Anyway, anyway," Cassandra said waving away the laughter. "They are my personal favorite fake married couple. And I love them both."

All the girls went "Owwwwww."

"Shut up!" Cassandra waved her arm again (Some wine flew out of her glass). "These are two special and beautiful kids. And I'm glad they're here. Raise your glasses all to Henry and Maggie Jones."

All the girls raised their glasses.

"Thank you both for tonight. (Maggie held my hand and laid her head on my shoulder. I smiled.) A night none of us will forget. Thank you. To the Joneses."

All the girls said, "To the Joneses…."

"To the Joneses…."

(echo….)

"To The Joneses…"

"Joneses…"

CHAPTER 76

—The Review from The Amsterdam Adult Entertainers Weekly Newspaper.

Cassandra's House Of Pleasure Gives Pleasure To A Group Of Men!

Well, it was certainly a hot time in the old town that night! And if you were one of the lucky friends of **Cassandra's House of Pleasure** it was certainly a night you would not forget. The girls put on a show that this reviewer can not help but call one word **"HOOT."** The extra "O" is for "Oh, wow."

The show began with an extremely **sensual** and **erotic** dance number by Emma (one of Cassandra's regulars). I couldn't help but readjust myself during her performance. **SEXY!** By the end, I couldn't help but be grateful after reminding myself how exceptional the prices are at Cassandra's.

Next Missy (all the performers were regulars) came out and sang a song about a woman that **fuck**ed around. All the audience got into that train of thought (Many sang right along). And it was easy to do considering the hot little number Missy was wearing. In the light of the spotlight, it was hard to leave anything to the imagination other than the concept of **taking off those clothes.**

Next on the menu of **sexual delicacies** was the raunchy show of one woman seducing another. It was an incredible turn on watching these two girls playing around with each other when we all knew they wanted nothing more than to **get it on!**

There were some other little acts here and there and then came the second act. Some of those highlights were Mistress Wang throwing her knives and working her whips. And many couldn't help but smile at the way she held her knives in her hands. **Stroking** them up and down and then throwing them near her beautiful assistant, Sue. You could tell that the two performers were **very close.** After they were done I couldn't help but close my eyes and picture their celebration for a show well done later up in the **bedchambers.**

Next, was a short excerpt of a play. Screw the symbolism of the work. If I was Godot and I knew such fine babes were waiting for me, I would have been there in two heartbeats. They wouldn't have to wait for me, that's for sure. I would also have made their short wait **worth their while** if you catch my drift. I'm sure they would have.

Following that was an **extreme** dance number. **FUCKING GREAT!** The women moved so in time you couldn't help but wish you were in between them as their **giant heaving breasts** kept tempo. Helping them move. Feeling their **naked** skin **rubbing** against you.

The show ended with the girls all welcoming the audience to join in the **LOVE.** And, guys, trust me on this one-you can't help but love women like this. So my advice to all the men who read this: if you're horny and want to give your boner some much-needed attention—**don't hesitate.**

Go right to **Cassandra's House Of Pleasure!!**

———

"I can't believe this!" I threw the newspaper aside. "They make the entire evening sound like a sex fest."

Toni Lyn leaned over and laid her head on my shoulder. We were in our room. I was sitting on the edge of the bed and she was sitting behind me. "It's ok. You did a great job. The girls know that."

"I was hoping for people to see a different side of them and…"

"But you did that," Toni Lyn reassured. "Everyone who was there saw that. They were seen as real people last night."

"But…"

She interrupted me. "The person that wrote that article had to do it that way. It's an adult newspaper. He has to make everything sound that way. If he said what really happened last night he'd probably lose his job." She wrapped her arms around me. "And if he really didn't like the show, do you think he would have praised it so much? He's trying to get the girls some business. And considering what a slow season it is right now, the girls will probably be very thankful."

She was right. She was always right (Except for maybe the safe thing). "What would I ever do without you," I sighed.

"I have no idea," She sighed in return.

I leaned my head back to meet her lips.

"Thank you," I said after we stopped kissing.

"For what?" She asked with a smile.

"For giving me a life," I replied. "For giving me a reason to live. For teaching me how to breathe. For everything."

"I don't know if I can take credit for everything," She laughed. "I love you, Mr. Jones."

"I love you, Mrs. Jones." I began to kiss her again and softly…

Ever so softly…

We began to make love…

Neither of us knew it was to be our last evening together.

CHAPTER 77

Henry James knocked on my door at exactly 11AM.

I didn't respond.

He knocked again.

Again I didn't respond… See, I was in my own world by this point and I knew in a second it was going to crash down again. The second he enters my rooms, my time with her in Amsterdam would end. I would wake up from the dreams. I didn't want the dreams to end. I wanted the days and the images and the moments and the touches to keep going like they should have. I wanted us to earn enough money to move out of the brothel, get a real apartment. We would find jobs. We would have a child. A beautiful child and we would stay together forever holding hands…. And the second, Henry James entered my apartment that part of me would disappear again…. And the me that was there in Amsterdam, was almost back. I was almost there again through those words, through those chapters. I was having conversations with her. And even at one point I swear, I truly swear, I saw her in my rooms. She was right there standing in front of me in my dusty living room in her white wedding lingerie holding her hand out to me. And all I had to do was to take that hand and I would be dancing with her again…. And I did… I stood up in my apartment and took her close and we danced. And when I closed my eyes, I could hear the girls singing again so sweetly….

As Time Goes By...

And… and… and… Henry James entered my apartment…

Time to wake up.

"You said you would be almost done with Amsterdam, by 11 AM so I thought I would come by and see how it was going." Henry James instantly began to walk over to the pages on my desk. He paused when he reached the desk. He looked at me a little stunned. He could see that something was wrong. I must have looked so pale to him. I was woken up again, but he would never understand what that meant to me… "Are you ok?"

"I'm fine," I mumbled at him. "I'm… fine. All fine."

He turned back to the pages on my desk. "How far are you?" He began to go through the papers and the words…. They were more than pages… They were all I had of a soul and he had the nerve to say, "A lot of dialogue, it seems. Some of these chapters, I really don't think can be considered chapters…"

"They aren't chapter," I said quietly. "They are collections of images. They are my dreams of that time…"

"Where are you right now?"

"I'm on our last day in Amsterdam," I said quietly. "I'm almost done."

He flipped through some more pages. "How could you remember all this dialogue?" He seemed amazed. "Did you make any of this up?"

"No," I stated. "I didn't make any of it up… I remember everything. Everything." It felt so early to me (on so many different levels) and for some reason I felt it was important to repeat everything.

"But there are over a hundred pages of conversations here alone. How did you remember all of this?" He asked, stunned.

I didn't tell him how I retraced those conversations a hundred times a day in my head. I didn't tell him how I could still hear her voice. I didn't tell him how I could close my eyes at any time and hear her laughter. I instead told him to "Shut up, Henry."

He, of course, did not shut up. "So how were you caught?"

"It wasn't a matter of being caught. It was a matter of being found," I sighed. "Both Toni Lyn and I knew it was only a matter of time…"

It was a slow night in the redlight district of Amsterdam. Only two of the prostitutes were working. Toni Lyn and I were playing poker with 3 of the other ones. We all had nothing better to do (Liz was in the office trying to fix the fussball table. Vicki was still in trouble with everyone at the brothel for that night). It also was an opportunity to earn some extra cash. I am lousy at poker, but poker is another gift in Toni Lyn's repertoire. Probably another talent skill by her family. I never asked her who taught her to play so well… I probably would have that night.

It was very humorous to watch her play. She always liked to wear a hat and smoke a cigar when she played. It was like it was all a requirement for her. She had her Cubs baseball cap on backwards and she was smoking a Cuban cigar. She was also wearing an old t-shirt and jeans. I was sitting next to her. The other 3 at the table were Cat, Alice and Ingrid. They were, of course, dressed in their working clothes… Or maybe it's better to say lack of clothes…. To tell you the truth I had no idea where they kept their money on their persons. Seriously where are pockets on sexy lingerie?.. But man, did they have a lot of it on them.

It was about 9PM and we were up by about two hundred American dollars when a knock came on the door. The girls instantly rose from the table and joined the girl in charge (It was Vicki that night) in a straight line in front of the door. Toni Lyn sighed and leaned back in her chair. She looked over at me and slightly smiled. "Why is it every time I've a great hand someone happens to knock on that door?"

I smiled back at her and slowly reached over and touched her face. I slowly rubbed my hand against her cheek. It was a natural motion for me. I didn't think much about it. I had no idea what was going to happen in the next few minutes. *At that moment, I just wanted to touch her. Something in me needed to touch her. She smiled and leaned her cheek more into my hand... She let out a little sigh and closed her eyes... And it was then that my soul left me. I left myself on that check, all my love; all myself was left with her. .... My soul went with her... It somehow knew what was going to happen when my hand moved away from the check of my great love... In just a short instant....*

The police walked into the parlor.

Everyone quickly reacted at the same time. The girls at the door all scurried around with hands over their heads stating in many different languages (This is a trained maneuver to confuse the cops, make it seem more difficult than it is actually is.) that this was ok. Vicki (as per her job) was already getting in the face of the first police officer stating that this was perfectly legal and there was nothing questionable going on here. The bodyguard on duty quickly walked up the stairs to notify the two women with their customers.

Toni Lyn and I did not react.

I guess we had become so complacent in our existence that we were never expecting to get caught yet (We both wouldn't admit we knew it was coming. We both just thought it would be another day.). We thought this was just another raid. No big deal. It wasn't until Jon walked through the door followed by some fellow Italians in suits that we realized that this was different.

"Holy shit," Toni Lyn exclaimed and quickly began to get out of her seat.

I quickly began to get up to, but… Unfortunately, Jon and the people with him were prepared for our reaction. Before I knew it, I was tackled to the ground and handcuffed.

I didn't struggle.

I didn't complain.

Strangely, it all felt very eerie… See, that wasn't me getting captured. That wasn't me getting kicked in the stomach. That wasn't me being arrested by cops. That was not me. My soul was still surviving in the last touch…. I left myself on her cheek… I was there until I could return to her….

Toni Lyn…

"I remember Toni Lyn arguing a lot," I said to Henry. He was making me breakfast. All he knew how to make was scrambled eggs. "I don't know what she was saying. Maybe I don't want to remember…."

Henry James walked out of the kitchen with two plates of eggs. He placed them on the table. I sat down in front of the food…. I didn't feel like eating. I looked down at the food and spoke. "They took me to the embassy. The embassy turned me over to the local authorities. Both my family and my country abandoned me. I was then put in prison for five years. What goes on in a jail in Amsterdam is… That… It's all… I…"

Henry James looked up from his food at me. This was something I haven't discussed with him yet….

"Have you seen Sylvia Plath lately?" I asked him.

He paused. He spoke slowly. "She's still having her little rebellion. She hasn't left her room in two days."

"What's she doing?" I asked. I still didn't look up. There was something about the eggs that captivated my eyes…

"You should go and see," He said. "It's stupid, but she's proud of it. The Happy Angels are going to have a field day with her soon… Why do you want to see her?"

"I want to do something different for the ending," I said. "Maybe something more poetic."

Instantly, Henry James was annoyed I didn't ask him for help. He ate the rest of his eggs in silence.

The dreams are over….

PART 5—GRAND RAPIDS

The lunatic, the lover, and
the poet are of imagination
all compact.
—William Shakespeare

*[The following is a copy
of the pamphlet given to a
dead who has gone 3 years
without a major incident.]*

Greetings!

You're still dead.

>>>

Our records show that you have gone 3 years without creating a major incident in heaven that could have jeopardized the angel/ dead relationships.

For learning to conform and not bring more grief upon your fellow dead, we are passing on to you THE MEANING OF LIFE.

WARNING:::

These facts should not be given to anyone else. Also, you should be prepared that the facts contained herein have been known to cause extreme depression.

Read at your own risk.

To begin with:::

The true creation story (all the goodbits we have learned so far).

God is from an extremely old race. They live on a different plane of existence from us.

For some reason, God was alienated from the rest of his race (Go figure). Some believe that was because of his lack of feelings or because of some kind of crime he comitted. Some, however, argue he is some kind of a mental patient who had gone inside his own head.

The point is God is alone.... and more than likely not by his own choice.

As God sat alone for a few days, he began to talk to himself. In a Freudian manner, he began to talk to his Superego and Id. These traits soon grew into characters. As time went on these two different sides became distinct and separate. They became the first angels and devils. Good. Evil. No emotions. Just pure beliefs. These sides would fight and argue for God's amusement.

However after a few decades of watching these parties fight each other, God became bored as well. So, he created a race that was a combination of both. God also gave this race a new power the older races in his head did not have. He gave them the power of freedom of choice... And to add an extra dash of spice, emotions.

(If you can't figure it out, that was us).

Man was created with the power to think for himself and act for himself. He was highly unpredictable. His unpredictability annoyed the angels and the devils and during the first centuries of its existence they would talk or work with the men to try and manipulate them to work normally in God's way. But over time, this only annoyed God.

God wanted Man to be free, so he separated the Angels and Devils from Man. So the Angels and the Devils had to stand by and watch (with their distinct morals in hand) as Man played in the spiritual wind.

However, God became bored with this and began to play with humans. He put obstacles in their way. He would create havoc and destruction through weather and the many other means at his disposable. Would this make the person great? Would it lead to suicide? It was all a game.

God was playing with his creation.

During the reign of the Roman Emperor Augustus Caesar, a special man was born. God found this man extremely interesting and would make wonderful things happen for that man at the slightest touch. No one could understand why water would change into wine for this man or why he could bring back the dead. God was playing with this man as well. All part of his little game. But to God's horror, some men destroyed Jesus and sent him into the nothingness. This devastated God. He liked Jesus and wanted to play with him more. So God brought him back into existence.

So Jesus went back to Earth. As you can well imagine, his returned presence there only caused more problems. So God decided to create a special place for him to live. Therefore, God created Heaven.

As time went on God met other unique men and women that amused him. And to reward these individuals God would send them as well to Heaven….

And that bring you up to date to where we are today. And this naturally leads into THE MEANING OF LIFE.

The entire purpose of your life….

The point of your existence….

The meaning behind all your pain....

"You're entertainment."

We are only here to entertain God.

Consider yourself a retired actor.

Over the years, God has created an elaborate scale. It ranges from one to ten. If your life has been entertaining enough to reach above a six, you get to go on to Heaven. However, if you are below the six line you must go back to earth and live another life.

This existence is our reward for a job well done. This immortality is his way of saying thanks for the memories.

We Hope You Enjoy the Rest of your FOREVER.

Chapter 78

I ripped the pamphlet up and threw it away down the street.

Fuck them all! Fuck them!

How the Hell is knowing that supposed to make me feel better?

Fuck them!

I turned and began walking to Sylvia Plath's place.

Fuck them all.

"SYLVIA!" I threw another rock at the window of her apartment. "For Christ's sake, Sylvia open your god damn door!" That pamphlet put me in a bad mood.

Her window opened ever so slightly. Then I heard that familiar voice shriek down at me. "Leave me alone I don't want to be happy. I've had enough happy, thank you very much."

"Sylvia," I shouted. "It's me. It's not the Happy Angels."

She opened the window wider and then her head peeked out. It was Sylvia, but she looked... She looked dirty. How did she get dirty? And how did she get so dirty so fast? Her hair flopped over the front of her head like a rag. "What the hell do you want?" She called.

"I need your help with something. Can I come up?" I asked.

"With your great book? Of course, of course. I'll buzz you in." Her head disappeared back into the apartment. I sighed and waited for that annoying little song... Oh, just a second.

A quick explanation-

When Rome switched over to Modern Rome, the Happy Angels made some changes they thought would be viewed as positive. One such change is they replaced all the buzzers and doorbells throughout the city with a little song. It was to remind the dead residents every day how lucky and special they were. The recording was of the Heavenly Choir (All the record stores are filled with their music—You actually have to go underground and to bootleg stores to get real music). And they are singing just one simple line:

"Welcome to the home of another blessed."

Sylvia opened her door quickly once I made it up the two floors. "I hate that song. If I could find a way to get people up here without a door, I would. I was thinking about a rope and pulley system, but when I asked for a rope the Happy Angels wanted a specific reason. God, I wish they would allow us to do our own work for a change."

"We don't have to listen to the song anymore. Lennon found a way to turn it off 3 days after they installed it."

She laughed at that and motioned me in. "I'm going to have to talk to John about that."

Her rooms were a pigsty! The ground was covered with newspapers and filth covered most of the furniture. And what was that smell? She waved her arms around her apartment showing off the mess. She was smiling wide. "Well, are you impressed?"

I smiled. "How did you ever pull this off?"

"It wasn't easy.... Look! Look at this!" She pointed at a spider web by her door. "An actual spider! I went back to Earth and got it. Isn't it great? Next week I hope to get some rats from the sewers in New York."

"Brilliant, just brilliant."

She waved her hand to blow off the compliment. "Let me get you a drink." She ran off to the kitchen. She called after herself. "It'll be a clean cup, I promise."

I took another look around the room. This truly was remarkable. I haven't seen a mess in years and here was one in all its glory.

"Take a seat," she called from the kitchen.

"Where?" I called back.

She laughed loudly at that and walked back into the room with two glasses. "Thanks," I said and took my glass. I took a quick swig. Plath always liked hard liquor.

"So why are you doing this?" I asked.

"The Great Unknown inspired me a few nights ago," She said. "I was walking around your building about two nights ago—I think it was about 3AM—when I…"

Sylvia Plath stopped in her tracks. Her thoughts on visiting her friend or the strict importance of writing disappeared from her mind. What was that smell? "It couldn't be," she whispered to herself. It was too good to be true. She breathed in the sweet smell again and let out a sigh. "Cigarettes," she sighed happily. The smell was coming from the alley near the building. She slowly looked into the dark alley. It was true…

"HI," The Great Unknown said. He took another puff on his cigarette.

Sylvia Plath couldn't believe the bliss that was in front of her. Screw the amazing possibility of talking with The Great Unknown, here were some actual cigarettes. She was so nervous and excited by the possibility of having one that she had a hard time getting out the words. "Could… I… I… have one?" She stuttered out.

The Great Unknown waved her forward. She lovingly took one of the cigarettes in her hand. She rubbed it between her fingers. The paper felt so smooth. "Camels," she sighed. She slowly lifted the cigarette and placed it in her mouth. Bliss. The Great Unknown leaned over and lit the cigarette for her.... And then.... Inhale... Ahhhhhh... She looked over at The Great Unknown. "Wherever did you get cigarettes?"

"I PICKED UP SOME ON SUNDAY WHEN I WAS BACK ON EARTH," The Great Unknown said.

"Why are you smoking them out here?" Plath asked. "You know you could get in trouble for this. They're illegal."

"YEAH, I FIGURED THAT," The Great Unknown sighed, "BUT THE ANGEL IN MY APARTMENT WOULDN'T LET ME SMOKE UP THERE."

Plath didn't bother to ask why an angel was up in his apartment. She was enjoying the experience too much to care about anything else. "Stupid angel…" Plath said absentmindedly.

"SHE SAID IT WAS A FILTHY HABIT," he sighed. "I DON'T THINK SHE WOULD KNOW REAL FILTH IF IT BIT HER ON THE ASS.

"So true, so true," Plath said.

"LIKE THEY'VE EVER SEEN A REAL MESS OR DIRT. I'D LIKE TO SEE HOW THEY WOULD REACT TO SUCH A DISPLAY. THEY'D PROBABLY FREAK OUT. KNOWING THEM, AFTER THAT THEY'D PROBABLY START WEARING GLOVES AND PROTECTIVE GEAR EVERYTIME THEY VISITED A DEAD."

"You're probably right," Plath said. This interested her. "I bet the angels would hate a mess…"

"Yeah, they'll hate this," I sighed.

"So how's the book going?" Plath asked. "I've been dying to come down to the AfterTaste to find out if you finally realized your stupidity."

I sighed even louder. "Thanks, Sylvia. Actually I'm on my last day and I'm right on schedule."

"Henry told me he's seen some of it," Sylvia said casually.

"And what did he tell you?" This might actually be interesting. Two important writers were discussing my work.

"He says you're forgetting something very important."

"What?"

"You." She pointed at me.

"What is that supposed to mean?" I asked.

"He says the book proves you haven't dealt with The Pain," she replied.

"The Pain"

That is the only name for it. In my opinion, it is complete bullshit. But here is the info on it anyway. There is a certain amount of baggage that comes with dying that it is believed the new dead have to get over. It has to deal with accepting one's death and finally separating oneself from the life left behind…. See, bullshit.

"What?" I asked annoyed.

"He says you're cold to yourself in the work and you never discuss the feeling of loss. He says it explains your lack of detail and development and…"

"That's bullshit," I replied.

"Sure it is," Sylvia Plath said (Is she being snobby to me?). "Sure it is. You've totally accepted the idea you're dead. (She is being sarcastic.) It's all a mature well thought out maneuver when you go back to your killer's jail cell and scare the shit out of him. How often do you do this anyway? Once a month?"

"I don't need to deal with this from you." I pointed at her.

"Avoiding the problem. So that's what worked for you over the last 3 years?"

I began walking to the door.

"Wait, just wait," she said slowly. "Maybe I can at least help you save this book. What do you need?"

I turned back to her. (What the Hell?). I still needed her help. (I can't believe she says I need to deal with The Pain). "I've reached a snag," I said.

"Well, where are you in the story?"

I sighed. I threw some newspapers off of one of her chairs and sat down. I'd just gotten out of jail in Amsterdam. I decided I was going to skip the explanation and details of my five years in that prison and get right to my return."

"Ok…" (I could see that this fact was connecting with her Pain theory. Move on. Move on.).

"First I worked my way across Europe. Then I worked my way across the Atlantic on a cargo ship."

"This is all good stuff."

"And then I hitched my way from New York to Michigan…"

"Building suspense, good. Make the reader want the reunion."

"Actually, I was going to skip all that too."

She looked up at me stunned. "Why would you skip all that?"

"I don't know…. I guess for me nothing is interesting unless she is in the story."

Plath laughed. "That's sweet, but not good storytelling."

I grimaced. (Control, control).

Someone knocked on her door.

"Just a second." She got up and moved over to her door. "Christ, it's Dickinson."

"Is she still on the pills?" I asked.

"She was almost off, but the Happy Angels got to her last week. They didn't like how she wouldn't leave her room so they spiked the food that was delivered to her room with the drug. After 3 days she was out and about."

Suddenly Emily Dickinson sang from the other side of the door. "Let me in Sylvia. I've brought a broom! Sylvia."

"Oh, my god," I moaned. Emily really did sound happy. She was actually singing!

"You see the evil in happiness?" Sylvia Plath said. "Ironic that they only way Dickinson could find happiness in Paradise was to have her personality, her self removed." She opened the door.

In bounded Emily Dickinson. She was wearing a bright dress covered with flowers, a large yellow hat and cleaning gloves. In her right hand, she held a green broom. She was living happiness. It was beaming out of every pore in her body (If that was possible she was accomplishing it). Even her teeth shown with a bright heavenly glow. "It's cleaning time, Sylvia."

"Go away, Emily," Sylvia sighed.

"You won't be able to get rid of me that easily, Sylvia." Emily pushed her way past Sylvia into her apartment. That was when she first noticed me. "Oh, my Saints in Heaven!" Emily dropped her broom and ran over to me. She wrapped her hands tightly around me and hugged. She happily swayed side to side as she hugged me. "Oh, I'm so happy to see you. So, so happy."

I struggled to get her arms off from around me (not as easy as you would think) and moved her a little back. "It's nice to see you too Emily."

"So how is the book going?" she asked quickly.

"Well…." I tried to answer.

"So why are you here?" She quickly interrupted. "Why don't you come to visit me anymore? All you do is hide out in your little coffeehouse and I never see you. You've got to come by more often. I so miss you." It was at this moment that she tried to give me a second hug. I quickly stepped back, avoiding her arms and looked over at Sylvia.

Sylvia could read the message of help on my face. "Emily," she began, "he came by to ask for some help on his book. So why don't you leave us alone and…"

"Oh, really," Emily responded in her very excited manner. "I'm all ears."

"Ok, well…" I tried to begin.

"Well," Emily interrupted. "I'm not all ears. Technically, I've only two. It's just an expression. A very odd expression. To tell you the truth I was never fond of it. I would not recommend using it in your book."

"I'll make a note of that," I responded slowly. The pills always have this effect on people. It's like speed but with a good dose of positive energy. A fast brainwash in a pill form.

"Emily, why don't you sit down and let him talk."

Emily quickly agreed. "Oh, I totally agree with you. That's a great idea. I'll just sit here….."

"See, what I want to do…."

"Well, maybe I won't sit here," Emily quickly corrected. "Frankly, I don't know how you could live in this filth, Sylvia. It's disgusting."

"Try again," Sylvia said as she angrily looked over at Emily. Emily didn't see the stare. She was too busy brushing the papers and wrappers off a leather chair.

I coughed and tried again. "I want to create the right…."

"I'll sit right here, Sylvia." Emily again interrupted.

Sylvia glared at her. "That will be fine," she said slowly.

"I just wanted you to know."

"And now I know."

"Yes, you do."

"So sit down."

"Ok." Emily sat down. "I'm sitting down now."

"That's great Emily."

Sylvia looked over at me and rolled her eyes. I'm amazed at how much patience Sylvia had for this. Most people would have been thrown out by now…. But I guess Emily Dickinson is different. "What is it?"

"Well, I'm jumping from this point to our reunion in Grand Rapids, Michigan. But I want to truly recreate what that felt like. I want them to feel it through the words I use. So I was thinking instead of writing a normal chapter, I would create a poem about the moment."

"Interesting idea," Sylvia said.

"Very interesting. I totally agree. Very interesting indeed." Emily quickly agreed.

"What do you have so far?" Sylvia asked.

I scratched the back of my head. "Nothing."

"Well, let's get out some paper and see what we can do…" Sylvia moved over to her desk. She sighed and threw off the piles of magazines on top of it. They scattered across the floor. Emily, after emitting a surprised squeal, jumped up quickly to clean the mess. Sylvia didn't even bother to tell her to stop.

Sylvia walked over to me and dropped the paper on my lap. "Take notes."

I suddenly had this feeling of being in college again with a strict professor glaring down my neck. Unconsciously I sat up straighter in my chair.

"Less is more," she first said. She spoke almost as if she was reciting a commandment.

"Ok," I responded.

"Write that down."

"I think I can remember that one. Trust me, with this book I've been living that cliche."

Sylvia glared at me. I sighed and wrote it down slowly. Sylvia began to pace around her room and speak at the same time. "In poetry that's true. However, you must choose your words carefully. It must come together like a puzzle in the mind of the reader. Let the words sing."

"You can sing my poems," Emily said. "I tried to think of my poems as little songs on paper."

Sylvia kept going with her lesson (she was in the zone). "Don't over express the moment though. Avoid words with strong feelings. Let those feelings be implied with other words."

"What do you mean?" I asked.

"'Love'," she explained, "is a great example. It is best to avoid the word 'love.' It can be implied with a look or a touch. It does not need to be spoken. It is viewed the same way in poetry."

"I don't agree with that, Sylvia," Emily interrupted. "Ever poem and every story is a different situation. In his story you're dealing with a couple that is truly in love. I don't think the word could be overused in such a poem. Let their love sing through the pages."

"One question I have," I asked," has to do with meter. I have a hell of a time writing in meter. So I thought I would go for a more modern feel to the poem to avoid the trouble."

Both Sylvia and Emily groaned. Sylvia was the first to comment. "I just knew the day we let that door open that all hell would break loose in poetry."

"So should I use meter?" I asked.

"It's your call," Emily said. "I'm sure either way will work."

Sylvia groaned even louder.

"Well, I came for help Sylvia. If you have some advice-give it to me."

Sylvia turned and quickly walked into her bedroom. She slammed the door behind herself.

Emily leaned over by me. "Poetry is her love. And she feels that her love is dying around her and there is nothing she can do about it. Post-modernism was hell on her. I still have hope for the future. But I'll give you some advice, ok?"

"Ok."

"Be true to yourself, the moment and your feelings. Let the words follow naturally. If you follow that path, you can't go wrong."

I sighed. I really didn't get anything out of this meeting. And I was starting to learn that I was dealing with an artform absent of rules. So how could I go wrong?

"Just let it flow," Emily said.

"I did that with an intro to my last part," I said to her. "It seemed to work for that."

"I can't wait to read it." Emily patted me on the top of the head (like you would a child after they said something good). She moved over to the door and picked up her broom where she left it. "Now I have some cleaning to do."

"Is she going to come out of her room?" I asked.

Emily shrugged her shoulders. "Who knows? Come back in a few days and maybe then we can help you. Maybe bring some notes on what you are planning to say."

"I can't do that," I sighed. "I promised myself I would finish the work quickly. I promised myself I would take 3 days to write it. The same amount of time it took me to fall in love. Today is the last day."

"A whole book in 3 days?" Emily looked up stunned.

"I haven't slept in days." I went to the door and walked out.

Emily began sweeping the floor again. She sighed. "He hasn't dealt with The Pain, poor boy...."

CHAPTER 79

I couldn't believe Henry James said that about me! How could he read
something like that in my book? I had dealt straightforwardly with all my
emotions. I talked about my love for her. I talked about how it felt to have
my parents ditch me like that. And through all that, he dared to say I still
didn't say enough? Like I had another side of myself to share…. And if
that was the case why talk about it behind my back? Why does he feel he
can't discuss The Pain with me? Is he afraid to bring it up with me? Why
would he be afraid to bring it up with me? He knows I think The Pain is
complete bullshit. I've mocked the concept of it a million times in front of
him. He laughed at my jokes. Why not bring it up?… I was asking myself
all these questions as I entered my apartment complex.

I walked up the stairs to my floor and… sitting on the carpet in the
hall…

Sitting on the floor of that hall against the door of The Great Unknown
was an angel. His angel. And she was crying… The angel was actually crying.

I was stunned. I paused and stared at the sight in front of me. Her
wings shook as the tears (which looked like liquid silver) covered her
hands and…. She looked up at me. "What is happening to me?" She
asked.

"I don't know," I replied. I slowly walked closer to her. Was this some
kind of a physical reaction after making love to a human?

The angel wiped some more tears away from her eyes. "I can't stop thinking about him. He haunts almost my every thought. Have you heard from him? Do you know when he'll be home?"

"He can't come home." I replied. "The Happy Angels are looking for him."

"Where did he hide?"

"I can't tell you," I replied. Was this a trick? Was she playing off my emotions? No… I've seen angels act before. They're all the same. This was different. She was really crying. She couldn't stop thinking about him?… It couldn't be, could it? I sat down near her.

"Is he ok?" The angel asked me (She was begging. I could see that in the way she looked and the way she held her hands. She really wanted to know).

"I think so," I replied.

"What is wrong with me?" She asked me again. "I'm so hurt without him. It's like I'm nothing without him."

Love? Could she actually love him? His angel loved him? I had to say the words aloud. "Do you love him?"

"Love?" The angel said confused. "That's impossible. Angels don't have emotions, just morals. We've always been that way. We don't…" Her words trailed off into nothing. She covered her face in her hands again and cried. "Damn them. I can't believe they did this to me."

"What are you talking about?" I asked. "Haven't you fallen in love before?"

She looked up at me annoyed. "Angels don't fall in love. I told you that is impossible…. Well, at least we used to not fall in love. There have been rumors going around for the last few years that the Superior Angels were going to add something to us to make us more interesting to God… I can't believe they did this without warning me. They gave us emotions and didn't warn us…"

This explained a lot to me. So, that was the reason they were such jerks before. And that explains why they seem strangely human now. This is why that one angel was so sympathetic to us and she was… Oh, my, this angel was really heartbroken. She looked over at me. "So now what do I do?"

"What do you mean?"

"What do I do to get rid of these feelings?"

I lightly laughed. "If it was only that easy."

She looked at me scared. "You mean there's no easy answer to get rid of this emotion?"

"Not at all," I sighed. "And some time you never get rid of it! Look at me. I fell in love in only 3 days and I'm still in love today…"

"I'm going to get those angels," She mumbled under her breath. "Those bastards…"

We paused quietly and sat there quietly together. An angel and me.

I= trying my best to think of how I was going to end my story.

She= busy trying to deal with all her new emotions.

"Can I ask you a question?" She asked me softly (Her voice sounded so lovely and warm).

"Sure," I replied.

"Earlier this morning at about eight I came by here and I heard this song coming from your room."

"Oh, that was Nat 'King' Cole," I replied. "I was using it for my book."

"It sounded nice," she said softly. "It reminded me of him…"

We paused again. She wiped away a tear.

"So you're writing a book?" she asked. I could see she was trying her hardest to move away from the conversation about emotions. Just like a human she was avoiding her emotions by trying to pretend they were not there. Interesting the changes going on here….

"It's my autobiography," I sighed.

"Everyone up here writes one," the angel sighed in return. "So where are you in the book?"

"I'm near the end," I leaned farther back against the wall. "I just got out of jail. See I spent five years in a jail in Amsterdam. I was put there for more political reasons then criminal. And the things they claim I did were all crap. Kidnapping. Robbery. Arson. If they would've just looked at the facts and allowed Toni Lyn to testify instead of rushing her back to America, I would've been…"

"How was that?" She interrupted me.

What?"

"Jail," She said even softer.

I looked at her. For once, I didn't shrug this off all together. "It was hard," I said slowly. "It was really hard."

"Then what did you do?" She asked.

"Well, I found my way back to the United States. I had to find my love and I had no idea where she was…"

"Your love?" She interrupted. I guess she really didn't know anything about me.

"Her name is Toni Lyn," I said.

"Where did you meet her?"

"I met her in Rome. She was working at the American Embassy… I had to hide out at the embassy… Well, it's a really immature and stupid reason, I don't want to get into it… Anyway, they hid me up in this little room and I snuck out to this formal party they were having and there she was and…. And I knew. From the first moment, I knew she was the one…. That was my third day in Rome… I guess technically I fell in love in one day… Funny, I've been saying that all wrong throughout the entire book…"

"Did she feel the same way?"

I laughed. "No, she took some convincing… but then we danced together. And we danced well and she fell for me… And then we spent the next two months running around Europe together."

"Where did you find her after you got out?" The angel asked.

"Well, that wasn't too easy. Because of all the news that was following our situation, her family tried to hide her away from the press. The last thing they wanted her to do was talk. It would confuse the situation. They liked the idea of me being in jail. They also forced her to marry her fiancé."

"She had a fiancé?" the angel asked confused.

"Well, technically, but she didn't love him. Actually she almost shot him once for me."

"I've got to read this book," the angel said to herself. "So where were they?" She asked me.

'Well, most people don't know this but many of the leaders of the big city Mafias own homes in the Grand Rapids area of Michigan. It's like a vacation spot for them. It's near the beaches, the taxes are low, it's conservative, real estate is inexpensive, and all the police care about are speeding tickets. So she was living in that area in her family's home…. It wasn't easy to find that out. I had to follow some very dangerous people around to get to her."

"That must have been some reunion."

I sighed. "It wasn't just a matter of us meeting each other again. It was a matter of recovering my lost soul."

"What do you mean?" The angel asked. This concept really confused her.

"Right before I was arrested I touched her cheek. For me, I left my soul there. To survive in the jail and on the roads I had to believe that I was with her right there. A part of her. I never left her. I didn't experience all the things that happened to me… that was only my body."

The angel decided not to contradict this thought. She shrugged it off because she knew how important it was for me to separate this from reality. This is so different from what a prior angel would have done. Before, angels were very quick to correct our errors. "Did it work?"

I shrugged my shoulders. "I believed it. And it made our reunion all the more amazing. I was becoming myself again just by being near her."

The angel looked at me quietly. What was she thinking? Was she trying to read my thoughts? "You're still in pain."

"What do you mean?" I asked her.

"How long have you been here?" She asked softly.

"3 years, why?"

"3 years and all that pain held in," the angel sighed. "You poor soul...."

What is up with this? First Sylvia then this angel. "I don't know what you mean."

"You haven't accepted the pain of your death yet. You haven't accepted the pain of the separation of life, have you?"

I was starting to get upset and she could see that. "I don't know what you mean."

She sighed. "Everyone's in pain and no one's happy." She pulled out of a pocket in her heavenly garment (Where are the pockets?) a pack of cigarettes. She offered me one. I turned it down with a nod. She lit up, inhaled and blew out slowly.

"Angels smoke?" I asked her. This was a first for me.

"I've been doing this since I met him," the angel replied with a small cough. "It helps me relax."

I slowly got off the floor. (Why is it my back still hurts every time I get up? Shouldn't that have been taken care of after my death? Unfair). "I got to go." I rubbed my back. "I have some writing to do."

The angel nodded and turned her head to the side.

I entered my apartment and locked the door behind me. And it was then that I began the reunion poem for my story... With the sound of an angel crying outside my door...

CHAPTER 80 — THE REUNION POEM

The moment of reunion breathes here-
In these words
As it did there
For the two lovers-

She-
Whipped by life—changed—older—sadder-

Him-
dirty—broken—older—sadder-

And then instantly-
Rebirth-
Luminous air-
Inhale the moment-

They tried to speak-
"It's...."
     "It's...."
          They kiss-

Watch the years strip away like the clothes-
The days, the hurt nothing more than fabric-

As easy to remove as slipping the arm out of a shirt-

And then they begin to speak-
Finding words quickly—almost like a hiccup-
Escaping trapped air-
Sad times only spoken through laughing joy-

She-
My parents forced me to
marry him. I don't love him.
I never would touch him.
And then one night... He
raped me. He... He got me
pregnant. I wanted... I... I
had... I love you... I couldn't
even write you. My family
knew people in the prison
and they said if I wrote you,
they'd.... I'm sorry... I... Jon
has a lover, I think. He's
always gone.... I thought I'd
never see you again.... I
stayed for the baby... Our
child. Make sure her life
turns out better than mine. I
have a daughter. She is
beautiful. At times I look at
her and see you. Like I am
seeing the possibility of what
she would have looked like if
she was our daughter. Is that
odd? You would like her. She
is so smart....

Him-
I was raped over a
hundred times- Everyday,
everyday I tasted my own
blood- I tried writing to
my family. None of them
of them would respond.
They didn't give a damn
for me. They didn't care.
I was all alone except for
the memories and my
dreams. You… My
family disowned me.
After I was let out of jail I
went to the embassy.
They wouldn't help me. I
was still an
embarrassment to the
country. So I worked my
way across the ocean on a
cargo ship. I then hitched
across the country. I
begged for food. I starved
most nights. I haven't
slept in a bed in weeks....
Absolute weeks....

And then they stopped-
Allowing the words of the other to sink in
Almost like water being drunk
Through thirsty lips-

Neither says a word again-
They begin to touch-
Remind that they were there-
She near him-
He near her-
Together-
Her face to his face-
His hand to her hand-
Reminding-

A soul was regained then-
It wasn't only his-
It was their's—And together it breathed-

Hold-
Hold-
Hold-
Don't ever let go-

CHAPTER 81

About two hours later Jon came home to find Toni Lyn and me together. He got out a gun and shot me.

I died.

THE END

Take A Breath…

Breathe In…

Breathe Out…

And Now For the Epilogues…

My Epilogue

"Jesus!" I swore. "What are you doing here?"

The Great Unknown was too distracted by the pile of pages laid out on my desk. "I CAME TO READ YOUR MANUSCRIPT."

"But... But you're supposed to be hiding," I moved forward (How the Hell does he keep getting into my apartment when I'm not here?).

"I WAS," He sighed. "YOU SAID YOUR BOOK WOULD BE DONE IN 3 DAYS, SO I'M HERE TO READ IT…. OH, HERE'S A GRAMMATICAL MISTAKE…"

I couldn't believe this. This man cared more about reading my book than his own safety. "I would've found some way to have gotten the manuscript to you after it was published… You didn't have to do this…"

He was engrossed in my work. (He had still to look up and make eye contact with me). "WHY DON'T YOU GO DOWN TO THE AFTERTASTE AND I'LL CATCH UP LATER…."

"But…"

"I'LL SEE YOU THERE…. SHUT THE DOOR BEHIND YOU…"

"You can't end a book like that!" Henry James exclaimed (I knew I should never have let him read the ending). We were all at the AfterTaste again at our typical round table.

"He's right," John Lennon agreed.

"How did you see it?" I asked John.

"James showed it to me." Lennon sipped his coffee. "It sucks. Horrible, fucking horrible."

"It doesn't matter," I returned. "I gave myself 3 days. My time was up. You all knew I was not trying to change life with this work. I was just telling my story."

The Great Unknown sighed and took my manuscript out of his backpack (He brought my first draft with him!).

"What's that doing here?" I angrily asked him. I was not ready to dive into all the eccentricities of the work with "The AfterTaste Round Table".

The Great Unknown was going to say something but he was interrupted by a still dirty Sylvia Plath (Who was surprisingly annoyed, so unlike her-sarcasm). "Didn't you listen to a single word any of us has said to you during the making of this book?"

"Yes, I did," I slowly responded. "But did I also mention to all of you on numerous occasions that I'm not as talented as any of you. I don't have the talent for description that James has. I can't convey power with my words like you and Fitzgerald. And I don't have the talent to weave a plot together like Woolf and Dickens. I'm not you. This is my story of my time with her. I had to do it my way."

"I DON'T THINK THAT'S IT AT ALL," The Great Unknown spoke. "I THINK HE'S AFRAID TO DISCUSS HIS REAL STORY IN A REAL FASHION."

"That's utter bullshit," I exclaimed annoyed. I looked around the table to find someone to speak up for me. Instead, it looked like a thousand light bulbs went on above the heads of the people around me. "That's not true," I stated again.

Maybe we should have bothered to get dressed. For some reason, it felt more natural to be nude around each other. Clothes only got in our way. Obstacles to tackle for us. It was almost like I was setting myself up for this. I just wasn't thinking and neither was she.

We were both just so happy to see each other again. So, so happy…..

"That would make sense," Dickinson agreed slowly. She was wearing all black today. The pills were starting to wear off again (They rarely last more than a week). That also meant it was only a matter of time until she would lock herself in her apartment again. "When he was at Plath's apartment he talked about how he didn't want to talk about his experience in prison. He also didn't want to talk about his experience trying to get back home."

I interjected at this point. "That's different! The story is about her and me. It's not about me. Everything is about her."

"What the fuck's going on here?" This was the first sign to us he was there. We were so into each other that we didn't even sense his presence. He could have been at that door for thirty minutes and neither of us would have known. We were just so happy to be near each other again. It felt so right to feel her alongside me again. Like going home....

Fitzgerald looked angrily at me and pointed. "Don't try to change the subject. This story is about you. This is the reason you got into heaven. In the long run she is only a supporting character to the reader."

"She's not a supporting character." I was getting so angry I could feel my hands beginning to shake. "My God, have all of you been missing the point? I've told this story at least a hundred times."

"It's a good story," Charles Dickens spoke up. You could tell by the tone of his voice that he was trying to calm me down. "Don't get us wrong, We're all your friends here. But you're the main character. You've told the reader so little about yourself. You must open up to the reader."

She got off of the bed. She ran over to him. She placed her hands on his shoulders. She spoke softly and slowly. "Listen, Jon... I'm sorry.... I'm sorry..... You know I love him. I've always loved him.... You knew from the moment that you forced me to marry you.... Time can't change that...."

He was staring directly at me. He never blinked. I swear he never blinked.

"IT SEEMS EVERYTIME WE GET TO SOMETHING JUICY ABOUT YOU, YOU SKIP IT OR BREEZE OVER IT. LIKE YOU WANT THE ACTUAL PAIN TO DISAPPEAR. THAT'S NOT HOW LIFE WORKS. YOU KNOW THAT, WE ALL KNOW THAT," The Great Unknown moaned.

"Listen asshole," I pointed across the table at the man, "of all the people here, you have the least right to criticize me."

I slowly sat up in the bed. He slowly looked down at his wife. He spat on her face. She grimaced. I began to get up from the bed. She turned her face away and began to wipe the spit off her face.

I quickly ran over to her. She fell into my arms. She was crying. I wrapped my arms around her like a blanket and held her on the floor.

Jon turned away and walked out of the room.

I wiped the tears off her face. They were warm…. So warm….

"LOOK AT ALL OF US," The Great Unknown said waving his arms around our circle of friends. "WE'RE ALL PRODUCTS OF PAIN. PAIN IS WHAT DRIVES CREATION AND CHANGE. PAIN IS WHAT MADE ALL OF OUR LIVES INTERESTING ENOUGH TO GET INTO HEAVEN. THE ONLY DIFFERENCE BETWEEN YOU AND US IS THAT WE HAVE COME TO GRIPS WITH OUR PAIN AND YOU HAVE NOT. YOU THINK IT CAN BE ABANDONED OR TOSSED ASIDE. YOU NEED TO ACCEPT THE PAIN THAT LIFE IS OVER. IT'S ALL OVER."

As I was holding her naked body, he was in the living room loading his gun. Her body felt so light in my arms. Light as a feather. She was lightly shaking in my hands. I felt like I was holding her shadow more than her. No, not her shadow. Her essence, her soul… I was caressing her soul…. Our soul….

"Fuck you!" I shouted at him.

"WHAT GOT YOU INTO HEAVEN IS THE FACT YOU ABAN-
DONED EVERYTHING FOR LOVE. YOU SUFFERED FOR LOVE.
YOU DIED FOR LOVE. FRANKLY AFTER READING YOUR
BOOK I CAN'T TELL IF YOU'RE ROMANTIC OR SIMPLY PIG-
HEADED." He slowly sipped his coffee. Everyone else at the table was
silent.

*She began mumbling to herself. She was asking why she had to be tortured
like this. What God had against her.... What was the point of her life....*

*Then she began mumbling that I should leave. I should leave now and
never look back....*

"WE'RE NOT ASKING YOU TO TELL US HOW MANY TIMES
YOU WERE RAPED AND BEATEN IN PRISON. WE WANT TO
KNOW HOW IT AFFECTED YOU. WE WANT TO KNOW
ABOUT HOW ALL OF THIS AFFECTED YOU. YOU TELL US
WHAT DRIVES YOU, YOU DON'T TELL US THE REAL REASON
WHY. THE PAIN IS HOLDING ALL OF THAT BACK. LET US
FEEL YOUR PAIN. OPEN UP TO US. FINALLY LET OUT ALL THE
PAIN YOU'VE BEEN HOLDING BACK ALL THESE YEARS. ONCE
YOU LET IT OUT THEN YOU CAN TRULY TELL US WHAT
YOUR LIFE WAS LIKE AND WHAT YOU FELT. YOU'RE HOLD-
ING YOURSELF BACK BY A DELUSION THAT YOUR STORY IS
NOT OVER. IT'S OVER. ACCEPT THE PAIN. IT'S OVER."

"I'm not leaving you. Ever," I whispered. "I'm not."
"You must go."
"I won't."
"Please."
"I'm your's."
"I love you."
"I love you."

"You must go."
"I can't leave you...."

"What are you talking about!?" I angrily asked. "You're fucking nuts!"

"I'M NUTS!?" The Great Unknown shouted. "WHY WON'T YOU EVER GO AND SEE HER?"

"I... I..." I couldn't say the words.

James laid his hand on my shoulder. Everyone was looking at me with a look I can only describe as warm patience. Like the kind a parent gives a child when the child is learning in front of their eyes.

Charles Dickens mumbled something to Woolf. I could read what he said on his lips. He said it was "The Pain."

I could hear his steps coming up the stairs. Even though neither of us said anything, we both knew what was coming. And neither of us did anything to stop it from happening.... It is as if we both decided quietly within our souls to accept the fate laid down before us. Neither of us could see another ending for our story.

I stood up angrily.

"What do you want me to say.... What do you want me to write..." I was beginning to cry. "Do you want me to tell you what it felt like to feel the bullet enter my skin and then feel my life drain away? Or do you want me to tell you what it felt like to hear her scream?" I wiped the tears off my face. I couldn't wipe them off fast enough. "Or do you want me to tell you how it felt to have her look down at me as she said goodbye? Or how it felt to see her say she loves me for the last time? Or would you like a detailed description of her painful expression as she lightly rubbed the side of my face as I slipped away?... What do you want?... Do you want to know how that feels to die in the arms of your love and there is nothing you can do to go back and change a thing?!... I can't change a damn thing! I'm fucking dead! Do you want to know how that feels knowing she is getting older and older every day and I'm not there? Do you want to know how it feels to watch all the time, all the time in the world slip by you and there is fucking nothing you can do to change a God damn thing because you're fucking dead!? I'm fucking dead. I'm dead… dead… Oh, God…"

The Great Unknown took another sip of coffee from his cup. He then slowly looked around at all the others. He then slowly looked back at me. "NOW YOU'RE READY TO WRITE YOUR BOOK."

THEIR EPILOGUE

Part One
—Goodbye To The Great Unknown…

"So how does it really feel?" Henry James asked me. We were walking home from the AfterTaste. It was evening and the lampposts on the corners lighted the street.

I looked down at the book that was in my hands.

There it was. My book.

Big and bold= **3 Days in Rome**.

My story.

"It feels ok, I guess." I replied slowly.

"So what's wrong then?" he asked me. He could tell something was up. We'd just spent the evening discussing and drinking to the work with the rest of the gang and yet for some reason I truly was not enjoying myself.

"Well, it feels like I never actually completed it. I feel more like I abandoned it. After that one night, I feel like I… What?"

Henry James was laughing. "You are a writer!… Who would have guessed it!? Most artists feel that way after completing a project."

I didn't join in with his laughing. "Maybe the whole idea of writing it so fast was a flop. Maybe I should go back and do it again. I know if I was to do it now I would have so much more to say…."

"Your idea was ok," Henry James sighed. "You made a very different book and considering you're talking about an artform that has been around for over a thousand years…. Of course, I'm only including the

English language in that. It goes back farther if you consider… Anyway, what I am saying is it's an achievement so don't get too sadden by…."

I interrupted him. "But there is so much I want the reader to truly understand and I really don't know if I succeeded in doing that. Do the readers know how great our love was? Do they truly know what I was thinking or feeling? Am I just a character on a page? Am I real to them? Is my story as real to them as it is to me? I would've written it so much differently now since… I feel so different since I…" (faced The Pain. C'mon you can say it).

Henry put his hand on my shoulder. "That answer is different for every reader. They'll each see it their own way. All we can do as writers is give them the story." We stopped under the lamppost by our apartment building… I sighed and….

Fighting?

Was that arguing?

What was all that noise?!

It was coming from inside the building. "What the Hell is that?" I asked Henry James (As If he knew more about it than I did).

Suddenly The Great Unknown was pulled out of the door by two Happy Angels (They got him! Oh, my God, they finally got him! Why the Hell did he come back to the apartment? I told him I would get a copy of the book to him).

"What's going on here?" Henry James asked in disbelief.

"THEY'RE TAKING ME AWAY," The Great Unknown screamed. "THEY'RE GOING TO MAKE ME FUCKING JOYFUL. LET ME GO!"

I tried to pull at the angel nearest me. He elbowed me away (Useless). "Let him go!" I screamed.

"Don't worry," the angel barked back at me. "Everything's going to be alright."

"What do you mean," Henry James argued back. "He doesn't want to be happy. He wants to no longer exist."

"We know," the angel replied. He straightened his wings. "It has been okayed. We're going to let him go…"

The Great Unknown stopped struggling. He looked up at the angels. His face reminded me of the look you would see from a hopeful child (I can't believe he really wanted this). "YOU'RE GOING TO LET ME END?"

"Yes," the angel replied. "It is what you wish, isn't it?"

The Great Unknown looked over at us. His face was bright with excitement. "THEY'RE LETTING ME DISAPPEAR…"

"God will like to talk to you too first, if that's ok," The other angel said (Saying this did not make him too happy. Was this angel bitter?).

The Great Unknown turned to us with a smile. "I GET TO MEET THE BIG GUY. QUICK! IS THERE ANYTHING YOU WANT ME TO BRING UP TO HIM?"

"Can't we do without spinach?" I asked.

"Country music!" Henry James exclaimed. I didn't know Henry James hated country music. I guess we have more in common than I thought.

"SPINACH, COUNTRY MUSIC, RIGHT," The Great Unknown said (as if he checked them off in the list in his head)

They began to lead him away slowly.

(He's going away. Why would he want this? Heaven isn't great, but at least it is something. Why would he want nothing instead of something? Why let everything go? I could never do that. I need this. I'm too used to this…. He was going to go away forever and I couldn't think of one thing to say. He helped me face The Pain and now he is going and I have nothing to say to him. Oh, God! Say something, damn it. You need to say something to him for all he did… I must say something). "Wait…"

He interrupted me (Even this did not change him). "YOU'RE WELCOME." How did he know? He laughed and pointed back at me." I LEFT SOMETHING UPSTAIRS FOR YOU IN YOUR ROOMS…. GOODBYE, MY FRIENDS."

Henry James raised his hand and slowly began to wave.

I waved with him.

Goodbye....

Suddenly they stopped walking. The angels let go of him. (What is going on? Was he going to come back? What were they whispering to each other?) Suddenly... I swear this is all true... The angels and The Great Unknown locked their arms and began walking away... No, wait...They were skipping and... Singing?

Yes! The Great Unknown was singing as he skipped away with the angels. The angels were singing too!

"We're off to see the Wizard!
The wonderful Wizard of Oz...."

"Are they skipping?" Henry James asked me. This confused him. All I could do was laugh.

"Yes," I laughed, "They're skipping."

And we stood there and watched as The Great Unknown skipped off to meet his maker with his arms locked with the two angels. And under that clear sky and under those stars strangely it all seemed to makes sense.

"Let's go in," I said softly after we were both sure they were gone (Gone for good... No more...).

We entered the building. "What do you think he left you?" Henry James asked.

I didn't answer. Of course, I didn't know.

Henry James followed me into my apartment and waiting for me on the desk was a present.... It was wrapped in white wrapping paper. It was a pretty good-sized box. I looked over at Henry James and back at the package. I slowly began to open it.

And inside the box...

Under some newspapers....

Were...

Books...

His books… The books of The Great Unknown.

I slowly picked one of them up…

They were all in one piece. Mint condition. I didn't know any of them survived. He already wrecked all the ones I have seen… These were perfect…

And there on the cover was the one thing that had spawned numerous debates, arguments, conversation, and jokes all over Heaven's Rome. The one thing that held him back from becoming more than an icon for his fellow dead…. It was his name. His all too human name…

Henry James leaned over to look at the book in my hand. He smiled. "It's a nice name," Henry James sighed. "A good writing name…"

Part Two—The Celebration….

A few days later I arrived at the AfterTaste to find almost the equivalent of a party! Woolf and Dickens were dancing to swing music (They were much better. Not bad, at all). And Fitzgerald was drinking over on the side with a young lady. They seemed to be having a great time talking to each other. (Fitzgerald seemed to be happy. Was he finally getting over Zelda?). There was a Hell of a lot going on. Every corner of the coffeehouse was filled with laughter and the sound of celebration.

"What is all this?" I asked Fitzgerald.

Fitzgerald looked up slowly. He looked annoyed to be interrupted (Maybe things hadn't changed too much after all). "God lost," Fitzgerald said and turned back to his conversation.

"What?" He couldn't have said what I thought he just said. Best to brush it off.

Suddenly Henry James walked in to the AfterTaste. I looked back at him. He looked just as surprised as I did. He slowly walked over to me. "What did I miss?" He asked me.

"I'm not too sure," I said slowly, "I think Fitzgerald may be drunk again though…"

"Mr. James!" Dickens shouted and ran over to us with Woolf in hand. "Did you hear the news?"

"What news?" Henry James asked, "What could possibly be this news-worthy?"

"The election!" Dickens replied.

"Yeah, so?" Henry James asked. "That was weeks ago. Don't tell me the results just got in." He turned to me. "That's longer than usual."

I sighed. "You know we would have results the same night if those angels got over their fear of computers. Frankly, I think it's ridiculous."

My Last Interruption.

Part 3—Why Angels Hate Computers...

Angels and computers don't mix.

If you put an angel in the same room with a computer, the angel will probably start destroying it.

This problem between angels and computers was first discovered in the late 1980's. See angels are so used to being around things with souls that when it meets something so sophisticated that does not exist—well—it irks them. The computer did not seem like a tool to them; it seemed like another creature. And no matter how hard the dead tried to explain this to them (Like angels would listen to humans anyway) they couldn't buy it.

It was like a living being to them that was not alive. What a concept! It confused them a great deal. So when the people arriving in heaven in the 80's demanded computers the angels that first got them were very.... Actually, this is a transcript of that fated first meeting.

SCENE—AN EMPTY WHITE ROOM.

There is a computer sitting on a desk by the wall. Slowly, the door opens and a very hesitant ANGEL sticks his head in. Suddenly someone pushes him from behind. He walks in and quickly looks around the room. He sees the computer and walks over to it. He spreads his hands and wings wide.

ANGEL
Welcome, to Heaven. You're loved.

The computer doesn't respond. This unnerves the Angel. He coughs and tries again.

ANGEL
Do not fear me. We all love you here in Heaven.

The computer again doesn't respond. The angel looks around the room as if to see if this is a joke. He walks closer to the computer and spreads his wings again.

ANGEL
Here, in Heaven you will find all your happiness.

The angel closes his wings. He slowly walks forward and looks down at the terminal.

ANGEL
It looks like a typewriter and yet it does so....
There's an ON switch.

He pushes the button and the screen lights up. The angel flies back in terror against the wall. The angel covers his ears as the computer boots up (making all the noises that a computer does while booting up).

COMPUTER VOICE
Welcome.

The angel gets up slowly. He is stunned.

ANGEL

That's my line. I welcome you.

The angel walks over to the computer. The screen is blinking: Hit Enter.

ANGEL
What will I enter? Where will I go? What…
How could this send me anyplace… Ok, stay
calm. It can't do anything to you….

He presses the button and the computer screen changes to a scene of a group of happy computers with smiles on their screens in a field.

COMPUTER VOICE
Welcome to the fascinating world of Computers.

ANGEL
No! I won't go! This is my world! You must stay
here. I can't go! Don't take me!

COMPUTER VOICE
In this program we will teach you how to use…

ANGEL
No, wait I don't want to go to your world. You
are in Heaven…

COMPUTER VOICE
Open and close files, start files…
ANGEL
Slave labor! Oh, my! No!

COMPUTER VOICE
And play games...

ANGEL
Games? Why would I be happy with games.
So is that how they appease the masses?

COMPUTER VOICE
Click on the ENTER key and we can begin your
journey to the future.

The Angel flies up in the air and back away from the screen.

ANGEL
The future. Oh my, oh my... The future... They want
me to hit enter. That must trigger it for real. Oh, my,
oh, my. This is all an evil plot to capture people. That
explains why it doesn't have a soul. I need to do
something...

The angel looks around and notices the plug in the wall.

ANGEL
The plug! That's it...

The angel slowly and (trying to look) casually moves over to the plug.
He reaches his hand out to the plug and...

COMPUTER VOICE
Hit ENTER and let computers help you make

sense of your world…

ANGEL
(screaming)
Mind control! Slave labor! Imprisonment!
I must save the Heaven! I must!

The Angel reaches over and pulls the plug. The computer turns off with a small hum… The Angel is panting in excitement on the side of the room. His breathing catches up…

Suddenly 3 other angels fly in to the room.

ANGEL2
You saved Heaven! You saved us all!

ANGEL
I only did what any normal angel would!

ANGEL3
You're a hero!

ANGEL
I am, aren't I?

END OF SCENE.

And it was then that the Holiday of "The Fall of Computers" was born. Every year on the anniversary in every city of Heaven, the dead must line the streets and watch the parade celebrating this "amazing victory." Numerous times the dead have tried to explain to the Angels how silly this all is and how everything was a misunderstanding, but they never listen. Angels never take the dead seriously....

So it is for that reason that many of the functions of Heaven (The election, the entrance... etc.) are still done by hand. So it was normal for the results of the elections (even though it is obvious to all since there is only one candidate) to take weeks to be official...

Part Four—The Punchline To All This....

"If God lost who won?" Henry James asked.

"Nothing won," Woolf replied.

Pause.

"I don't understand." I shook my head confused...

"Well, you know on the ballot how you have two choices—God or that other choice."

"Sure," Henry said... Suddenly he began to laugh. He began to laugh loud and hard. This was a very happy Henry James. "And people checked the other box?" He began to wipe the tears of laughter away from his eyes.

"I guess the broadcast of The Great Unknown had created quite a little stir among the people. He has changed things..." Woolf said. She grabbed her drink off the table and drank some more. The song changed to Glen Miller's 'In The Mood.' "Oh, I love this song," she said to herself. She began to tap her feet to the beat. Henry James watched her.

"What's the other choice?" I asked. "I don't remember. I really never bothered to actually read the blasted thing. I just pull the lever and walk out as quickly as I can..."

"That's the funny thing," Dickens said.

"I get that," I sighed. I wanted in on this joke.

"It's just like the last choice on the ballots in the USA," Woolf laughed. "Now do you see?"

"I never voted while in America," I sighed. "I liked to be in the majority. So, what's the choice?

"Well, it's... Weeeeeee..." Woolf wasn't able to finish her thought. See Henry James grabbed her hand and took her to the dance floor. I watched as he stepped on her toes... Over and over again. Henry James is a lousy dancer.

"Here let me show you," Dickens said. He grabbed a newspaper. He pointed at the headlines. "Here's the other choice."

I laughed.

Oh, my....

I laughed at what got more votes than God.

I'm sure the angels when they prepared the ballots didn't catch the implication of the phrasing they used on the ballot. But in the long run, it worked so well... It all came together so very well....

None Of The Above

HER EPILOGUE

I went to her house.

I watched as she put her daughter to bed. She was right about her. She is beautiful. She looks like her mother. She named her Juliet. Just thinking about that makes me smile. I watched as Toni Lyn ran her hands through Juliet's hair and tucked her up in her blankets.

Toni Lyn then turned on the nightlight and turned off the main light. She walked out of the room leaving the door open a crack. A small crack....

I watched as she walked down the hallway and down the stairs. She was wearing a red bathrobe and she had her hands wrapped around her body almost as if she was hugging herself. Like I did that one day....

She turned off the lights in the living room. Then she turned off the lights in the family room. She was about to turn off the lights in the kitchen, when she stopped. She stopped... She turned around. It was like she was looking straight at me. She couldn't see me. I know she couldn't see me.... She can't see me. But she stood there for at least a minute staring at where I was standing. She rubbed her hand slowly against her cheek just like I did when I left my... How could... So close.... Near.... Let me.... No.... She can't... No.... She can't.... Can she?.... No.... Please.... I can't...

She smiled a little.

A tear fell from her eye.

She wiped the tear off of her cheek, turned off the kitchen light and wandered into the living room. She walked up the stairs and I followed.

She checked on her sleeping daughter and I followed. She went to her bedroom and I followed.

I watched as she undressed. The moonlight from the window shone on her skin. Her skin glowed in that light like an angel... She was my angel.

She laid down on her bed. She snuggled into her blankets and rolled over on her side. I...

I...

I climbed into bed alongside her. I snuggled up against her and wrapped my arm around her. She sighed softly and leaned back into my body. My nose was up against her hair. It smelled so, so wonderful. She felt so, so wonderful.

"I love you, Mrs. Jones," I whispered to her.

"I love you, Mr. Jones," she whispered back.

And we both fell asleep.